CALICO

Raine Cantrell

DIAMOND BOOKS, NEW YORK

This book is a Diamond original edition,
and has never been previously published.

CALICO

A Diamond Book / published by arrangement with
the author

PRINTING HISTORY
Diamond edition / July 1993

ISBN: 1-55773-913-7

Diamond Books are published by The Berkley Publishing Group,
200 Madison Avenue, New York, New York 10016.
The name "DIAMOND" and its logo
are trademarks belonging to Charter Communications, Inc.

PRINTED IN THE UNITED STATES OF AMERICA

10 9 8 7 6 5 4 3 2 1

To Ange and Kathy, special daughters, special friends, who have found their own McCreadys in Jim and Bob.

CALICO

CHAPTER 1

"M-maggie! Maggie! Come runnin' with your gun. They stole your groom."

The door to the one-room cabin burst open before Mary Margaret O'Roarke could move. Pamela Burton stumbled inside, clutching her side. "I ran . . . all the . . . w-way." The young woman's chest heaved with every breath she drew.

"Was I hearin' you right?" Maggie turned from the cracked mirror over the washstand. The dreamy look brought on by her approaching wedding disappeared. She felt as breathless as Pam looked, swaying for a few seconds. But Maggie never let any feminine weakness show, and wouldn't do so now.

"Oh, Maggie, you look so . . . so pretty."

"Never mind me. What happened to Quincy?"

"Your groom was nervous as a church mouse waiting for you," Pam explained, fanning herself with one hand. "Pa said for him to take a walk around, but Quincy didn't want to get his boots dirty. Then the circuit preacher arrived, and Miss Mae showed him into her parlor when in they came from the back door." Pam spread her fingers and rested her hand over her heart. "Five of them, guns drawn, mean and ugly sounding. Two grabbed hold of poor Quincy and dragged him outside. Miss Mae was near to fainting." Wringing her hands, she added, "I didn't know what to do first. But Pa's getting together some men to go after them."

Maggie winced as Pam's voice climbed with shrill excitement. She knew the girl's father had declared his intent to see an end to the lawlessness in the rough New Mexico mining camp. Andrew Burton hadn't been able to do much in the few months he'd been there. First Maggie's uncle had been murdered, and now her groom had been stolen just minutes away from their wedding. With Quincy gone, it could mean the end of her dreams.

A low growl came from beneath the single wooden bunk built against the corner of the cabin, causing Pam to flinch.

"Hush up, Satin," Maggie ordered, ripping out the flowers she had labored to secure in her short riot of red curls. She tossed them into the washbowl with a stab of regret, then comforted herself with the thought that they had looked silly. Maggie knew she was not a woman for frills no matter how much they mattered to Quincy.

Quincy. For a moment Maggie forgot Pam, forgot what happened. Quincy loved her. He had told her so. He was going to take her East and show her how ladies dressed and behaved. Her hands would never be raw and scraped or stiff with the numbing cold of mountain streams again.

"Maggie? Are you all right?"

Coming to with a start, Maggie nodded. "That I am. You'd be knowin' I'm hard enough to handle all that comes me way."

"You don't look hard today. You look soft and pretty, the way a woman should."

With a shake of her head Maggie denied the glow that Pam's words brought to her. Soft and pretty? She eyed Pam, who was still twisting her hands together in a helpless manner. Maggie shuddered. Is that what Quincy expected from her? To be soft and pretty and helpless as Pam? If she was, she wouldn't be getting her groom back for sure.

"Did you get a look at them, Pam?"

"Not at their faces. They were all wearing dark bandannas over their mouths and had their hats pulled low so I couldn't even see their eyes. Don't think anyone had the time to get a good look at them. It all happened so fast."

"What about their horses?"

"Horses? Maggie, I was so busy fanning Miss Mae that I didn't even think about watching them ride off. Anyway, what good would seeing their horses do? Horses all look alike."

"Alike!" *Saints save her from weak-kneed females.* Maggie finally realized she was wasting time while the thieves got away. Without a care for the half-done buttons up the back of her new calico gown that was to have been her wedding dress, Maggie lifted her gunbelt off the stubby bedpost and strapped it on.

"Can't understand why someone just didn't shoot them."

"They couldn't, Maggie. None of the men there had their guns. It wouldn't have been fitting for a wedding." With a delicate shudder Pam gnawed her lower lip. "Maggie, don't you think you should change? I mean," she explained, motioning with one hand, "you're sure to ruin your gown." Maggie's glaring look silenced her, but Pam knew that Miss Mae would be hurt after she had rushed to make Maggie's wedding dress.

With a shrug Maggie said, "Guess you're right. But I can't

be worryin'. McCready ain't gettin' away with stealin' me groom.''

''McCready! Oh, Maggie, what makes you so sure that he had anything to do with this?''

''Know that polecat better than anyone. He's behind this. I'll cut that snake's liver out and feed it to him this time.''

Pam gasped, one hand clutching her throat. Maggie had picked up a wickedly honed knife from out of the clutter on the table and tucked it into a sheath concealed in her boot.

Wisely, Pam refrained from answering her. She knew that Maggie's wasn't an idle boast. Maggie had learned to skin hides from her father before she had learned to ride, and could, if she was of a mind to, skin McCready alive before he downed a glass of that whiskey he was so fond of.

Maggie straightened and buried her regret for the second time today. She had thought this day would be special, a new beginning. Here she was once more forced to defend what was hers. She lifted the Beal Army Model revolver from its holster. The .44 caliber gun with its eight-inch-long barrel and polished walnut grips was made the year she had been born. Twenty-one years of use, first by her father, then herself, told its own tale of the lawless lands she had lived in.

While Maggie fiddled with her gun, Pam sighed with pity to see the discarded black kid high-buttoned shoes. Maggie was never going to be Quincy's ideal lady if she refused to give up her worn boots to wear proper shoes. But then, Pam reminded herself, the last few weeks of trying to turn Maggie into Quincy's idea of a lady had been just that: trying.

Satin crept out from under the bunk, and Pam cringed when the dog dragged forth the mangled remains of a bustle only to drop it as Maggie headed for the door. Pam stood aside to let her pass, wincing, then refusing to listen to the plans Maggie had for McCready's body. She wouldn't have minded making a few plans of her own for the man, but McCready wouldn't look twice at her. The Lord knew she had tried, but with his wicked smile and those incredible blue eyes holding her a breathless captive, he had stated flatly that sweet, nice, respectable young women were not for the likes of him. Pam squeezed her thighs together, flushing with the warmth that filled her at the thought of McCready.

Satin's muscular furred body brushed Pam's skirt and forced her flat against the rough-logged door. Another low warning growl came from the mongrel bitch's throat. Pam heeded the warning. Satin hated anyone getting too close to Maggie.

Shutting the door behind her, Pam followed Maggie and the trailing dog across the wooden bridge over the swift flowing waters of Mineral Creek. She was embarrassed when Maggie, with her accustomed lack of understanding for proper ladylike behavior, hiked her hem above her knees. Shaking her head, Pam thought that if McCready was behind the kidnapping of Quincy, as Maggie believed, he had gone too far this time. It didn't take the brain of a peahen to see that Maggie was riled, stomping through mud ruts without care, heading down the gulch to what passed for the street.

Pam thought about calling out to Maggie and telling her that the back of her gown was only half-buttoned. With Maggie's short hair, the flapping gown revealed an indecent amount of skin. But an angry Maggie meant no one in Cooney Camp with a lick of sense tried to tell her anything or tried to stop her unless they had a death wish.

In the four months they had lived here with her father, Pam had witnessed Maggie taking on hard miners who outweighed her and coming out without a scratch. Her first sight of Maggie, who she thought was a young boy, had been of her straddling a mud-strewn man while she fed him a handful of the mud that covered them both. It was later that she had learned the man called Maggie as crazy as her uncle and as likely to wind up dead if she didn't stop thinking she was as tough as a man. Maggie was strong, but even as Pam sometimes envied that strength, she would never give up her own dainty ways.

Tents, log cabins, and shacks crowded against one another along the main street. Ahead, Pam saw Maggie's shouted command stop a group of mounted men. Since her father was among them, Pam hurried closer to hear what was being said.

"Where's the sidewinder, Andrew?"

Lean as a pole fence, Andrew Burton tipped his hat back, revealing the same straw-colored hair as his daughter. He and the men with him didn't ask who Maggie called a sidewinder. They all knew what she thought of McCready.

"Well, now, he was over to Miss Mae's with us. No one wanted to miss your wedding. But after those men grabbed hold of Quincy, he headed back to the Rawhider."

"Likely laughing himself into a fit over pullin' this off," Maggie muttered.

"Ain't so sure, girl," Ira Jarvis said, rubbing his sparsely whiskered chin. "Know all 'bout his threats to stop the weddin', but he was a mite taken back when those men busted in and stole Quincy."

"An' you believed his actin'? The man comes from a long line of Scot thieves. Did you expect him to be admittin' that he planned this? You all know that varmint wants me mines, and he'll do anythin' to stop me from gettin' enough money together to open them. Didn't he undercut me freightin' prices so that I had to close down? But I swear I'll fix him. That Scot reiver won't win with his lies."

"Now, Maggie," Ira cautioned, "don't be lettin' that temper of yours get you into—"

"Maggie's right."

The simple statement drew all attention to Lee Warren. He walked his horse up from the back of the group. "It was McCready who insisted that all weapons be left at his saloon. If we'd been armed, those men would've had a fight on their hands when they came for Quincy. And McCready's the one that delayed opening the door so we could have our guns and let them get a good start on us. Funny, too, he ain't riding with us.''

Several men nodded, and reluctantly Ira had to agree. ''Gotta point. But Mohawk and McCready were friends. Don't see Maggie's uncle trustin' a scoundrel.''

''More's the pity he did,'' Maggie said, turning to Lee. ''Thank you for agreein' with me. I'll hope that you find their trail. I'll catch up after I see McCready.''

''Want me to come with you, Maggie? Don't cotton to you facing him alone.''

Maggie heard the iron beneath his softly voiced offer. She studied his lean, dark face, the features cut as sharp and clean as a knife blade. She took no offense at his words. Lee was one of a handful of men who had come to know her, accepted her as she was, and respected her abilities, even if at first he tried to be more than friends. She shook her head and stepped back out of the way, remembering the rumors that followed Lee's arrival in the mining camp four months ago just when the Burtons arrived. Lee's claim to be a miner was riddled with holes. He didn't know enough about mining to fill one of Miss Mae's thimbles. Now, if someone had told her that he rode the outlaw trail, she wouldn't have fluttered an eyelash. Lee was mighty comfortable with his gun, as she had seen for herself when he joined in the hunt for her uncle's killer. Satin whined at her side, and Maggie absently scratched behind the dog's ear.

''All right, girl. Let's go find that bastard.''

Pamela smiled at each man as he rode by her. She debated with herself over following Maggie down to the Rawhider saloon to witness the kill. Wisdom dictated otherwise. Pam headed for the three-room log cabin that housed her father's mercantile. Her delicate stomach couldn't stand the sight of blood. Especially if it was going to be McCready's.

Maggie walked in the center of the road that wound its way

through the canyon. The Mogollon Mountains cast their rugged shadows over this second mining camp. Clairmont on Copper Creek had been the first. Her uncle had told her tales of the constant Indian raids the miners suffered while they exploded the ledges of the canyon in hopes of finding gold-bearing ore. A sudden chill swept over her. The same sense that had warned Mohawk Pete when the Apache would attack and kept him alive, the sense he claimed she had, now warned her that trouble was coming.

She shrugged it off in seconds. She knew from the moment the news of her uncle's death reached her that she would have trouble aplenty. Pete's claims were rich. How rich, no one really knew. All she needed was enough money to begin mining them. Money that marrying Quincy Kessnick was going to provide.

And McCready wasn't going to find a hole to crawl into anywhere in the New Mexico Territory if he didn't return her groom.

Dutch Malone, the Rawhider's barkeep, six feet tall and half as wide, barred Maggie's way up the three planked steps leading to the saloon.

"Step aside and let me by."

"Maggie, I can't let you inside with a gun."

"I know that lyin', cheatin', no-count jackass is hidin' in there. You afeared I'll shoot him on sight?"

"Yeah. That's a first thought. The second being that you might be the one to get hurt."

"Then come inside with me, Dutch, and see that I don't, if it'll set your mind at ease. But around you or over you I'm goin' inside."

Dutch planted his hands on his hips, glaring at her. He liked Maggie, truly he did, but when the boss put him between them, like now, he wished he had stayed in New York.

"Ah, Maggie, 'pears you're in a fine temper."

"That I am." She tried to dodge around him, not wanting to

draw on Dutch since he was only following McCready's orders, but Maggie knew that if Dutch didn't want to step aside, nothing short of shooting him would get him to budge.

"Dutch, you and Pete were such good friends. How can you be protectin' that polecat from me? I never thought to see the likes."

"Don't be turning that Irish charm on me, Maggie. The man pays me a fine wage to see that his orders are carried out." Folding his massive arms across his chest, Dutch stood firm. "Since you're the one reminding me that I was good friends with your uncle, I need to say that McCready wants to see you safe and settled, Maggie. More than once I've heard him say that you needed a man to be . . . er, well, helping you. Even Pete said as much."

Maggie felt her rage build to another level. So McCready thought she needed a man, did he? The thought stopped her cold. She did. Why else had she considered marrying a tenderfoot like Quincy? Damn McCready's hide!

The deepening flush that stained her cheeks warned Dutch that Maggie's temper was about to explode. Seeking to calm her, protect McCready, and save what he could of his own body from harm, he offered her a compromise.

"Tell you what, Maggie. I'll let you by if you swear to me that you won't kill him right off."

"That lily-livered coward," she muttered, glancing away. "You know what he did. He has to pay for it."

A man of unmeasured patience, Dutch waited with ease. He knew that with every second gone by, Maggie would calm down. He couldn't hope for more.

"McCready can't be facin' me like a man, can he?" she asked.

"He's all the man he needs to be. Now, do you promise me, Maggie, so I can step aside, or do we stand here till sundown?"

"All right. You win, Dutch. I'll promise not to kill him right off."

"At all."

"Dutch!"

"At all, Maggie."

"You're a sight harder on me constitution than findin' a pinched-out vein, Dutch." Her sigh was followed by a careless shrug. "If that's the way of it, that's the way of it. I'll promise."

Dutch smiled, then leaned over to pat Satin. He was the only man beside her now deceased uncle that the dog allowed to touch her. His gaze followed Maggie as she passed him up the steps. A smothered laugh had her spinning around, her eyes as chilling as a mountain runoff.

"You'd best have a damn good reason for laughin' at me."

His expression was suddenly sober. "Never. I wasn't funning you. Just realized that you're wearing a woman's trappings, Maggie. You're right pretty all cleaned up, even if you're toting iron. Don't recall ever seeing you dressed like a woman before."

"Ain't likely to see it again. This piece of fancy goods was for me wedding dress." Maggie wanted to call the words back, understanding that she was admitting defeat of her plans. A narrow-eyed glare was pinned on Dutch. "It will be me wedding dress. Frills don't change me none. I'm still Maggie." She pushed open the thick wooden door of the saloon and stepped inside.

Smoke stung her eyes. Built without windows, the interior of the Rawhider would have been near dark but for the round coal oil fixtures suspended from the raw wood beams overhead. The bar, no more than three twelve-foot planks supported by empty upended flour barrels, ran the length of the left wall and stopped short of the corner, where a few steps led to McCready's rooms. Four tables filled the right side of the saloon. Against the back wall was McCready's pride and joy, a piano.

The man himself was hunched over at the far end of the bar, his hands wrapped around a glass, his eyes focused on whatever liquor the glass held. The flickering light from the fixtures cast shadows on his shoulder-length brown hair.

Maggie's distaste for his totally black-garbed figure was echoed in Satin's growling. With a back kick Maggie slammed the door closed. She knew that McCready was aware of her standing there, watching him. He didn't turn, didn't say a word or make a move to indicate that he cared.

Patience was not one of Maggie's virtues. But she tried. She counted all the way to ten and faltered. McCready's action had upset her plans. Anger forced her to act.

McCready lifted the glass to his lips, and Maggie drew her gun. She fired, shooting the glass from his hand.

Liquor and glass splattered over the planks of the bar. McCready's swearing, aimed at the ceiling, was drowned in the roar Dutch cut loose as he burst inside behind her.

"Maggie! Damn, you promised me!"

She didn't bother to turn. "Look for yourself. Didn't harm one hair on his proud head."

"Boss?"

"You can leave, Dutch. I'll take the price of that drink out of the miscreant's hide. Just make sure no one else comes in. This is between the Irish barbarian and me."

"Irish barbarian!" The words exploded from Maggie, and Satin howled. She didn't dare ask what the other word he called her meant. McCready would only laugh at her.

"Shut her up and yourself as well, Maggie."

"Don't be givin' me orders."

"Do it."

"Look me in the eye an' say that, McCready." Maggie knew Dutch left them; she felt the draft caused by the closing of the door across her bare back. Hushing the dog, not on McCready's order, but for herself, she stepped closer to the end of the bar.

"Have you any idea how much that fine liquor cost by the glass?" McCready didn't expect an answer. He slowly brushed the shards of glass from his vest and shirt, refusing to look at Maggie. His breathing was deep and even, his control barely stretched. But he really didn't trust himself around Maggie. Actually he had to thank the most merciful saints that she had not decided to shoot at any part of his anatomy. Maggie never missed what she aimed at. His best panama hat had the bullet holes to prove it.

"Turn around, coward."

"Ah, there's men that would be calling you out for saying as much. But I'm in a generous mood and more than willing to forgive your asperity. Holster your gun, Maggie, I'll not be fighting with you. In honor of your wedding my shirt's new, and I'll not have you spoil it with blood. It's detriment enough that you have me reeking of damn expensive whiskey. In addition, my dear termagant, I'm unarmed."

"If someone cut out that silver tongue, you would be." Maggie refused to ask what he had called her. McCready was always using words she didn't understand. But she holstered her gun, not on his order, nor out of fear of him, but simply because she knew she could outdraw him if the need arose.

Still not turning to face her, McCready sniffed the air in a loud, exaggerated manner. "Violets?" he murmured. "Am I truly in the august presence of O'Roarke and smelling sweet violets?" A quick shake of his head was followed by denial. "It simply cannot be." A frown denoted the serious nature of his own query.

There was no help for it. McCready straightened to his full height and faced her. His breath lodged somewhere in his throat. "Oh, my," he managed to say and barely that.

Each of his muscles tensed, and his silver tongue deserted him. "By the bones of the bonny prince!" he uttered as both oath and prayer. "Miss Mary Margaret O'Roarke's a woman and surely a sight to tempt a saint."

"Since you'd be kin to the devil himself, McCready, I won't be worryin' about temptin' you." But she was struck by the strange way he continued to stare at her. McCready never had looked this way. Maggie frowned, her eyes narrowed in concentration. She felt as if she were a honeycomb he was thinking of stealing without getting stung.

"My own eyes can't be lying," he murmured.

Maggie no longer cared. She reminded herself of why she was here. "What did you do with Quincy?" To show she meant business, Maggie spread her legs in an aggressive stance.

McCready groaned and closed his eyes for a moment. If Maggie knew what he was thinking, she would shoot him one inch at a time. It took strength of will not to cover that most vulnerable rising pillar of masculine pride.

"McCready," she warned.

"I never touched him. Never mind that mealy-mouth. He is—"

"Don't be callin' Quincy names."

"He's no more a pilgrim needing your protection than I am, Maggie." His gaze targeted hers, believing her eyes were the safest place for him to look. "You've had yourself a bath. I can finally see the color of your hair isn't the grand shade of a mud slide. It's shiny copper with gold ribboning through. Now, if you would take pity on these starved senses of mine and let it grow—"

"Long? Like yours?" Maggie couldn't help the unladylike snort. McCready was always going on about what was wrong with her, but for an unexplained reason she found his bantering exciting.

"Ah, Maggie mine, you've a nasty sting to your voice. It wounds me something fierce." With a flourish he placed one hand over his heart. The racing beat beneath his fingers confirmed the feeling of being poleaxed. McCready could find no other way to describe what Maggie had done to him. She remained unmoved by his gesture, squinting owlishly at him, but her mongrel shook her head as if to tell him his ploy was not going to gain him the sympathy he sought.

"Where is Quincy?"

"Quincy?" His hand dropped to rest elbow up on the bar, his palm cupping his chin. "Ah, yes, Quincy. The illustrious supposed-to-be-groom," he drawled, his smile then framed by deep creases.

"Faith and begorra, McCready! Take that whiskey-smooth drawl and drown it in the fancy liquor you're so fond of."

"If you speak to Quincy as you do to me, Maggie mine, it's no wonder the man ran off."

"Quincy didn't run off, you loggerhead. He was kidnapped. And you," she admonished, pointing one finger at him, "you put those men up to it."

"Now, Maggie, don't be accusing—"

"Enough!" Dropping her hand to her side, she gazed up at the ceiling, fighting not to shoot him and be done.

Cocking his head to the left, McCready's smile deepened. Maggie's skirt trailed crookedly behind her. "Did you forget your bustle?"

"Me what?"

"The bustle, Maggie," he explained with patience. "You tie it over your petticoats—you are wearing petticoats, aren't you? Not that it matters to me, you understand, but Quincy would certainly care." Her blank stare had him adding, "That little rounded-shaped cage lifts up the train of your gown that's dragging behind you. Didn't anyone come to help you get dressed?"

"Didn't want anyone," she snapped, stung by his pity. "An' never mind what I'm wearin' or not. It'll be off in a thrice once I'm married." She ignored his choking. "If you don't tell me where you hid me groom—"

"You know," he continued in a soft voice, as if she had never answered him, "I've heard of a jealous suitor stealing off with the bride on her wedding day, and seeing you, believe it, but never did I hear of someone stealing the groom."

"It wasn't *someone*, as you well know, McCready. There were five of them. Five men that you paid."

"I'll admit I was there. The man didn't put up a fight, Maggie. Didn't protest a bit at being stolen from his own wedding. Can't understand that," he said with another quick shake of his head that lifted his shoulder-length hair. "Do you think the man reconsidered and believed he was being saved from a fate worse than death?"

"Is that the choice you offered him?" Maggie hid the hurt his stinging question caused her. Her chin angled up. She knew she was not the sort of woman a man wanted for a wife. If she had not known, McCready had made it his sworn, solemn duty to point it out to her at least once a day for the past few months.

"Since you're upset, let me atone. Share a drink with me, Maggie. It'll calm your bridal nerves."

"Ain't got them."

"Well, then, have a drink with me so I can mourn the passing of Czar Alexander. That's who I was drinking to when you shot the glass out of my hand."

"Zar Alexander? Don't recall the name. He be one of the tinhorns you knew?"

McCready had to swallow his laughter. "No, Maggie. He wasn't even a friend, but the Czar of Russia." At her confused look, he added, "He was like a king. The man was assassinated last month, and I've only learned of it. His dying marks—ah, never mind."

Shifting her weight, Maggie stilled her impatience. She had a healthy respect for grief, even if she didn't quite understand McCready's.

"Sorry as I am to hear his dyin', I won't be drinkin' with you over someone I couldn't be knowin'."

McCready knew he had touched her stiff-necked pride, and strangely the baiting game lost its appeal. "Well, there's happier things to drink to. Garfield's inauguration as our president. Or the completion of the second transcontinental railroad right in our territory of New Mexico.'' Maggie shook her head, but he wasn't giving up. "If you'd like, we could have a drink of commiseration for those poor souls in Kansas whose legislature passed a law prohibiting the sale of liquor except for medical or scientific purposes.''

"None of them are a reason to drink with the likes of you.''

McCready's tone became serious. "Then a last offer. Have a drink with me as a toast from one old friend to another.''

Maggie grinned and glanced around the empty saloon. She needed a bit of her own back. "Don't see any old friends or any new ones.''

"You've wounded me to the quick.''

"I'll do more than wound you. I promised Dutch I wouldn't kill you right off. But I'm slowly regretting that rash promise, McCready. If you had brains beneath that mop of hair you're so vain over, you'd know that I won't rest till I find out what you've done with Quincy.''

His answer was to walk around the end of the bar to fetch himself a new glass and the bottle. Pouring out a stiff belt, he sniffed the bottle and then held it high to check the level. Half-full. The amount reassured him that he had enough to fortify himself for what was coming. But as he sipped his drink, McCready found his gaze drawn back to Maggie. He couldn't seem to stop himself.

She waited for him to answer, sliding her hand up to rest on the protruding butt of her gun. Moments went by and she wondered if he had heard her declaration. She stepped closer to the bar, a frown once more marring her forehead. McCready was staring at her, his dark blue eyes intense, his thin lips compressed, his breathing labored, and a dark flush creeping up to color his clean-shaven cheeks. Maybe all the wicked living he had done was catching up with him. Maggie studied him as she would a new rock sample, looking for clues to its composition. In seconds the color deepened over his cheekbones, and she wondered if he was about to have a fit like the miner who up and died in the street two days ago.

Most puzzling of all was why that should alarm her.

"What's bedevilin' you, McCready?"

"You don't want to know." His words crackled with tension.

Maggie stiffened her back. "You haven't been dippin' into that bug-juice you serve to the go-backers?"

With a visible shudder McCready muttered, "Heaven and saints forbid."

"Well, it don't take much to see that somethin' is wrong with you. Wouldn't be havin' an attack of conscience for ruinin' me weddin' day?"

"No," he managed to choke out, shifting his stance, only to change his mind and come out from behind the bar. He wanted to get closer to Maggie.

"You're lookin' mighty hot and sweaty all of a sudden," she observed, narrowing her eyes. She didn't know what to make of his strange look and strange behavior. Never once had his silver tongue deserted him. Not even when Mica Bob hit his strike and brought his mule into the Rawhider for drinks. Unable to put a name to what it was that exactly bothered her, Maggie shrugged it off. McCready with his fancy words and dark moods made her uncomfortable. But he sure did look hot and sweaty.

Hot and sweaty didn't come close to what McCready was feeling. He was fighting his own reaction to seeing Maggie dressed for the first time as a woman. He knew she was tall, barely four inches shorter than his own near six-foot height. He knew and filed that fact away because he liked his women petite and cuddlesome. He just never realized that Maggie had a small waist, or gently flaring hips that could cushion a man's ride with ease, or breasts so lushly full they would fill his hands, along with skin that rivaled the color of sweet cream. The corner of his mouth twisted with sheer exasperation.

How dare Mary Margaret O'Roarke keep herself hidden away beneath baggy pants, shirts, and a jacket that would easily stand on their own, plus mud and a stench that would curl a mule's ears?

Just how dare she!

All this time he had been regretting his promise to Mohawk Pete. He had waited, hoping and praying—for he did believe the Lord indulged his sinner's prayers—that the good Lord was going to take pity on him as a reward for his costly sacrifice. And what did he get, aside from the laughter that was likely shaking the heavens? Maggie slicked up with bows and lace for Quincy Kessnick. Maggie—a woman.

He moved with an unfocused gaze and slow deliberation to stand tall and started toward her.

Satin's hair rose. Growling at the danger McCready presented, she moved to stand in front of Maggie.

"Satan hates me."

"Her name is Satin, McCready. You know, just like the fancy goods *your* ladies wear."

Leaning down to caress the dog's head, Maggie whispered her praise. "Good, good girl." And to him, "How many times do you need to be reminded of her name? Much as it irks me to be admittin' it, you're right. She does hate you. Almost as much as me an' with less reason. Since you won't tell me where Quincy is hid, I'll go lookin' for him meself."

Standing straight again, Maggie glared at him. "I'll give you a last warnin'. Nothin' you do will stop me from marryin' him. I'm gonna have the money I need to open those mines."

"Maggie, you can't. The claims belong to me."

"Don't be startin' with your lies again. Me uncle wouldn't gamble one claim away, much less all of them. And if he did, the only way you won was to cheat him."

Shaking his head, needing the abrupt motion to clear his thoughts, McCready drawled, "Maggie mine, not again. You've left me no choice. I've tried to tell you since Pete died that the claims belong to me. Not only the claims—but you do, too.''

''What devil's tale are you stirrin' up now?''

Her reaction was less than he hoped for. Struck with lightning inspiration, McCready reached inside his vest pocket and pulled out a folded piece of paper. Holding it to the side by two fingers, in case Maggie took it in mind to shoot at it, he nevertheless waved the paper. ''This is no tale.''

Firmly then, he stated his case. ''You forced my hand by pushing for this marriage when you learned that the circuit preacher would pass through. You can't marry Quincy Kessnick. You, Maggie mine, can't marry anyone.''

The wicked laughter was long gone from his eyes, and his gaze was most certainly focused. On her. Only her. Maggie squinted at him through the smoky haze drifting down from the overhead fixtures. She couldn't utter a sound. There was a rising lump in her throat that wouldn't allow her to swallow, and her breath seemed twisted inside, unable to get out. Now it was McCready who stood with his legs spread, sure and arrogant that he held a winning hand.

''Did you understand me, Maggie? You can't get married today or any other day.''

''The hell I can't!''

Shooting a look at the blackened ceiling, McCready asked for guidance. Looking back at Maggie, he whispered, ''I'm trying my best to prevent you from committing a sin.''

''Sin?'' she repeated softly, sensing that he was taunting her but unable to walk away until he showed his full hand.

''Bigamy, Maggie. That's what sin I'm talking about. I had to save you. Someone did, and the good Lord and Pete chose me. I had to get rid of Quincy before you did something that would make you burn in hell. Seeing you now makes the mere thought a sin of its own. And,'' he added, grinning, ''we have to come to an understanding.''

"Understandin'?" she parroted, swallowing past the thick lump that was choking her.

"Yeah, Maggie. Between you and me. This most valuable and treasured piece of paper, duly signed and recorded in the county records, is for a proxy marriage between one Mary Margaret O'Roarke and C. V. McCready."

CHAPTER 2

"Liar!"

"Not about this, Maggie mine."

"Give it to me."

McCready glanced at the paper he held as if giving consideration to her demand, then glanced back to Maggie's blanching face. "Don't take offense, lass, but I'd be a fool to trust you near this. Besides, Maggie, you can't read it, can you?"

Brazenly she tossed her head. "No. I can't read. But Pete wouldn't—" Maggie stopped. Her uncle's last words to her when he had left for his diggings burst vividly from her memory. *"Don't worry, girl. I fixed everything for you."*

"Maggie?" Concerned for her continuing pallor, McCready started for her.

"Don't take another step. I don't want the likes of you near me."

"Admit it, then. Your uncle lost his claims fairly to me. No matter what you think is true, or what you believe about me, Maggie, I didn't cheat him to win. And this," he stated, once more waving the paper, "proves that he was worried about what would happen to you."

"You're a liar, McCready."

"At times." He answered with candor, without hesitation. "But this isn't one of those times. Pete said that if I would marry you by proxy, he would make sure that I knew which of his seven claims were to the gold. You wouldn't believe anything I've tried to say these last few months since he died. You just pushed and pushed until you backed me into a corner."

She raised her hand as if to do that very thing, shuddered, and dropped it back to her side.

"Maggie, listen to me. When Quincy came along and you decided to marry him, I had to protect what's mine. I had to protect you just as I promised Pete."

Shaking her head in denial, Maggie whispered, "Married? To you?" Her husky voice had a deep, choked quality to it. Still shaking her head, disbelieving every word McCready spoke, she felt a pounding begin over her left temple. Hog-tied to McCready? Shackled by marriage?

"Aye, Maggie, married to me. I came up to your cabin almost every day since Pete died. You either refused to open the door or weren't there."

"I was doin' me grievin'." Rubbing her forehead Maggie gazed around the room, feeling the pull to look back at McCready's face. "Married?" she repeated yet again.

"Legal as can be. Of course, it would be nice since the preacher's here, ready to perform a ceremony, if we were to make sure that no one doubts it's true. Miss Mae went to a great deal of trouble—''

"Never."

"Pardon?"

"You heard me—never, McCready."

He shrugged. "You'll need time to get accustomed to the idea. Mohawk Pete was your only relative. That made him your legal guardian. You're underage, Maggie. Well, you were until two days ago. This proxy marriage took place three months before he died."

Seven months! McCready knew about this for seven months and never said a word. "Why would Pete trust you?" It just couldn't be true!

"Why not me?" he countered, daring her now with his look to add further insult.

Maggie violently shook her head. She wanted to wrap her arms around herself, as if that would protect her from this verbal battering. She was frightened and didn't dare give McCready that knowledge, or he would use it as a weapon.

"You . . . are me . . . h-hus-band?"

McCready's engaging grin died aborning. Maggie's pride and spirit had disappeared. He never knew that she could fear anyone or anything. Nothing had daunted her. But her eyes, those damnable, haunting eyes accused him, revealing for a brief moment her vulnerability. He could not falter now.

"In the legal sight of man, if not God, I am."

"You only want the gold claims."

"I've made no secret of that, Mary Margaret. You're the only one who knows which of those seven claims is for gold. The assay report on one shows a rich vein that men would kill to possess. And I admit, after seeing you dressed like a woman, Maggie, my . . . er, greed, shall we say, is no longer for the gold alone."

Her eyes, the green of ancient jade, snapped to life. "Think I'll make it easy for you? You figure some piece of paper's tyin' me to you? Let me set you on the right path, McCready. I'll make meself a widow before I'm your bride.''

''Would you now?'' His voice was soft, almost friendly, but utterly pitiless.

The look of his eyes sent shivers up her spine and a loop of heat curling around her belly. Never once had McCready ever gazed at her like he was coming off a steady diet of roots and berries and she the perfectly sizzled steak set before him. Maggie felt an attack to her senses that sent panic streaming through her.

''Mary Margaret,'' he chided, shielding his eyes with lashes that were thick and curling, ''why would you desire to take this to that extreme? Widowhood isn't at all what you want, much less need. Black won't suit you.'' The lie slid off his smooth tongue as his imagination peeled the finest of soft cashmere from the lush body in front of him. Or silk, he amended, thinking of its sensuous quality against skin.

''You can't be knowin' what I want or need, McCready.''

He forced his thoughts from their licentious path and reasoned with her. ''Think about Pete. Think about his gold. If you kill me, Maggie, you're sure to end up in jail, then, more's the pity, hung. I'll be gone, that's true, but someone is sure to come along and find that mother lode. Pete had big plans for you and that gold, didn't he? Would you deny what he wanted?'' McCready started to tuck the paper back into his vest pocket.

''Hold it. I might not be able to read it, but I'll find someone who can. You think you can flimflam me? Think again. Hand it over.''

McCready glanced from her outstretched hand back to her glittering eyes. ''No deal, darlin'.'' He patted his pocket and gave in to the urge to get closer to her. He managed all of three steps. There was a flicker of fear again in her eyes, something he had never seen or hoped to see from Maggie. But then, today seemed to be winning him prizes for firsts with Maggie.

He watched the way her hand curled around the butt of her gun.

"Think before you do something rash, Maggie. Shooting me would be too easy. You might," he taunted, "enjoy finding yourself married to me."

A remembered flash of Cora Ann's smile after she had spent a night in McCready's bed cost Maggie her breath. If that reminder wasn't enough to add weight to his taunt, she recalled the Desert Rose teasing her that playing duck and goose was simply the best when played with McCready. Well, she wasn't taken in by simpering females and their gushing praise of his masculine charms. His women could have him!

"McCready," she intoned in a deadly voice, "I'd sooner be married to a mule. Matter of fact," she stated, then had to stop, fighting for the spirit that had never deserted her. She gave him a thorough once-over from the tip of his square-toed boots up the indecent fit of his pants across the snug pull of his vest and shirt, lighting her gaze on one shoulder. "A mule is better lookin', better mannered, and a sight easier to handle."

"Try a little sweetened sugar and less of the salt and vinegar you're so fond of spitting out, Mary Margaret, and then see how easy I am to handle."

"When mules talk, boyo." She turned around, disgusted with him and herself. Maggie took a few steps toward the door only to stop when he bit off her name with a choking sound. A quick look over her shoulder showed McCready staggering before he grabbed hold of the bar. She thought he was going down to the floor, but he recovered. Maggie stared. He appeared to have some trouble drawing his breath. One of his hands suddenly clutched his side, the other hovered near his mouth.

"Dutch!" she called. "Dutch! Get in here. McCready needs you," she bellowed in her best mule-skinner's voice.

But Dutch didn't come bursting through the door. She hesitated, wishing McCready to the devil and yet unable to just leave him. Then he doubled over, and her choice was made as it would be for any helpless critter. Much as she hated him, Maggie didn't want him dying by any means but her own hand.

She rushed to his side, bracing him upright. "What ails you?" Her gaze took in the fever bright glitter of his eyes, and the flush that was once again stealing up to shade his skin. "Damn you, McCready, answer me."

He barely managed another choked sound. His head fell forward, his cheek coming to rest on the upper slope of her breast. Maggie reacted instantly, shifting her body so she was more to his side.

McCready kept his head low, hiding the unholy light of satisfaction in his eyes, and leaned heavily against Maggie. Her arm held him firmly around the waist, the position pressing one lush breast against his chest. Her shoulder barely fit beneath his arm, but it gave him free access to slide his hand into the gaping back of her gown.

Stiff as a poker, Maggie angled her head to glare up at him. "Don't be tryin' none of your dandy's tricks."

"Support . . . that's all," he mumbled.

He *was* a trifle unsteady. Maggie knew McCready never got drunk this early in the day, so she let this go by, even if his fingers couldn't seem to light in one place on her back. She could feel the heavy, erratic beats of his heart. But damn if he didn't make her stomach feel like a bevy of butterflies had taken up home there.

Maggie, she warned herself, this is McCready. And McCready is a liar, a cheat, totally untrustworthy. She eyed him with those thoughts.

"Ah"—he sighed—"I'll be cold in hell, Maggie mine," he whispered, nuzzling his cheek against her shoulder.

"McCready—"

"Maggie." Laughter rode his voice. "You've got freckles."

"Take your hand—"

"Now, tell me, Mary Margaret," he asked, his voice now low, silky, and challenging, "are they all over?"

''That's it!'' Maggie yanked his arm off her shoulder, gave it a good twist, and shoved his body backward at the same time. Satin leapt up, teeth bared to grab hold of his arm, pulling his hand away from her mistress. The dog's added strength helped Maggie's second shove send McCready sprawling on the sawdust-littered floor. He was stunned for a moment, and that was all Satin needed. She planted herself on top of him, once more baring her most impressive teeth.

Smacking her hands together, then wiping them down the sides of her gown, Maggie glared at him. ''Keep that sidewinder pinned, girl,'' she ordered Satin.

Maggie had had enough. She had reached the limit of being able to hold back her fear that McCready might have told her the truth. How could she prove he was lying? They couldn't be married. She detested him and all he stood for. Lazy no-count tinhorn!

With a graceful turn that twisted the dragging trail of her gown around her boots, Maggie ignored his mutterings. Yanking the entangling cloth free, she walked away.

''Maggie! Maggie, come back here!'' he yelled. ''Get this devil's bitch off me.''

''Get her off yourself. Use your silver tongue to slide your way out of this. Or tell me the truth, McCready. You were lyin' to me about us bein' married, right? I know that you are. So did Pete. He never would've tied me to a stingy thievin' Scot like you.''

''He did! Tie you to me, that is. An' I'm no more a—''

''Tell me where you had those men take Quincy.''

''I don't have him here.''

''That's no damn answer. Stay with him, girl.'' She gave him a cheeky grin. ''Seems you're stuck, McCready.''

''If I am, expect payment in kind, O'Roarke.''

Maggie stopped in the act of hooking her thumbs in her gunbelt. She was still. Looking at him, startled by the fierce challenging gaze that met her own, Maggie had no time to attempt to hide the fear and hurt she felt.

"If you told me the truth and we are married, McCready, I'll be payin' for it the rest of me life. Why I don't kill you now and be done with it is beyond me. But I'll swear this, sidewinder, I'll find a way to prove you're a liar, a cheat, and a thief."

"Maggie, I didn't want to tell you this way. I tried to talk to you—"

"The day I buried Pete?"

"I wanted to protect you. But you left me no choice."

Maggie wasn't going to be fooled by the soft sincerity in his voice, but Satin whined and looked at her.

"Don't you be turnin' traitor, too. What Pete did to me was enough." Saints be! What was she admitting?

"Maggie, you are *my* wife."

"Only if you catch me, McCready," she taunted, having regained some of her spirit and knowing that she had only herself to depend upon to help her out of this.

McCready didn't miss the flash of excitement in her eyes. The corner of his mouth tugged up the beginning of a smile. "I'll catch you, Maggie. What's more, you'll like it when I do. I'll hogtie you so tight that you won't have room to move, much less think. And then, Maggie mine," he promised with all the male arrogance that too many easy women had enforced, "then I'll make you understand what being my wife means."

"You can try, boyo. You surely can try."

She stood a moment more, legs spread, hands on hips, her chin angled for battle, and McCready felt heat melt his bones. She was exactly what he had called her: barbaric. The fire of her passionate denial only settled matters. He wanted her.

Maggie's leaving broke the spell, her laughter floating back to him as he cradled his hands beneath his head. He longed to deny the underlying desperation he heard along with her taunting laughter. But McCready lived by few enough rules. One was that he never, ever lied to himself.

Maggie was afraid of him.

Satin pawed his chest and forced him to look at her. He thought about freeing his hands and closing them around the dog's throat to throw her off him. Satin inched each of her large paws upward until they rested on his shoulders. She cocked her head to the side.

McCready smiled. "There, lass, that's a good girl."

He spoke too soon. Satin's teeth were once again bared. The dog resettled her considerable weight over his chest with her rump planted on his knees.

McCready sighed. "What we have here is a Mexican standoff, Satan."

Deep and low came her warning growl.

"All right. All right. Satin. Satisfied? 'Tis a cursed life I lead, girl. I've had some possessive females wanting my body, but none were ready to rip my throat to keep it." He eyed her tongue lolling to the side. "Wouldn't you like to be petted? Not by a woman's soft hand but by a man's strong one?" Satin's ears perked up.

"I've found something that you want, right?" He slid one hand out from under his head, his gaze never leaving that of the dog's. Satin didn't growl this time, her ears laid flat back, and he could feel her body tense to spring. McCready put his hand back beneath his head.

"I'll be damned if I understand why Mary Margaret named you something soft and pretty while she refuses to look like a woman. She's got deep secrets, girl. Secrets I intend to reveal, just like I'll find out how many of those adorable little freckles she has."

Satin lowered her head, butting her cold nose against his chin.

"Am I to assume the idea finds some favor with you?"

The dog watched him with unblinking eyes.

He inched his hands out from beneath his head, and up came Satin's head.

"Yeah. I get the message. It's all right for me to talk, but no moves, huh?" Before he cradled his head again, Satin settled down. "Ah, Maggie my own," he crooned softly, "for every minute this devil's bitch has me pinned beneath her, you my love, are going to find yourself experiencing the very same attention."

Two hours later, when Dutch opened the door to the saloon, his heart stopped. McCready was sprawled on the floor, his arms flung out to the sides, and Maggie's dog lay beside him. Maggie had lied to him. Dutch didn't want to believe it, but the proof of his own eyes was impossible to deny. She had killed McCready and left her dog so Dutch would know it was her.

The floorboard creaked as he stepped closer. Satin rose, hair on high, attack ready, until Dutch spoke to her.

"Easy, girl, I just want to see how she managed to finish him off."

McCready lifted one thick brow, then opened his eyes to find Dutch's hulking form bending over him.

"You're alive."

"There's no need to reveal your disappointment, Dutch. And it's with no thanks to you deserting your post. It should cost you a month's pay for leaving me at the mercy of that creature."

Looking him over, Dutch straightened. "You ain't bloody, so I guess it couldn't have been all that bad. And I had damn good reason to leave. I had the feeling."

"A week's pay, then," McCready conceded, knowing Dutch's *feeling* was nothing to toy with. "Can you get the beastie away so that I might once more stand like a man?"

"Ain't fair, boss, losing my pay. You're lying there—"

"I didn't have a choice, man. The mongrel was lying on top of me, barely allowing me a decent breath, much less a move."

McCready eyed Dutch's hand, absently patting the dog. "Don't be rewarding her. Get her the hell out of here."

"Sure thing, boss. C'mon, girl," he coaxed, holding the dog by the ruff. "Go home to Maggie."

Once Dutch had shown Satin the door, he returned to the end of the bar to watch McCready finish brushing the sawdust from his hair and clothes. There was a tight set to his boss's mouth that boded ill. McCready poured them both a drink, sipped his, then demanded to know where Dutch had been.

"Unlike you, I'm not trusting those men you hired away from Quincy to kidnap him. Figured if they sold out to you, they might sell back to him. Went up to the cabin to make sure they were gonna keep him there until I went for him. It was a good thing, too. He was set on upping the ante to bribe them into letting him go."

"I paid them plenty to—"

"I know. I know, boss. But Quincy was talking money. Big money for his freedom. Double what you paid them was the last I heard. I warned them but good just what you'd do to them if Quincy showed his face around here before you were ready for him." Dutch shook his head. "Still can't understand why you didn't just tell Maggie the truth. She wouldn't want to tie herself to a man who'd do anything to get those claims. She should've been told that Quincy planned to have himself kidnapped, and when she came looking for him, they were going to demand she sign over the claims for his life."

"They're my claims, Dutch. Stop forgetting that."

He eyed his boss. Ah, McCready was sure getting touchy about Pete's claims. Dutch decided to abandon talk about them. "You got to admit, boss, that Maggie sure looked pretty dressed in a gown. Didn't she?"

The drink that McCready was nursing burned his throat. The glass hit the planked top of the bar. Liquor sloshed over his hand. "Don't," he grated from between clenched teeth, "dare mention that creature's name in my saloon if you value your hide.''

"Didn't say a thing about Satin, boss. I was talking about Maggie looking so damn good she—"

"By the bones of the bonny prince, shut up!" McCready's eyes closed tight. Once again he saw Maggie's luscious figure so firmly implanted in his mind that he knew he would never forget it. One of the sins on his most unforgivable list was being duped. Maggie's offenses through the last year had multiplied until he gave her a priority listing of her own. One that demanded for the sake of male pride that he take some revenge.

Dutch sensed he had stumbled onto something more than all the past heated confrontations between McCready and Maggie. Like a man probing a throbbing tooth, he couldn't resist another gingerly made thrust.

"That woman's got a right fine figure. Surprised me, I'll freely admit."

"Dutch."

Ah, he was right. McCready's voice was soft. He sipped his drink, cupping the glass to warm the liquor, and kept his gaze pinned to the bottles lined up neatly against the wall.

"I did some thinking while I rode out to the cabin. Figure with the right educating in manners, she'd be a woman any man would be proud to have on his arm."

"I'm fair warning you."

"Yes, sir," Dutch continued, ignoring him, "Mary Margaret has finally grown up." Smacking his lips, Dutch turned and watched as McCready opened his eyes and faced him. It was a shame that the good Lord had seen fit to give a man as good looking as McCready a jaw soft as butter. Not in its shape, Dutch noted, it was manly enough, but the lightest tap knocked him cold.

"I did warn you not to mention her name."

"But I didn't." Hands raised in protest, Dutch grinned.

"Did the dog affect your hearing, man? Not one sound came from these lips of mine that sounded like the name we've all been calling her. I said Mary Margaret."

McCready dropped his head forward, defeated. He couldn't hit Dutch. He needed him for an ally. And if the Lord had stopped laughing long enough to see the serious matter at stake, Dutch would never know the licentious thoughts he was having about her. Maggie. A groan escaped him.

"If I didn't know better," Dutch stated, his brow deeply furrowed as he rubbed his chin, "I'd say you've got the same guilty look about you that usually marks your scheming."

"You've been too long in the wilds, man. You're seeing what isn't there."

"Maybe so, maybe so. What are you going to do about the female whose name I can't be mentioning?"

A furious pounding at the front door of the saloon interrupted them. McCready motioned for Dutch to see who it was while he stepped behind the bar and broke the seal on a fresh bottle of his special whiskey.

"We're not open for business, Dutch," he called out just as the man lifted the wooden bar across the door.

Dutch nodded to show he heard him, but now he was really worried. McCready never turned down a chance to make money. Never. Dutch always blamed it on his Scot forebears.

Opening the door part way, his body blocking entry, Dutch looked at the two men, heard what they wanted, and closed the door. "Boss, it's Abe and Jimmy Keystone, wanting to know why the door is barred."

Without looking, McCready reached behind him, lifted a bottle of Dutch's homebrew, and tossed it to the barkeep. "Give it to them with my compliments."

Dutch nearly dropped the bottle he had just caught. Oh my, McCready was in a bad way for him to give away free liquor. Dutch did as ordered and once again barred the door before he took up his place standing opposite McCready.

"That's the second bottle you've opened today," Dutch said, tipping a bit into his own glass. "You want to tell me what's wrong? I mean *really* wrong. I know this has to do with Maggie." He met McCready's glower with a steadfast gaze. "I know that I agreed to help you, but I still can't figure out why you couldn't tell her the truth about Quincy. She wouldn't marry a man just for money."

"That's how much you know Maggie O'Roarke. Kessnick has money that Maggie wants to work all the claims. How could I be living with myself if I failed to protect her from such a lying schemer?"

Dutch choked, then swallowed the liquor in his mouth. He set his glass down and gripped the edge of the bar. "And what would you be calling yourself if not the same?"

McCready ignored the twinge of guilt that made itself felt. "It isn't the same at all. I'm keeping my sworn word to Pete. He wouldn't want Maggie tied to a man that agreed to marry just to get his hands on those claims. Once I had Quincy drunk enough and heard that he had no plans to stay married to her, I had to rescue Maggie. He bragged long and hard about the eastern mining syndicate that he was fronting for. When he realized that Maggie wasn't about to sell the claims to him, not that she can, mind you, but that's when he decided to marry her."

"So, you're still saying that you acted with the noble thoughts of sacrificing yourself to save her? And you'd be having the purest of intentions toward the girl?"

McCready tossed back his drink and moved to refill his glass.

Dutch stopped him. "I've rarely questioned you, but this time you owe me an answer."

Having long ago made a satisfactory deal with his conscience, McCready wasn't easily cowed by the threat in Dutch's voice. A guilty conscience needed no accuser.

"Be satisfied with this, Dutch. My intentions don't matter. I settled the question of Maggie marrying anyone."

Slapping his boss's back, Dutch poured his drink for him and even handed McCready the glass. "I knew you'd do the right thing and tell her the truth. Maggie's smart enough to understand." Tipping his own glass in salute, Dutch neatly downed his drink. Lowering the glass to the bar, he glanced at McCready's untouched glass. "You did tell her the truth?"

"Did you know that telling the truth shames the devil?"

"What are you saying?" Dutch's meaty hands curled into fists.

"Well, my friend, there are those who will say that the truth may be blamed but cannot ever be shamed."

"The last time you got to recalling that fancy learning of yours was the night we got run out of Virginia City."

"A ways back. But a most pleasant memory."

"Hamilton Baker didn't think so. You took him for almost thirty thousand on the turn of one card. Couldn't blame the man for raising the question of where that ace came from, either. You were mighty clumsy in those days."

Thinking of the hurt in Maggie's eyes, McCready knew he was still clumsy.

"Seems to me," Dutch went on, unaware, "that every time one of your schemes starts skidding the wrong way, you get to pulling out those confounded sayings."

Grinning, McCready faced him. "It was a most memorable night, Dutch." But under the man's steady regard, his grin faltered, then died. "Almost as good as the night we met in New York and—"

"Never mind trying to lead me down that false trail. Pete was my friend, too. I made him the same promise that you did to take care of Maggie and watch out for her. So, I'm asking you once more, Mr. McCready. If you've done something to hurt that gal, best be telling me now."

He couldn't continue to meet Dutch's gaze. Looking heavenward, and knowing there was no answer forthcoming, McCready sighed. "Dutch, I told Maggie that as her legal guardian, Pete married her off by proxy before he died."

"That must have jury-rigged her sails just fine." But gazing at his boss revealed one unhappy-looking man. "It can't be bothering you that Maggie hates you a bit more?"

With a serious tone McCready admitted, "Actually, it does. And you're right. She did look pretty all dressed up like a woman."

Dutch found himself stepping away from the bar. It wasn't the words themselves, but the lust, as pure as the gold from Mohawk Pete's first claim, that was wrapped around the last words McCready spoke. He took the measure of a man whom he topped by a few inches and outweighed by a good seventy pounds. Something told him he was going to regret pushing McCready into telling him the truth. But he wasn't a man who would run from knowing.

"Now, what would a man like you be wanting with Maggie when you have Cora Ann and that new songbird, Rose, to be fighting over who spends the night with you? You don't need Maggie. You don't want Maggie." Dutch stopped. In his mind he once again heard McCready's earlier confession. He told Maggie that Pete married her off by proxy. Dutch reverted to a string of blue curses learned on the New York docks. When he was done, he took a deep cleansing breath, released it, then asked, "Who did you say Maggie was married to?"

"You don't want to know." McCready turned and rested both elbows on the bar. He knew that Dutch wouldn't let it be. He was deliberately allowing himself to be vulnerable. Perhaps he should renegotiate the deal with his conscience. Sure enough, the big man lumbered out from behind the bar to plant himself in front of McCready. But he had to give it one last try.

"Dutch, we've been friends for almost ten years. We've been in some rough spots and had a few narrow escapes. But there's been times when we've had—"

"I know all that. Answer me."

"You only knew Pete for three years. Yes, I know he's the one that tipped us off that Cooney Camp would be the next big strike with money to be made freighting. But where the hell does your loyalty—"

"Never mind my loyalty. Leave it out of this. Who did you say little Maggie is married to?"

"Dutch, back off."

Dutch noted the soft, soft voice. He thought about it for just a second and decided against its warning. "You're gonna tell me, McCready, and without any of your lies."

"Do you know that you're the second one to call me a liar today? I must be slipping. But frankly, I'm getting damned tired of hearing it."

"Then stop doing it." With a quick shift of his body Dutch assumed a fighter's stance. "It's thanks to you that I've boxed my way through more than a few barroom brawls. You know that I'm always one of them that walks away. Unlike you. Friendship is the only thing that's stopping me from taking a piece of you now. I won't be asking this again. Who is married to Maggie?"

McCready saw the red flush creep up from Dutch's stiff white linen collar at an alarming rate. He eyed Dutch's fists. The scars and protruding knuckles forced him to swallow. He knew he was already suffering the condemning guilt of the damned. With a mental shrug he answered.

"Me." And braced himself for the blow that was coming.

CHAPTER
3

High on the rim of Silver Creek Canyon, Maggie knew that a further search was hopeless. The other men had already turned back when she caught up with them, but she had insisted on continuing even if the trail they had followed had been carefully wiped out.

The sturdy mustang mare stood quietly as Maggie studied the open land dotted with scraggly brush. She was being stubborn and perhaps a bit foolish to sit here, wasting the last of the daylight when she should be heading back to the mining camp.

But Satin was the only one waiting for her to return.

A wave of loneliness overcame her. Since Pete had died, she had no one to trust, no one to count on but herself.

It sickened her now to remember that before she had Pete buried, people were claiming friendships that she knew had never been. Debts, more likely owed to Pete than the demands that he was the one owing them, surfaced faster than a good panner collected his poke of gold from his placer claim. And she thought herself so smart, finding Quincy, convincing him that she couldn't sell what Pete had left her, but that if he married her, he would be well paid.

Smart maybe. But McCready had proved smarter. If he wasn't lying.

Just the thought of being married to McCready set off those funny flutters rising in her belly again. Damn the man and his smooth ways.

"Aye," she whispered, "*smooth* is the devil's own word for the man."

His voice was smooth, never a rough edge to it, just like the whiskey he favored. His hands were smooth enough to deal off the bottom of the deck while you watched to catch him. And that fancy talk of his could make a person as crazy as Cockeyed Charlie. McCready was a handful of trouble she could do without. Him and his fancy ladies lording about with those cat-got-the-mouse smiles.

She knew it was only feeling a bit raw herself that had allowed curiosity to surface about McCready. What did he do to cause those women to fuss for his attention? Pamela, she recalled, was a sensible-to-a-fault female most of the time, but she melted and ran like honey if McCready so much as breathed the same air as she did.

That's what being a woman got you, she decided. A man like McCready was all set to call the shots with his wicked smile and sweet talking. Well, it would never happen to her. She had horse sense. She would never let McCready get close enough. And if he tried claiming some rights with his lies of their being married, Dutch could go polish the bar glasses with the rash promise he had forced from her. She'd fix McCready's silver tongue but good.

She had to. There was no one else who would do it for her.

Restless, Maggie shook off her black thoughts. Her nose itched. "A warnin' for sure," she muttered, glancing around as a chill laced itself up her spine. She slipped her rifle from its boot beneath her leg, and set the weapon across her lap.

The mustang's ears flattened as Maggie whispered to the mare, then perked high to capture sounds that Maggie couldn't hear.

Maggie didn't trust people, but her horse and dog had never failed her. The ripple of tension that passed over the mare's hide was all she needed. Dropping the knotted neck rein, Maggie kneed her mare to a walk, glancing behind her.

There was no shelter to hide someone. Yet a feeling persisted that she was being watched. She needed to get off the rim of the canyon, where she presented a perfect target.

Maggie looked down. The mustang veered from the edge of the canyon just as a shot whizzed damn close to where Maggie's back had been seconds before. Furious, she brought up her rifle, sighting the deep clefts of the canyon wall across from her. She couldn't see anyone in the dusky light.

Gently squeezing the trigger, Maggie decided to pepper the wall, but a second shot echoed and grazed the rump of her horse. Caught unaware, Maggie tumbled to the ground when the mare reared in pain. The rifle fell from her hands a few feet away.

The rapid fire of the repeating rifle kept her pinned in place. In moments the painful whinny of her horse and the drum of the mare's hoofbeats were faint sounds.

Maggie ignored the sting of her cut cheek and the scrape on her chin as she pressed her face to the bare rock. Now she was truly alone.

Her only safety lay in the last feeble rays of the descending sun that would give her the shroud of darkness. She urged it to hurry, for Maggie found that she was too scared to pray.

Far to the northwest, in Santa Fe, Thadius Cornwallis watched the same setting sun as he patted the fattened envelope resting securely in the inside pocket of his jacket. He stroked the fine cashmere and wool blend material of the lapel. Thadius prided himself on wearing only the finest of cloth. A smug smile played around the cigar he was never without. He accepted another glass of the Milwaukee beer from one of the Staab brothers, nodding as he listened again to the story of their being chosen the sole agents by the Schlitz's brewery for the New Mexico Territory. Thadius did not know which brother was which. They were not important in his scheme of things, so their names did not matter.

But Thadius made it a policy to smile and listen to everyone. A smart man never knew when he would be offered the perfect tidbit to sell to those men whose rewards kept him in grand style.

William Berger, head of the mining exchange, and a real estate and insurance firm, motioned for Thadius to join him. For less than a heartbeat Thadius's small eyes, set like a pig's, revealed a flame of hate. But he excused himself and began to cross the room to William, knowing he was the last man here this evening who still had to offer more than verbal thanks. Thadius knew to the penny how much Berger stood to make on the completion of the Southern Pacific joining with the Atchison, Topeka, and Santa Fe line to form the second transcontinental railroad.

It was Thadius's business to know such information. Know what you wanted from a man, find out what he wants, and give it to him. Thadius's rule. One of his few. He had learned to live without a conscience, having decided at the age of eleven it was baggage that he could easily do without.

William watched the portly man's progression through the

crowd. He noted each of the men whose hands Thadius paused to shake. All of them men whose palms Thadius had greased to bring about the final stages of his latest scheme. His satisfied smile irritated William as he finally reached his side.

"A token," William said, handing over a thick wad of banknotes.

"Generous," Thadius murmured, sliding the money into his inside pocket, then patting the bulge it formed.

"I can afford to be, can't I."

It wasn't a question, but a statement that required no answer from Thadius. "What's on your mind?"

"I spoke to Walter Jones, that assayer I told you about. He tested the sample. It weighed forty-seven ounces and is worth about seven hundred dollars. I want that gold mine, Thadius."

"Yes. I thought you would."

"You knew I would. I heard a distinct *but*—"

"Well, now, William, I've never been one to bother you with the sometimes difficult problems that I encounter—"

"And you will not begin to now, Thadius."

The command grated on Thadius. But this time, for the first time, he had the upper hand. "As you wish. The owner refuses to sell, so I've decided to pass."

William eyed him with amusement. "You are telling me that? I'm not one of your gullible marks, Thadius. If that sample tested out as pure as Walter claims, we stand to make a fortune."

"You just made one on the railroad," Thadius pointed out. "But I'll admit you're right." Sucking noisily on his cigar, he hooked his thumbs into his vest's pockets and rocked back on his heels. "However, in this case, the owner is proving troublesome."

William Berger was of an equal height to Thadius, but without an excess bit of flesh on his bony frame. He patted his thinning brown hair, his dark eyes narrowed as they snagged

Thadius's gaze. "You wouldn't be thinking to claim there are problems to up the ante, would you?"

Shifting the sodden tip of the cigar to the left side of his mouth, Thadius took exception. "Didn't I cut you in for a tidy profit on that deal—"

"Not here. But yes, yes you did."

"And who was it that put you wise to buying the land up in Deming before the rail ever laid a piece of track near there, William?"

"You did, Thadius. I do not deny that you've made me money. I expect you to make me more. I want that gold claim. When you are alone and see what I have given you to show my gratitude, Thadius, I believe you will find that I have been more than generous for what you did."

"Never doubted that for a moment. Always could count on you. But since you never wish to be bothered with all the little annoying details—and in this case there are plenty—I can't offer you a cut."

Thadius turned away, the conversation at an end. But William, with his eye on the governor's mansion, knew he needed more money than he had amassed to have his desire come to fruition. Money bought power. He reminded himself that the kind of dirt men like Thadius generated was wont to stick to one's feet. No matter how necessary they were to the scheme of things. The assay report tantalized him. William broke his own law of never getting involved personally on Thadius's level.

"Perhaps I've been hasty, Thadius. A good friend and business partner should extend help when it's needed. Why don't you tell me about the problems you're having?"

Inwardly Thadius smiled. Now he had William hooked. He faced him, knowing his fish so well, and didn't waste any more time.

"It was to be clean. An accident, a jumped claim, and the deed done. But this man of mine, damn good I must say, faced a shotgun held by a woman. Can't do business with a woman. Never works, as you well know. The creatures can't be decisive, don't think with logic that makes any sense to a man, and likely can't see past their next fancy to buy. It set my plans back a bit with her refusing to sell. But I told you my man was good. He offered to marry her.''

William's smile never reached his eyes. "It's a temporary solution that would work."

"Temporary is right," Thadius agreed, lowering his voice so that William had to lean closer. "A week or two, we had figured, just long enough to refile the claims and make out a will."

"And once again I hear a *but*."

"Someone else is claiming to own the mine."

"A problem, just as you said. But tell me, Thadius, won't someone suspect another death so close to the first?"

"Don't know what you're babbling about, man."

"You know. Don't ever forget that I've known you long enough to understand exactly how you work, Thadius. You do not leave things to chance. If this woman is in the way, she'll be removed. Permanently. If not by your front man, then by the other one you've already had in place as a backup."

"Think you've got me all figured out, Berger? Don't." But Thadius had a moment's fear. William shouldn't know such things about him. He'd always been careful to cover all his tracks. "I never said there was anyone else down there to negotiate for me. Watch your mouth—you'll have us both swinging from a rope." After removing his pocket watch, Thadius flipped open the case, glanced at the time, and then snapped it closed. "I've got another appointment that I'm already late for."

William was not a physical man, but he gripped Thadius's arm. "You always get what you go after, friend. I want this to remain a private deal between you and me. And, Thadius, I never want the thought to cross my mind that you'd close me out of a deal this good.''

"I hope I heard you wrong." Thadius stared at William. "Don't threaten me. You talk and it's my neck. But I've protected myself, William. No rope stretches without me having company."

"I'm well aware of that. Just as I'm aware that miners meet with all kinds of accidents. But those were men, not a woman."

Rocking back on his heels again, Thadius eyed his companion with mockery. "Are you developing a conscience? Didn't know you could afford one as yet, William. This woman isn't one in the sense that you're thinking. And you never wanted to know the details before. Let's keep it that way."

William stepped back and away, heeding the underlying threat that had been returned. Thadius had spread a net in the territory that no one was privy to. Yet there was a nagging in his mind that forced him to ask another question.

"Why are you taking this delay so well, Thadius?"

"Didn't believe I was."

A shrewd measuring look met his statement. "There's more to this than what you're telling me, isn't there?"

"Common sense. Use yours, William. Why would I? Any delay costs me money and time. It costs my investors the same."

"Just how rich is this one claim?"

Thadius removed his cigar, contemplated its stubby length, and smiled. "There's enough for us to share." His smile remained fixed in place as he thought of seven staked claims that had tested out to be rich veins of either silver or gold. But no one else had to know. This was his big chance to hit the mother lode without having to share it. He knew William's greed and his desire to see himself in the governor's chair. Thadius had made it his practice to sniff out those men whose greed for land, riches, or power could be used to his advantage.

Slapping William on his back, Thadius laughed softly. "Never fear. I've always come through for you. You get your cash together. You'll be needing it."

William Berger watched Thadius weave his way through the crowd and leave. His thoughts raced even as he began his own leave-taking. There was more to this gold claim than Thadius had told him. He was sure of it. Now he had to find a way to act on his knowledge. Thadius had made him money, had helped him gain a measure of power.

But Thadius was all for himself, and William never forgot that simple truth. And Thadius was dangerous. William never forgot that, either.

It wouldn't hurt to have someone of his own to see to his interests in Cooney Camp. He mentally ran through the list of names of those who owed him favors or debts. When he reached back far enough, William found a name he could use.

A name he recalled recently mentioned for having a stake in Cooney Camp.

CHAPTER
4

Maggie would never forget the last few hours. She was close to dragging herself the last feet to her cabin. The walk back from the canyon left her chilled to the bone, aching with scrapes and trembling. What remained of her wedding gown after she had slashed off the cumbersome material tangling around her boots would serve for rags.

If she wasn't so furious, she would give way to the tears burning in her eyes.

But Maggie was angry. Whoever had been shooting at her had kept her pinned on the canyon rim long after dark. Someone either wanted to frighten or kill her. She knew it had something to do with the claims her uncle had left her.

Satin rose from the shadows near the corner of the cabin, whining as she nuzzled Maggie's hand. Maggie thought of McCready pinned down by her dog, but the attempted grin failed. McCready had been as helpless as she. Helpless. She shuddered to understand what that meant.

Maggie held on to her anger, refusing to allow room for any other feelings. Someone had tried to kill her.

After opening the door and slipping inside, she set her rifle in the corner, then barred the door. As she lit the lamp on the table, she wished she had let everyone know that McCready had won those claims from Pete. Someone might have used him for target practice and gotten lucky.

And the attempt on her life would never have happened.

Maggie slid the glass chimney back on the lamp just as the deepest level of her mind rejected the thought that McCready tried to have her killed. It just wasn't the man's way. She couldn't even question why she believed this.

At the moment she couldn't do more than pull out the roughly made wooden bench and sit.

She stared at her trembling hands. Fear finally shoved aside anger to take hold, sticking in her throat like cotton. Her laugh was bitter. Now, she thought, now that I'm safe, I get scared.

Shivering gripped her body, and she wrapped her arms around her waist. Satin rested her head on Maggie's lap, soulful eyes looking up. Maggie sniffled, wiping her nose with the back of her hand. The need to cry with Satin her only witness to her weakness nearly overwhelmed her.

Stroking Satin's head, she closed her eyes. The past, along with the days ahead, stretched out in the wretched weariness of her mind. Quincy's disappearance was forgotten, her uncle's murder set aside, and the loneliness that Maggie thought she could live with swamped overburdened senses.

Maggie knew she was strong. Physically and in spirit. Everyone who knew her told her so. Everyone believed it. There were times she believed it herself.

From the first, when she had trekked the mountains far to the north, her small footprints barely covering half of those made by her father, she had heard those words over and over.

"Keep up, Maggie. I warned you how it would be. You have to be strong, girl, or it's back to the home for you."

So she learned how to be strong. Maggie vowed never to go back to living with the orphans. They had no families, no one to care about or to call their own. She had a father and an uncle.

Seven years old she was, forcing cramped legs to keep moving when another step seemed impossible. She had learned to swallow bile like the first time she had to gut and skin the still-warm body of a rabbit her father had shot for their supper. She had not cried when her father had cut her tangled hair because there was no time for her to be brushing and braiding it. And she had never let it grow long again.

A long-buried memory surfaced of a corn husk doll that was so briefly in her possession, traded along with a hunting knife for a new pair of moccasins to replace her worn-out boots.

But these were old hurts. Things she believed she had forgotten.

The fear inside expanded as Maggie realized what she was doing to herself. Now was the time to be strong, not weak.

She had to remember that with every difficult skill she learned, there came a freedom she was loath to relinquish. A freedom she had embraced eagerly. Boy's clothing made movement a joy. Riding astride allowed her to feel the power of the horse beneath her. Using a knife and a gun with unerring skill had protected her and freed her from dependence on anyone.

She knew how to survive beneath a baking desert sun and in the cold of mountain nights. Maggie had learned to never need another person to do for her.

But she had broken her own rule. She had needed Quincy Kessnick and his money.

Behind her closed eyelids she saw herself flattened on the

rocky ground again, sweat—not from heat but from fear—pouring from her body. She listened to the echo of the crack and whine of bullets that kept her pinned down. Maggie had admitted that she needed someone then. She needed to know that someone would care if she died. That one person might worry about her.

It was a secret weakness that she was ashamed of acknowledging, even to herself.

Satin raised up with her paws on Maggie's leg and licked her cheek. Leaning her head against the thick, soft fur of the dog's neck, Maggie took what comfort the animal offered.

A few moments later the dog growled. Maggie froze, gripping Satin's fur coat with both hands. She darted a quick look at the empty rifle in the corner even as she released the dog and drew her gun. Someone was coming up the path to the cabin.

"Maggie? Maggie, open up."

The sound of McCready's voice and his fist pounding the door sent a flood of relief through her. She set the gun on the table and went to unbar the door, unwilling to question herself for trusting him.

"Where have you been?" he demanded, pushing the door open.

Maggie had already turned her back on him, her whispered command stopping Satin from attacking him. She urged the dog down, and Satin stretched out on the floor, her eyes pinned on McCready.

"I asked where you've been," McCready repeated. The nagging fear that had twisted his gut and sent him up here to see if she was all right churned into anger.

"I was lookin' for Quincy." Maggie turned and took her seat on the bench. She looked up to find McCready still in the doorway, her eyes widening when he stepped inside. The lamp light revealed his face; right cheek marred with a purpling bruise, his left eye nearly shut, and his nose swollen. "What happened to you, McCready? Get caught between a rock and a hard place?''

''Dutch took me down,'' he snapped.

''Were you wantin' somethin' to come here so late?'' She watched him close the door and slide the bar in place. Her gaze darted to the gun within easy reach and slowly her hands unclenched.

''Yeah, you might say that. Ira found your mustang with a bullet crease on her rump.'' McCready had avoided looking at her face, almost afraid of what he would find. But he couldn't avoid it any longer. The torn clothes were bad enough. The scrapes and scratches hollowed out his stomach for long seconds. But it was the glimpse of fear in Maggie's jade-green eyes that filled his mouth and throat with a cottony dryness he had trouble swallowing. ''And you? What happened to you, Maggie?''

''Someone tried to kill me,'' she answered truthfully, her voice raw with fear and exhaustion.

The words themselves took a few minutes to sink in. Not so the knowledge that Maggie trusted him enough to open the door to him. McCready didn't eat up the short distance between them because of either reason. It was the way Maggie spoke. There was a disbelief that someone had tried to kill her underscored by the fear that it was true.

He braced one hand on the table, kept the other clenched at his side, and leaned over. He studied the black rings that captured the fractured shades of green in her eyes. McCready found himself beset with the sudden urge to throttle her for putting herself in danger and hold her close at the same time.

He did neither one. Maggie never needed anyone. She had told him so plenty of times. Proved it to him when he had dared to doubt her. Maggie made her feelings plain enough, but right now his need overpowered Maggie's wants. He had to destroy the breathing space between them and touch her.

The fingers of his hand uncurled at his side, and he slowly

raised it, half fearing that she would bolt away from him. He brushed the back of his hand over the scratches on her cheek. While his own face ached from the pounding he had taken, the sight of Maggie's injured skin sent a new level of pain spreading inside him.

"McCready?" she whispered, unable to hide the tremor in her voice.

"Hush, Maggie mine." Why hadn't he ever noticed the innocent vulnerability in the purity of her features and the clarity of her eyes? Maggie, he was discovering, had the face of an angel, a body that was a benediction for the hungry, and eyes turning wary as a cornered puma.

A muscle clenched in his jaw as he made an obvious effort to control the fierce rush of fury inside him. How dare anyone try to hurt her? But with it came a rush of guilt that he had caused Maggie to run off and search for Quincy.

Maggie sat as still as a fawn being stalked by a winter-starved wolf. She couldn't make him stop stroking her cheek. She couldn't find her voice. She couldn't even move away from him. Being honest, Maggie didn't think she wanted to move. McCready's touch was gentle. No one ever touched her like this. She found she had a strange intense longing for his touching to go on and on.

She stared up at his eyes. The one that wasn't closed revealed a blue as dark and deep as mountain nights. She didn't understand why she thought it appeared guilty. Maggie blinked, and it was gone. She locked her fingers together in her lap to resist the urge to reach up and soothe the bruises that marred his handsome face.

Faith and begorra! What was happening to her? A strong sense of being safe was easing the knots of fear and tension that had captured her. Why? She struggled to understand how McCready's touch could make her feel this way.

McCready didn't like her. He badgered her. He baited her into losing her temper every chance he had and a few he made himself. The man teased her unmercifully. McCready was a thief, she had to remind herself. And a liar. He cheated at cards. He drank. He had women chasing after him. He was as smooth and slick as a wet rock and twice as hard.

Then why by the saints, knowing all this, was she taken by a tremble that erupted when he leaned closer? Maggie shut her eyes. She was breathing McCready's scent. Warm whiskey. Night-brushed sage. Blending together until the room began to close in on her.

Behind her eyelids she was tantalized by the sight of his lips. She didn't want to think about what his cocky grin did to her stomach. What was he doing to her? She felt almost boneless. And hot. Oh, Maggie, she groaned to herself, wrong thought to be having. Heat and fire were already climbing as his hand slid around so that four fingers rested on the side of her neck, and his thumb began circling her chin.

"Maggie?"

It wasn't his whisper that made her think about moving now. It was the fine tremor she felt from his hand. His thumb was no longer drawing circles on her chin but rubbing back and forth beneath her lower lip. Get a grip, Maggie, she demanded of herself. Don't let him come any closer. You can't be tempted by this man. For the sake of all you own, it's McCready that's touching you!

"Ah, Maggie mine," he breathed over her slightly parted lips. "I've been wanting to do this for a long time."

His slow, soft drawl ruffled her nerve ends. McCready's thumb was coaxing her lower lip open with tiny strokes while his fingers rubbed the sensitive skin behind her ear. Maggie couldn't help the little shiver he called forth. She opened her eyes, scowling. And nearly groaned aloud. McCready wore that cocky grin that made her stomach roll over. Anger was her only weapon.

"I should've figured you'd be one to take advantage when me guard was down."

"Is your guard down, Maggie mine?" His eyes brightened as the thought and his grin became a satisfied smile.

"You'd be knowin' it, McCready."

"That and a bit more about you. But I'm not taking advantage, Maggie," he said, his voice whisper soft, unwilling to give up his prize. "I've not taken a blessed thing from you. Yet."

"An' you won't," she promised, shaking her head to rid herself of his hold.

Gambler's instinct came into play, and McCready wisely folded. He released her and stepped back.

"You never said why you came here." Maggie dragged in a deep breath she hadn't known she needed. Turning away from him, she stared at the flickering lamp flame.

"I was worried about you."

"Why? You never were before. An' you'd be knowin' I can take care of meself."

"It's the truth, Maggie."

"Ha! The truth? You wouldn't know the truth it if was sittin' in the bottom of a whiskey glass starin' right up at you."

"Is that what you think of me?"

Maggie sensed she had hurt him the moment he spoke. She looked up at him only to find herself puzzled by his expression. Watchful and waiting. What would he be waiting and watching for? She shook her head and rid herself of the question. McCready couldn't be hurt by anything she said.

"Well, boyo, you've seen for yourself I'm fine, so be off with you."

"Not so fast. You can't stay here, Maggie. Not alone."

Eyes narrowed, Maggie studied him from the tip of his boots up to his long, disordered hair. Her mouth thinned when he hooked his thumbs into his pants pockets and met her glare with his own.

"You're gettin' to be as pesky as a horse fly an' 'bout as wanted, McCready."

"An' you're a fine-looking filly for me to be pestering."

"No."

"No?" he repeated with a silky warning. "You're forgetting you're my wife, Maggie."

She rubbed one finger over the gun grip, shaking her head. "I won't be listenin' to your passel of lies again. It's best you go while you can still walk."

"Don't threaten me, Maggie."

"I'm not. I'm warnin' you. This is me cabin. A body can't be blamed for protectin' its own. Someone tried to kill me. For all I know—"

"Stop right there!" McCready made a visible effort to control the flush of anger rising to a dangerous degree. "If you thought I had anything to do with that, you'd never have opened the door to me, Maggie. I know it and you'll admit it. You can't stay here now. If anything happened—"

"Right. You and your claim would be floatin' down the river without a landin' in sight. Selfish to the core, ain't you, boyo? Well, Satin's here an' you ain't wanted."

McCready's hands slid deep into his pockets to prevent him from grabbing hold of her and shaking sense into her.

"I promised Pete I'd look out for you. I can't keep that promise, Maggie, unless you help me. Just come down to the Rawhider for a few days."

"No."

"For tonight?"

"Not an hour, McCready."

"You're my wife. You're supposed to obey me."

"What I am is tired, McCready. Tired of listenin' to you. Go home." Maggie flipped the gun over and, in doing so, fixed the barrel so that it pointed at him. She motioned Satin to her side, splaying one hand over the dog's neck.

"If I could find out what happened to me bullwhip, I'd be addin' it to what's here. This is all the protectin' I need from the likes of you."

"And if someone took your dog and weapons away, Maggie, what would you be using then?" His pockets had grown too tight to contain his hands so he threaded his fingers through his hair. "You don't make sense. You were scared when I first came. Don't think about denying it. I saw the fear."

Her shrug infuriated him even as he noticed that she slid her gaze from his and pinned it on the wall behind him.

"There's no shame in admitting that you're not as strong as you think, Maggie. I can't leave you here alone. So you leave me no choice once more. I'll stay here."

The shelf above the bunk in the corner held one spare blanket. McCready started for it, ignoring the click of the gun hammer being pulled back. He ignored her hissed warning, ignored Satin's growl, and reached for the blanket, figuring Maggie was too good a shot to hit him.

But she didn't shoot. From the clutter on the table she lifted a box of cartridges and then rose and took up her rifle.

"What the hell are you doing?"

"If you'd be plannin' to stay, I'll be leavin', McCready."

"It's your cabin."

"Nice of you to be sayin' so."

With a sound of disgust he threw the blanket down on the bunk, eyeing her and cursing himself. Exhaustion had her standing with slumped shoulders, her head bowed, her grip on the rifle so tight that he could see her knuckles whiten.

"The stove isn't lit, and you haven't washed those scrapes, Maggie." He waited, but she didn't answer, didn't even look at him. "Can't you give in with a woman's grace and admit that you need someone?"

Her head snapped up, and she pinned her gaze on him. "I don't need anyone." He had to be the devil's spawn to be knowing her shameful admission. Maggie backed up and leaned against the wall, the rifle slipping in her grip. She felt her strength drain and didn't think she could stand up much longer. What did it take to get rid of this thick-headed mule of a man?

"I'll leave as soon as I get the stove going and heat some water for you."

"Go away, McCready."

"When I'm finished." He eyed the mangled bustle on the floor and mentally bit his tongue not to tease her. The easily given concession to Maggie's feelings surprised him.

The barrel-shaped wood stove yielded cold ash, and Mc-Cready scraped a place for the kindling he took out of the wood box. Dried chips of bark caught as quickly as he lit them. He knelt there, feeding the tiny fire, and asked himself what had possessed him to come up here and stay to take care of Maggie. Especially when she didn't want or need him. There were no answers for himself, no clear-cut ones, that is, and with a slight shake of his head, he rose and went to the washstand.

Still woven into a garland that could only have been for Maggie's head, crushed wildflowers lay at the bottom of the cracked washbowl. McCready gripped the edges of the wash-stand, staring down at the flowers, seeing Maggie—a fragile, womanly Maggie—and her dreams in their place. And he knew that he was responsible for tearing apart those dreams as easily as she had torn those flowers from her hair. Flowers for her wedding . . . the thought swamped him with guilt.

What was Maggie doing to him to make him feel guilty? He had acted to save her life, but telling himself this once more didn't make the guilt disappear. Telling Maggie when he knew she wouldn't believe him was not an answer, either.

"Did you love Quincy?"

Maggie was no more startled than McCready as he faced her. "What?" she asked.

"Did you love Quincy?" he repeated in a flat voice.

"Them knocks that Dutch gave you made you daft. You know why I wanted to marry Quincy. I've not the spit left to be fightin' more, McCready. Leave it be or tell me where you hid him so I can get him in the mornin'."

"You can't marry him. You're married to me. And I'll be leaving now, seeing as how you're too tired to be fighting with me."

Maggie used the last of her strength to open the door for him, but McCready paused.

"I'll be back, Maggie. This isn't over."

CHAPTER 5

"Kidnap Maggie? You've lost your wits."

"It's the only way, Dutch. You've got to agree to help me. How else can I keep Maggie safe if she isn't where I can keep an eye on her?"

"Can't this wait till morning, boss?"

"Three-thirty is morning," McCready responded as Dutch sat up, blinking and yawning.

Keeping his eyes averted from the brightly turned-up lamp, Dutch shoved aside his blanket and, with his hands rubbing his face and threading his hair, mumbled, "Let me talk to her. She'll listen to reason."

"Only if you kicked her charmingly rounded posterior first."

"Seems to me that you're mighty taken with Maggie's body since yesterday. Can't say that I like it."

The warning didn't make McCready stop his pacing. "Can't say that I much care. Will you help me?"

Dutch felt his sleepiness disappear. He yawned, stretched, and rubbed his rumbling belly through the gap of a missing button on his union suit. "Let me see if I got this plan of yours straight. All I do is get Satin away so you can get Maggie 'cause you know and I know that she won't go willingly with you anywhere. Then I tell everyone that Maggie left the dog with me since she changed her mind about marrying Quincy and lit out for one of the claims. You figure that Quincy'll get tired of waiting and leave. Right so far?"

"That's about it."

"Not so fast, boss. You're figuring to stash Maggie up at your cabin. That's near a day's ride from here. So tell me where will you be while I'm lying through my teeth?"

Pausing, McCready rubbed the back of his neck, but he refused to look at Dutch. "Around," he murmured.

"What's that?" Dutch leaned forward on the edge of the bed, cupping his hand over one ear. "Say again. I didn't catch that."

"I said around."

"Around here? Around Maggie? Around where?"

"Right, Dutch. That's all of it."

Gripping his knees, Dutch eyed McCready. "You're fixing to seduce that girl, and don't be trying to flimflam me otherwise."

"I'm fixing to save her life." McCready bit the words off, his body aching from both the physical pounding he had taken from Dutch's hands and the one his senses had taken from being near Maggie. He rounded on Dutch, this time meeting his direct gaze. "You had to see her, Dutch. Maggie looked, well, beaten. Even when Pete died, she didn't look as if she didn't have a friend in the world to turn to.''

''Murdered.''

''Right,'' McCready agreed quickly. ''Pete was murdered, and I don't intend to see Maggie end up the same.''

''It's not just the gold anymore, is it?''

''Nothing else but the gold.'' McCready knew his voice lacked conviction.

Dutch chose to ignore it, forming his own conclusions. ''Well, it seems to me that saving her life is a point we agree on. It's from there we take different roads on how. You know,'' he suggested, stifling another yawn, ''Maggie could stay here.''

''No. Wouldn't work. She'd be vocal in protesting her confinement.'' McCready draped his lithe body into the corner chair, booted feet crossed at the ankles, his head resting in the hands clenched behind his neck. With his eyes closed he added, ''Too many people would know that she's here. Between the two of us, we couldn't check out every stranger that comes into the Rawhider.''

''But along with us she would have Cora Ann and the Rose. Not only for company, not to mention me, but they'd help sniff out—''

''Maggie has no desire to further her acquaintance with them. And you've heard what Cora Ann and the Rose had to say about Maggie. Remember, this is Maggie's life we're talking about. I don't trust anyone, Dutch.''

Dutch stared at the floorboards, his chin sinking onto his chest. ''Boss, you're not going to like what I'm thinking.'' McCready's groan was his only response. ''Just hear me out. I think you're missing something. Something important.''

''Sleep, for a start.''

''You stole mine. It's only fair that you shouldn't get any. Now, just listen. You said that with Maggie gone, Quincy will give up and leave.''

"A reasonable conclusion you will agree."

"Maybe. But Quincy was up at my place with those men when someone was shooting at Maggie. So how could Quincy be involved with it? The man couldn't be in two places at the same time."

McCready opened his eyes and sat up. "Why the hell do you think I want to kidnap her? I told you it was to save her life. I know someone was shooting at her while we held Quincy."

"You're worked up. I might even say you're angry."

"Damn right there."

"Well, I had to be sure that I heard you right. The mines are a prize for any man that's greedy and don't mind how he gets his hands on them."

"You don't," McCready grated from between clenched teeth, "for one minute think that I shot at Maggie?" The pressure he put on his swollen jaw sent tentacles of pain shooting up the side of his face, but seeing Dutch's clear steady gaze pinned on him, McCready found that he didn't dare relax.

"I didn't say anything about you. If I thought it was you, McCready, I'd have stopped you myself."

"Nice to know whose corner you're in."

"I've always been in yours," Dutch claimed with a serious note. "But right now, Maggie needs me more."

"Then you'll agree to help me?"

A soft knock at the door stopped Dutch from answering him. Grabbing hold of his pants from the floor, Dutch knew, with the lamp turned up bright, there was no way to ignore whoever it was. Snapping his suspenders in place over his union suit, he called out he was coming. A burst of merry laughter answered him, and he shot McCready a look of sheer exasperation. "Cora Ann," he murmured, opening the door.

McCready eyed the dynamite package of feminine charms in a sprite's body that was Cora Ann Avernel. Her disposition, drunk or sober, was that of the merriest of widows, which she claimed to be, and with McCready's live-and-let-live attitude, he never bothered to dispute this with her. She showed up one day four months ago, riding a spirited sorrel, asking for work. McCready played five hands of poker with her and hired her on.

Cora Ann didn't walk into the room—she glided. And with the smile of a naughty child who knows her every transgression will always be forgiven, Cora smoothed the folds of a soft blue cashmere robe over her hips, eyeing McCready from beneath her thickly curled brown lashes.

"You've kept me waiting."

There was husky promise, pouty reprimand, and a decided female possessiveness enriching this accusation. McCready studied the perfectly shaped petite body that had given and taken pleasure from every hour they had shared. Unfortunately for Cora Ann and perhaps himself, he noted whimsically, Maggie O'Roarke had suddenly consumed all his thoughts.

"You're mistaken," he finally answered

Cora Ann chose to ignore this. She glided to his chair, leaning over to tap one finger lightly against his chin. She leaned over to give him a view of bare breasts through the gaping robe along with a whiff of delicate lavender that she favored. She made no comment about his bruises, having already rendered her opinion to Dutch about his heavy-handedness rearranging McCready's handsome face, and received in turn both men's warning to stay out of what she didn't understand.

With her luscious pink mouth glistening from a slow swirl of her tongue, and very sure of her welcome, Cora Ann settled herself on McCready's lap.

Dutch motioned to McCready to leave.

"That won't be necessary. Cora Ann is going."

"Why?" she demanded. "I told you I missed you. Come back to my room with me," she whispered, caressing the soft skin behind McCready's ear, then bit the lobe. "I've something delightfully special just for you."

There was that sound of her possessiveness again. On McCready's list of the unforgivable, which Maggie's sins headed, there rested the one of any woman's possessiveness. With a charmingly lazy smile he removed Cora Ann's fingers from his neck, kissed their tips, then set his hands on her hips to lift her up and off him.

"Darlin', you're mistaken, on all counts." Patting her bottom, he added, "Be good and leave. Now."

For a moment a militant gleam entered her doe-brown eyes. "It's the Rose, isn't it? I know she's taken all your time lately. Well, just so we understand each other, McCready, I won't stand for it."

"Dictating to me, love?" he queried in a soft voice.

"And why shouldn't I? I'm entitled after what we've—"

"No. You'll leave. Tonight."

Cora Ann's eyes widened, and she opened her mouth only to close it. There was no mockery in his voice, none of the seductively sympathetic amusement that so often coated his speech and made her feel stroked to hear it.

"You can't mean that."

"Oh, but I do."

"McCready, the Rose isn't for you," she insisted. "You should know that her interest lies elsewhere. Lee Warren for one and Andrew Burton for another."

"A woman of extremes," McCready admitted in a distracted voice, ushering Cora Ann out of the room. "I've never asked nor expected to be kept apprised of your or Rose's choice of bed partners."

"I don't want to leave, McCready. We've gotten along fine together until she showed up."

"Dutch, coffee's in order. We've got plans to finalize."

"What about me?" Cora Ann asked, no longer pouting but beginning to believe that McCready meant what he said.

Dutch had remained quiet all this time, but now he stepped forward to whisper to McCready. "If you won't be around, I can't deal and tend bar, and Rose is no good at cards."

"Then let her stay."

Dutch stood with Cora Ann as McCready left them. "Well," he said, "you heard the boss."

"Yeah, I heard him, but I don't like it much. There's something troubling him, and I aim to find out what it is."

"Woman, if you're as smart as I think you are, you'll keep out of this."

"Maybe, Dutch. Then again," she stated with a shrug, "maybe not."

Less than a minute later, having made her decision, Cora Ann was knocking at the Desert Rose's door. Where Cora Ann was dark and petite, the Rose, one Molly Prentice, lately of Denver and Tucson and before that the London slums, was a statuesque blonde. Gifted with a voice that was whiskey smooth and smoky hot, the Rose, so dubbed by a past lover for her between-the-sheets performance rather than her stage presence, finally opened her door.

"Wot's you be wantin'?"

"We've got to talk." Cora Ann pushed her way inside. "Now, close the door and listen to me."

Dutch eyed the two-inch-thick steak laced with laudanum. The sky was filling with light streaks that peeled back the night. It was almost five o'clock. Maggie, he knew, was an early riser and would, upon waking, let Satin outside. He stood twenty feet from the cabin door, out of sight but within calling distance to the dog. He still had his doubts about McCready's plan succeeding, but he couldn't come up with a better one.

If only he didn't feel as if he were betraying Maggie, not to mention Satin's trust.

The early-morning stirrings from the mining camp below

reached him just as he spotted the door of Maggie's cabin opening. Against the shadowed dark wood of the cabin, Dutch could make out Satin's alert stance. He should have given some thought to the dog finding his scent this close. It was too late to do anything but pray that Maggie wouldn't notice, or if she did, believe it was merely a small night creature caught in the open that had attracted the dog's attention.

He held his breath, waiting for the door to close behind the dog so that he could call to her. Satin, in a complete spirit of uncooperation, refused to move from in front of the cabin.

Dutch waved the steak high above his head, wishing for a slight breeze to bring the scent of the meat to Satin.

The only breeze came from the one he was creating, feeling like a fool.

"Satin," he whispered, "come here, girl."

A deep-throated growl came in response. Dutch sighed. Now what? The dog was not going to come willingly toward him any more than Maggie would go willingly to McCready for his protection.

Once more Dutch eyed the steak that was to have been McCready's dinner, since he had refused to part with his own. He had less than an hour to get rid of Satin before McCready showed up. They both wanted Maggie gone before Quincy was released and returned to camp. Dutch had to make his move now. He flung the steak toward the dog, hoping for the best.

Crouched as he was, he waited and watched Satin. For minutes that seemed longer than they should have been, the dog merely lifted her head and sniffed the air. Chilled air, Dutch noted, feeling the damp cold seep from the rocky ground to the hands he used to brace himself. He'd be old and likely crippled by the time Satin decided to investigate that damn piece of meat.

Once more he tried whispering, coaxing the dog to come to him. He was well aware that if Satin caught McCready's scent coming up the trail before she dined on that steak, his boss would be jumping higher than a kangaroo rat. He, himself, had bet on one that could easily top six feet.

His patience was rewarded. Satin decided it was safe to approach the steak. She darted toward it, yipped, and backed away, only to return and repeat the process twice more.

"Hurry up, you mangy critter," Dutch muttered, shifting his uncomfortable position. "That's the best meal you'll ever have. Aged four months and trimmed by my own hand, not that you'd be caring how tender that meat is."

Satin nudged the steak with her paw, sniffed, and once more backed away. Dutch couldn't wait any longer. He rose, determined that the dog would eat that steak or he'd die trying.

The dog looked up as he approached, her tail wagging after a moment. "Good girl," he murmured. "Now, let's you and me play with that chunk of meat. I'll throw and you catch."

It was too late to worry about the chance of Maggie seeing him. Satin came to his side, allowing him to pet her, but when Dutch reached down for the steak, she bared her teeth.

"Not at me, you forsaken excuse for a dog! Use your teeth on that steak."

But Satin only set her front paw possessively on the meat, tongue lolling, her head dropping forward while her haunches rose in the air.

"We can't play here, girl. Ah, McCready, the risks I take for you." Dutch hunkered his considerable weight down and slowly, very slowly, reached out with his hand for the steak. Satin, enjoying this, used her paw to inch the meat away from him.

Dutch lunged.

Satin snatched the steak and trotted a few feet before dropping it in front of her.

The lapsing time made Dutch desperate. He could hear McCready's whistle from below the trail. Crouched down on all fours, he steadily made his way toward where the dog waited. He pleaded, he cursed. He coaxed and promised, then cursed some more. Every time he got close enough to grab for the steak, Satin snatched it up and trotted off. With the meat held firmly between her jaws, Satin shook her head back and forth, as if making sure her prize was dead, before holding the steak between her front paws and tearing off a few chunks to eat.

Neither Dutch or McCready had any idea how much laudanum would be enough to put the dog to sleep. Dutch had finally stayed McCready's overgenerous hand while he dropped the liquid over the meat. Now he wished he hadn't. Satin showed no sign of stopping her play.

They were halfway down the rocky trail, and Dutch heard McCready's cheerful whistle coming closer. He backed down a bit more, hoping that Satin would follow him. For once his action and prayers came together. Satin came after him with the remains of the steak dangling from her mouth.

Dutch cursed his own luck that she was still alert and standing when McCready was in sight. The dog dropped the piece of meat, ears straight up and attack ready, as McCready, carrying a napkin-covered tray, neared them.

Two pairs of eyes were pinned on Satin. The dog eyed the steak, then McCready while issuing a low rumbling growl.

"Hell of a choice, ain't it, girl?" Dutch muttered, hoping his boss had the sense to remain perfectly still and, above all, quiet.

McCready had to have heard his silent wish, for when Dutch shot a glance over his shoulder, McCready was frozen in place.

One of Satin's ears drooped a bit, and she tilted her head to one side, rubbing the offending ear with one paw. Dutch watched with bated breath. The dog shook her head, and he wished that it wasn't a pesky flea but the drug finally taking effect. Guilt flooded him when the dog began to whine, her gait unsteady as she started toward him.

"Easy girl, easy," he offered in comfort, once more inching his way to her.

Unexpectedly Satin stopped and turned back to grab hold of the steak, tearing at it, tossing it from side to side, all the while a deep, threatening growl issued forth from her throat.

"She knows," Dutch whispered, thinking that McCready had been forgotten as he reached the dog's side and tried to touch her.

With a snarl Satin backed a few steps. Panting, she dropped the meat, her head falling forward. Her back legs refused to support her, and down she went. But when Dutch attempted to lift her in his arms, she lunged for McCready, throwing him off balance.

Dutch gave McCready credit for nerve. The man didn't move while he struggled to maintain a grip on the dog's fur. Satin had more strength than he thought, for she managed to get within a nose of McCready's feet before Dutch flung his considerable weight on top of her. With one hand clamped over her nose to keep her jaw closed, Dutch fought for breath.

"You're running late, Dutch."

"That's all you've got to say? And I'm not late—you're early, you son of a bitch."

McCready ignored the last. "Is she down for the count?" He glanced up at the still-closed cabin door, realizing that they were in full view of Maggie should she open it.

"I can't tell. You hold her while I get up."

McCready knew it was a perfectly reasonable request. The look Dutch gave him said as much. But he had no desire to tangle with Satin's teeth. Not after seeing the way she had torn into that steak.

Swallowing a lump, he offered a compromise. "We can spare a few minutes more and be sure."

"No way. You either hold her so I can get up, or I let go and you'll take your own chances. It's not my throat she wants."

"No give?"

"No give, boss. As it is, I may never forgive myself for doing this to her."

McCready set aside the breakfast tray. He didn't want to ask who Dutch meant, Satin or Maggie. He didn't want to know since he was doing a bit of regretting for all this himself.

Hunkering down in front of the dog, McCready took a steadying breath, released it, and placed his hands over Dutch's. At his nod Dutch eased his hold, sliding his body back and away.

Dutch eyed Satin, for he had felt the bunching of the dog's muscles, but feeling a twisted sense of justice, he figured that McCready had coming whatever the dog did to him.

McCready's hold wasn't as Dutch's had been. When the dog whined again, he barely kept his hands in place, swearing at himself. A look at Dutch showed him kneeling and rubbing his hands over his massive thighs.

Satin gave a long shudder. Another smaller one followed, then she didn't move.

"I guess it finally worked, Dutch."

"Guess so."

"Where's the sack?"

"Down below, behind that clump of rocks."

McCready could no longer ignore the censure in Dutch's voice. "Well, what are you waiting for? Go get it so you can carry her down."

"Sure, boss." Dutch lumbered to his feet, started down the trail, but stopped and looked back. "You've got to know how lousy I feel about this."

"Spare me. You've only done this to a poor dumb dog, but I've got to do this to Maggie," McCready snapped, his voice taut with exasperation and a few other emotions, among them, shame.

It seemed to placate Dutch, for he nodded and went to retrieve the sack.

McCready glanced at the covered breakfast tray he had prepared and intended as a peace offering to Maggie. How peaceful, she wouldn't know until later. He closed the door on his conscience.

There was no other way to protect Maggie's life.

CHAPTER
6

McCready stood beside the bed in his cabin watching Maggie. She lay snugly enfolded in a drug-induced cocoon while sunlight dappled her fine-boned features like the spots on a newborn fawn hidden in a thicket. Within the confines of his pants pockets, his fingers tightened, fighting the urge to touch her. Dutch had left with the pack mule and horses; they were alone.

A bit of the lace-edged cotton of her chemise peeked from the open throat of her linsey-woolsey shirt. With a gentle rhythm, her breathing made her breasts rise and fall. She appeared sweet, vulnerable, and innocent, but he had no illusions about the snarling, spitting wildcat he would have to contend with when she finally awakened.

As the need to touch her became stronger, McCready lifted one of her hands that lay slack outside the quilt. Work-rough, bruised, and callused, nails broken to the quick, there was nothing soft, nothing feminine about the strongly made hand that he held. But it was all too easy to imagine this same hand, softened with delicately scented cream, returning the sensually seductive caresses he burned to offer her.

What was Maggie doing to him? He found himself leaning over to rub her palm against his cheek, understanding the sudden tender protectiveness that surged through him, but not why he was feeling this for Maggie.

And if she knew, she would likely laugh at him. The thought was sobering, and he set her hand down but didn't move away. McCready gazed at the faint bluish shadows that lay beneath the gold tips of her lashes. Proof enough of the sleepless night she had had. The laudanum-induced sleep he caused gave her the benefit of much needed rest, but he doubted that Maggie would appreciate the gift.

Sap spit from a log in the fire, drawing his attention to the coffeepot he had forgotten. McCready went to the fireplace built into the far wall and nearly singed his fingers to pull the pot back before it boiled over.

There was none of the scattered clutter of Maggie's cabin here. From the neatly stacked logs and filled wood box, to his favorite books arranged on a shelf, all was in order. Airtights of peaches and peas, jars of tomatoes, green beans, and pickles filled two open shelves in the corner cupboard. The flour, sugar, and salt were stored in crocks alongside the bottom of the cupboard. A basket of fresh eggs, meant for the free lunch offered at the Rawhider, sat on the table. Pickled beef, dried venison, and bacon should see them with enough to eat through the few weeks he thought they needed to get rid of Quincy. If luck was with him, Dutch might discover who had shot at Maggie a lot sooner.

Retrieving a cup for himself, McCready poured out the coffee. He opened the bottom of the cupboard and was about to take out a bottle of whiskey when he thought better of it. He needed to keep a clear head to deal with Maggie.

He stood gazing out the unshuttered window, sipping the coffee, wondering if he had made a mistake in estimating the strength of his willpower to be alone with Maggie for even a few days without attempting to bed her.

With a shake of his head, McCready dismissed peeking through that mind's door. Maggie would certainly have plenty to say to him, but he doubted he would hear an invitation to share the mutual pleasures of sex.

The restless prowl of masculine hunger had him shooting an angry glance at her, resenting the hint of a smile on her lips as if she knew what he was thinking and enjoyed torturing him. It made no sense. How could he be angry with her for casting innocent allure that tempted him to forget he would never take a woman against her will? The bitter memory that surfaced sent him bolting from the confines of the cabin.

Maggie felt the tug on her senses to awaken. She turned on her side, cupping her cheek with one hand, refusing to heed its call. She drifted lazily through a misty-colored world where warmth cradled her, making her feel safe, and she snuggled deeper into its welcoming arms.

That did it! Singed, fried, and done to a turn, McCready swore and damned himself for the stupidity of believing he would get any rest stretched out on the bed with Maggie nestled tight against him.

They hadn't started out that way. At first he had been careful to keep his distance until she had wiggled and squirmed her way to his side. Putting his arm around her wasn't going to hurt anyone, not even when she burrowed her face against his chest with one leg flung over his thighs and wore that darn hint of a smile.

He couldn't take any more. Shooting up from the built-in double bed, he shoved back his hair, muttering, "The hell with a clear head. I need a drink."

He wasn't quiet. Truth be told, he knew he was deliberately making noise, wanting Maggie up and snarling. Tossing off a quick drink, he built up the fire, then poured out another one. "Wake up, Maggie," he called. "I need the sharp side of your tongue, Irish." Anything would be a relief from the emotions plaguing him.

Maggie slept on.

McCready finished his drink, lit the lamp, and turned it up so with the fire burning bright the shadows were chased to the corners. He broke open a fresh deck of cards, shuffling, then packing them into place with sharp raps on the table. Maggie stirred, rolled onto her back, arms flung to the sides, murmuring.

Tilting the bottle to fill his glass, McCready wondered what happened to his idea of gifting her with sleep. He eyed the full pail of well water and knew he was losing what few wits he had left.

He hummed, dealt himself a hand of solitaire but couldn't draw one card from the remaining pack. The level of the bottle steadily decreased, and still Maggie showed no sign of waking.

McCready tossed the cards aside, drumming his fingers to the tune he sung. Maggie murmured again, but he couldn't make out what she was saying.

"No you don't, Irish. I'm not coming near you." He turned his chair so that his back was toward her. Maybe without the tempting sight of her in view, he could find some peace.

A cottony dryness filled Maggie's mouth. Her eyes fluttered open, closed, and stayed that way as she tried to swallow. An angry buzzing came to her ears, then a sharp rap. She struggled against the bonds that drew her back to sleep. With her eyes still closed, she felt alongside of her to test the place she rested. The bed wasn't her own. Wriggling her nose, she inhaled the scent of wood burning and something faint that she didn't know. The buzzing had softened, and she realized that someone was humming.

Despite the dryness of her mouth Maggie tried to call out. She heard the scrape of a chair against the wood floor and didn't understand the cowardly urge to keep her eyes closed and flop over onto her stomach when footsteps neared.

The gentle touch on her cheek told her who it was before she opened her eyes. McCready. The mist lifted and she remembered opening the door to him this morning. But Maggie knew morning was long gone.

"What happened?" she croaked.

He didn't bother to answer but went to fetch her a cup of water. He had his wish; Maggie was finally awake.

Maggie managed to push herself into sitting with her back braced against the wall. She couldn't seem to fight her eyes wanting to close, but when McCready returned and cupped the back of her head with his hand, holding the cup to her lips, she managed to keep them open.

"Don't gulp the water, Maggie mine. I'll get you more."

"Do it, McCready. A lot more." She glanced around and knew without asking that this was his cabin, the one everyone knew he had, but not where. Like a greedy child she finished the second cup of water, impatient to shake off the feeling that wanted to drag her under again.

"More?" McCready asked.

Maggie shook her head.

"With your mouth all puckered up like that you look unspeakably sanctimonious, Maggie mine. Reminds me of a schoolmarm I had."

Having no idea what he meant, Maggie ignored this. "Tell me why, McCready. You tricked me like the low-down thievin'—"

"Spare me the litany of your pet names." Walking away, McCready set the cup on the table and lifted up the lamp. He was worried about Maggie. She had not attacked him. There wasn't even much heat in her voice. After setting the lamp on the small bedside table, he leaned over and peered into her eyes.

Disconcerted, she frowned up at him. "What are you lookin' for?"

"I want to make sure you'll live. Since I went to a bit of trouble to get you here to keep you alive, don't you agree that it would be a pity if I had accidently killed you?"

McCready saw the fear before Maggie shoved him away. "Maggie, you know I wouldn't—"

"I know nothin', but you bein' a snake. It was the food, right? Smilin' an' fakin' your carin'. 'I was worried 'bout you,'" she mimicked his words of the morning when she opened the door to him. "'Can't be sharin' your breakfast, Maggie, it's all for you. I was worried an' wantin' to prove we can get along.' You'll pay, McCready. You'll pay for every lie."

Maggie searched for a weapon, but she couldn't reach the lamp on the table unless she went through McCready. Grabbing one of the pillows from behind her, she threw it at him. "Rotten gully-raker!" She was incensed that he merely smiled and caught the pillow, which he tossed to the floor. She managed to scramble to her knees, landing a few feeble punches on him.

"Faith and begorra! I'll have your hide for a saddle blanket. You'd rob bees of honey an' sell it back to them, you gin-shepard!" Maggie landed a solid blow to his stomach. McCready winced but didn't move or try to stop her. She could feel her strength returning; the fury she felt for his fooling her so easily boiled her blood. She wanted McCready's hide and anything else of his she could get her hands on.

"Tinhorn," she grated from between clenched teeth, aiming

a blow to his groin. But McCready's hand blocked her. "You loose-in-the-rump parish stallion!" Maggie went for his chin. McCready jerked his head back, and her fist slid harmlessly past his shoulder, but her strength ebbed and she fell forward.

McCready was there to catch her. "You run down yet?" he asked, grateful that his fear of having given her too much laudanum was groundless. He would rather have a spitting, snarling Maggie than the helpless companion of the day. Maggie struggled. "Stop it, now. You'll only hurt yourself."

"Let me go, McCready," she demanded hotly. The soft feather tick offered little support to her knees. Maggie felt the grogginess she was trying to fight return. Having McCready's hands on her didn't help. "You whiskey-swillin' hog," she muttered, running out of names to call him.

"Now, Maggie, I'll be the first to admit that I like my whiskey, but a hog? No fair. I'm taking exception to being called a hog. I'm a generous man, Maggie mine. I'll share my whiskey and anything else you'd be wanting."

"Fair? You think I'll be fair after what you did? It's war, McCready. Open huntin' season on you."

With a wave of his hand he indicated the cabin. "This, then, is your battleground for as long as it takes."

Maggie gulped. "Long as it takes?" she repeated. The words lit another fire inside her. "You can't keep me here!" No matter how she pushed and twisted, he refused to let her go.

"Remember that we're married, Maggie. I can keep you here as long as I like with none to stop me."

"You'll have to tie me down," she declared but with a panicked note. She had forgotten his devil's claim of their being married. Maggie angled her head back to look up at him.

McCready smiled. "Tying you up offers several pleasing possibilities."

"What? Spoutin' more of your devil's tongue?"

"No. I was just thinking that if I were half of what you called me, Maggie, I would have certainly taken advantage of your charmingly vulnerable state.'' The aching fullness that strained to be closer to Maggie's body had him adding, ''I would have thought that your first concern upon waking up in my bed would have—''

Maggie wiggled her hand free and clamped it against his mouth. Her eyes were wide with understanding what she had stopped him from saying. But she was fully dressed. Except for her boots. Even for the whispered prowess of McCready, sex was impossible if she was fully clothed. But his cocky know-it-all grin was back. The sass and fight seeped out of her. Her hand slowly slid down from his mouth to his chin coming to rest on his chest.

''Tell . . . me.'' She had to swallow. She even had to find the courage and drag it up to ask, ''Did you . . . I mean, was I . . . could you really . . . No, you wouldn't.'' With a shudder she closed her eyes, giving up a pitiful groan.

McCready let her suffer. After all, he reasoned, he'd been through the torture of the damned all day. Stroking her tangled curls, he rested his chin on top of her head, drawing her closer to his body. ''Maggie,'' he murmured, ''would it have been so bad if I had?'' Another shudder rippled over her in answer. His lips pressed a light kiss to her hair, sure that she couldn't feel it. She felt good in his arms, just as she had when she was curled up trustingly against him and sleeping. But it played hell with him to know that she didn't want to be there.

''You have no morals,'' she whispered, unable to keep herself from sagging against him. Her legs felt like loose gravel. Her stomach turned into a stage for the fluttery sensations to dance on.

''Not a one, Maggie mine.''

''I wouldn't be proud as Lucifer to admit it.''

''But you see, O'Roarke, I'm trying to prove I'm not all the liar you call me.''

''You belong locked up with the key thrown away.''

''Not me, Maggie. You.''

Her green eyes flickered up in groggy confusion. She wasn't sure she heard him right. He had both his arms around her, his forehead touching hers. Maggie noticed the dark stubble on his cheeks and chin. His shoulder-length hair brushed her cheeks. Maggie licked her dry lips. She didn't like the way his eyes followed the tip of her tongue. McCready was dangerous. Her body was telling her so.

"McCready? Why do I belong locked up?"

He was lost in visions of her tongue gliding against his own lips. Maggie's fingering the bruise on his cheek ended his distraction as she repeated her question.

"To keep you alive, that's why. It's the only way, Maggie mine. You stay locked up, and I'm the man with the only key."

Maggie didn't like the way McCready was staring at her. His eyes were too dark, too intense, and her flesh seemed suddenly hot, then cold. Her heart was beating too fast, and the tiny flutters spread to other parts of her body.

McCready stroked her spine, lingering to rub the small of her back. "Maggie, there's a time to stop running and a time to stop being alone. Understand?"

Only a bit, she thought. She was aware now of the shape of his lips. He tilted his head to the side, but managed to bring his mouth closer. His lips were slightly parted, hovering near her own. Maggie turned aside. She had to get free or McCready would have her locked up in more than his cabin.

Maggie's breath caught at the shock of his warm mouth skimming the shape of her ear. She couldn't breathe without his scents filling her. The shimmery sensation spread with the slow slide of his lips down the side of her neck. He nuzzled the hollow of her collarbone. Maggie knew she was still groggy, and tired. That she couldn't summon the will to fight him made her miserable. That was the only reason why the small murmur escaped her when he pressed her closer to him.

Rock-hard. Sun-hot. Maggie felt him over every inch of her body. He pressed a lingering kiss on her forehead, across her fluttering eyelashes, down to her cheek. She was surrounded by McCready. He just seemed to be everywhere.

His mouth found the corner of hers. One hand cupped the back of her head, bringing her around to face him.

"Maggie, I won't hurt you."

She heard the rich promise in his voice. The underlying heat of pleasure. She wasn't reassured. This was her enemy. She couldn't forget his trickery. McCready would use every bit of his snake charm to get what he wanted. Maggie felt her head clear.

"I'll be—"

His lips touched hers, shaping them to fit his larger mouth. His tongue, as arrogant as the rest of him, stole the moisture from her mouth. Maggie had had enough. She opened her eyes and pulled back.

"McCready," she whispered, "I'll be needin' to use your bucket."

"What?" he murmured, dragging his lips over the sweet generous shape of hers.

"The honey bucket, McCready. You've got to have one. And I need it."

McCready's head snapped up. "Now?" Maggie's guileless gaze lay in wait for him. She nodded, then bowed her head. "Of course I've got one. I'll just—"

"Leave, boyo. That's all you have to do." Maggie still wasn't sure that he hadn't taken advantage of her. She didn't know what she would feel if he had. The only thing she counted on was that McCready was not going to stay in the cabin.

He had already decided that for himself. He released her and pointed to the rounded wooden tub leaning against the opposite corner from the bed. "Under there."

Maggie hid her smile when he helped her to stand.

"You're sure you'll be all right alone?"

"Go on, McCready."

The door barely closed behind him and Maggie moved. She thought about shoving the table in front of the door, but she didn't want to lock herself in; she wanted to get out. The bar was missing to bolt the door from the inside. The latch was in place but there was no tie to fasten it. McCready thought he had her. She'd show him.

"Damn him!" There wasn't a gun in sight. She eyed the wood box, but using a log to knock him out was too chancy. McCready wouldn't go down easy. She knew he wasn't going to give her much time. Maggie headed for the drawer in the cupboard. Forks and spoons rattled as she searched for a knife. Not a one.

If she was desperate enough, she could stab him with a fork, but his hide was likely so tough the darn thing would bend before doing any damage. There had to be something. . . .

Turning, Maggie stared at the whiskey bottle and cards on the table. McCready was a gambler down to the bone. He had taken his biggest gamble in believing that she would meek as a mouse accept his imprisonment.

She glanced over at the bed. It didn't matter if he had taken advantage of her or not. He would. And her betraying body would help him every step of the way.

McCready liked his bed kept warm. Maggie's eyes glittered as she turned to the fire. She'd make sure he had no complaints.

CHAPTER 7

The cold snap of the mountain air cleared McCready's head. He stood a ways from the cabin, hands in pockets, gazing up at the brilliant stars spread against the velvet night.

From his memory came the fancy and fable that had given names to the constellations. The heat of July was ascribed to the rising of Canis the Dog with its bright star, Sirius. And Boötes, with its bright star, Arcturus, whose risings and fallings near the equinoxes were believed to portend great tempests. A fitting star for his Maggie.

His Maggie? With the taste of her lingering on his lips he had no trouble accepting this. Dutch's accusation was true. He did want to seduce her until her senses were pleasure-drenched with himself.

Look at the stars, he reminded himself. It's a safe distraction that won't tie your gut in knots and keep you randy like the parish stallion that Maggie called you.

But the scattering of stars had him remembering Maggie's freckles and his intent to discover every one of them. With a snort of disgust, McCready raked his hair back. He had to stop thinking about her.

There above him were the twins, Castor and Pollux . . . McCready inhaled smoke.

He glanced behind to the cabin. Faint light rimmed the two shuttered windows. The smell of smoke was stronger. He wondered if Maggie had overfed the fire. If she had, she . . . His thought died. That wasn't smoke from the chimney that he smelled!

McCready ran. Fear wrapped itself around his chest like a thick leather belt, tightening belt hole by belt hole until he saw black spots dance in front of his eyes.

He shouldn't have left her alone. She had passed out and knocked over the lamp. He cursed, threw off the bar to the door, and plunged inside.

''Maggie!'' The thick smoke haze stung his eyes into tearing. He gagged on the stench of burnt goosefeathers. He swiped at his eyes with one hand, extending the other in a blind search for Maggie. He felt the shape of a chair and spun around, overcome by coughing. Dropping to the floor, he crawled his way to the bed, sure he would find Maggie there. He offered prayers to a deity that he was sure had forgotten him. He promised to mend his ways, if only she wasn't hurt. He'd give up whiskey. Never lie. Close the Rawhider on Sundays. Anything, so that Maggie was all right.

His shoulder hit the side of the bed. His throat was so tight with fear he couldn't utter her name. He felt the top of the bed for her body. His fist came away with a mass of soggy feathers.

It took him moments to realize that the haze was lifting. It took him seconds more to understand what he held. Burnt, wet feathers. He reached out with his other hand smoothing over the bed and knew the pile was small enough to be no more than the pillows. The fear holding him in its grip slipped a notch.

There were no flames. No fire. Maggie hadn't passed out and knocked over the lamp. McCready threw the mess he held against the wall. He came up in a crouch. Swallowed repeatedly until he felt moisture in his mouth.

"You Irish bitch! Where the hell are you?"

Maggie heard his bellow. She winced as another unseen rock jabbed her stockinged foot. She wanted to run. She looked behind at the light spilling from the open cabin door and knew McCready would come after her. But Maggie didn't know what lay before her. She could break her neck. The thought crossed her mind that if McCready caught her, that would be his first choice. No, he'd keep her alive to get the mines.

Maggie knew time was past for her to move. She had not planned her escape well. A bone-chilling cold made her wish for a blanket. But how could she think about food, warmth, and water while McCready's kisses were still hot on her mouth? Face it, Maggie, she told herself, steering clear of a clump of brush, you're running from yourself as well as McCready.

Small rocks tumbled down. Maggie spun around to see how close McCready was and lost her footing. She went down hard on her knees. Panting, ignoring the scrape on her hand, Maggie scrambled down a rock face, frantic to find a place to hide. McCready surprised her. He had discovered her ploy faster than she would have believed, and was gaining on her.

But why run? she asked herself, crouching down at the base of the rock. McCready would go right by, and when he was far enough away, she would head in the other direction. Maggie gritted her teeth and huddled to keep her body heat. McCready mustn't take long. She had to be up and moving before she was too cold.

She could hear him, hear his breathing somewhere above her, the grate of his boots against the rocks. The good Lord would not have blessed *that man* with eyes to see in the dark. Not if there was any justice! She closed her eyes, imagining him standing there, searching for her.

Maggie would kill for a sip of his whiskey. Rubbing her arms wasn't helping. And she didn't need memory dragging up the sound of McCready's voice when he burst into the cabin calling her name. He sounded afraid, afraid for her. Fool, she chided herself, that's just what he'd like you to believe. But the thought wouldn't leave her.

She glanced up, only to find the dark massive rock blocked her vision. What was McCready doing? Why wasn't he moving? Her stomach rumbled and she pressed her hands against it.

Maybe he had given up searching for her? And maybe those stars would drop like stones and hit him, she amended in the next breath.

Damn him! Where was he? She couldn't remain where she was. The stone held the cold of night just as it held the heat of the sun in the day. She had to believe she had made good her escape. Bracing her hands behind her, Maggie pushed herself upright. She still couldn't see above her, but she listened and heard no sound that would warn her if McCready was close.

Now or never. Maggie pushed off the rock to run.

McCready's strong arm snaked around her waist and hauled her up against him.

There was an instant when Maggie thought to fight him. The instant before he spun her around, holding her arm to the side and wedged his shoulder on her belly. It astounded her that McCready could lift her, but he did, hefting her over his shoulder so she hung head down.

"Ah, Mary Margaret," he muttered with a light pat to her bottom, "you'll lead me a merry chase. You're like the Queen of Diamonds, never to be trusted. But I like spirit in a woman," he observed with a cheerful voice. Taking a firm grip on her legs, he bounced his burden. "All secure?" Her grunt pleased him as he began the climb to the cabin.

"You know what gave your hiding place away, don't you? It was your stink," he said without waiting for her to answer. "The goose you tried to cook up there turned out to be your own." McCready ignored the stitch in his side. "I'll admit I expected better sport of you, Irish."

Maggie, swaying to and fro, heard his disappointment. She damned it and him. Better sport? She'd give McCready more sport than he had ever had!

"I hope you'll be gracious in your defeat, O'Roarke, and concede this first hand to me. I'll even admit that for a minute or two you had me worried." Liar, whispered a little voice that McCready chased quickly. Maggie had drawn the battle plan and picked the site, feeble as it was. But he had won the skirmish.

He made an effort not to pant to save his pride. He knew it wasn't his strength but Maggie's weight that was slowing him down. The thought of setting her free to walk back was rejected as fast as it came. He couldn't chase her again, and he had a feeling that she knew it.

"Won't . . . be . . . long . . . now, Maggie."

His labored breathing only had Maggie worrying that he would fall. She had no room for pity. He had decided to haul her back like she was a side of beef, so McCready could suffer for it. But her satisfaction was short-lived.

"I need . . . to think . . . of a fitting . . . punish-ment . . . for your escape."

The words she dismissed, but the shift of his hands on her thighs made her tense.

"Easy, girl," he soothed, grinning for all he was worth. "I won't be . . . too hard . . . on you."

Hard? On her? Maggie couldn't summon another thought. She refused to grab hold of any part of McCready's body.

The constant swaying motion and blood rushing to her head, arms, and hands were making lights dance in front of her eyes. If he slowed down any more, she would likely pass out before he reached the cabin.

Maggie smelled their destination long before she saw the light. McCready didn't hesitate at the door; he walked right in and dumped her in the middle of the soggy mess on the bed.

She sprawled where he dropped her, groaning. McCready hunched over, gripped his knees, and drew in heaving lungfuls of air.

"If . . . you move . . . I'll . . ." *Breathe in and out, and damn her.* "Yeah . . . I'll use . . . the belt on you."

Maggie believed him.

It was hard not to, when he straightened and, with his gaze never leaving hers, opened the belt buckle.

"Found sense in your . . . flight, O'Roarke? Good. Don't trifle with me." McCready slid the belt free and let it dangle above her.

"Now, McCready . . ." Maggie found that she could move. Right into the far corner, where she scrunched up like a mouse.

"Looks like you're wearin' war paint, McCready, with those smoke streaks on your face."

"You're none too pretty yourself." He had to swallow his chuckle. He couldn't believe Maggie was cowering away from him as if she believed he would use his belt on her. Chuckles became laughter that couldn't be contained. He looked at Maggie's blazing eyes and knew she was about as cowered as he was.

"Checkmate, Maggie mine."

Her hands curled into fists. "What's that?"

"I've got you and you've got nowhere left to run." McCready turned his back on her and shrugged out of his shirt.

Maggie stared at the wall. Her own shirt smelled of smoke,

and the back was damp from lying on the bed. She was still cold. Maggie didn't bother to look when she heard the bar slide across the door, nor did she move when McCready returned to the bedside.

"Get up." He didn't expect her to obey him, but she did, watching him with wary eyes. "Take off your shirt, Maggie."

"Why?"

"It should be obvious, even to you."

"You'd be thinkin' I'm hidin' a weapon?" Maggie refused to let her gaze drop below his nose. "If I had—"

"Maybe you are," McCready snapped, giving her a light push with the heel of his hand so her back was against the wall.

Maggie was too shocked to fight him. He ran his hands from her shoulders to her wrists. He slid his hands under her arms and stroked down her sides to her hips. His gaze pinned her in place as surely as disbelief when he shaped her breasts and spanned her rib cage. She uttered a choked sound as he spun her around, sliding his hands into her pants pockets quickly and just as quickly running them down her legs. One finger traced the length of her spine. She felt his full hand span her hip then palm her bottom.

"Nothing's where it shouldn't be."

Maggie wasn't cold anymore. McCready left behind a flush that stole inside her. She turned slowly and found that she couldn't understand the expression in his eyes. But she had no trouble understanding his warning.

"Don't goad me, Maggie. Don't dare me, either. I'll call your bluff every damn time."

She knew she was at the end of her rope; it was the reason that she nodded meekly. The reason why she couldn't figure McCready at all.

"Truce?" he offered, reaching for the buttons on her shirt.

Maggie slapped his hand away.

"You need dry clothes, O'Roarke. Stop being stubborn. Try being grateful that I didn't take a belt to your backside."

"I'll tend to meself."

"Fine." McCready knelt beside the bed and reached beneath it for the small trunk holding his clothes. "When you've changed, you can help me clean up this mess." He flipped open the top and withdrew two clean shirts along with pants for himself.

Maggie eyed the shirt he handed her. "Where's the rest?"

"That's all you're getting until your clothes get washed and dried."

"You'll be freezin' me—"

"There are plenty of blankets." McCready took his clean clothes to the fire. He added a few logs, for Maggie's sake, not his. Cold and exhaustion had fled his body the moment he put his hands on Maggie. Wearing an angry scowl he kicked off his boots and stripped his pants. It took every bit of willpower not to turn and look at Maggie when she made a choked sound. He didn't trust himself to see her watching him, but he could almost feel her gaze on him.

McCready admitted it weakened his resolve when he heard the rustle of her clothing falling to the floor. He refused to let the image of Maggie's body and how it felt to him enter his mind. The woman would have him on his knees if she knew how much he wanted her.

He needed something to appease the hunger prowling his gut. And he expected that Maggie was hungry, too. Too bad they didn't hunger for the same things.

After fastening the buttons of his fly, McCready lifted the bucket of water, swearing when he found it smelled as bad as himself.

"You finished, O'Roarke?" he asked, gathering his clothes into a small bundle. She didn't answer. He turned and found Maggie perched on the edge of the bed, leaning against the wall. "O'Roarke?" Her name came out with a stifled groan. His shirt barely draped Maggie's thighs, and she, uncaring of him, had those long legs stretched out in front of her. "O'Roarke!"

His shouted command made Maggie shake off her exhaustion and face him. Face him, but not look at him. She directed her gaze to the stone of the fireplace behind him.

"Gather up your clothes. I won't sleep with this stink in here."

Maggie lifted her shirt and rolled it tight. "Here, McCready." She threw it at him. The shirt fluttered open and fell to the floor between them. Her pants and socks followed.

Hands on hips, McCready waited for the last, and when it wasn't forthcoming, he went after it. Towering over her, he extended his hand. "There's one more."

Maggie didn't argue. She took the crumpled chemise from between her and the wall and handed it over.

"I'll be needin' one of those blankets, McCready."

"When we're finished," he snapped, his gaze sliding down her bare legs, long enough and shaped to make a man sweat. "Get up, O'Roarke. I'll need your help to roll the tick."

"An' what happens if I don't want to help?"

"Defiant to the last, Maggie? Try it and see."

Maggie thought for a moment, tempted to call him, but there was a dangerous glint in his eyes, and she couldn't deny her need to sleep.

Before she moved, McCready had opened the door. Barefoot and dressed in his shirt, Maggie wasn't going to run. At least not tonight, he amended. He threw their clothes outside, then helped her roll up the feather mattress. He didn't bother to tell Maggie that tomorrow he intended to see that she repaired the damage she had done. He didn't say anything while they grunted and tugged the large soggy bulk out the door.

Maggie was shaking when she came inside. She took a blanket from McCready and wrapped it around herself, looking for a place to lie down.

McCready poured himself a drink. "Want one?" he offered, understanding her searching gaze. "Take the bed, Maggie."

"Ain't a proper bed without rope springs. Never saw one with full boards in their place. Don't look comfortable for a body."

"Oh, but it is. For me. I like a hard bed and a soft body beneath me, Mary Margaret."

"Well, don't be thinkin' to have me there, boyo." But Maggie said this without heat. She had heard the coaxing temptation in his tone. She hated the image he created with those few words. Hated them, for it was far too easy to see herself there. Maggie pulled the blanket tighter and squeezed her thighs together. She had to get away before McCready had his way with her.

McCready suffered for his teasing remark. He sipped his drink, but warm whiskey wasn't the taste he craved. It occurred to him that he didn't want Maggie going to sleep. He wanted her awake and as aware of him as he was of her.

"Would you like something to eat first, Maggie?"

"No!" She hadn't meant to yell but the thick-headed man didn't understand that she had to shut him out of her sight.

"Don't be testy. I'm a passable cook."

"Sleep is all I want."

"Since my bed doesn't appeal to you, you're welcome to stretch out in front of the fire." McCready set his glass down and tossed her the quilt that had been on the bed. "That should cushion your soft bottom."

"I'm not soft, McCready, an' don't you be thinkin' it." She knelt with her back toward him to fix the quilt in place. Biting her lower lip, she said without turning, "Will you have a blanket?"

"Ah, Maggie mine, are you offering to share yours with me? Before you answer, you should know the thought holds a great deal of appeal to me."

"Why?"

Her voice was so soft that McCready wasn't sure he had heard her correctly. Raking his hair with one hand, he finished his drink.

"Can't you tell me why, McCready?" Maggie didn't know why she had asked him. She already knew the answer. He wanted the mines and would use himself just like one of those snake-oil drummers to sell shoddy goods.

The temptation was there for McCready to show her with action, not tell her with words, why he wanted to share her blankets. He gave thought to it. Just long enough to become fully aroused, which was mere seconds. But he knew he would be on Maggie quicker than a greenhorn raking in his first winnings, just as greedy and proud as the devil she called him.

And it was pride that had him say, "You'll find out, Maggie mine. Before we leave here, I promise you'll find out why." Turning down the lamp, he fetched the last blanket from the chest and settled himself in front of the door.

Maggie slowly settled herself before the fire. She didn't like the strength in McCready's promise. He'd left no room for doubt that he would indeed show her why the sharing of her blankets held any appeal for him. But she wore a smug smile that he didn't know the idea held more than appeal for her.

She wasn't finished with McCready.

CHAPTER
8

"I can't fix it!" Maggie declared, hands on hips. The morning sun added glints of gold to the copper color of her hair, but the blaze of her eyes rivaled the sun's heat. She kicked aside the makeshift blanket skirt and tried to move past McCready.

He grabbed hold of her upper arm. "I can't believe this. You're a woman. You're supposed to be able to sew."

"Who wrote that into law, McCready? You? I get by for what needs doin' for meself."

"Yeah. I already know how selfish you are." The uncomfortable night spent tossing and turning added a sharpness to

94

his voice. "Well, I've got news for you, Maggie. You are going to repair my feather tick. I don't care how you do it. I do not care how long it takes you. But you will fix my mattress."

If she didn't get the point from his insistent voice, she certainly knew it from the cunning gleam in his eyes. Maggie grated her teeth together and stared pointedly at his hand still gripping her arm. The back of his hand was pressed against her breast.

McCready suddenly released her as if he had become aware of the same thing, only to capture the ends of her shirt collar. Maggie tried to pull away. McCready gathered more of the collar into his hands. Her heart was beginning to thud uncomfortably. The wee flutters were once again dancing inside her, had been, she admitted to herself, ever since she awoke to find McCready at her side this morning. It hadn't sweetened her disposition any to find that he made good on his boast of the night before and had made breakfast. Maggie made him taste everything, not trusting him. It surprised her that he did it willingly.

She let out a hiss of breath. The man didn't understand what his being this close did to her. His head was as thick as the stout cabin walls.

"Say you'll do it, Maggie."

She squinted up at the sun.

McCready closed his eyes briefly, offering a prayer for patience. "Are you trying to make me angry?"

"Try, McCready? Don't need to. Seems to me that around you it comes right natural."

He twisted the ends of the collar and jerked her flat up against him. McCready grinned as her chin shot up. "I warned you last night, didn't I, Maggie?"

"Stuff that warning in the hole in the mattress." Her pulse was dancing to the tune the little ones played. Little ones that seemed to make themselves at home when McCready's body touched hers. She didn't like feeling a tight, grabbing sensation deep in her middle.

"Well, what's it going to be?" he prodded, angling his head so that his mouth hovered over hers. He craved a kiss and would have taken it, but pride once more dictated that Maggie had to give willingly.

The teasing glint was gone from his eyes from one heartbeat to another. What Maggie saw replace it was dark and dangerous. She felt the same excitement as when she scraped her knife blade against bedrock and found alluvial gold. His breath teased over her mouth like a breeze tickles the leaves in summer. It was a sinful mouth, and she had to get away from it and him before he clouded her mind.

"McCready," she murmured, "I'll make a deal with you."

"I'm listening, but make it a good one. I'm not in a mood to be generous."

"You wash and I'll try to fix your mattress."

"Not good enough. Offer me more to sweeten the deal."

"More?"

"You've been allowed to go along without paying for your actions, Maggie." He couldn't resist brushing his lips over hers. It was a little sip to ease his need. He felt her tremor, but as he kept his eyes on hers, he could see it wasn't from fear. He nipped her bottom lip. "You keep on forgetting that you're my wife, Maggie. A wife should take care of her husband's belongings."

He waited to see if she would reject him again. No matter the need churning inside him, he would not force her.

Maggie had her hands flat on his chest. He was hard and warm. She leaned away to escape his tantalizing mouth, but the effort cost her. Her lower body nestled the blatant shape of his manhood. She had found something else that was as arrogant as everything else about him. Be kissed or burned, but make up your mind, her body demanded.

"I'll do it." Maggie found herself free. She wished she

could take enjoyment from his stunned expression. But she couldn't. Submitting to his demand to repair his mattress and wash their clothes was hard to swallow. Maggie was more afraid that McCready would know why she had done it.

"I'll be gracious and heat the water for you, Maggie." He started for the cabin, then turned back. "You won't try to run?"

She glanced at her bare feet and the bulky blanket that she wore. "Not likely."

McCready accepted the silent vow in her eyes. Maggie would run as soon as she was given another opportunity.

"Why don't you know when McCready's coming back, Dutch?"

"I told you, Cora Ann, the man has business away from here. I'm not his keeper. He didn't tell me how long he'd be gone." Dutch set out a glass in front of her and, without waiting, poured out a drink. Cora Ann belted it down, and he refilled the glass. He cursed McCready for leaving him to deal with a vicious dog and two irate women.

"Why don't you tell me what's wrong? Maybe I could help?"

They both looked over when the Rose began another mournful tune. Dutch knew she was missing McCready, for her singing left a lot to be desired tonight. But there was nothing he could do about it. When Cora Ann asked again where McCready was, Dutch knew he had had enough.

He slapped down the bar towel. "You married to the man, Cora Ann?"

"No. But I'd like to be."

"Then don't ask me again. McCready will be back when he's back. Not a day before. If you can't keep your nose from poking into this, I'll try seeing how business improves without a whining woman around."

"You can't fire me! McCready said you had to keep me on last night."

Dutch leaned over the bar. "McCready ain't here. I am. You're trying my patience till there's little left. Go deal cards, Cora Ann; it's what you're best at."

She took the bottle and glass. With a swish of her plaid, corded silk gown she settled herself at a table. "Play something cheerful!" she yelled to the Rose, wincing when discordant notes were followed by a rousing tune.

Three men, miners all, left the bar to join Cora Ann. She nodded to Abe and Jimmy Keystone, twin brothers whose faces were as browned and creased as walnuts. Slick Tobell made a fourth.

"Any of you see McCready today?" she asked, so distracted over McCready's disappearance that for once she didn't eye the pokes they set on the table.

Slick answered her. "Seen his horse in the lean-to when I brought in my mule. Man can't go far on foot."

Breaking open the deck, Cora Ann agreed and began to shuffle. "But he's not over at Miss Mae's, and no one's seen him all day. If he was dead, we'd all know about it."

"How's that, Cora?" Jimmy asked, cupping his ear, for he had lost part of his hearing in a dynamite blast last year.

"Why, boys," she answered with a cheerful note, "the bastard who shot McCready would be bragging all over."

"Since you're mentioning bastards, Cora Ann, look who just walked in."

Cora Ann looked where Slick pointed. Quincy Kessnick stood in the doorway, his dark shrewd eyes searching the faces of those present. Behind him were the four hired guns that McCready had bribed to kidnap him. Cora Ann glanced at the Rose, who kept right on playing, but she was the only one who didn't know Quincy was here.

She shot a look at Dutch, but he gave a sparse shake of his head, warning her to let him handle this. Quincy was almost as tall as McCready but heavier built. His mouth, Cora Ann decided, was wide and full and downright intriguing but for the tilt at the corner that hinted at cruelty. She didn't understand how a man who was so exacting could even think about marrying the likes of Maggie O'Roarke. Returning her gaze to the cards she held, Cora Ann knew she would keep it to herself just how exacting Quincy could be.

"Dutch," Quincy called, "I won't hold you responsible, for I know you're only hired help. But where's McCready?"

"Gone."

"Ran out, did he?"

Dutch barely spared a glance for Ryder Balkett, the man at Quincy's right. "He didn't run. McCready had business elsewhere."

The Rose stopped playing and turned around. She took note of the mean-looking bunch at the door and dismissed them as potential customers. The only move she made was to perch on the edge of her stool, ready to run if any shooting started.

"And Maggie," Quincy demanded, "did she also have sudden business elsewhere, too?"

"Wouldn't you know it? That's just what happened. Left her dog with me and took off to one of the claims."

"Without McCready?"

"I wouldn't know." Dutch turned and broke open the seal on a bottle of whiskey. He set out five glasses. "Why don't you boys have a drink on the house and then leave Cooney Camp? There's nothing here for any of you."

Quincy motioned Ryder forward. "I want to know where McCready is," he murmured. "And if he's with Maggie. If Dutch won't talk, go after Cora Ann."

"Right." Ryder and his cohorts moved to do Quincy's bidding. Hitching his gunbelt, he swaggered over to the bar. Ryder had to admire Quincy for not holding it against him that he had taken McCready's money along with his own.

"This is business, Dutch, nothing personal," Ryder warned.

He grabbed hold of Dutch's shirt, expecting his grip to put Dutch at a disadvantage by forcing him to lean forward. But Dutch's solid bulk didn't budge.

"Henry, grab hold of him," Ryder ordered a hatchet-faced man. "Jess, you help him. Sonny stands by me."

Dutch took a deep breath and released it. He saw that the miners were rising, ready to come to his rescue. He didn't want anyone getting hurt, so motioned them to stay put.

"I can handle this, boys," he assured them. Dutch jerked free of Ryder's hold. He shot a quick look over his shoulder to see the position of the two men behind him. Swirling around, he rammed both men in the groin with his meaty fists. In the next few seconds he grabbed hold of Ryder's shirtfront, hauling half of his body over the bar, broke a bottle, and held the jagged edge up against Ryder's throat.

"Now, you understand that this is nothing personal, Ryder. I just take exception to being roughed up for the likes of Kessnick."

From the corner of his eye, Dutch saw that Quincy was fingering his fancy vest's pocket. There was a double barrel derringer concealed there. "Wrong move," he told Quincy, shaking his head at him.

Slick confirmed it would be a foolish move. He had his gun out and aimed at Kessnick.

Dutch then turned back to Ryder. "We have a right fetching dilemma, boy. You can try for that iron on your hip, like you're itching to, and I cut your throat before you draw. Or," he continued, grinning, "if you're of a mind to, you can back off and take the trash that's groaning behind me and leave. But don't take long to make up your mind. I can't keep my hand steady for long."

Ryder's eyes darted frantically from side to side, looking for help. He hoped Quincy would make a move, but within seconds he knew he was on his own. The glass pricked his skin, but he swallowed anyway.

"You win," he muttered to Dutch.

"Smart choice." But Dutch didn't remove the glass. "You two hombres get out from behind me and haul your tails outside. You can help them, Sonny," he ordered to the man who had waited at Ryder's side. Once they were moving toward the door, he looked at Quincy.

"I'll be sure and tell McCready that you stopped by."

"Do that, Dutch. And tell him this isn't over. No one gets away with stealing from me. No one cuts into my deal and lives. I'll find Maggie and marry her. Those mines belong to me." Quincy elbowed aside the three men and left.

Dutch released Ryder. "Have a drink to wash the fear out of your mouth, boy. I've got another job for you."

Ryder rubbed his throat. "Crossing Quincy again?"

"Nothing else," Dutch answered, pouring him a drink. "Now, listen good to what I want you to do."

CHAPTER 9

"So that's how you managed to kidnap Quincy. You bribed his men," Maggie said, pushing aside her finished plate of beans and bacon.

"It's true, Maggie. 'The devil rules over lovers of temporal goods belonging to this world, not because he is lord of this world, but because he is ruler of those covetous desires by which we long for all that passes away.'"

"That nonsense from your fancy books?" she asked, gesturing to the shelf above him.

"I take offense, O'Roarke. Yes, it is something I read in a book, but you malign the words of Saint Augustine to call them nonsense."

Maggie was about to ask if he knew the man but stopped herself. McCready's wicked gaze lay in wait like a trap ready to spring on her. Shrugging it off, she rose to clear the table. She wasn't thinking about McCready's claim that she should be able to do a woman's work. She was simply sharing a chore as she had with her father and uncle when they were alive. McCready had cooked, she would wash the dishes.

Alerted by her willingness, McCready watched her every move. She was once again dressed in her baggy pants and too large shirt. It didn't matter. He now knew what was beneath them.

"There's more coffee," Maggie said, holding out the pot.

"No, thank you, Maggie. I've had enough."

"No reason to be so stiff, McCready. You could've just said no."

"I wasn't being 'stiff,' as you called it, but simply being polite."

She straightened from where she had crouched before the fire and turned with hands on hips to face him. "Are you tellin' me I've got no manners?"

"No, Maggie, that is not what I meant," he answered without hesitation, knowing how much he could hurt her. He had learned several things about Mary Margaret O'Roarke today. Things had angered him, things that endeared her to him, and a few that had him raking his hair in frustration.

He saw that his answer satisfied her, for she went back to washing their few dishes.

Leaning back in his chair, cupping the back of his neck with his hands, McCready stared at the ceiling, ruminating on his association with Maggie. She was a woman who didn't know the meaning of the word *quit*. Swearing and cursing, she had tackled the repair of the feather mattress. When he had ventured to suggest that his point had been made to have her fix what she had ruined and that she should stop, for it was never going to be slept on, Maggie found her own way to prove him wrong.

While he had examined the crooked stitches, she had searched for and found a variety of wild herbs and added them to a few small branches of cedar. Crushing them together, she stuffed them into the mattress and sewed it closed.

Thinking about her smug smile that brought his own smile in return, McCready caught himself grinning. Maggie then surprised him with her knowledge of the medicinal use of wild plants, learned, she said, from other miners, trappers, and Indians. She informed him of the blending of cultures, although those weren't her words or understanding, that had given Indian cures to Spaniards, then to the Anglos that followed once the Santa Fe Trail had been opened.

But when she went on to tell him about taking care of a fever-stricken father when she was ten, McCready found his anger growing. He knew that Maggie didn't know what she had said to make him angry, and McCready didn't enlighten her. There were other tales she told him, leaving him to draw the conclusion that Maggie had learned her independence at such an early age, it was ingrained in her to fight any one and any way to keep it.

He thought of his own childhood, spoiled and pampered by Maggie's standards, if he would tell her about it. In his own mind he knew by comparison to many men, he had grown up with having every monetary need met. A succession of tutors and masters of dance, fencing, and equestrian skills had been hired with the express order to raise him after he had outgrown a nanny.

The stern face of his first valet, Frederick Beamsworth, came to mind, and McCready found that he still had a soft spot for the English gentleman hired to teach him his manners and the proper form of dress and to care for him in his excesses. Beams had tried to fill the roles needed by a lonely boy.

But no one could feed the hunger inside him. While Maggie

had roamed wild trekking the mountains with a father who wanted her, he had learned to maneuver his way around the drunken bouts of a woman whom had given him life and loathed the sight of him.

That knowledge had been the grand discovery of his fourteenth year, although he hadn't learned the full reason. He had dutifully attended the musicals, afternoon teas, and a host of other tiring social functions with the hopes of receiving one nod, one smile, one bit of notice from his mother.

It had never happened. Within the two years that had followed, he had gained attention of another sort with his drinking, gambling, and women. He had often wondered, during that time, if his mother had known that her dearest friend had seduced him. When the doors of polite society were finally closed to him, he had earned what he desired: his mother's attention.

The scathing words exchanged in that interview were burned in his memory. The result had been his leaving with a cash settlement to make his own way.

McCready glanced around his cabin, one of the few places he called his own. His gaze skimmed the massive stones that formed the wall of the fireplace, then lowered to find Maggie quietly watching him.

"You've come back from where the wee folk had you," she murmured.

"The wee folk?"

"That's what me father said when he'd get that same look in his eyes."

"Did it bother you, Maggie, when he was lost in his own thoughts and shut you out?"

"At first," she answered with a touch of sadness.

"Do you miss him?" He watched as she drew her knees up and wrapped her arms around them. He sensed that Maggie was sharing with him what she hadn't shared with anyone else.

"There's times when I do. Just like I miss Pete. But they both taught me to get along on my own."

"A woman shouldn't have to—"

"Maybe for some that's true, McCready, but not me." She rested her chin on her knee and looked at him. Even sitting with his long legs stretched out in front of him, McCready was powerful. His bruises had faded, just as the swelling on his eye had almost gone. He hadn't shaved and the beard shadow suited his hard-jawed face. A longing to touch him swept through her, but Maggie was no longer caught unawares by it. She had suffered through the day with the feeling never quite leaving her.

"How long you figure on keepin' me here, McCready?"

"Until it's safe for you to go back."

McCready's slow grin as he looked down at her made the wee flutters shimmer and stir inside her. Maggie looked away. "That ain't much of an answer. I can take care of meself. Never needed no man to do it. Can't see why you don't believe me." Maggie nibbled her lower lip. "I'd be missin' Satin. What did you do with her?"

"She's safe with Dutch. You know he'll take good care of her. I'm surprised that you didn't ask me about her before this."

"I wanted to. Truth is, McCready, I was scared of what you'd done to her."

"Your high-ranking opinion of me is enough to drive me to drink. I didn't hurt her, just as I wouldn't hurt you." He stood and stretched, catching her puzzled expression. He laughed a soft, rough kind of a laugh. Maggie, for all her lack of poise and polished feminine charms, played hell with his good intentions. Reaching down, he opened the cupboard's door and took out a bottle. "Share a drink with me?"

Maggie eyed the bottle he held. The wee ones were still stirring about inside her. But McCready had a fondness for whiskey that might put him to sleep. Didn't her father often tell her that the fairy folk had a fondness for gold and good whiskey? Just like McCready. Maybe, if she had a few drinks with him, McCready and the wee ones would go to sleep and leave her be.

She found herself smiling and nodded. She started to rise to join him at the table.

"Stay by the fire, Maggie. I'll join you there," he murmured in a voice filled with promise.

Stepping into a hunter's snare couldn't have made her feel more trapped. Pride wouldn't let her show him that she was afraid. Her blood sizzled softly, and instead of feeling frightened, Maggie felt excited by the challenge. And she had nothing to worry about, she reassured herself. She could handle McCready and his liquor. For sure, a little voice reminded her, didn't you prove that last night?

Torn between hope and doubt, she sighed. It was too late. McCready settled himself beside her on the quilt. She took the glass he handed her and drained half.

McCready told himself not to be alarmed. Maggie knew what she was doing. But not to be outdone by her silent challenge, he finished his drink and without asking topped off her glass and refilled his own.

Maggie glanced from his wicked mouth wearing a cocky grin up to his eyes filled with amusement. If the boyo thought that he could drink her under the table, she'd make sure that he woke with a head that he wouldn't want to call his own.

"To us, Maggie," he suggested, touching his glass to hers. "And to friendship."

"We ain't friends, McCready. We got business 'tween us an' nothin' more."

"I'll place a bet on our becoming friends, O'Roarke. And there's our marriage to think about. You don't know how that will turn out."

Marriage again? Maggie wished he hadn't said that. She stared at the glass cupped between her hands. Why did he have to remind her about it? She didn't want to remember his claim.

"Drink up, O'Roarke. You're falling behind."

Calling herself a fool, Maggie nevertheless downed the whiskey. This time she held her glass out for more. "We've got business that needs settlin'."

"What?"

"Your claimin' Pete's mines, for a start."

"We can talk about that, Maggie. We'll work out something pleasing to both of us. Is there anything else that you want to discuss?"

"Anythin' else?"

"That's what I said. Here we are, warm, safe and alone. It's a pleasurable feeling. And Maggie, I like mixing business with pleasure." Once again he toasted her with his glass. "Truth is, Maggie mine, I make a habit of it."

Just his mentioning pleasure kept her quiet. She had to finish her drink quickly. The wee ones hadn't been given nearly enough whiskey to make them stop their fluttering about inside her. The fire at her back was making her warm. At her side McCready sent flickers of flame shivering over her skin with the delicate touch of his finger tracing the shape of her shoulder.

He bothered her terribly, she admitted. Maybe it was his size. There weren't many men she couldn't look in the eye. Maybe he never let her forget that he was a man. It could be that cocky know-it-all grin. Every time she had caught his lips creasing into it today, she had wanted to accept its wicked invitation to share. She couldn't ignore the way his eyes lingered on her face filled with an amused gleam that she in turn longed to slap away. She didn't like McCready thinking he knew something she didn't. And there was no denying to herself that his drawl, so slow and lazy-sounding that she was forced to think of soft things, made her want to touch his long dark brown hair.

Mentally straightening her spine, Maggie determined she had to do something to deal with it.

"It won't work, you know," she muttered, wondering as she spoke if she was making a mistake.

"What's that, Maggie?" he asked with a soft, lazy drawl.

"You figurin' on gettin' me soused so you can have your way with me."

"Ah, Maggie," he uttered, burying the urge to laugh. "You're mistaken. Face me," he ordered in the unequivocal way that one might speak to a child. He counted off the seconds before she did. He took her glass and set it aside with his own. "You've had enough."

McCready cupped her shoulders and dragged her closer. "I told you I wouldn't hurt you. And if I wanted to"—he groaned and forced himself to use her words—"'have my way with you,' Maggie, I wouldn't want you drunk." His gaze targeted her mouth where the edge of her teeth worried her lower lip. "Maggie, I wouldn't find seducing you half so pleasurable unless you were very aware and able to share the pleasure with me." He saw her eyes widen, only to be shielded by her lashes. The fire cast a halo around her hair, and its glow shot through the short red curls and turned them golden. McCready remembered all those freckles that he had promised himself he would discover. Freckles and feminine secrets he was growing more sure that Maggie had never let any other man discover.

"What's wrong?" she croaked. The amusement was gone from his eyes. The blue color darkened, and as it did, a decisive gleam made her sense danger. "McCready? What's—" She ended with a cry as he hauled her across his lap. "What the hell do you—"

"That, Mary Margaret, about sums up where you've put me. But no more." He dragged her head down.

He closed his mouth over hers in a taunting kiss, catching her when her lips were parted. McCready felt the moment's stiffness of her body in rejection, at the same time the heated softness of her mouth took fire under his. For a few shattering seconds he wasn't trying to prove anything to her, and she wasn't fighting him. For one moment the kiss seemed to demand total intimacy from each of them.

Maggie wrenched her head away. He saw her stunned look and flushed skin, heard her splintered breathing. He was in no better shape. But he had learned that he had to be wary of the effect she had on him. The desire that lay beneath the tension between them had the power to make him forget everything but Maggie.

He felt her hands shaking where she still gripped his arms. Her eyes opened with a guarded look as if she was desperate to protect herself from whatever he would do next. McCready had never had a woman afraid of him. And he wouldn't begin with Maggie. He came to his feet in a controlled rush, dumping her on the floor, then grabbed the bottle and glasses.

"It's time you went to sleep."

She waited until he set the bottle and glasses on the table before she stood up. Who did he think he was kissing her and stopping as if it meant nothing? And how dare he toss her off as if she were the gravel in a miner's pan!

McCready turned just as she rushed at him. The next thing he knew he was shoved hard and landed on his butt. Her smug smile stung him, but it was the brushing motion that she made with her hands that infuriated him. His hand snaked out and grabbed hold of her ankle. Her startled cry was cut off as she landed beside him. McCready lost no time in pinning her in place with one leg thrown over hers.

"You're fast, Maggie, I'll give you that. But you've got to learn to keep your eyes on who you're fighting with."

"If I was a man—"

"Maggie, ah, Maggie mine, then this wouldn't be half the fun." His soft laughter slowly died. He took her mouth in a quick, hard kiss, but it wasn't enough. "Maggie?" he whispered, not wanting her to stop him when need rolled like thunder through him. "Give me your mouth."

A flash of Quincy's shocked face when she had told him no more kissing and reinforced it with her fist crossed her mind. She was strong enough to push McCready away. If she wanted to. . . .

A deliciously hot shiver walked up her spine. "Take it, McCready," she whispered back, feeling the little flutters inside dance to a quickened tune.

"I only awaited the invitation." He kissed her lightly, teasing her mouth with the barest touch of his own. But Maggie trembled against him, one of her hands clenching his shoulder, the other gripping his arm. Her mouth didn't understand his lips' demand to lead. It was as mobile as his own. Just as aggressive. Just as warm. She had told him to take, but Maggie was the one who was taking him deep.

McCready was no stranger to desire or women. He liked them. But Maggie stunned him with this scalding desire that made him want to lose himself in her. She parted her lips for the sweep of his tongue, and McCready felt the power of need down to his bone, tumbled along with emotions that tried to surface.

It was blinding curiosity that had Maggie clinging to him. She wanted to know why her body softened to fit the hard swell of his chest, the taut curve of his belly and the power of his thigh. And his taste . . . her mouth couldn't get enough.

She quivered helplessly when his hand slid up her arm and shaped her shoulder before he cupped the back of her head. His fingers held her still, then angled her head up so that her mouth mated more fully with his. Her body wanted to curl around his, and she strained upward in a slow, rhythmic motion. She was losing herself in the scent and feel of McCready. Heat unfurled through her at an alarming rate. Maggie felt as if she had swallowed a pepper patch. She knew he would take everything that she was, everything that she had, and still demand more.

McCready licked the corner of her mouth.

Maggie's eyes flew open, then narrowed. "Stop that."

"Why, Maggie?" he asked absently, rimming the shape of her bottom lip with the tip of his tongue.

"I told you to stop, McCready. It's . . . well, it's wet."
And shivery. And felt good. Too good.

He tilted his head back to stare at her. "What's wrong? Or is that another of your whimsical compliments?"

Maggie closed her eyes. "I don't know. Is it?" She had heard of being in tight spots, but she was in a hard one. The floorboards beneath her wouldn't yield, and McCready was as hard and unyielding on top of her.

"Maggie, I've never had a woman tell me how to kiss her before you."

"Didn't say that."

With a rueful smile McCready slowly understood that she was afraid. "Do you want me to kiss you?"

Frustrated, Maggie looked up at him. "I didn't say that."

"Ah, I understand," he murmured, then nodded. "What we deal with here is a woman's fancy. Caprice . . . 'Hard is my lot that here by fortune place—'"

"I'm the one on the floor, so don't be whinin' about hard. An' no one put you here but you."

"I must watch the wild vicissitudes of taste, but the truth, Mary Margaret, is that I'd rather be tasting the wildness of you." He lowered his mouth and at the last second kissed her cheek.

"Stop mumblin' things I can't be knowin'."

"Somewhere in there were a few of my favorite lines of Samuel Johnson."

"All sounds like hog swill to me. Get up. I've made me choice. I don't want to be kissin' you." She pushed him and knew that his moving aside had allowed her to stand up, for he stood right beside her.

"Then maybe this is something you will understand, Maggie. Since you can't make up your mind about my kisses, I'll do it for you. We'll play, Maggie," he promised. "I'll chase you—"

". . . an'," she prompted when he didn't finish.

McCready smiled and leaned closer to her. "And then you'll chase me until one of us is caught."

Maggie found herself backing away until the edge of the table stopped her. "Try it. Just try it. This O'Roarke can handle the likes of you, McCready."

"If only you would, Maggie mine. It's becoming an unbearable desire."

Instantly Maggie was braced for battle.

The mere thought of stalking her now, of ruffling her belief that she could win, tempted him beyond anything else had in the last few years. But McCready knew the stakes he was playing for and turned his back.

She had dared McCready and won. Maggie wanted to crow. She had made him back down. But the flush of winning excitement drained just as quickly as it had come. Why was she suddenly feeling as if she had lost something? It was only McCready and them damn fancy words of his that were driving her mad. Those words and the wee ones and his evil whiskey.

Maggie glanced up at the shelf of books. She eyed the bottle on the table. McCready had plucked her up just like a miner grabbing in a stream for a nugget only to find it was fool's gold, and he threw her off just as fast. The man needed his proud tail feathers trimmed.

It took the time of her heartbeat slowing for Maggie to figure out a way. And the best thing was, she said to herself, smiling, she wouldn't need a knife to do it.

Unaware of the revenge being plotted, McCready presented Maggie with the opportunity to carry out her plan the next morning.

Maggie discovered that sometime while she slept, he—like

the thief she had called him—had sneaked out of the cabin and barred the door from the outside.

The morning had brought second thoughts. The barred door chased them. There was no hesitation in her. She dragged the large wooden tub to the center of the floor, eyed its distance from the door, then decided she wanted it closer. McCready was not going to be able to miss seeing what she had done when he opened that door.

"Leave me locked up, will he?" she muttered as she set to work. "He'll have to let me go after this. I can't be fightin' him an' meself."

Within minutes she surveyed her handiwork. And then began to worry.

CHAPTER
10

McCready met Dutch in a ravine almost an hour's walk from his cabin. The sun had already begun baking the earth. McCready's cotton shirt clung damply to his skin. He had asked little while Dutch told him what had happened with Quincy, but he was angry by the time he finished.

"Why the hell involve Ryder again? The man proved he can't be trusted. I told you Quincy would have to give up if there was nothing for him to find, didn't I? And the hell with his threats. They're as empty as he is. He'll hang around to see if he can bribe Ryder again. But you didn't think about the risk to Maggie, did you?"

Beneath his bushy brows, Dutch calmly watched him. "You finished?" he asked, putting the cap back on his canteen. McCready nodded. "You didn't give me a chance to tell you what I hired Ryder to do. Believe me, I never forgot about Maggie's life being in danger."

"Dutch, I didn't mean—"

"I'd hope not."

"Go on," McCready encouraged, impatient to get back to Maggie. She'd be furious that he left her locked in the cabin with the windows shuttered so she couldn't escape.

"I told Ryder to dress in your suit and ride your horse out of camp this morning. He made sure that a few of the miners saw him. Since it was dawn, no one could have gotten a good look, so stop worrying that someone recognized him. I even lucked out with curious Cora Ann swearing that you were back at the Rawhider last night."

"How?"

"Well, she heard Ryder and me in your room, and naturally she knocked, thinking it was you. I mumbled some to leave us alone, then opened the door to her. From the back Ryder looks a bit like you, and I made sure she didn't catch more than a glimpse. She'll tell everyone that it was you."

Raking his hair, McCready paced in front of the rock where Dutch sat. "I still don't see how this is going to get rid of Quincy."

"Easy. If your head wasn't filled with thinking about Maggie, you'd see how easy it is."

"Leave my thoughts about Maggie out of this."

"Sure, boss. Whatever you say. But Quincy had the place watched. I think it was Sonny. The other two couldn't have been up to spending the night on their feet after I got done with them." Dutch stopped and joined McCready's laughter. He accepted his boss's clasp on the shoulder as a sign that all was forgiven for his not following his orders to the letter.

"I would guess that I'm getting as touchy as Maggie," McCready said by way of apology.

Dutch let it pass, anxious to finish. "Now, Ryder rode north to Santa Fe, and Quincy followed him. So you don't have to stay locked up in the cabin. I'll be back with the horses tomorrow, and you take Maggie home. Then we can sit and settle the matter of Pete's claims." McCready had stopped pacing. Dutch waited a moment, then added, "And we can't forget that Maggie needs to be told the truth—"

"Maggie's not ready to come back."

"Oh? It's Maggie that's not ready? McCready, I'm ashamed of you. You never used to lie to me."

McCready winced at the implication that he lied to everyone else. "I'm not . . . All right! I'm not ready to take her back. She still hasn't told me about the claims. You know that Maggie won't give her trust to anyone easily. I'll need more time."

"No offense meant, boss, but that's a barrel of belly-rot. The only time you need is to see to your own—"

"Don't say it, Dutch. Friends or not, I won't take that kind of talk from you."

"All right. I'm quiet." Dutch held up his hands. "Step back and tell me what you think of my plan."

"It might work. Only time will tell. Meet me here in two days. Quincy will either have been long gone or be back."

"You're sure that you don't want me to bring the horses?"

"I can't trust Maggie." McCready didn't tell him about her escape. No sense in having Dutch laughing at how easily she had fooled him. But it was a sore spot. "Did you bring Maggie's clothes?"

"Couldn't."

"Couldn't or wouldn't, Dutch?"

"When I say I couldn't, that's what I mean. I've had my hands full taking care of Satin. That dog misses her. She has to be coaxed to eat. Thankfully she doesn't seem to tie eating that steak with me. I think she's saving her revenge for you, boss.''

"Well, if everything works the way it should, that devil won't have a chance at me."

"Maggie giving you a . . . *hard* time?''

McCready stared at Dutch. There was no sign of malicious intent in his eyes, but McCready sensed that Dutch used the word deliberately. He refused to give him the satisfaction of responding to the goad.

With a shrug Dutch also let this pass. "Now, as I was saying, I've got to take care of the dog and listen to Cora Ann's whining about where you are. Then, there's the Rose. Without you her playing is suited to a five-dollar funeral. You got the best of this setup, McCready. You've only got to deal with Maggie."

Only Maggie. Dutch's words lingered in McCready's mind as he made the climb up to his cabin. If only he did have her.

As he got closer, McCready heard Maggie singing. He shook his head. Maggie was singing? Not cursing, not swearing, but singing. He couldn't catch all the words, but he had heard that rousing tune sung by enough men to know that cheerful though her voice was, the song was a curse to him. It told the tale of a young man with gambling fever in his blood. He had lost all his earnings and told the men around him a sorrowful tale of needing money for the doctor for his darling gal. The men had never heard him cry over losing before, so they took up a collection before he reached the door. He blessed them and thanked them, clutching the money tight. And before a man could blink, he'd bet it all.

He paused in front of the door just as Maggie sang the last and heard her replace poor Johnny with his name.

"Poor McCready was a liar, what a liar he could be,
But with gambling fever in his blood, he's a thief for all
    to see.
Those miners they was angry, those gamblers they was
    rough.

They gathered round McCready an' strung him up.
Strung him, strung him, strung up sure enough!''

She didn't have to sound so gleeful adding a resounding
''Yahoo!'' It was his gambler's superstition that had his hand
touch his throat when Maggie repeated the last line. She really
was an Irish barbarian.

The thud of something hitting the floor forced him to throw
off the bar, shove open the door, and rush inside, only to stop.

Maggie swirled around on the table. The chairs had been
kicked over. McCready's gaze fell to the wooden tub he'd
nearly fallen into. The whiskey fumes hit him, but he stood his
ground.

She knew he was back. A delicious shiver walked its way up
her spine, and Maggie turned, very slowly, to find McCready
just standing there. No, she amended, frowning. He wasn't
exactly standing still.

''You're back,'' she mumbled, leaning forward and bracing
her hands on bowed legs to peer down at him.

''That's right, Maggie, I'm back. Had yourself a little
party?'' He could kill her. It wouldn't be impossible at all.
There wasn't a man in the New Mexico Territory—hell,
anywhere—who would hold him responsible. He didn't bother
to count the broken bottle necks, for rising from the wooden
tub were enough fumes to verify that she had smashed every
bottle of his best whiskey.

Maggie blinked, trying to make him stay still. ''Come to
dance?'' she asked, smiling crookedly at him.

''Up there?''

''For sure. It's where me an' the wee ones are.''

Her whispered confidence lost something with the series of
hiccups she tried to hide. McCready, deciding he had better
check to be sure, sent a searching glance around the empty
cabin. ''Maggie, I hate to be the one to tell you this, but there's
no one here. Just you. And me.''

A quick shake of her head sent the room spinning. "Oh, you can't see 'em," she whispered, holding one hand over her eyes and leaning dangerously over.

He was a man with a great deal of control, McCready told himself as he stepped close to the table's edge and braced himself to catch her when she fell. He wouldn't strangle her. Yet. But Maggie, lifting her head high, saw him and reared back.

"Go 'way, 'Cready." To add force to her demand, she managed to stand straight.

"No, Maggie mine. I'm not leaving. Leaving you alone tends to set loose havoc. But I want you to tell me where the wee ones are." McCready inhaled, trying to determine how much whiskey Maggie had drunk before she decided to break every bottle. She avoided the hand he held out to her, and afraid that she would fall and hurt herself, he dropped his hand to his side.

In a soft, coaxing tone he said, "Show me where the wee ones are, and I'll get rid of them for you."

"Here," she answered, rubbing her belly in circles. "An' down here." Maggie dragged her hands over her thighs. "Your fault. You bring 'em out."

"I bring them out? Don't blame me for this." McCready closed his eyes for a moment, groaning at the urge to replace Maggie's hands with his.

Maggie started laughing. "You're movin'." She cocked her head to the side and covered her mouth with one hand to stifle the laughter. "Can't fool me."

Whatever anger he had at that second left him. How could he remain angry when she wore a lopsided smile and wagged her finger at him. "Maggie, I don't want to fool you. I just want you to come down from the table before you hurt yourself."

Even with the door open McCready felt the whiskey fumes getting to him. A twinge of guilt wormed its way inside him.

He had not left the windows open so that Maggie couldn't climb out and escape.

"Come to me, Maggie. I'll help you."

She eyed the four hands he held out and began humming the song she had been singing.

McCready edged around the table, trying to get his hands on her.

Maggie wavered back and forth, almost lost her balance, but managed to evade him.

Twice around the table was enough for McCready. He waited until Maggie had taken another turn and her back was to him, then leapt up onto the table, hoping it would hold their combined weight. "Maggie," he whispered, "I'm—"

"I'm drunk." Wide-eyed and solemn, she gazed at him over her shoulder.

"I know that, Maggie."

"Do?"

He nodded. "Yes, I can see that for myself. Was this your idea of revenge because I left you alone or some whim you indulged?"

She lowered her head, trying to make sense of what he had asked. The only word she grabbed hold of was *revenge*. McCready wasn't going to like knowing that's why she broke his whiskey bottles. But he was wrong about why she did.

He touched her shoulder. "'Cready? You're makin' the wee ones dance."

Holding one arm out to the side ready to catch her, he could only murmur that he was sorry, then asked, "Does it happen often?"

"When you're near."

McCready drew on the last store of his patience. "Then come off the table, and I won't be near you anymore. The wee ones will leave then, won't they?"

"I keep tryin' to make 'em go."

McCready knew it wasn't a plea for help, but he jumped

down and braced himself, then grabbed her wrist and pulled
her off the table. He staggered as Maggie fell against him, but
he managed to keep them both upright. Within his loose
embrace Maggie sighed and flung her arms around him.

His destroyed stash of whiskey was forgotten. Maggie's lips
were pressing against his. Definitely more potent, and infi-
nitely smoother, they pressed and parted, and he couldn't help
himself. He took her mouth, sweeping the whiskey-warm taste
of her up and inside himself, hungry enough to forget that she
didn't know what she was doing.

Maggie knew the wee ones had somehow gotten hold of
McCready's whiskey. There could be no other reason for the
seeping warmth that trickled from her breasts to her thighs.
With a cry she freed her mouth and sagged against him. She
closed her eyes but could still see McCready's face. Into the
whiskey-induced cloud came the certainty that no matter what
she tried, nothing was going to get rid of the flutters that
danced inside her the same way McCready's fingers played on
her back. *Not whiskey. Not kissing.*

The gold, Maggie, a voice whispered. *You've still got the
gold.*

McCready beat the feather mattress after he had cleared the
wooden tub out of the cabin and put Maggie to bed. The tick,
hanging on a rope strung from the corner of the cabin to the
empty corral's fence, took the punishment he longed to deliver
to her bottom.

"Two damn days!" he yelled, taking another swing with the
broom. "I had to tell Dutch to wait two days before he comes
back."

Sweat rolled down his face, and he used his forearm to wipe
it away, having long since discarded his shirt. With a glance at
the cloudless sky, he asked, "Did that woman have any idea of
the strain she'd put on me without my whiskey?" He remembered her smug smile as he had tucked her in. "She knew, all
right, she knew."

Muttering to himself, he gripped the broom handle tighter. Suddenly he realized that even when Dutch met him in two days, the man wouldn't know that McCready needed whiskey. His next swing split open the repair Maggie had labored over, and the feathers went flying. But he didn't curse, he didn't once swear. He dropped the broom and started for the open door.

Beating the feather tick no longer satisfied him.

The sight of Maggie, curled tight in the quilt on his bed, stopped him. Male instinct said she wanted him as badly as he wanted her. He couldn't take his revenge with violence. Maggie would be expecting that from him, and what's more, she would be ready to fight him.

His smile smacked of the devil's own. "Mary Margaret O'Roarke, you're not going to like how you will pay for my whiskey. But, I swear, pay for it you will."

And as the long hours of the night crawled by, and Maggie blissfully slept on, McCready kept adding to his list of her sins, compounding the debt that she owed him.

"You owe me, Cornwallis!" Ryder shouted, banging his fist on the gleaming wood desk that belonged to Thadius. "I damn near killed that horse to get here an' tell you what's been happening in Cooney Camp. You're the man with his hands in every bit of dirty laundry in the territory. An' you tell me that I ain't got money coming?"

Thadius lit his cigar, then shifted the papers in front of him to buy time. Lowly hirelings like Ryder were never supposed to know he was the man behind their doings. He gazed at the ash on his cigar and said, "Sit down. We'll discuss this, Ryder. I'm not unreasonable, but I'm curious as to how you knew about me. Care to explain that?"

Shrugging, Ryder sat. "Ain't no big deal. I searched Quincy's bags before I said I'd work for him."

"And what did you find?"

"The letter you sent telling him what to do."

"You can read?"

Ryder came up out of his chair. Threateningly he leaned over the desk. "Yeah. I can read, little fat man. So what?"

"Sit down. Please, sit down," Thadius implored, mopping the sweat from his brow. "I didn't mean to insult you. It is unusual to find a man of your . . . well, your talents able to read."

"My ma was a Bible-reading woman, an' she taught me."

Thadius nodded, but he was silently acknowledging that he had made a mistake and judged Ryder too fast. He would never again commit anything to paper linking him with Cooney Camp. But Ryder was going to be his means to an end, not Quincy's. He could not let Ryder know how upsetting his news was. Damn Quincy! The man's failure to follow simple orders to marry a backward girl, and have her make out a will before he killed her, was costing him time and money. But he would have to wait to deal with Quincy's incompetence when he showed up.

He didn't need this along with the additional pressure from William Berger. The man was obsessed with gaining possession of that gold mine to realize his political dreams. He glanced at the gun slung low on Ryder's hip as the man sat down again. Perhaps he could use Ryder to rid him of all three problems. Berger had lost his usefulness. Quincy had unwittingly revealed his involvement, and Maggie O'Roarke was an unnecessary obstacle.

He knew that Ryder was waiting for him to offer money. It went against Thadius's grain to pay for something twice, when the first time didn't see the job done.

Thadius flipped open the box on the corner of his desk. "Help yourself, Ryder. We have business to discuss."

"Ain't a smoking man. An' I'd rather hear about the money I got coming."

"In good time." Smiling, Thadius leaned forward. "There is a man I want you to see in Cooney Camp. Andrew Burton."

"The mercantile owner? What's he got to do with you?"

"Now, let's talk money, Ryder. Then I'll explain what you have to do to earn it."

William Berger had made his decision. Thadius was stalling. He didn't trust anyone but himself to gain possession of that gold mine near Cooney Camp. A three-day growth of beard along with the store-bought clothes marked him as one of a hundred drifters in the territory. His altered appearance ensured him that no one would recognize him.

After snapping closed the loaded cylinder on his gun, he sighted it beyond the fire. Tomorrow would see him in Cooney Camp with Cora Ann Avernel working for him. There were times when he missed being the man of action. It sweetened the reward he was after. He had to eliminate what stood in his way. First Quincy and his supposed-to-be bride. Then Thadius.

It had been a long time since he'd set up such a smooth double cross. He settled his head on his saddle, dreaming of gold and all it could buy.

CHAPTER
11

"Hang it, McCready! Your damn whistlin's got me wishin' I was grinnin' at the daisy roots."

He smiled, then continued his whistling.

The morning had crept by, just as Maggie herself had crept around the cabin, restless and filled with the dread of what he was going to do. She knew he thought it was the whiskey that made her mood surly, but Maggie knew better. It was the dreams of his mouth and the hot look of his eyes that had plagued her sleep and made her long for freedom.

And he watched her. The moment she went near the open window to study the dark clouds piling in the distance, he was on his feet behind her.

She couldn't take much more. Careful not to touch him, Maggie slipped away and returned to her place by the fire. Desperation for something to do had driven her to make biscuits, and she moved the short-legged cast-iron spider back from the coals so that they would not burn. In a kettle beans, venison, and wild onions simmered. She gave it a stir, staring at the stew.

"Needs more salt."

"You didn't even taste it, Maggie."

"Some things you just know by lookin'."

McCready was giving her the crock before she could move. Maggie took it, unable to avoid touching his hands. Her gaze locked with his, and her memory supplied a flash of seeing this same look in his eyes once before. The day she had confronted him in the Rawhider. McCready was not only eating her alive with his eyes, he attacked her senses and sent panic streaming through her again. Her breath caught in her throat. The crock slipped from her hands, spilling the salt before it shattered.

McCready didn't glance at the broken crockery. He couldn't drag his gaze away from the glittering awareness he glimpsed in Maggie's eyes. He felt himself being pulled by more than the desire he felt for her. Maggie was stirring emotions that he had thought long dead and unneeded.

"McCready?" she whispered.

"Yeah, Maggie. I know just what you mean. Some things you just know by looking."

Awareness melded with feminine curiosity in the ancient green of her eyes. The quick little catch of her breath, the parting of her lips, and the slight forward move she made, all invited a kiss. But for once McCready didn't act on it. He knew kisses weren't going to be enough to calm the fever that was building by seconds inside him.

Maggie didn't ask what he meant. She knew. Her hands curled into fists and her belly tightened. She didn't want to be kissed by McCready, did she? She shouldn't want him to kiss her again—want it so badly she could taste it.

She remembered that he told her she would like being married to him, that he would make her understand what being his wife meant. Maggie wasn't sure she was ready to find out.

McCready had reached the same conclusion. But there was still the matter of his whiskey to be settled between them. He slowly straightened and crooked his finger at her. "Come with me, Maggie. I want to explain how you'll pay for my whiskey."

"Whiskey? Pay?" Was that near mewling voice hers? Maggie shook her head. She wasn't afraid of him, was she? It was the sight of his crooked finger motioning her to come that shredded the last of the webs he skillfully entangled around her with his nearness. She joined him at the table.

"Let's imagine that there is a bottle on this table, Maggie. And you watch me pour out a glass. Please," he said sarcastically, "note, I must use both my hands, one to hold the bottle, the other to hold the glass. Now a man sometimes likes to sip and contemplate his whiskey. He uses both hands to do so. With me so far?"

Maggie glanced from the cupped hands up to McCready's watchful eyes. She didn't trust the glitter within their blue color, but she nodded that she understood his motions.

"Good, Maggie." He gave her a beaming smile of approval. "Now, as I was explaining, here I am holding my glass, and I lift it to my lips to drink. Then I set it down. A serious drinking man could stretch out a bottle for hours, but we need to remember that I don't have a bottle of whiskey anymore. Do I?"

What was he getting at? She shook her head, then added a weak, "No."

McCready leaned forward, his gaze once more targeting hers. "Did you give a thought as you broke my bottles of whiskey as to what I'd be doing with my hands and mouth if I couldn't drink?''

Maggie's hands clutched each other tight on her lap.

"Where's that quick stabbing tongue, Maggie mine?''

Stuck to the roof of me mouth, she wanted to answer but couldn't. The glitter in McCready's eyes seemed brighter. Maggie knew this boded her no good.

"You'll have to pay, O'Roarke. I'll need something to keep my hands and mouth busy. Fair enough?''

Maggie swallowed. "If I had me knife, I could teach you to whittle.''

"Not good enough. That would keep my hands busy, but not my mouth.''

"You could whistle, McCready. Much as it drives me crazy to hear it, you could do it.''

"Ah, it does my heart good to know that you're so willing to be accommodating about this, Maggie. I had hoped it would be so.''

The crafty look he wore alerted Maggie that she wasn't going to like his payment demand. She had seen that same look on a hundred miners' faces when someone asked about their claims.

"To make sure there is no misunderstanding between us, we are in agreement that you owe me for breaking my supply of whiskey." McCready was betting on Maggie's honesty to get her to say yes. She made him wait, but patience was on his side, since he wanted everything spelled out for her.

"I owe you, McCready. An' as soon as me mines are producin', I'll pay you.''

"Now, Maggie mine, I'm the one who is going to set the terms here, not you. Besides," he added, sitting back and crooking one arm over the back of the chair, "I can't wait that long.''

"Oh.''

He watched her squirm in her chair, but to her credit she didn't try to get up.

"So, you see my predicament. I—"

"Stop usin' them big words. An' I found a way. I'll cook and wash. Drive me crazy to do for the likes of you, but I'll pay what I owe."

"Not good enough, Maggie. That keeps you busy, not me."

"You cook and wash?" she suggested, holding on to the hope that he would agree. The crafty look was gone from his face, but in its place was the look McCready wore when he held the winning hand. Her whole body was tensing, and Maggie didn't know if it was from fear or excitement.

"No, Maggie, that doesn't work, either. My way will give us both something to do at the same time."

"It will?" Faith and begorra! What was the man thinking of?

McCready savored the moment and let her wait after he nodded. He couldn't decide if he should tell her or show her. Given Maggie's volatile temperament, no matter which he chose it could end with the same results. McCready shoved his chair back and rose, coming around the table before Maggie could move. At her side he hunkered down, bracing one hand on the back of her chair and the other on the table in front of her.

"Maggie, you agreed to pay me. And this is how. Each time I need a drink, you'll have to kiss me."

"Kiss you?" she parroted. With her eyes closed she didn't see his nod or his satisfied smile. All Maggie thought about was his knowing that she had wanted to kiss him. Devil's own that McCready was, he had figured out a way. She felt the quickening of her heart and the wee ones dancing with glee. Her body was against her mind.

She opened her eyes but kept them on the table, studying the hard strength of his hand. She had to keep his hands and mouth busy, that's what he said. There had to be more rules to this payment. She had to know where he'd be keeping his hands.

McCready lifted his hand from the back of her chair and lightly smoothed her hair. "Well? Are you going to do it or welsh?"

"I've never welshed in me life, McCready, an' if you'd not be knowin' that—"

"I know, Maggie. I counted on it."

The ring of truth was in his voice, and Maggie had to face him. "You figured this for a time, didn't you?"

"No. How could I? You broke the whiskey, Maggie. I'm just collecting on the debt you owe me." He found himself swallowing and hesitating a moment before he asked, "Do you find the thought of kissing me distasteful?"

"I wouldn't be sayin' that."

"Then you like kissing me?"

Maggie knew she was in hot water, hot and deep. She'd be a fool seven ways to Saturday to admit she liked his kisses.

Avoiding answering his question took some thought, but she found a way. "You like drinkin' for hours."

"I've been known to."

"Would you be . . ." Maggie rubbed her hands on her thighs. "Well, would you be lookin' to kiss me that long?"

Leaning his forehead against her shoulder, McCready hid his smile. The hand stroking her hair hadn't told him that Maggie was trembling. But this close he couldn't help but feel the effect he had on her.

"Maggie, let's make this easy. We'll try it and see."

"You're known to have a powerful cravin' for whiskey."

"But I'm beginning to understand that I have other cravings just as strong." He swept his hand from the table to her far shoulder, urging her around in the chair. Sliding his fingers from her hair down to the slender curve of her neck, he angled his head so that he could look up at her face.

"Maggie—"

"It's the damn mines, isn't it?" she blurted. "You'll do anythin' to have them. Take them, McCready. Take them and to hell you'll go. But you'll not—"

"For once, Maggie, you're wrong about me. I've wanted to kiss you since you walked into the Rawhider dressed to marry another man. I wasn't thinking about the mines; I was thinking about you. How you would feel beneath me. How your lips would taste. How many freckles you have. You can't know how many times I've seen myself counting them with kisses. And there is one more promise I made you that day that I haven't carried out."

Maggie shook her head and closed her eyes again. Her body was flushed from the inside out. She didn't need to ask about the promise; she recalled his words when she had ordered Satin to keep him pinned in place. He had sworn then that for every moment the dog held him down, he'd have her the same way. Maggie tried backing off the chair, but he held her still.

Now she faced not only being held captive in his cabin, but by McCready himself.

But was he lying to her? She didn't know. Could a man lie with his touches and kisses? There was only one way to find out.

She opened her eyes and stared directly into his. There was no gentle amusement, no glitter, nothing but serious regard.

"All right, McCready. You'll have your payment. But we set rules about it."

"No rules, Maggie," he stated with utter calm, convinced that he had won.

"None?"

"Not a one."

She licked her bottom lip, then sunk her teeth into it. "Well, what're you waitin' for?" Mccready stood up abruptly, and Maggie's gaze followed the rise of his body. She knew she wasn't small, but she felt that way as he towered over her. No man's body had ever held curiosity for her. But suddenly

McCready's did. The thought of his arms around her own body, pressing intimately against her, sent an arrow of sensation sliding from her breasts to the pit of her belly. She swallowed hard and looked away from his clear, penetrating eyes.

Silence stretched and then stretched some more, leaving Maggie feeling uncertain and breathless. She glanced up at McCready, only to find him watching her with unnerving intensity, as though he knew exactly what she was thinking.

For a moment McCready lost himself in the darkening green color of her eyes. Her lips were full, the soft curves a silent invitation to a man's hungry mouth, and he knew that hunger. His body hardened in a single wild rush, forcing him to bite back a curse and a groan. But there was no way to take back what he said. Not when Maggie seemed to be willing to pay it.

With one finger he tilted her face up and brushed his thumb over her bottom lip. Her breath caught, then rushed out over his skin.

"Stand up, Maggie." But even as he ordered her, he was lifting her from the chair, drawing her against him. Need sank little claws of demand for him to hurry. But he tried to slow himself down. Tried to remember that he liked his women petite and soft. Maggie wasn't petite, and as he stroked her back, pressing her breasts against his chest, he knew she wasn't soft. There was strength in the slender body he caressed, and the only softness she had was where she needed it. Her mouth. The lush curves of her breasts. And the softest heat now hidden from him.

Maggie braced her hands on his shoulders. She had always thought of McCready as soft. But the warmth of his body, the strength of his shoulders made her feel like she was touching the granite of a placer strike. She gazed up at his eyes, and the glitter was back, like gold running through quartz, just as sharp and bright. Maggie heard the tearing sound of his breath and knew she wasn't alone with the strange feelings McCready caused.

"Maggie," he breathed, bending down to her mouth, brushing it lightly when he felt her trembling. He wanted to know the heat and taste of her. With aching slowness he again whispered his mouth over hers, repeating the caress again and again until he lingered a bit longer and felt the hardness of her teeth behind the warmth of her giving mouth.

But he remembered Maggie's taking and giving with a hot wildness that was unlike any he had known.

She shut down on the battle waging inside her. His mouth wasn't lazy now. Hard and hot, his lips took from hers while his fingers pressed her back. She moaned when his tongue slid over hers. She uncurled her fingers to clutch at his shirt, then slid them up into his hair. The scrape of his teeth against her bottom lip had her gasping. There was a too new desperation spilling through her and she wanted to fight it. Her body betrayed her and strained against his while her mouth burned to match his need.

McCready lost himself. He knew how a woman clouded a man's senses, how she caused his body to throb and burn. But Maggie . . . her almost dazed surrender made him know a desire so knife-blade sharp that it sliced through him. There was no coyness, no need for him to seduce. Maggie was as direct and honest about what she wanted from him as if she had spoken.

His body had no trouble answering the pleading cry of hers to be closer. To fit thigh to thigh, belly to belly, breast to chest, and mouth to mouth. There were, he was fast finding out, a great deal of advantages to kissing a woman of Maggie's height. He didn't have to bend to reach the delicate lobe of her ear or trace the taut line of her neck. And when he claimed her mouth again, he fit himself in the cradle of her hips, cupping her bottom to hold her there and ease his aroused flesh.

He brought his mouth down on hers, harder and rougher than

he had meant to. His emotions broke free of his control as raw, explosive passion dictated to him.

The excitement built inside Maggie until she didn't think she could stand it. Kissing McCready was better than finding gold. It was watching the eagles soar and closing your eyes, wishing you were up there with them, carried on sweeping air currents, free. He made her forget everything. Everything but the hot churning within her body.

When his mouth released hers, she wanted to pull him back, but his lips raced down her throat. Instinct sent her head tilting back to give him what he wanted. The scents that melded and were McCready's alone drifted over her, then his mouth was at her ear, his teeth tugging and nipping before he whispered something she didn't understand. Words didn't matter. The sound of his rough voice made her tremble. She dragged his lips back to hers with a soft moan of desperation.

She explored his back while the hot caress of his skilled mouth had her wanting his hands on her body. There were so many things she didn't know, but her body was telling her that McCready could teach her.

She felt him pull her shirttail free, then slide his hand over the thin cotton chemise that offered no shield to the heat of his touch tracing the line of her spine. The frenzied mating of their mouths subtly changed to a slower, deeper rhythm, just as his caresses became unhurried. He drew his palms around to her sides, stroking up and down, the heels of his hands pressing against her breasts. Shivers of desire ran down her belly.

With his mouth still covering hers, McCready backed her up against the wall before she could stop him. Her arms were around him as if they belonged there. Strained against her, his body throbbed until it was one sweet ache. He could sense each change as it flowed through her. The unbridled passion in Maggie stole his breath, and he lifted his head, watching her lean limply back against the wall. Maggie's pulse was wild beneath his hand where he cupped her throat.

But he hadn't finished his seduction of Maggie's mouth, making it wholly his. She tasted of him, her breath tore as his did, and every sound of desire he called from her was an echo of his own.

Biting the tip of her tongue distracted her from feeling each shirt button that he opened. But the cool air touching her bared skin and the heat of McCready's mouth trailing along the edge of the thin cotton chemise had Maggie tense. His murmured "Trust me" broke into the passion that nearly consumed her.

The wall at her back left her nowhere to retreat, but he felt her instant withdrawal and slowly lifted his head to look at her.

"Why?" he asked, trying to make sense of her frozen state. Her eyes were still passion-dazed, her lips swollen from his kisses, and her body throbbing as fiercely as his.

Anger surged through him at her continued silence. He gripped her shoulders, pinning her tight to the wall. "Tell me why, Maggie?"

"You. You want me to trust you." He had made her need him. He had to know just by looking at her that he only had to touch her, kiss her, and she would be helpless to stop him. He made her want to give. And he wouldn't have to ask. It shamed her. That anyone, especially McCready, could have any power over her pride and her will shook her to her soul.

Infuriated that tears burned behind her eyes, Maggie shoved his chest and was thankful that he gave her breathing room. "Do you want me to say more? Do you want me to tell you that I want you?"

"Nothing would please me more, Maggie, than to hear you say it. But not like this. Not when you hate the thought of it."

"Let me go, McCready."

There was an underlying plea for him to let her go that went beyond this cabin and his presence. With regret he shook his head. "I can't, Maggie, even if I wanted to."

"It's the damn mines that you want."

"No. There's you. I want you. I told you that, and you

wouldn't believe me.'' He lifted his hand to her face, and she stiffened and shut her eyes.

"You won't win. I won't let you win.''

The way she looked at him made him feel as if he had shattered something smaller and definitely more fragile than himself.

"I can't even tell you that I'm sorry, Maggie.''

"Don't bother, boyo.'' She glared at him, dragging up anger to give her strength. "I'm the one sorry enough for both of us.''

Without another word he walked out of the cabin.

CHAPTER
12

Within minutes of meeting with McCready, Dutch decided that he was in a rare mood. He had seen McCready like this few times in the past, but when he did, Dutch had learned not to argue with him.

McCready had a dangerous glint in his eyes that warned of a man ready for a fight. No, Dutch amended, McCready was not just ready to fight, he was spoiling for one.

He could only guess that things were heating up with Maggie. He tried to warn McCready, but the man wouldn't listen then, and he doubted he would listen to anything he had to say about Maggie now. But he wished he could see McCready, wound tighter than a two-dollar watch, fly apart.

"Well," McCready asked, "what are you waiting around for?"

"Just making sure that you didn't forget anything you needed. Don't hardly seem worth the trip to bring you eggs and whiskey."

McCready knew that Dutch was angling for an explanation of what had happened to all the whiskey he had helped store at the cabin, but he wasn't about to give it to him.

"That's what I need. That's all you are to bring to me tomorrow."

"Don't think I can do it. Not tomorrow anyhow. Satin's pining something fierce for Maggie. The dog doesn't want to eat. Can't tempt her at all, especially not with steak. I even tried to take her outside—"

"Are you deliberately trying to let her get away from you?"

"No me, boss. I made a collar for her with rope and just figured that a walk might perk up her appetite. Didn't do a bit of good. She still refused to eat."

"If you're trying to make me feel guilty, Dutch, you're doing a hell of a good job."

"It ain't that. I don't need to put any guilt on you, boss. You've got enough of your own without me adding to it."

McCready closed his eyes briefly. Dutch was right. He did have enough guilt of his own. And he had to go back and face that guilt in the form of one Mary Margaret O'Roarke the way he couldn't do it last night. He had thought himself a man unafraid to face anything that came his way. But once he had walked out of the cabin last night, he couldn't make himself go back inside. The cold ground in front of the door had made a sorry bed, but then, he had been so restless it wouldn't have mattered where he tried to sleep.

A glance up at the sky showed the dark clouds that had begun piling to the north yesterday were moving slowly toward them. Rain would cool things off, he thought, raking his hand through his hair.

"So, it's all right with you if I wait—"

"No. Christ, no! I need the whiskey, Dutch. If you could go back to camp and get it now, I'd wait."

Lumbering to his feet, Dutch shook his head. McCready had it bad. His own words came back to him from the other day when he had asked McCready if Maggie was giving him a hard time. It appeared to him as if she wasn't anywhere near done, judging by the way McCready behaved.

He, too, saw the threatening clouds and felt the urge to get back to the Rawhider before the rain hit. "You know, boss, I'm getting a feeling that things might be stirring up in camp."

"I thought you said Quincy followed Ryder out of camp north to Santa Fe?"

"That he did, just like I figured he would, and he ain't come back."

"Then why the feeling?" McCready had a healthy respect for Dutch's feelings. He didn't get them often, but when he did, it was worth paying attention.

"This time I can't answer you. Just take it as gospel."

"What I'm taking is a hike back up to the cabin. You, I expect to see here tomorrow."

Dutch had a serious decision to make. He could bring McCready his whiskey, but that would prolong his staying up at the cabin with Maggie. He could also risk his friendship and his job and not come back at all.

"A right fetching dilemma," he murmured to himself, hurrying now to ride back to the Rawhider.

Maggie had let the fire die. The damp from the coming storm was already seeping into the cabin, but she didn't care. She told herself she wasn't worried about where McCready was, couldn't care less if he ever showed his face again. But the truth was, she did care. The man was a burr under her skin, and she knew how to pluck those out even if it pained her. Why, then, couldn't she get McCready out of her head?

The coffee in her cup had long since cooled, but Maggie drank it anyway. She had to find a way to escape. There was no other way to get rid of McCready. Once free, she could take off and be lost in the mountains long enough for him to forget about her and her mines. True, that move would cost her the chance of marrying Quincy and getting the money she needed to open the mines.

"Damn him!" she yelled, throwing the cup across the room. Inactivity ate at her. She couldn't sit here hour by hour and not do something. She stared at the closed door, then shifted her gaze to the shuttered windows. There had to be . . .

Before she finished her thought, she was up and moving around to the chair. Hefting it chest high, she carried it over to the window and rammed it against the wood. The shutter flew open.

Maggie's mouth hung open, and she dropped the chair, barely missing her foot. Leaning over the edge, she saw no broken wood. It had never been barred at all.

"An' here I sat, fool that I am, while McCready's been gone." Yet, she didn't climb out the window, cautious now that she knew she hadn't been entirely locked in. She knew she didn't trust McCready. It would be just like him to be lying in wait for her. If she knew one thing, she knew that McCready would do anything to get his hands on her again.

But as she studied the rocky land around the cabin as far as she could see, Maggie began to understand that McCready might not be there at all.

She couldn't wait any longer. Since he hadn't come back into the cabin last night, she had no way of knowing how long he had been gone. He could be returning while she hesitated.

Freedom was so close that she could taste it, but Maggie spun from the window and grabbed a blanket. She still had no weapon, for McCready kept the knife locked in his chest. A fork would have to do. This time she wasn't recklessly going to run without food. She couldn't take the dinner no one ate, but the hard biscuits would keep her from starving until she found her way back to her cabin.

After shoving the biscuits into her shirt, she fumbled with the buttons, urged now by an inner warning that she had to hurry. Tossing the blanket out the window, Maggie hoisted herself over the ledge and out.

The last time she'd run, she had no time to plan, and McCready had found her. Luck didn't seem to be riding with her this time, either. She headed around the back of the cabin, trying to forget the storm that was piling up grief faster than a miner's unshored diggings. There were few things that Maggie was afraid of. Gully-washers with their thunder and lightning topped her small list.

To the far north, jagged peaks were being smothered by the darkening clouds. She glanced to the south, to the mesas rising like cones with their tops cut off, and thought of the Indians that still roamed the land. But the Indians posed less threat to her than McCready did.

Maggie looked back and saw she hadn't come far enough from the cabin. But before her was a narrow path between boulders. Hitching the blanket over her shoulder, instinct warned this was not the way to go, but she was still in view of McCready's cabin, and that meant if he came back, he could see her.

Not twenty feet farther Maggie knew why she should have listened to her own inner warning. She was on the edge of a crevice that was almost fifteen feet wide. She didn't even think about jumping. She backed away, just as the first rumbles of thunder pealed in the sky.

Squeezing her eyes shut, Maggie told herself she was not going to be afraid. She would find another way. But the only other way was back past the cabin.

And she didn't care if she had to crawl her way to get by it.

Lightning split the sky. Maggie felt her belly hollow out. She wasn't going to be given the time she needed before the storm came. Without boots she would be a fool to try to run, but desperation breeds fools, she decided, making a run for the back of the cabin.

Flattened against the wall, she listened, but the repeated rolls of thunder foiled her. She couldn't hear if McCready was inside. A careful peek around the corner revealed nothing but the empty corral.

Well, if she was a fool for running, she'd be a bigger one to stand where she was.

Maggie rushed forward only to stop short, swinging her arms in circles to keep her balance. McCready's back filled her vision.

And even with the crashing roar of thunder she heard him calling out to her.

Maggie turned tail and ran back to the boulders, frantic to find a place to hide. There wasn't a crevice to hide a prairie dog, much less someone her size.

Forked lightning seemed to point its bony fingers at her, and this time the thunder rumbled like laughter. Even the storm seemed determined to give her away to McCready.

Wind swept fat raindrops against her. For a few minutes Maggie kept her fear at bay and searched for concealment. A few straggly yucca bushes didn't offer any hope.

"Maggie! Answer me!"

She dropped flat and covered her head with the blanket, praying the small outcrop of rocks would at least hide her legs. *Don't let him come this far.* The wind edged its way beneath her blanket, and she knew that the very elements were against her. The rain pelted down, and the ground shook as the thunder claimed the land. Maggie shook right along with it. Fear wormed its way from inside to chill her flesh.

She wasn't sure if the wind carried McCready's voice or if he was going away from the cabin, down the path she had tried to use the last time. It was her call to make. She could go back to the cabin or face her own fears and ride out the storm in the open. A choice from hell, but one she couldn't wait any longer to make. Rivulets of water were crawling beneath her. The force of the rain and wind already soaked her clothes.

Maggie scrambled to her feet and ran for the cabin. Only there was no cabin to see. In the few minutes she had hidden beneath the blanket, the dark roil of clouds unleashing their fury had blotted out every bit of light. The solid torrent of rain left her floundering for direction. As desperate as she was to reach safety, Maggie closed her eyes with every strike of lightning.

The terrifying panic was closing her throat so she could not make a sound beyond a single whimper. Her legs gave way, and she huddled under the soaked blanket, hugging her knees tight while silent screams clawed their way from inside her.

McCready was forgotten. There was nothing but Maggie and fear. And the storm that seemed to intensify its rage.

The sound of naked violence hurled her back in time. Maggie was twelve, spouting up as tall as her father, scared to tell him about the bleeding that wouldn't stop. She didn't understand why she bled without there being pain. She knew she hadn't hurt herself. But when a second shirt of hers had to be torn up, her father discovered her secret and told her what was wrong. It was her fault they were caught down in the gully washing out the rags she had made. The storm had caught them there, and she followed her father up the rock wall that offered little in the way of handholds.

She remembered the scraggly little bush jutting from a tiny crevice that she had reached for. She had bitten her lip and tasted her blood in fear as the roar of water rushed below them. Her father had motioned her over and away from the bush, grabbing hold of it himself. Maggie was braced between two small ledges barely wide enough to hold her toes and hands. The rock face was cold as she pressed her cheek against it, her eyes wide and staring at her father. He had smiled, she recalled, the last smile before the bush tore free and he disappeared down into the churning waters below them.

"Papa!" The scream from the past clawed its way free with her scream now.

McCready shook his head. It wasn't more than the scream of the wind he heard. Soaked and still standing in the rain, he knew he was being a fool to hope that Maggie would come back.

He still didn't understand how she got by him. And that is the only way she could have left. One of the reasons he had built the cabin here was the crevice that extended for over a thousand feet in the back of the cabin. No one could climb it, up or down. Not even Maggie. But there was no getting away from the fact that she had managed to leave.

Raking the rain from his hair, he turned to the door, yet something stopped him from going inside. He knew he did not have Maggie's skill or knowledge about the land, but he knew the surrounding area well. There was no place for her to hide while the storm continued.

He remembered that the fire was dead when he returned. Wherever Maggie was, she was long gone.

He was the devil's own, but a fool just the same, for he found himself rounding the cabin, swearing at the gray torrent that hindered his sight.

McCready slid and went down on one knee, cutting it on a rock, before he could stand. The instant sting of the cut was washed by the rain. He couldn't fight the need he had to make sure that Maggie wasn't here. Even if she didn't need him for anything, he had to satisfy himself that she was safe.

By touching the slippery, cold stone he felt his way, rain stinging his skin as it renewed its force. He tried to call her name, but the wind whipped the sound from his mouth and blended it with its own wild wailing.

He argued with himself to turn back, for it was impossible to see even with the near constant flashes of lightning. But he went on a few feet more, still trying to call her, driven by icy tendrils of fear. He tried not to think of how cold it was, how quickly the wind stripped the heat from his big body. "Maggie!" he yelled. *"Maggie!"*

The ground was treacherous between the slippery rocks and churned mud. There was no sense to the certainty that Maggie was somewhere nearby. He knew it but kept looking.

At first when his boot kicked at something soft, McCready didn't understand what he'd found. It wasn't until he dropped to his knees, wincing as another rock hit his cut, that he tore the covering aside and found her.

CHAPTER
13

Outside, the storm had nearly spent its fury. In the silence and firelight McCready broodingly watched Maggie. She was finally warm and dry, despite the occasional shiver that racked her body. Wearing his clothes and covered by the quilt, she sat propped up against the wall, sipping from the steaming cup of coffee she held.

McCready would have killed for whiskey. Not for his cut knee that was more bruise than anything else, but for Maggie. She's fine, he told himself, sipping from his own cup. Any fool could see it. Even him.

So why do I feel she's still lost somewhere?

Easy. Even for a fool like you. She hasn't said a word from the moment you found her.

And her eyes. He couldn't avoid looking at them. The fire lent them a luminous quality, but they stared blankly at what only Maggie could see.

Her cheeks had taken on a flush that he hoped came from the warmth in the cabin. He turned his gaze to the fire, trying not to recall the sight of his hands stripping Maggie's sodden clothes and drying her skin, or the way her breath had turned ragged and her nipples tightened when he had bundled her into his shirt.

His own breath shortened when he found that Maggie was looking at him. Something in her eyes made the blood simmer wildly through his body. Even as he warned himself, he felt the rush of his body changing to meet the honest femininity of Maggie herself. He was filled with a need that was as basic and necessary as breathing itself.

And he wasn't going to do anything about it. Sometime in those frantic minutes of his search, he had made up his mind to take Maggie back. He'd find another way to protect her if Quincy returned or there was another attempt on her life. He could only guess that his conscience had finally caught up with him, just as Dutch had been warning him would happen one of these days.

"McCready," Maggie said, clearing her throat of its husky intensity. "I owe you."

"You don't owe me a damn thing. If it wasn't for me you wouldn't have been trying to run, would you? And the storm would have played out just like it's doing now."

Nervously Maggie plucked at the quilt. She knew what had to be said to McCready, she just needed to gather up the courage to do it.

"Want more coffee?" he asked, turning to fill his own cup.

"Bet you'd like whiskey in its place."

"I won't deny it. But this will do." Holding up the pot, he glanced over his shoulder to where she sat. "Yes?"

She nodded and held out her cup. But after he had poured, Maggie reached out and touched his arm. "I need to talk to you."

His gaze remained on her hand. He told himself that she couldn't burn cloth and skin, but he felt scalded by her lightest touch. Carefully he set the pot aside.

"Maggie?"

"Yeah?"

"It'll be better if I sit over by the fire."

There was a feverish light in his eyes when he looked up at her, and Maggie didn't lie to herself that it was from anything but the same ache in her. She had been so grateful when he found her that she couldn't speak. He couldn't know what it meant not to be left alone with her terror. But even with her mind still filled with reliving the nightmare of her father's death, she had been aware of McCready. The heat and strength of his hands. The ragged sound of his breathing. The pulse beating wildly in his throat that she had longed to touch but didn't. She had shied away from watching him strip off his own wet clothes, too shaken by her own discovery that she had needed McCready and he had come. A new tension had filled her, even as she questioned why he didn't yell at her for running and getting caught out in the storm or for the soaking he took along with her.

Truth was, he hadn't said much of anything for the last hour or so. He started to jerk his arm away, and she tightened her hold. Setting aside her cup, Maggie turned to him, but as she opened her mouth to speak, he placed one finger against her lips.

"Maggie, you're playing with fire," he said flatly, taking her hand off his arm.

She didn't pretend not to understand. "Maybe I like to. Or

maybe I'm just cold. It could be," she added with a rueful smile, "that I haven't the sense of a mule, McCready."

She reached out and cupped his cheek, and this time he didn't push her away. "I haven't mentioned this lately, but Maggie, you're right. Dig-your-heels-in mule stubborn."

"Nice of you to notice."

His narrowed blue eyes swept over her slender body. "Oh, I'm a right noticing kind of man, Maggie. Right now I'm noticing things that would make you run and blush."

There was a warning for her, but she wasn't about to heed it. She watched his eyes darken, and her gaze drifted down to his chest. Half the buttons were undone on his shirt, revealing a light mat of hair. It looked soft and Maggie wondered how it would feel to touch. Her mouth went dry and she licked her bottom lip with the tip of her tongue.

"What things, McCready?"

"That I've come to crave the sight of your smile as much as your kisses. Kisses only lead me to wonder how it would feel to have your mouth on my skin." He reached out and with the tips of his fingers stroked her cheek. "It's the same way I want to taste yours while I'm counting all those darlin' freckles.

"And that sassy pink tongue. There's a reason for a man to gamble all his winnings, Maggie. I'd like to feel that all over every damn aching bit of me." His thumb brushed the quick pulse in her throat. "Enough?" He watched her lick her lip again and slid one hand behind her head, angling it back so she had to face him. With his gaze locked on hers, the words feathered over her mouth.

"I can't help but notice how tight your nipples are. From the cold, Maggie? Would they get like that for a man's hand, for his mouth?"

Maggie's lips parted, but she couldn't make a sound. Her breath caught, then rushed out. No one had ever said such things to her. She didn't even know that men thought about women this way. *Not men,* a little voice corrected. *McCready.*

''I told you that I wanted you that day in the Rawhider when I saw you dressed as a woman for the first time. The mud and men's clothes you used to hide behind were all gone. And I felt poleaxed,'' he gently informed her in a voice rich with passion. The slight tremor sliding through her brought his slow smile, but even as his body curved over hers, he wouldn't touch where he burned to, wouldn't take her mouth.

''Did you know that I was furious with you?''

''Why?'' The word creaked out like the turn of a rusty key, but Maggie couldn't help it.

''I felt . . .'' The curve of her brow invited his lips, and he placed a light kiss there, dragging his mouth to briefly touch her temple. ''Cheated, Maggie, that's what I felt. I never noticed till that day that you had a small waist or gently flaring hips that could easily cushion a man's ride with ease or breasts so lush that they would fill my hands.''

Once more he stroked her cheek, barely touching her. ''And you've got skin to rival the color of sweet cream. Did you know,'' he whispered, tilting her face up so that he was brushing her mouth with every word, ''that those long, long legs of yours have kept me awake nights wondering how they would feel locked around me? You cost me sleep, Maggie, and I didn't have a drop of whiskey to cool the fire.''

McCready leaned back and cradled her face within his hands. ''There you have it, Maggie. As honest as I get. I want you like hell's on fire, but I won't take.''

Maggie's eyes closed as she savored his passion-laden voice but hid from the bright knowing glitter of his gaze. For once she didn't think that McCready was lying.

Those few moments of hesitation cost her his warmth. He was up and away before she could stop him. Maggie stared at his back. He stood to the side of the fire, one hand on the mantel, the other clenched at his side. It distracted her to feel the tiny stretching of the wee ones inside her, for they had been slow to awake tonight to McCready's heady nearness. But now that they were awake, there would be no peace.

"McCready," she called out softly. "I'm sorry that you hurt your knee, but I'm glad that you found me."

"Don't," he stated flatly, turning to face her, "be so sure of that, Maggie. And don't worry about my knee. It'll be fine."

"Tonight, in the storm . . ." Maggie raised her knees so she could wrap her arms around them. It seemed important to tell him how the storm made her feel, but before she spoke, he did.

"I wondered why you hadn't gotten far."

"Did you? It wasn't for lack of tryin', boyo. I'm . . . storms . . ." Maggie swallowed, unable to understand why the words seemed to stick in her throat.

"There's no shame in being afraid of something, Maggie," he said, pierced by the vulnerable look of her innocent eyes. Did she understand half of what he'd told her? He turned back to the fire. It didn't matter if she did. He was taking her back.

No shame. Maggie repeated those words to herself, thinking McCready might be right. No one would hear what she said but him, and if he dared to tell anyone, she'd deny it.

"My father died in a storm like this one. Washed away in a gully. I never found his body." Tears choked her throat. "I've been scared of storms since then."

He wanted her body, and she was handing him her secret fear. *Damn you, Maggie! Don't trust me.*

Maggie watched him. The firelight lent streaks of gold to the dark brown of his long hair and caressed his skin the way she longed to. Clutching the quilt tighter around her, she took what warmth she could from it, wishing it was McCready's arms wrapped as tightly.

He felt her gaze on him and resisted the urge to turn around. But he couldn't continue to ignore her confidence and said, in a too husky voice that he couldn't help, "If you're worried, Maggie, I won't tell anyone."

She brooded over the way he stood, not making another move toward her. How could he say those things to her and leave her alone with them? From memory she dragged forth the sight of Cora Ann's smile along with the Rose's teasing sigh that hinted of all the delights they shared with McCready. She'd had a taste of them herself and wanted more. There was a time to take bait and a time to leave it in the trap. She had to decide what she wanted. "McCready?"

"What?"

The word was as tart as green apples, and Maggie shifted to come to her knees. She kneaded her thighs, finding the courage to ask what she had to.

"You've not said a word about us bein' married."

"No, I haven't."

"You told me that you'd be teachin' me what bein' your wife meant. What's more, you said I'd be likin' it."

"Did I? I don't remember, Maggie."

Frowning, she hesitated, uncertain what to say to that. "But you threatened me."

"Then I apologize."

"Oh." She wasn't the one who was mule stubborn. He was. How did a woman go about getting a man to come to her? The question startled her. When had she decided that? Maggie shook her head, as much in confusion as she did to rid herself of plaguing questions.

"You said you'd been wantin' to kiss me, McCready. I'd figure you can't be wantin' it all that bad."

Tension coiled his body, but still McCready didn't turn around. "Maggie, how many men have you been with?"

She asked about kisses, and he asked a dumb question that he already knew the answer to? Maggie sank back on her heels. What was wrong with him?

"Can't count them all?" he asked with anger sharpening his tone.

"There was my father and Uncle Pete. But you know—"

"Not those men. That's not the kind of *being with* I mean."
He raked his hair, fighting the answer that was rushing at him,
hoping he was wrong. There was no delicate way to ask, and
with a shrug, he tossed a look at her. "What I want to know
is—"

"I'm not that dumb, McCready. You're talkin' about the
way babies get made."

Indignation flooded her eyes, and McCready bit back what
he'd been about to say. "Yeah, Maggie, that's what I meant."

Once again she saw the fire highlighting the planes of his
face, the curve of his mouth, and the sheer power of his lithe
body. Maggie watched him with a fascination that she didn't
try to hide.

"You keep looking at me like that, Mary Margaret, and I'm
going to feed all that hunger in your eyes." His gaze moved
over her face, lingering with frank male intensity on her parted
lips. Even though his shirt was a bit big on her, it didn't conceal
the harsh rise and fall of her breasts.

"You didn't answer me, Maggie. How many men?"

"Not a one," she answered honestly, feeling the coil of
unknown tension as if a band squeezed her belly. She couldn't
keep kneeling there, watching him. Not when need urged her to
satisfy it and touch him.

Maggie came to her feet slowly, dropping the quilt, for once
wishing she knew a woman's ways. She felt clumsy dressed in
his shirt and pants and with her feet bare. But she didn't let that
stop her. She was walking toward something both exciting and
dangerous.

"Think about what you're doing, Maggie. I said I wanted
you like hell's on fire. That's hungry, little one."

"I'm not so little, McCready. I'm big and sometimes so
clumsy—"

He reached out and pulled her up against him. "No. You're
not, Maggie. I just want you to understand that if I start kissing
you, it doesn't stop there. I'll want everything you have to give

a man, and I'm going to want it until I'm too damn tired to breathe.'' Maggie had resurrected his conscience, and now he couldn't close the door on it.

"Don't you understand? I get hard just watching you." To prove his point, he took hold of her hand and dragged it against his violently aroused flesh. *"Now, do you understand?"*

She understood that she had never wanted a man before.

"Truth, McCready?"

"A man can't hide what he's feeling the way a woman can."

She couldn't help but look at his mouth with a hunger she had never felt. The dark beard stubble only made the smooth line of his lips more inviting. Maggie lifted her gaze to his eyes. They burned. And she knew he meant his warning. McCready wasn't going to stop with kisses. He'd take all she had to give. *Deep waters, Maggie. Aye,* she answered herself. *But these aren't the same cold ones I've stood in to pan for gold. They're so hot I can feel the heat in my bones.*

She sensed the hard beating of his heart. Felt the wild pulse of the flesh pressed against her hand. Maggie lifted her head a bit more, just enough to taste his breath on her lips and take his scent into herself.

"You know what I understand, McCready? I understand what it means to be caught between a rock and a hard place. If I walk away, I'll fight the little devils clawing at me belly for something only you can give them. If I stay, I have nothing to protect meself—"

"There won't be any babies, Maggie. There are ways to prevent—"

She brushed her mouth against his. "Then show me. Show me all the ways there—"

His mouth settled over hers with the same hard hunger that racked his body, sinking deeply into the giving warmth of her mouth, teasing her with deep, thrusting motions of his tongue.

Maggie stroked his body as if she would never get enough of

touching him. McCready paid her back with the same rough caresses that were just as greedy, setting off a wildness that excited himself along with Maggie. Her hands slid down his hips and played over his thighs with the same bawdy, unhurried tantalizing way she explored the secrets of his mouth.

Her body rose to meet his, and Maggie heard his soft frenzied groan as she rubbed against him. She nipped his lip, craving the heat of his mouth, driven by forces she had unleashed.

McCready heard his gruff sound of need. He brought one hand to the back of her head and held her tightly while he ground his mouth on hers. He knew he should slow down, wanted to, but she opened so hungrily to him that his savage response shook him. He grasped her bottom, grinding his hips against her. The need to sheath himself inside her scorched him from the inside out.

"Maggie, Maggie," he whispered, dragging his mouth across hers, unable to stop.

She sensed there was more he wanted to say, but she couldn't wait to find out. All she wanted was to hold him and feel his arms around her. She needed to fill herself with the taste of him, to feel the hardness of his body against hers. She smoothed his hair before her hands settled on his shoulders. Kneading him, she made soft, approving sounds, glorying in touching the hard muscles of his arms.

McCready took. Everything. All he had wanted and found that Maggie still had more to give with her mouth. Pleasure expanded as he urgently savored her, tasting and caressing and luring her deeper and deeper into the passion ripping him apart. When he was breathing as harshly as she, he lifted his head and, holding her hips, rubbed her against the hard length of his arousal. He was shuddering, with no thought to try and hide from her. Holding her tightly, he fought for control.

"My God," he whispered, releasing an explosive hiss.

Afraid he would let her go, Maggie nuzzled his neck. She

closed her eyes to feel him stroking her hair, trembling even as his big body shuddered again.

She nipped his skin lightly, instantly soothing it with her tongue.

McCready's fingertips scored down her back, sending a delicious shiver deep, deep inside her. He threaded his fingers through her short curls, tugging gently backward until she had to look up at him.

"Sweet, Maggie." His mouth dipped for a tiny taste of her lips. "Soft and giving. You deserve better than a hard floor—"

"But you," she whispered in return, "said you liked a hard bed and a soft woman beneath you."

His slowly formed wicked smile stole her breath. She offered her mouth to his once more, disappointed that he took no more than a light kiss. She watched him, filled with uncertainty. This was all too new. She didn't know how to tease and play, but she wanted to learn. Wanted it as badly as she wanted him to kiss her again so that she couldn't think, couldn't talk.

Maggie suddenly found herself pulling free of him. "You promised me that we'd play," she said, backing away from him. "You said you'd chase me—"

"I will." Without warning he took a step toward her.

"Oh. Your knee."

"Never mind my knee. It won't stop me, Maggie. Nothing will."

Maggie opened two buttons on her shirt.

McCready stopped. He read the desire in her eyes but remembered her innocence. "All right, Maggie mine," he said in a lazy drawl. "We'll play." He saw the start of a provocative smile on her lips. "But I name the stakes. And, Maggie, this is a game where the winner takes all."

CHAPTER
14

Maggie's fingers hesitated over the next button. McCready wasn't going to play fair. He was already shrugging out of his shirt, tossing it aside, his eyes never leaving her.

"Chicken already?"

Her chin came up at the taunt. "Are those the rules? Me shirt goes next?"

He caught the trembling of her hands and saw the heat flushing her cheeks. "Not quite. I have to catch you first, Maggie mine. Then the shirt comes off."

"There's a lot more of you than I'd thought, McCready." But the nervous betraying tremor in her voice didn't stop her from looking her fill. From his navel to his collarbone a masculine pelt formed a ragged wedge. His beltless pants dipped teasingly lower when he put his hands on his hips. The edge of Maggie's teeth scored her lip.

"Tell me, Maggie mine, are the wee ones about?"

She gulped and nodded.

McCready offered a satisfied smile. He shifted his weight, standing with legs spread, and cut Maggie off from any place to go but the bed. For every step forward that he took, she managed two steps backward.

The backs of Maggie's knees hit the edge of the bed.

"Bad move, Maggie mine."

She wasn't fooled by the softness of his voice. His eyes watched her like the craftiest of hunters. But Maggie had been jumped before and knew a few tricks of her own.

With a playful growl McCready lunged for her. Maggie leapt for the bed and would have made it but for McCready's pants sliding down her hips. Trying to keep hold of them cost her her freedom.

"A forfeit, Maggie," he whispered, holding her tight.

"Take it," she demanded but was already offering him her lips.

McCready bent and took the hard velvet tip of one breast in his mouth. The shirt did nothing to protect Maggie from the fire that streamed through her body. A broken sound of pleasure escaped her, only to be repeated when she felt his hands on her waist, kneading her flesh while his mouth suckled her breast.

Even as she shivered to feel the hot rasp of his tongue through the shirt, McCready moved his hands and gently tugged on the pants that seemed to beg to accommodate his desire to see them gone. The drag of the cloth along with the heat of his hands over her hips and thighs made her knees weaken. Maggie clung to his upper arms to keep her balance. Every time she touched McCready and felt the warmth and hardness of his muscles, it surprised her, but this time there was no cloth to stop her from caressing him.

McCready tore his mouth from her and began kissing and love-biting a path to her ear. He licked the fine sheen that sprang from the heat of her, tempted to take the softness that nothing concealed, but Maggie was shaking and clinging to him. His tongue traced the sworls of her ear, and with a light kiss he pulled back.

"Game point's mine."

"But not the game, McCready." Maggie kicked the pants free and slipped from his loose embrace. She danced away to the center of the room, smiling and giving a saucy toss of her head.

She was a breathtaking sight with the firelight adding its gold to her copper curls. The shirt that ended mid-thigh revealed the long length of her legs, and McCready felt a clenching in his gut that warned him his body wasn't going to take much more playing.

Maggie tried to gather her wits. McCready looked dangerous with his eyes narrowed and the shadows playing over his bare chest.

She placed the table between them, taunting him with her smile. McCready readily took up the game, and for a few minutes darted back and forth while Maggie managed to use the table for protection. His speed forced her to rethink her plan as his fingers closed within inches of her shirt.

Maggie made a move to the right, praying her timing was good. McCready came around to chase her, and Maggie heaved herself up on the table, barely grabbing hold of his arm.

"Now it's me turn to be claimin' a point."

McCready looked from her hand on his arm up to her eyes. He could easily shake off her grip, but the flaring excitement bringing to life the ancient green shade of her eyes brought his own smile and nod.

"Your point, Maggie. What'll you have?"

"Your pants, McCready."

"Fair enough. Do you take them off or do I?"

"I . . . no . . . you . . ."

"Can't make up your mind? Maybe this will help. I'm not wearing a damn thing under them, Maggie."

She gulped and closed her eyes. It was what she wanted, wasn't it? He'd taken off hers. But when she looked at him and found that glitter of amusement back in his gaze, the answer she thought to give him got swallowed. Maggie let go of his arm, motioning him away so she could get down from the table.

You're no coward. Tell him to shuck down.

I'm not ready for this.

But her body told her she was.

Maggie rubbed the sides of her thighs, then planted her hands on her hips. "Well, McCready, go on."

His hands hit the buttons so fast she could barely follow his moves. She blinked and found him kicking them aside.

Swallowing was no longer a choice. Her mouth went cotton dry. "Sweet heaven, McCready, you're a splendid sight."

"And who, Maggie mine," he asked, with a quickening anger, "would you be measuring me by?"

Maggie bit her lip, hesitating. Then, with a decided twinkle in her eyes, she threw back her head laughing.

"Maggie," he warned, advancing on her.

She stopped instantly. "I wasn't laughing at you. I didn't lie to you. I've been with no man. But, McCready, I've seen me share of jackasses and horses an'—"

"Are you comparing me with a—"

"Don't take on, boyo. It's a favorable thing I've said. You're fitted for a hell of a ride, McCready, an' that's the truth."

"Am I now?"

"For sure."

"Then you won't take offense, Maggie mine, when I tell you

that I've been thinking the same about you." McCready didn't laugh at her stunned expression. He couldn't. She tossed her head proudly, and his conscience reared once more, telling him he should be ashamed of taking advantage of her innocence. But Maggie's gaze reflected the heat of his own.

"You did me a favor by ridding me of those pants, Maggie. And doing a favor for an unscrupulous man like me is quite as dangerous as doing injury to a good man. There's only one more piece to go."

Maggie looked down at her half-unbuttoned shirt and turned tail.

McCready caught her easily. Maybe too easily. He spun her around and took her mouth in the next breath. Maggie came to him with all her woman's heat, all her softness, all that generous giving. The game was over, and they both knew it.

She gave. And gave. Before he could ask. Before he knew he needed. There was a gentle drumroll of rain on the roof, but he could barely hear for the beat of his heart.

Maggie followed his teasing, maddening mouth. She made a ragged sound that was frustration and need in one. Her tongue sought out and found his for a wild, hungry kiss, and his arms closed tighter around her, arching her into his body. Again he moved, bending her supple body more deeply to his, satisfying her instinctive need to match a woman's heat with his hard need.

Maggie felt her world spinning, and she with it in the consuming hot darkness that was McCready's taste spreading through her. And then he was spinning with her, slowly turning, holding her tight, and Maggie felt herself being lowered to the floor. McCready didn't break the kiss, and she felt his weight, the ripple of his muscles, the blunt ridge of his arousal, the hardness of his thighs. She trembled even as she pressed against his big body.

"You're trembling, Maggie."

"You are, too."

He stroked her hair back from her face. "I know. I almost didn't have the strength to take us both down." His voice was filled with both desire and laughter. "Maggie, let me get the quilt."

Her hands tightened on his shoulders. She slowly shook her head, almost afraid of what she wanted to say.

But he read the question in her eyes. "Tell me. Whatever it is. I ache, Maggie. Ache for you. If I can say that, can't you tell me what's wrong?"

She closed her eyes and whispered, "I want to be the soft woman beneath you, McCready."

"Maggie. Maggie, look at me." He cupped her chin, waiting until she opened her eyes and stared into his. "Maggie, if you get any softer, I'm going to sink into you so deep, so hard and fast, that it'll be heaven and hell rolling together. But I'll hurt you, and that I won't do. That's why I'm getting the quilt."

With dreamy eyes she watched the supple play of light and shadows on his body as he moved and came back beside her. For a minute, staring up at his towering dark form, Maggie grew afraid. She felt exposed lying there. But McCready's eyes were so intent with desire that she couldn't move.

He spread the folded quilt and gently urged her onto it, quickly settling himself beside her, coaxing her to come into his arms. His knuckles grazed her breasts as he undid the buttons on her shirt.

Maggie watched him, her belly tightening when he reached the last one, and his hands splayed wide over her too sensitive skin. He moved aside the cloth and slowly angled his hand down to draw the nipple into his mouth. Her broken cry of pleasure made him shudder.

Flicking his tongue over the swollen tip, McCready forced himself not to think of the deep pulsing need of his own body and concentrated on pleasuring Maggie.

She was sweet heat. More potent than the best of whiskeys. The taste of her lured him like a high-stakes poker game where he risked the pleasure and pain of his own savage arousal for more of her rippling broken cries. Her breaths whispered warm and promising over his shoulder, and the rain-washed scent of her filled him until there was room for no other.

Pleasure burst over Maggie, filling her with a recklessness that had her hands streaking over him. She wanted the same power over McCready that he had over her. She wanted to know she could make him tremble as she did, make him as mindless, make him burn.

Her breasts were hot and swollen, their tips hard and aching for more of his caresses. She arched against his hand stroking down her body, burning and shivering, needing something more and unable to tell him. Her lips pressed frantic kisses on his shoulder, then her teeth closed over him in response to the feelings raging inside her.

McCready lifted his head, and his hands stilled on the flare of her hips, while he fought to control the violent shudder ripping through him.

His purely male smile shocked her almost as much as her biting him. Restless need had her twisting against him, and she couldn't speak.

"Tell me, Maggie." Her head rolled from side to side, but her eyes told him what he wanted to know. "It's all right. You can bite me all you want. You don't know what's coming, but I do, and it's making you angry as hell, Maggie, that you're trembling out of control and tied in knots at the same time. You blame me, but you don't want to stop. You don't, do you, Maggie?"

She turned to his chest in answer, raking him lightly with her teeth, licking the salt of his passion, and heard his unbridled groan.

McCready bent his head to her shoulder and repeated her love-bite. "Take what you need, Maggie. I will."

Her fingers worked through the ragged wedge of his chest hair and found the pebbled tip hidden beneath. Without thought, she returned the sweet torment he had given to her, listening to his dark whispers, feeling the wild ache grow deeper, then deeper still. Maggie fell back against the quilt.

The restless moves of her legs drew his hand, and his mouth tugged rhythmically on her breast, soothing and teasing her. His teeth lightly raked her nipple, but he knew Maggie was too aroused to feel it. With hunger he watched her rosy nipples pout and beg for his mouth, but her pleading cry broke over him.

He fitted his palm over her pale, soft triangle of curls and eased his long fingers between her legs. "Maggie, hold me," he whispered against her mouth.

Maggie felt the gentle move of his hand, the easy rocking that sent fire streaming through her. She turned to him, her fingertips finding his hot flesh and lovingly tracing it. Her breath broke as pleasure showered through her.

Beneath the firelight, McCready saw the desire that misted her skin. She melted against his hand, softly, repeatedly, and he took her mouth with the same gentle gliding penetration as he took her body. Her throaty cry of passion was his to drink, and his caresses deepened as he called forth the small hard nub of desire from her sleek softness.

Maggie felt her body tightening, racked by the intense shivers from the hot intimate touch of his hand. She called to him, his name the only sound she could make, pleading for something, anything to ease the whiplike coiling that held her.

Slowly McCready rose over her, kneeling between her legs, wanting to be sheathed in the heated silken softness where pleasure shimmered again and again from his touch. Her total trust pierced him, making him tremble with emotion that went deeper than passion, more powerful than the need ripping at him.

Maggie watched him through dazed eyes that widened as his teasing fingers were replaced by the hard flesh she had held. Shimmering ripples of another pleasure took hold of her, and she closed her eyes, feeling him gently ride the waves of passion that brought him deeper and deeper into her body.

His mouth moved against her neck, biting her with hot restraint. Flame shot through her, filling her even as he did. Completely. She moved her hips in a sinuous motion, measuring him again and again, caressing him with the same heat that spread inside her. Her fingers dug into the clenched muscles of his arms, and she cried out.

He drove into her her, rocking her with the force of his need, giving all he had, and still she wanted more.

There were no words, not even his name, only passionate sounds she made of desire's demand.

Hot with hunger, his mouth mated with hers. Reckless now, he could almost feel his control snap, and he sated himself with her generous giving. There was fury, darkness, and Maggie's cries filling him.

She knew her power as a woman. His anguished groan. The driving thrust of his powerful body. Her name on his lips. The violence of need. Her body was coiled, tense with the passion that was answered by his pouring himself into her, endlessly, spinning her with its fury, bathing her with its complete possession.

The tremors faded slowly. Maggie felt the shift of his body and held him tighter. "Don't leave me," she whispered.

"I couldn't if I wanted to. And I don't want to, Maggie."

He angled his head to the side, and she saw the fire reflected in his eyes. Before she could say a word, he was talking.

"I've never had a woman so giving as you. Nothing held back, Maggie. I just had you and still want you," he said, his voice taking on a harsh edge. "But you're tender and sore, and I'll take you again and again just like I said. Until I can't breathe."

"Yes."

"Yes?"

His lean hips moved, and Maggie lost her breath with the

rush of fire that started all over again. She drew his face to hers, licking his lip with her tongue. "Yes," she murmured, taking his mouth just as his body pinned her again under its hard weight. He began moving, and her eyes blazed as he drove into her, taking all of her again, just as he whispered he would. Sweat gleamed on his body, and Maggie could feel the sheen on her own. The hot slide of their bodies brought sparks to flame, and she clung tightly to him, for there was no peace. He was driving her higher, rocking against her, then harder still, and she thought she would die. She fiercely arched into him, telling him the only way she could that she needed more of him.

The savage light of his eyes should have frightened her. It didn't. His teeth scored her neck; she found his shoulder.

"It feels like your blood's on fire, doesn't it, Maggie? A burning that goes all the way to the soul. That's what you do to me."

Twisting, hearing his dark voice, Maggie fought for the fulfillment she knew was waiting. He rose up slightly, pinning her hips still, feeding the wild hunger, until he was driven to have her mouth. She was helpless beneath him as he drove into her, grinding his body against hers as if he had to become a part of her.

Maggie wanted to scream. She had no breath. No voice. Nothing but savage blows thundering through her, impaling her as he did, shuddering with the same tormented cry that ripped McCready. *A burning to the soul.* She knew it was true. Fire stretched between them, both hell and heaven, wrapping them in its flame, taking him, taking her, until there was only one.

She lay spent beneath him, shocked by the passion that rocked through them. Now she fought for breath, just as he did, holding him tight against the world that still spun around her.

The spinning stopped, and the night faded with hours consumed in learning the slow, shimmering caresses that taught her the pleasures of McCready's body even as she learned her own.

And as dawn slowly stole the night, as slowly as McCready unraveled her once more, she learned that her need of him carried no shame, for he was as vulnerable as she and as needing.

Still joined, sleep finally staked its claim, but just before Maggie closed her eyes with his kiss on her lips, she knew that need could turn to the beginnings of love.

And McCready blessed the education found in countless bedrooms that had taught him how fragile the barrier of a woman's innocence was. Knowing how Maggie lived, it was no wonder that there had been no pain, no blood. His darling innocent wasn't even aware that there should have been.

But Maggie had gifted him with her trust. And she gave it as she gave herself, with nothing held back. He had told her he could prevent there being a child.

He hadn't.

The only excuse he offered himself was that she was a fever inside him that left no room for logic. It was feeble at best. He promised himself he'd be more careful.

CHAPTER
15

"Bein' a lady, learnin' to read, an' havin' me mines open are me only dreams." Cradled on McCready's lap, Maggie toyed with the top button of his pants. "What's yours?"

Tucking her head under his chin, McCready didn't answer her immediately. *No one had ever asked him about his dreams.* He tugged the edge of her shirt to cover a little more of her thigh. Maggie, he'd found, wanted everything from him. She gave the same way.

"Don't you have any?" she asked, sensing his tension.

"I'll live yours for a little while, Maggie mine."

"You can't. Every one has dreams of his own." His hand on

the back of her neck prevented her from looking at him. She
felt hurt. Whatever he asked her to share with him, she had.
Her body, her fears, her past, and now her few dreams. To feel
him withdrawing, although he didn't move, forced her to
realize that he'd made no more promises than the gift of their
shared pleasure with each other. *But we're married*, she
reminded herself. What other promise was as important? What
other promise could matter? She nuzzled his throat.

"Maggie," he whispered, pressing a kiss to her hair, "I
could teach you to read."

Distracted by the way her lips could speed up his pulse,
Maggie didn't answer. Her tongue stole into the hollow of his
throat.

"Maggie, did you hear me?"

His abrupt move that had her off his lap and standing beside
him left her surprised.

"No more, Maggie mine."

"Not at all?" she asked with a smile that was as wicked as
the one breaking over his lips.

"You're insatiable. I'm almost sorry I was the one to
introduce you to the—"

"What does that mean, McCready?"

He saw the flare of hurt and the beginnings of anger in her
eyes. "It means to be unsatisfied, Maggie. Like a thirst that
doesn't quit no matter how much you drink."

A flush stole into her cheeks as she thought of the night past.
"Meself had enough, thanks." She turned her back to him,
burning to hear his rough laugh.

"I didn't," he murmured, coming to stand behind her.

"Don't be givin' me your lies, McCready."

"No lies, Maggie. There haven't been any since I kissed you
last night." With one finger he drew a small circle and
adjoined a line to it on her back. He felt her shiver, and his
smile broke, for he knew just how sensitive Maggie was. His
own flesh hardened at the memory, and he repeated it.

"What's that you're doin' now?"

"Teaching you . . . to . . . to read."

"On me back?" Maggie shrugged off his hand and stepped away from him. She had had enough of McCready and his fool's games.

McCready was right behind her. Cupping her shoulder, he drew her back against his chest, ignoring her small effort to be free. "Listen to me, Maggie, I said I could make that dream come true." The exposed skin of her nape invited a kiss, a nip, and the soothe of his tongue. He was rewarded by a deeper shiver that joined his.

"Never heard of no learnin' the likes of yours."

"Trust me, Maggie. You *will* like my way. What's more," he promised in a silken voice against her skin, "so will I."

Maggie had to fight to keep her mind on what he was saying. His voice was promising other things, sending shivers deep inside, wiping away the hours in his arms, and leaving her with new needs, harder cravings.

"You could—" Her voice broke as he nuzzled her neck, tilting her head to the side.

"Yes, Maggie? What could I do?"

"A stick. From the fire. The floor would do."

McCready murmured agreement, sliding his hands around her waist. "But my way is better. You won't forget anything that I teach you, Maggie." His fingers splayed over the flat plane of her belly, and he couldn't stifle his harsh groan. "You're like a fever, Maggie. And I'll be damned if I know how to get rid of it."

"Show me."

Still holding her with one hand, he used the other to draw an *I* on one hip. "I," he breathed into her ear and followed it by spelling out *want you*.

"What did you do?" She couldn't think again. His palm cupped her intimately, and she knew the coil had already begun holding her in its grip.

"Want you. I want you, Maggie." She was twisting and turning, bringing his lips to hers, teaching forgotten while they repeated the lessons already learned.

But when the shimmering ecstasy left them bathed in soft flames, Maggie found that McCready's teaching skills brought rich rewards. By the time the afternoon's light descended, she had learned to write *I want you*. But Maggie mumbled an apology when her letters seemed to follow their own erotic pattern. She had found that McCready's blunt, hot flesh truly helped her form the perfect *u*. And she kept on saying she was sorry that her tongue seemed quicker than her fingertips to learn the making of all those strange shapes.

McCready accepted the apology, even if her eyes were full of sass. He was in complete agreement that she was learning fast. He had no choice. She was killing him, but he was dying with a smile.

Dutch was not smiling. He was polishing the same glass for the last ten minutes. He was aware of it but didn't stop, for he was watching Cora Ann cuddle with the stranger that rode in late last night. Trouble was, Cora Ann didn't look too happy about it, and when he called her away to find out if she wanted the man gone, she said no.

On a quick look the man appeared to be a drifter. The top of his head, including the high crown of his hat, had barely come to Dutch's shoulder. He wasn't young, and Dutch made that judgment not on his thinning brown hair, but the man's brown eyes. They were cold and hard, for even when he smiled, like now at something Cora Ann said, the smile never reached his eyes. That bothered Dutch, that and the way Cora Ann hadn't left him since he had walked into the Rawhider. And for all his questions, he'd only found out that the man's name was Bill and he had a pocketful of cash to spend.

It was more than enough for Cora Ann, but not for him. And he had his worries about McCready that kept getting in his way. The man would likely be hitting a slow boil along about now that Dutch didn't meet him with his whiskey. He could only hope that McCready didn't take it out on Maggie's soft hide. But he felt it was the wrong time for him to be leaving.

Cora Ann motioned for another bottle of whiskey, and Dutch set one out on the bar, still watching the man and trying to figure out what about Bill didn't fit. He looked as if he could use the gun he wore. Dutch had seen his share of green broncs looking to make a reputation, and this man wasn't one of them. Besides, there were no guns in Cooney Camp that would make a man's reputation. Well, there weren't any but Lee Warren, and he kept a low profile. This man was as quiet.

But as Cora Ann took the bottle and walked back to the table they shared, Dutch saw that he'd been caught staring. For a moment there was warning in the man's eyes for Dutch, then it was gone.

Slick walked in with Lee Warren and ordered up a bottle just as the Rose came down the steps. Lee had eyes for no one else, and within minutes the Rose was playing and singing for him.

"Bodes no good," Dutch muttered, leaving his place behind the bar. "Cora Ann," he called out, "you tend to things. I'll be in back." He headed for the storeroom where Satin was. The dog had the sense to sit and listen while he sorted out his feelings from facts.

Cora Ann turned back to William Berger once Dutch was out of sight. Slick, Lee, and a miner she didn't know were clustered around the piano and the Rose, so she didn't need to worry that anyone would hear them.

"I keep trying to tell you it was a mistake for you to come here. You see the way Dutch's watching you. Sending word to me would have been fine. But it wouldn't have mattered. I don't know where Maggie O'Roarke is."

"But Dutch does."

"He might," she answered, filling her glass. She made the

mistake of looking up at William's face. His eyes had a way of narrowing and appearing so cold that goosebumps broke on her skin. "Don't think I can get Dutch in bed. He doesn't mess with the Rose or me. Dutch would rather take off to the big towns and find his own women."

"I'm not leaving until I have what I want."

"But Dutch isn't going to tell you or anyone more than he told Quincy." This time she hoped he would add something more to the little he had told her. Cora Ann scratched her nose, for it was itching as it only did when someone lied to her about money. She knew that McCready was claiming that he had won old Pete's mines and now owned them. But Maggie had been planning to marry Quincy to get the money she needed to open the mines. It was anyone's guess who really owned them. And she didn't understand why William thought she would believe his story of being partners with Quincy. He knew she was a woman who watched out for herself. She knew who Quincy's boss was, even if William didn't. Give a man what he wanted in bed or anywhere else that tickled him, and he'd tell you how many visits he'd made to the outhouse, if you wanted to know.

Below the table William's bony fingers squeezed her knee.

She knew it wasn't a signal to go upstairs. William wouldn't even bother to ask.

"Pay attention to me, Cora Ann. I want to know where Maggie O'Roarke is. And I want to have that information by tonight."

"But I told you—" She winced as he increased the hard pressure of his grip.

"You owe me and don't you forget it, Clarissa."

"Cora Ann. Clarissa is as gone as if she never was."

"There's a Texas marshal that believes differently. I didn't tell you that he was up to see me a few weeks ago. Just stopped by in case I had any word from you."

"You know that I didn't cheat that cowboy. When he pulled

his gun, I had to protect myself. You saw us fighting. You could have helped me get the gun away from him.''

''But I couldn't get involved. I told that to the marshal. Said it was an accident, but you can't blame him for not believing me. It was his brother that you shot.'' He leaned closer. ''I don't care how you find out. Just do it.''

''Work and more work. I'm sick of work,'' Pamela muttered in her father's mercantile. There were supplies to be sorted, but once Ira had helped her father unload the freight wagon, and they'd left, she refused to do another bit by herself.

''Ira was only looking for another grub stake. Pa had to give him enough so he wouldn't stay. But he won't give me the money to leave this back of nowhere. Sometimes, I swear I'll dry up and rot here.''

She peered into the small mirror propped up behind the counter, trying to decide if Miss Philippa Gosling's face wash was really turning her skin to feel like silk. That's what the advertisement in the *Daily New Mexican* claimed. True, she reminded herself, she had only been using it for two months. Maybe it took more time to work. Sighing, she turned.

Sugar loafs waited to be stored. The ready mades had to be sorted, pants from shirts, and the near empty pickle barrel moved to make room for the new one.

Pamela turned back to her primping, bored, and wishing that something would happen. Things had been quiet in camp with both McCready and Maggie gone. Well, there had been a little excitement stirred up that night that Quincy had come looking for Maggie and McCready, but she had been asleep and didn't hear about it until snippy Cora Ann told her.

And everyone was worried about Maggie. Even Pamela's father. Why he would think that she would know where Maggie went was too much to understand. But he was right in saying that it wasn't like Maggie to take off and leave Satin behind. She had even gone up to Maggie's cabin yesterday afternoon only to find that nothing had been touched, nor was there any sign that Maggie had been back. The strange thing was that both her mare and mule were still in camp.

Strange thing, and that's all there was to it.

The cowbell tinkled over the door, and Pamela whisked the mirror under the counter before she looked up.

She offered her most timid smile to the man that filled her vision, frightened that he walked so softly. The dust coating his clothes said he had ridden hard. The look in his eyes told her that she had better not ask from where or why.

"Can I help you?"

"Looking for Burton. Andrew Burton."

"That's my father. But he's not here right now. Why don't you come back—" Pamela's words were lost in her cry as he hauled her forward across the counter.

"Where is he?"

"He . . . he took a load of supplies up to Clairmont. The-there aren't as many miners now, since most of them have come down here to Cooney Camp, but Pa has his regulars that he delivers supplies to and . . . and . . ." She stopped herself when she realized that she was babbling and he was no longer listening to her. "Please, you're hurting—"

"When's he expected back?"

"To-tonight." She wished she could swallow and spit in his eye. Maggie wouldn't have hesitated a moment. But she didn't have any moisture in her mouth.

"You tell him," he demanded, twisting the cloth of her gown in his fist, "that Ryder's looking for him. An' if you know what's good for you, you won't be mentioning me to anyone else. Got that?"

"Got it," she repeated in a high squeak. "Yes. Now, please, I—" Pamela found herself released as suddenly as he had grabbed her, and she collapsed across the counter like a discarded rag doll. What had her father gotten himself into this time? She had to get out of this place.

Slowly dragging herself to stand, Pamela stared in shock at the way her hands were shaking. That man, Ryder, had meant to frighten her—and he'd accomplished it. She tried to fix the lace edge of her collar, and tears came to find that he had torn it.

For the second time she wished she were Maggie. Maggie would have gutted him before he put a hand on her. She glanced at the gun concealed beneath the counter and used a few of Maggie's more colorful swears for her own stupidity in not making a grab for it. The man wouldn't have dared to be so rough with her if she had been holding a gun.

But Pamela knew she hated guns and hating touching them.

Once again she heard the bell above the door tinkle, and this time she didn't think. She grabbed the gun and pointed at the towering man that filled the narrow doorway.

"W-what do you want?"

Larson Vladimir glanced from the wavering gun pointed now at his belly, now at his heart, to the petite young woman who was trying to steady it. "Please. I mean no harm. I come to look for Mary. Mary O'Roarke. You can help me find her, *ja?*"

After what just happened to her, Pamela wasn't quick to set aside her weapon. She held her arms straight out, both hands gripping the gun, watching the man come toward her. He had to duck to avoid the leather bridles and straps that hung from the rafters.

But when she looked at his kindly but puzzled blue eyes, and saw that he kept his big hands away from his sides to show her that he carried no weapon, Pamela began to feel foolish.

She set the gun back under the counter and straightened. "A woman alone can't be too careful around here. I had a most unpleasant experience just minutes before you walked in, and it left me quite shaken."

"There is no one here with you?"

"Well, my father usually is, but he had to take supplies to

Clairmont. This is our store, Burton's Mercantile. And forgive
me for not introducing myself. I'm Pamela Burton.''

"A woman so pretty like you should have her man with
her."

Pamela's eyes brightened, and she forgot all about Ryder.
"My man?" she asked, practicing the soft, sweet drawl that
she had heard Cora Ann use.

"You are married."

"No." She lowered her lashes.

"There are no men here?"

"Oh, yes. There are plenty of men. But not the type who
know how to court a lady."

"*Ja.* That is the right way of things."

"Not that I complain, you understand. It just gets so lonely
sometimes to have someone to talk to."

The flare of interest in his eyes made her blush. She was
disappointed to see it disappear in seconds. He didn't have the
dark, sometimes dangerous look of McCready's blue eyes.
This man's were the blue of a still clear lake. Thick blond curls,
the color of new corn, framed a face that was as ruggedly cut
as the mountains. But when he smiled, it added a gentle
softening that invited her to smile with him. He was young
enough to be interesting, but old enough to be called a man.
And he had all his front teeth, and they were clean, too.

He was looking better and better to her.

"Have you just arrived in Cooney Camp?"

"*Ja.* I just come. I am Larson Vladimir from the territory of
Washington." And proudly, "I am the owner of a sawmill."

Pamela's smile widened. He was nearly as big as Dutch, but
she could see there wasn't a spare bit of fat beneath the fitted
white shirt he wore under his black suit jacket. He was so polite
and cute with his slow way of talking that she forgot he had
asked about Maggie. Although she herself often forgot that her
name was Mary Margaret.

"You are not still afraid of me?"

"No, Mr. Vladimir." He nodded his approval, and Pamela knew she had been right to use his last name. This was a man who not only appreciated a lady, but might also, with a little of the right encouragement, be pushed into taking her away from here. She continued to smile at him, thinking that she was going to leave Cooney Camp and whatever trouble her father had gotten himself into far behind. And Larson Vladimir from the territory of Washington was her answer.

"I have a fresh pot of coffee on the stove in the back. I don't usually ask a strange man to share a cup of coffee with me, but since you've just arrived and I'm still shaken, I hope you will join me."

She smiled so sweetly and yet looked so sad, that Lars found himself saying, "I would be pleased to have coffee with you."

He watched the gentle sway of her slender hips as she came out from behind the counter and walked toward the back of the cluttered store. He followed, hoping that Mary O'Roarke was very much like this charming young woman with the eyes to make him blush. Lars brushed the dust from his pants legs. He wished he had found a place to take a bath. But he would not stay long. After all, it was not proper for a young woman to be alone with a man unless he had first spoken to her father.

And as he sat sipping his second cup of coffee, talking and laughing with her, Lars forgot why he had come to Cooney Camp and needed to find Mary O'Roarke.

"Will you stay for supper?" Pamela shyly asked as the hour grew late. "I just know my papa would love to meet you and hear all the exciting things you've done, Mr. Vladimir."

"*Ja.* I will stay. I will be pleased to meet your papa, too."

CHAPTER 16

"Supper, McCready. I've got to eat somethin' an' so do you."

McCready pushed aside the shirt from Maggie's hip. "Roast haunch for me." He nipped her skin and lightly pinched her bottom. Maggie's squeal only made him lock his arm around her legs. "And a little," he whispered, moving to softer game, "essence of love."

"McCready! Mc . . . Cready . . ."

He planted a kiss on the damp triangle of curls and looked up to where she sprawled on the tangle of blankets. Her eyes were already clouding over, closing even as he watched, and he knew if he wanted she would give herself to him again.

"Maggie," he called softly, resting his chin on her thigh. "Look at me." He waited for her eyes to focus and smiled. "You are right, Maggie mine. We will eat supper . . . first. Then I'll want my dessert." The tremor that rippled over and through her had him hesitate for a moment. With the greatest of reluctance he forced himself off the bed. "Stay. I'll fix something for us."

She watched him slide his powerful legs into his pants. And she waited until he began buttoning his fly before she called out to him.

"McCready?"

The teasing taunt of her voice made him keep his eyes on what he was doing. If he didn't, he would be climbing back on that bed with Maggie. As it was, he was having the devil's own time trying to close his pants.

She called him again.

"What?"

Maggie smiled to hear the edge in his voice. "I was just wantin' to know if I get dessert, too?"

His head came up slowly, the pants forgotten. "Christ!" he almost hissed. "You're gonna kill me, Maggie."

"But you can't be smilin' an' dyin' at the same time," she sassed back, pulling the quilt to cover her legs.

"Can't?" Instantly he forced his lips into a stern line.

Maggie's laughter filled the cabin and the empty places inside him that he didn't know needed to be filled.

"Supper," he muttered, moving away from her.

"McCready. You didn't answer me."

"No. I know I didn't. I don't want to. I'll just leave you to wonder about it." Her soft, knowing laughter ruffled his nerve ends.

"But, McCready, I already know."

Death. She would be the death of him, and he had no one but himself to blame. With a rough shake of his head, he knew it wasn't so. Maggie was life and laughter with her fresh innocence that never learned the games of manipulation. Still, he couldn't forgive the damage she did by planting the sight in his mind of her learning what pleasured him just as he had learned the sweet secrets of all that made Maggie what she was.

He nearly sliced off his finger while cutting the bacon, and when it was sizzling in the pan, he felt as if he were hearing the sound of his own blood.

But when he set the bacon and beans on the table, his thoughts already on the coming dessert, he found that Maggie's playful mood had been replaced by a serious one.

"We have to talk about the mines, McCready."

He should have stayed in bed with her. It was the one thing that he had avoided talking about each time she brought it up. Kissing her silent had worked well, but with her already seated across the table from him, he wouldn't get around to her fast enough. Maybe she was right. It was time they talked about them.

Maggie stared down at her plate, pushing the beans into small hills. "You've got to admit that Pete didn't lose them to you."

As an opening he thought it lacked finesse. But at least she had given him the benefit of not being called a liar again.

"Why, Maggie?"

"They belong to me. They're all I have." His silence grated on her. It was a mistake to talk to him about the mines. He wasn't going to admit that they weren't his. But even as she thought this, McCready offered another way.

"Take half. I'm in a generous mood."

She wasn't going to get angry with him. He'd like that too much. And she was aware that he only had to look at her now with that hot intensity that said he wanted her, and she would be helpless against him.

"Would you be wantin' the gold or silver?"

"Silver? There's silver, too?" His fork hit the tin plate.

"Pete never said anything about silver, Maggie. Is this one of your—"

"It's nothin' but the truth, McCready." Her gaze was steady, directly on his when he looked up. She nodded to make sure he understood that she was telling him the truth.

"No one—"

"No one knew but Pete an' me. The gold that got him killed, well, he had a chunk of it with him. By the time I found him, it was gone. Pete an' me figured it was gonna assay out close to five, maybe six hundred dollars."

"And the silver, Maggie?" Even as he asked, McCready was refiguring everything he'd known about Pete's gold mine. And since Maggie had opened the door to his conscience, he felt the worm of guilt snake its way up for not telling her the truth.

Maggie pushed the plate aside and lifted her cup for a sip of coffee. She set it down carefully, stalling, while she made the decision to trust McCready.

"Near as rich. All three of the claims."

"Three!"

"That's what I said, boyo, three. There's only one gold an' the other three claims might have some decent pickin's, but I never went back to them."

"Do you know what kind of money you're talking about, Maggie?"

"If I don't, McCready, I'd best hang up my pick an' send me mule to pasture."

He wanted to wring her neck. Not for the smug smile, but for knowing this and not having the sense to realize how dangerous the knowledge was to her. It took him minutes before he calmed down to answer her.

"Maggie, what you just told me is more than enough reason for someone to want you dead." He hated saying it the moment he was done. Her face lost its color and her eyes reflected fear.

"I'm sorry, Maggie. I didn't mean to remind you, but you're the only one who knows where the mines are, true?"

"True." Maggie didn't hesitate over the small lie.

McCready's elbows hit the table, and he dropped his head into his hands. "What a mess."

"Not so," Maggie said. "All I needed was the money to open them. These ain't no pan an' rocker mines, McCready. Lumber's needed for shorin' an' men for diggin'."

"And?" he prompted when she stopped.

Maggie kept her eyes on the table where she was drawing the letters he had taught her.

It took McCready a few moments to understand what she was doing, and he reached out to cover her hand with his own. "Tell me why this isn't a mess?"

Say it, Maggie. Just tell him what you're thinking. You had no trouble doing that while he loved you.

"I was figurin' that with us bein' married an' all, that you'd be puttin' up the money." She looked up at him. "For half, just like you said."

But McCready wasn't telling her that it was a good idea. He wasn't saying that he'd give her what she wanted. He wasn't saying a damn thing. Maggie shoved back her chair. She took her plate and his and went to the fire, but McCready had not set the kettle on with water to wash them. A glance showed her the bucket was empty.

"We need water, McCready."

"Maggie, listen, I—"

"That's all right, boyo. I'll get it meself." She set the plates down and grabbed the bucket. "Don't be worryin' that I'll run. I won't."

"I wasn't worried, Maggie. I just want you to understand that I . . . ." McCready turned and found himself talking to an empty room.

Maggie shivered in the night air. All she wore was McCready's shirt. "Damn him!" She stubbed her toe and limped over to the well. In spite of the cold she would wash his touch and smell right off her. The hell with McCready! The man was quicksilver trouble and nothing else but. Stubborn. Arrogant. Pigheaded. Ah, why was she tiring herself out trying to call him names?

Why didn't he say something? The question plagued her as she sent the bucket down the well, and by the time she pulled it back up, she still didn't have any answer.

The night air and icy water did more than chill her; it cleared her head. Maggie glanced back once to find that the cabin door remained closed.

She knew McCready was a greedy man. He had proved that every time he made love to her. But she was just the same. He laughed with her and made her laugh. He made her feel so good that she had to return pleasure. Was that all they had?

She hurried to button up the shirt, truly feeling the cold, and quickly filled the bucket again.

The fire was built up, and for a moment she thought he was gone, but then saw him lying on the bed.

The sight of his shirt clinging to her damp body told him what she had been doing outside. And the set of her mouth told him what had been going on inside Maggie as well.

Telling her the truth was no longer an option to be considered. He'd have to find another way to smooth things over with her.

Maggie set the kettle on, but being in the cabin with McCready again only made her ask herself what she had said to silence him. The last thing she had mentioned was their being married. McCready had told her it was so. He had a paper to prove it. It couldn't have been that. So it had to be her asking him for the money to open the mines. But Dutch had told her that McCready had plenty of money.

There was no sense to be had from recounting all this, and with a sigh Maggie gave up.

"Maggie, come here."

"The fire's warmer, boyo."

"You said you had a dream of being a lady, didn't you? Well, Maggie mine, ladies learn to be obedient."

"An' learn to bow prettily so they don't fall over, an' they never wrinkle their—"

"They curtsy, Maggie. That's what ladies do. Men bow."

If he had sounded in the least like he was poking fun at her, she would have let him have it, but he didn't. Nor did he sound teasing. Trying to follow McCready's moods was like trying to follow a played-out vein that might, if you stayed with it, pay off with a bonanza. Maggie tried very hard to sidestep where her own thoughts were taking her. McCready didn't help.

"You're halfway to being a lady, Maggie. You're just as soft, as sleek, and as graceful as any woman I've seen."

"No more games, McCready."

"No games. Back to as honest as I get, Maggie."

The husky edge in his voice warned her what she would find if she turned around. Maggie faced him. She blocked the firelight so he was bathed in shadows and nothing else. She lost her breath somewhere and couldn't find it for moments.

Mines and money were forgotten. McCready was as naked as Adam and twice as proud. He had a right to be, she thought, following his gaze to where his shirt clung damply to her breasts.

"Maggie, it's time for dessert."

She closed her eyes against the whisper and the promise that drifted across the cabin to her. The fire at her back couldn't touch the blaze that came from his eyes. She felt herself weakening, and fought, but was already thinking of the haven she would find in his arms.

"Maggie?"

"I've not made up me mind."

"I have. I'm hungry enough to forget my pride, Maggie."

She didn't need his coaxing to make up her mind for her. Her body quickened at his soft drawl. But she had pride, too.

"I'll be havin' your answer about me mines first."

The gleam in her eyes told him she meant it. But he couldn't lie. He wasn't thinking about the damn mines. "Yours, mine, just be generous with me, Maggie. As I'll be with you. We'll share, *everything*, Maggie, equally and together."

"You've the devil's silver tongue, an' that's no lie."

"So sure? Come to me, Maggie." He was ready to tell her that he would sell his soul to the devil.

Satisfied that she had gotten what she wanted from him, Maggie slipped the shirt off over her head.

Wearing nothing more than her Irish pride, she went to him.

Cora Ann was drenched in fear. Listening at Dutch's bedroom door, sure that he was asleep, she tiptoed down the steps and made her way to the storeroom. A low warning growl made her hesitate, but she had William's threat to tell where she was and jammed the key she had taken earlier from behind the bar into the lock. Just before she turned it, Cora Ann slipped the bolt on the back door and opened it.

The dog's growls intensified, and she was shaking as she began to turn the key. Somewhere in the dark William was waiting to follow Satin to Maggie.

Flattening herself against the wall, she unlocked the door. Taking a deep breath, she shoved it open. Satin shot out and disappeared before Cora Ann sank to the floor.

She flung the key outside, knowing it was foolish. Dutch would know that she was the one who let Satin out. Once he saw William gone, he would have to know.

Gathering herself to move, she thought of her packed bags waiting upstairs. William promised to leave her horse saddled out front. Before morning she would be gone from Cooney Camp.

Pamela sniffed prettily into her hankie. At the rate Lars was apologizing, she would be away from Cooney Camp by nightfall.

She drew her handmade quilt closer to her chin and looked
at Lars. "I don't understand all that you're saying. You took
advantage of me, Lars. I was an innocent . . . there is no
other way to make things right but for you to marry me." She
hid the gleam in her eyes beneath a calculated sweep of her
lashes. Lars owned his own mill plus stands of timber. He told
her he'd bought part of a shipping line to ship his lumber and
planned to own it all within two years. But he was not
forthcoming with an offer of marriage.

"If my father had not been detained, this never would have
happened." The tears were very real when Pamela lifted her
gaze to his. "I thought you were a gentleman. I would never
have let you stay for supper otherwise. And when you began
telling me all those stories about your mill and how lumber is
cut, I felt safe with you. I let you hold my hand. I let you kiss
me and . . ." She wailed, louder this time, for she had taken
the biggest gamble of her life and was not getting what she
wanted.

"I did not mean for this to happen. I could not leave you
here alone when you were still afraid that the man Ryder would
come back and hurt you." Cradling his head in his hands, Lars
rocked back and forth on the edge of the bed. He couldn't think
clearly. He didn't know how he'd wound up in Pamela's bed,
taking from her what only belonged to her husband.

"Didn't you . . . like me a little, Lars?"

Her timid voice cut through his own pain. "Never have I
done such a thing. But *ja*, I liked you more than a little. You are
a fine young woman, Pamela. You will make a man a good
wife."

"Then why won't you marry me?"

Her reddened eyes were no match for the flush that colored
Lars's skin. "You try to understand, *ja?* I cannot marry you."

Despair filled her. She glanced around her room, searching
for a clue as to why he kept insisting that he couldn't marry
her. The rough chinked log walls were all covered with lace

curtains in an attempt to bring back the civilized world she had to leave behind. An ornately flower and fruit carved lady's slipper chair sat in one corner, its upholstery almost hidden by the satin and lace-edged pillows from her bed. The top of her polished bureau held an array of creams and perfumes, her one good bonnet, and bits of ribbon. Her gaze was drawn to the corner of the four-poster bed, where she cringed beneath its crocheted canopy. Everywhere she looked, virginal white mocked her for what she had lost.

Pamela saw that Lars was already gathering up his shirt, tie, and jacket. He was going to leave her. And with him went her chance to get away from there. A rage spread through her, shaking her with its force.

She had tried pretty; she could lose nothing more by letting anger free.

"Mr. Vladimir, look at me," she demanded, deliberately letting the quilt slide down to her waist. "Tell me why! Damn you! I've a right to know why you can't marry me."

CHAPTER
17

William Berger knew his plan was simple and risky. Once Cora Ann set the dog free, all he had to do was follow her to where Maggie was hiding. If he hadn't been straining to hear a sound, he would never have known that the back door to the Rawhider had been opened. What he hadn't counted on was that the dog would move like a shot once free of her confinement. He lost sight of her in the dark.

Cora Ann had told him where Maggie's cabin was, and he allowed that the dog might go there. He urged his horse forward, letting him pick his way. After the bungling job Thadius had done, he was going to succeed.

He swore softly as his horse's hooves clattered over the wooden bridge. Just as he reached the other side, a howl rent the night.

He wasn't alarmed. He believed everything Cora Ann had told him about Maggie and her dog. It was natural for the animal to howl when she didn't find who she was looking for up there.

But the howling continued. It steadily grew in volume. Cursing under his breath, William abandoned his horse and began to make his way on foot, determined to make his plan work, whatever the cost.

Within the shacks and tents of Cooney Camp, miners woke. Most of these men had heard that howling once before when Mohawk Pete had been found murdered.

Down below in the Rawhider, Dutch muttered and turned in his bed, trying to ignore Satin's latest ploy to gain his attention. It was minutes before he realized that the sound was drifting in from his window, not coming up through the floor. In the following seconds he knew the thumps he heard were coming from the hallway outside his room.

"By the saints in heaven!" he roared, tossing off his blanket. "Can't you wait till you get to your room?" Still swearing, he grabbed his pants and pulled them on, confused by Satin's apparent freedom. He knew he had locked the door.

But when he stepped out into the hall expecting to find either the Rose or Cora Ann and some man, there was no one. Scratching his belly, Dutch shook off the last vestige of sleep. Satin was outside, and someone was sneaking around downstairs! His bellow shook the rafters.

Cora Ann dropped her two carpet bags and ran.

Still bellowing, Dutch made a leap for the fleeing shadow before it reached the door. His fist closed on a handful of cloth just as his body slammed something smaller and much softer than himself against the barred floor.

He heard air whistle by when the body sagged, and he was forced to hold it up. For a few seconds he was stunned.

The string of curses told him who he had long before he hauled her back to the bar and shoved her down to the floor. Planting his bare foot on the squirming woman, Dutch lit the lantern.

"What the hell is going on, Cora Ann?"

Satin's howling split the night. Dutch raised Cora Ann to her feet and glared at her. With one hand on her arm he held her still.

"What did you do to Satin?"

"Nothing. I . . . I . . ."

"Talk, damn you!" he yelled, shaking her.

"I f-felt sorry for her and, and, l-let her out." Dutch's shaking of her body was nothing to compare with the inner quaking that racked her. She was done for, and she knew it would take a small miracle to get her out of this.

Dutch was torn between wanting to beat the truth out of her and going after Satin. The echo of a shot made his decision. Cora Ann only confirmed it.

"I didn't mean any harm, Dutch. I swear it."

"The hell you didn't. You were born stirring up trouble. It was that man, wasn't it? Knew I shouldn't've let him hang around. Move," he ordered, pushing her ahead of him.

"Where?"

"Your room. And hurry. I'd like to hear the tale of why you did this, but if something happens to Satin, I'll take it out of your hide. That is, I will if Maggie don't get to you first."

Wild-eyed, Cora Ann grabbed the edge of the bar trying to prevent him from carrying out his plan. "You don't understand! Dutch, please let me go," she wailed. "I'll be gone and you'll never see me again."

"Up the stairs or I'll carry you there."

Cora Ann backed up the stairs, pleading, crying, and when these didn't work, she cursed him all over again.

Dutch ignored her. He crowded her down the hall to her room, pushed open the door and shoved her inside.

The edge of the bed stopped Cora Ann from falling. "What are you going to do?" She'd never seen Dutch in such a rage. And fear of William Berger rapidly left her.

"Lock you in where you can't do no harm," he answered. He took the key and pulled the door shut with a force that shook its frame. A kittenlike cry made him look up to find the Rose staring open-mouthed at him. "If you don't want the same, get back where you belong!" he shouted over Cora Ann's furious pounding and wails.

The Rose's door slammed just as he twisted the key in the lock. To make sure she'd stay put, he took the key with him to his room. He had to find Satin before that son of a bitch killed her. Or the dog found Maggie and McCready, he added, pulling on his boots. Carrying his shirt, he returned to the bar, took his gun, and shoved it into his waistband.

And as he ran toward Maggie's cabin, he knew he had better find that dog, or Maggie would skin him and pin his hide out to dry.

William's shot wounded the dog, slowing her down as he intended. Her pitched yelp finally cut off the howling. But he wasn't going to have time to search for her. The shot had awakened the whole mining camp. He could see shadows of men moving up toward the cabin carrying lanterns.

He had to get away without being seen. As long as no one knew it was him, he could stay in Cooney Camp until Maggie returned. Cora Ann couldn't give him away. She was long gone.

But the only way back down was the way the muttering miners were coming up.

A little action to sweeten the reward. His words came back to haunt him. That didn't include being at the end of a rope.

But William had not gotten where he was by being afraid.

He waited until the men were milling about the front of the cabin, listening to one yell out that no one was inside. Keeping flat to the wall, he made his way along the side and when the first man's back came in view, William knew he would once again succeed.

He snuck in behind the men, smiling to hear the angry muttering, and when he heard it reach the proper pitch, he yelled, "There's fire down below!"

In a collective rush the men ran. Everything they owned was in the tents and shacks that lined the surrounding area. William had counted on that. But once again he found that he had lost the dog in the ensuing melee. Not a whimper was to be heard.

Dutch heard the trampling rush of miners and braced himself at the end of the wooden bridge to stop them.

"Move, Dutch. There's fire!" more than one man yelled.

"Ain't no fire. It was a trick to get you away from Maggie's cabin. The son of a bitch that shot Satin is up there."

Ira pushed his way through the crowd and with him came Slick. "Ain't no one up there. Not even the dog."

The lanterns' light showed Dutch the nods of most of the men. "Dammit!" He pounded his fist on the wood rail and heard the crack. "Ira, stay at the Rawhider. Tend bar. I've got business. And whatever else you do, Ira, don't let Cora Ann out."

"McCready business?" Ira called out, coming off the bridge.

"Maggie business," Dutch returned.

"What'd ya figure she'll do to Dutch iffen something happened to Satin?" Slick asked Ira as the panic of the fire left them and they ambled their way to the Rawhider.

"Figure Maggie'll have his hide. Skinned neat as can be an' staked out in front of the Rawhider for all to see."

"Yeah. I sorta figured the same."

Dutch knew the men were speculating about what Maggie would do to him. But he couldn't worry about it now. He had to lose time going back to get his horse along with Maggie's and McCready's.

The lean-to wasn't barred, and Dutch fumbled until he found the lantern and lit it. The restless stampings of the horses distracted him, but when he heard a loud snore again, he knew he wasn't alone. Drawing his gun, he headed for the only empty stall.

A man had to have finished off a keg of whiskey to sleep through all the excitement. But when Dutch held the lantern high and light shone down at the man sprawled in the straw, he amended his estimate. A barrel more likely to put this big man down so soundly.

Dutch kicked his boot, then kicked it harder to rouse him.

With a roar and two fistfuls of straw, Lars bolted upright. Light blinded him. He threw aside the straw to shield his eyes with his hands. "Who is there?"

"Never mind who I am. Who the hell are you?" Dutch lowered the lantern, not out of consideration, but to show the man the gun which he held. "I'm waiting for an answer."

It was too much for Lars. Twice now he had had guns pointed at him in Cooney Camp. But this man meant business. There was no wavering in the hand holding the weapon on him. Lars slowly raised his hands high.

"Larson Vladimir, I am. I come from the territory of Washington."

"And you just up and decided to sleep in here?"

Lars colored and lowered his hands, deciding that the man would have shot him if he wanted, or demanded his money by now if he was going to rob him. But he was not going to tell this man or anyone what happened with Pamela Burton after he explained why he could not marry her and she threw him out.

"The door was not locked. There was no place to go so late," he offered lamely.

"Likely. But what are you doing in Cooney Camp? You ain't a miner and you ain't carrying a gun."

"*Ja*. This is true. I come to look for Mary O'Roarke."

"Mary O'Roarke? Oh, you mean Maggie. Well, you wasted your time, fella. She's not here." Instinct built over the years told Dutch that he didn't have to worry about this man. He lowered his gun, then stuck it back in his waistband. Besides, he had figured he had a good thirty pounds more on him.

But when he left the stall to saddle the horses, Lars stumbled out after him.

"Wait. Please. You tell me where she is, *ja*?"

"Can't do that. But if you want to tell me what you're wanting with Maggie, I'll tell her for you."

Lars wanted nothing so much as to leave this place. He took the measure of the man that was near his equal in size and weight.

Dutch quickly smoothed the saddle blanket over his horse's back before he slung the saddle on. He caught the man's hesitation to speak.

"Name's Dutch. I tend bar over at the Rawhider. You fixing to stay in Cooney Camp for a while, go over to Miss Mae's an' tell her I sent you. She'll give you a room."

"You will be seeing Mary O'Roarke soon?"

"Sooner than I'd like. But don't ask to come with me. You can't." Dutch eased the bit into the horse's mouth, slid the ear straps in place, and began on McCready's horse.

Lars had made three wrong decisions yesterday. He should have refused coffee, supper, and the invitation to bed Pamela Burton. He could add a fourth wrong decision or have his first right one by trusting Dutch with his reason. Lars quickly chose to tell Dutch why he wanted to see Mary O'Roarke.

"Mister, you'd better have proof," Dutch demanded, curling his hands into fists. "If you're lying," he yelled over Lars's repeated, *ja, ja,* "I'll break you into matchsticks and grind you up like sawdust!"

"Here. You see." Lars reached into his jacket and showed Dutch the papers he had.

For the second time that night Cooney Camp was treated to the sound of Dutch's enraged bellow.

Maggie was dreaming of balloons and escape. She had fallen asleep while McCready was reading to her from the Lakeside Library twelve-cent edition of Jules Verne's *The Mysterious Island—Dropped from the Clouds*.

Desperate Confederate soldiers made good their escape from a Yankee prison camp and were drifting without direction when they sighted the mysterious island. She tossed and turned, reliving the soldiers' desperation, while being frightened for them. McCready and his fancy books had opened a new and exciting world to her.

Chilled, she snuggled closer to the warmth of McCready's body curved spoon fashion behind her. His sleepy murmurs were a quick soothe, and with a smile touching her lips Maggie hoped that when the next adventure was printed, she would be able to read it by herself.

After all, McCready said she was a quick learner.

Thunder rolled off the mountains. Maggie burrowed against McCready so hard that he woke and had to clutch the edge of the bed to keep himself from falling off.

"Easy, Maggie mine," he whispered, gently pushing her over to make room for himself. "I promise I won't let the storm inside."

"Did you hear yourself, McCready?" she asked, stifling a chuckle.

"I heard. Now, go back to sleep. It isn't a fit time for a man to be awake." He slipped one arm beneath her sleep-warm body and cradled her close. Kissing her ear, he blew on it, trying to distract her from her fear. He couldn't tell Maggie how much he cherished her trust; the emotions that shimmered inside him were still too new to be spoken aloud.

He kept whispering to her, smiling to feel the tension that held her ease. Maggie's sleepy response was an absent pat on his arm. The drumming roll sounded closer and brought McCready fully awake.

That wasn't thunder he was hearing. It was horses.

Besides himself only Dutch knew the way to the cabin. And McCready knew, big as Dutch was, he couldn't ride more than one horse at a time.

He was off the bed and fumbling in the dark for his pants to find the key to the chest. He should have built up the fire after supper. But the few coals were covered by ash, and now he didn't want light showing from the cabin.

"Maggie, we're getting company. Get dressed." He dragged out the chest from under the bed and managed to unlock it. Carelessly tossing aside his clothes, he finally grabbed the solid form of his rifle.

As he rose from his crouch, Maggie scrambled off the bed. "Faith, McCready! Give me a gun."

"There's one and it's mine," he snapped, pulling on his pants. He cracked open the rifle and shoved the cartridges in. "Get under the bed if there's shooting."

"Under the bed?" she parroted. "McCready, go to the devil. I'm no silk an' satin female."

"You're a woman. Act like one, Maggie. I've got no time to argue."

"No!" She grabbed hold of his arm before he could move. "You'll not be doin' this to me, McCready. I'm Maggie. You ain't changin' me. I'll fight beside you."

"Then get dressed, darlin', or we'll have one hell of a party."

But when Maggie spun around to get her clothes, he pulled her back for a quick hard kiss.

"For luck, Maggie mine. And there's my hunting knife in the chest."

He was stationed by the window when Maggie came to stand alongside him. "Could be Dutch," she offered, still feeling a warm glow for his trusting her with a knife. Nothing pleased her more than to have McCready accepting her just as she was. It would be a fine marriage they'd be having.

McCready peered out through the partially opened shutter. The thin crescent of the moon offered him little light to see. But he could hear that the hoofbeats were slowing as they neared. Using the barrel of the rifle, he edged a bit more of the shutter open, bracing the stock of the rifle against his shoulder.

"You'll not be takin' offense for me askin', McCready, but can you shoot the damn rifle?"

"It's a fine time to be asking me that. But I get by," he whispered back.

"That might not be good enough since there's more than one. You need to be hittin' what you're aimin' at."

"Trust me, Maggie. I haven't failed you yet." In the next breath he ordered her to be quiet. Three moving shadows were coming toward the cabin.

Maggie fell silent when she sensed his tension. But his head and shoulders blocked her view out of the window.

"Can you see?" she whispered in his ear.

"That's funny. There . . . Oh, forget it, Maggie. Put down the knife. A blind man could see that it's Dutch leading horses."

McCready was in the act of turning around to Maggie when Dutch bellowed his name.

"Get the hell out here, McCready!" Dutch roared, cursing as he dismounted and ground tied the horses.

"Never heard Dutch cuss so. He could make a bull-whacker sound like a preachin' man."

McCready was of a similar opinion, even if he would have phrased it a bit differently. "Maggie mine, I think you'd be better off staying inside until I find out what has Dutch a mite upset." He handed her the rifle with no more thought than the absent peck he gave her cheek.

"If you think Dutch's *a mite upset,* McCready, you've been away from your whiskey too long."

"Don't remind me."

Hitching his pants up, McCready went outside.

"McCready," Dutch said, advancing on him, "you're as useless as a four-card flush. I oughta haul your ashes out back and toss them over below and beyond." Poking one finger into McCready's shoulder, Dutch took a breath and lashed out. "I've followed you in dumb places and tight spots. I've fought by your side. I've protected your back, but this time you've done it. This time, McCready, I'm coming after you."

"You've got me," McCready grated, pinned as he was between Dutch and the cabin wall. "Trouble is, you're not making much sense, Dutch. I'll bet you've got Maggie biting her lip inside to hear you carry on."

"Maggie! I'll give you Maggie, you bastard!" His fists came up between them.

"Since you are one of the few people who know the truth about my mother, I won't take offense for what you said. But I'm not a boy, Dutch. Back off."

"Do it, Dutch," Maggie ordered, motioning with the rifle. "I like you, but you're not hurtin' him."

"Hurting him? Maggie, McCready's a snake that couldn't be hurt if I pounded him into the ground and threw alkali on him. You can't protect him. If you knew—" Dutch stopped. Without warning he swung at McCready.

"Dutch!" Maggie screamed, just as McCready ducked to avoid his blow. She yelled his name again, leveling the gun at his belly. "Back off. Even you couldn't be missin' from here. You got somethin' to say, say it. Tell me, if it's so bad. But don't beat on him."

"I can't." Dutch turned his back on McCready, shaking his head. "Maggie, it's time you came back."

She lowered the gun. "Can't you be tellin' me why?"

"I'm not the one that needs to talk to you."

"McCready?" Maggie looked at him, hoping that he would tell her what was going on.

"Go inside, Maggie, and give Dutch and me a few minutes."

"Sure you'll be—"

"I'm sure. Just go." McCready waited until she closed the door. "I want you to tell me what happened, Dutch. You owe me that much, if nothing else."

Maggie stood by the open window until they were out of sight. Whatever Dutch was telling McCready was bad news. She had never seen Dutch in a rage tearing into McCready. Maybe someone had robbed the Rawhider. But that didn't make sense. Dutch wouldn't be mad at McCready for something that wasn't his fault.

She couldn't stand around and wring her hands over it. Her time with McCready in this cabin was coming to an end. Every instinct she had said it was so.

A short time later McCready came back inside the cabin. "Maggie," he said without looking at her, "we're going back to Cooney Camp."

"Figured that. You'll be needin' your boots."

"Yeah. Right. My boots." He was relieved that she didn't fire questions at him. He had no answers to give her. It wasn't until he sat on the bed that he saw what Maggie had done. The quilt and blankets were rolled, the fire smothered with ashes. Pots and kettles were stacked aside, and his clothes were out of sight. He assumed she had put them back into his chest. Maggie was standing by the table, dressed in her clothes, quietly watching him. He couldn't meet her gaze.

"Will you be wantin' to take your rifle with you?"

He heard the layers of hurt and bewilderment in her voice, but he still couldn't look at her. "Yeah, Maggie. I'll need it."

"You won't be sharin' what's wrong with me?"

We'll share, everything, Maggie, equally and together. As if he had heard her repeat his words out loud, he knew she was thinking about them.

"Maggie, I just can't."

She ignored the plea in his voice. "Why won't you tell me what's wrong? I told you I ain't no silk an' satin female."

He shook his head and concentrated on pulling on his boots.

Maggie took a quick look around. She had lost so much in this cabin, not all of it bad. She had found more to tip the scale of good things. But the first time she had asked him to share with her what was wrong, he refused. What else would he hold back from her?

"I'll be waitin' outside." But even as she said it, she lingered by the door, hoping he would stop her or at least look at her. When he didn't, she felt the weight of the scale tip back to losses. Only for the life of her she didn't understand why.

CHAPTER
18

The three of them rode back slowly to Cooney Camp since the horses were winded from Dutch's hard ride. Dutch thought about McCready insisting that Dutch be the one to tell Maggie about Satin. McCready had enough of his own to sort out with her.

He spared yet another glance to where Maggie rode in the middle, worried that she was so quiet. She hadn't asked one question when she came outside and mounted up. She just sat and waited until McCready joined them. It wasn't a natural state for Maggie.

McCready wasn't any better. He hadn't even looked at

Maggie. Now that Dutch had had a chance to digest everything that McCready told him, he knew this was going way beyond a right fetching dilemma.

This went all the way to a hard blow, tempest strength.

Dutch was no coward, but he kept holding off what he had to do until a crack of light broke the far horizon. The only thing he had in his favor was that Maggie didn't have a weapon at hand. He pulled up and stepped down from his horse before they knew what he was doing.

"Maggie, I need to talk to you." Dutch waited while she walked her horse back to him.

"I'm here."

"Yeah, well maybe you'd better get down while I say it."

It wasn't Dutch's request but McCready's continued silence that left her without the strength to argue. She got down. Holding the reins, she stood by her horse.

"Maggie, you know that I like you. You know that Pete and me were friends," Dutch said, wishing he didn't have to do this.

"Just say whatever it is."

He shot a look at McCready, wondering if he heard the almost lifeless sound of her voice. But McCready gave no sign that he heard, and Dutch knew he had to get this over with.

"Maggie, there ain't no nice way of doing this. Satin—"

"Satin?" Guilt that she hadn't even asked about her dog cut through the hurt that kept her quiet. "What happened?"

"We were getting along just fine. I took good care of her, and she—"

Maggie slapped the reins against her palm.

Dutch heeded her warning. "Cora Ann let her out tonight. Nothing would have happened to her. She ran up to your cabin, but there was a man either following or waiting for her. There was a shot. I don't know if she's hurt. I couldn't find her after the howling stopped."

Maggie was already in the saddle, yanking the horse's head around.

"Maggie, wait!" Dutch called, but she was letting the horse stretch out, and McCready was right behind her.

Dutch had no choice but to follow them.

Maggie didn't hear the horses behind her. She leaned low over her horse's neck, crooning to her mustang to give her heart and get them to Satin.

Pete had given her the pup after two men tried to jump a claim they'd been working. Maggie remembered holding the squirming ball of fur who wouldn't stop licking her, and promising that nothing would happen to take the dog away from her.

But McCready had. To protect her life, he'd said. But if he cost Satin hers, she didn't know if she could forgive him.

"Where's she heading?" Dutch yelled to McCready as they raced side by side after Maggie.

"Not to camp," McCready answered, wondering the same thing himself.

Maggie let the mustang pick her pace around the base of a mesa. If Satin was hurt, she knew there was only one place the dog would go. She headed deep into the Mogollon Mountains, riding over flat stretches of land and through twisted canyons. Maggie knew she was running her horse out, but she was desperate to find Satin.

It was a thought that McCready echoed as he kept his eyes on her fleeing form. He'd lost track of where they were and suspected that Dutch was as lost, but Maggie seemed to know where they were headed as if she had made this ride many times before. She wasn't slowly picking a trail around outcrops; she was riding hard. And she by-passed canyons only to turn down the next tortured opening. A suspicion grew inside him that Maggie was heading for one of the mine claims. Guilt ate at him that Maggie trusted him, while he couldn't return the same to her.

A spread of soft glowing colors like the muted shades of a watercolor announced dawn. McCready was better able to see Maggie, still leaning low over her mustang's neck riding away from him. The sense of loss stunned him. He wanted to call out to her, but she wouldn't hear him, or if she did, Maggie wouldn't stop to hear anything he had to say now.

And when they got back to Cooney Camp, she wouldn't want to listen at all.

Maggie followed the small meandering stream deep into the canyon's belly. Concealed in a thicket of cottonwoods was her lean-to. She was off her horse before the mustang fully stopped and running toward the trees.

A whimper from the dark interior was all the reward Maggie needed for her wild ride. There was no way to hold back her tears as she knelt beside Satin. Burying her face in the dog's fur, Maggie whispered her name over and over.

McCready dismounted, no longer speculating about where Maggie had led them to. He didn't care once he heard her crying. When Dutch made a move to follow her inside, he stopped him.

"Give her time alone, Dutch."

"I feel responsible if that dog's been hurt."

"It wasn't *your* fault," McCready answered.

Dutch had the strange feeling that McCready was about to add something, but he didn't. He took the horses to water, glancing back to where McCready settled down with his back against a tree. There wasn't anything else he could do but wait as well until Maggie came out.

But Maggie wasn't thinking about either one of them. She ran her hands over Satin's fur and found where a bullet had grazed her haunch.

"It's me fault, girl, an' no others that this happened," Maggie whispered, thankful that the wound wasn't deep. Satin had done a thorough job of cleaning herself, for Maggie didn't find blood. "You're a smart girl for thinkin' to come here."

But Maggie couldn't stop blaming herself. She had felt the same way when Pete died. If she hadn't left him alone, he might be alive. If she had let McCready have the mines, no one would have shot at her, and he wouldn't have taken Satin away from her to protect her life.

"That's why he took you, girl. To protect me. But you're the one who got hurt."

Maggie rose to her feet. "Come outside, girl, an' let me wash you. Then we'll head back home an' find the bastard that did this to you."

She felt both McCready's and Dutch's intense gazes follow her down to the stream, where she knelt to take a drink and wash her face before she bathed Satin's wound.

Dutch broke under her silence before McCready did and rose to go to Maggie.

"Sorry ain't enough to say," he began. "I can see she was lucky it was only a graze. Satin will be fine. Won't you, girl?" he asked, hoping for more response from the dog than he was getting from Maggie.

Satin heeled as Maggie once again came to her feet and started back to the horses.

Dutch grabbed hold of her arm, ignoring the growl from the dog. "Maggie, please. Say something. Yell. Curse me. If I had a knife I'd hand it over for skinning, but——"

She looked up at him, her eyes cold with suppressed fury. "You got a name?"

Dutch swallowed against the rage bubbling beneath the even edge of her voice. "Bill."

Maggie shrugged off his restraining hand. "You said Cora Ann let Satin out. What's she got to do with him?"

"I'm not sure. He rode in late the other night, and she spent the time drinking with him. I know he spent the night with her and hung around the next day like he didn't want her out of his sight. I stopped her from leaving after she let Satin out."

"Where is she, Dutch?"

"Locked in her room."

Maggie walked off, only to find McCready waiting for her by the horses. She glanced at the three sets of reins in his hands and knew he wasn't going to let her ride out without talking to him.

McCready tipped back his hat. "What do you plan—"

"What I'm doin' is none of your business, McCready. Hand over me reins."

"You're not accusing me of having something to do with this."

Since he was telling her and not asking, Maggie felt her back go up. "Is that what you're sayin'? You didn't know who was after me and me dog?"

Her eyes held his, caught with the morning sun and glittering with its heat. "That is exactly what I'm telling you, Maggie. The truth."

"Once I figured you wouldn't know the truth if it was in the bottom of a whiskey glass. News for you, McCready. I'm back to wonderin' the same."

In a very calm but most deliberate motion, he reached out and gathered her shirtfront in his hand, uncaring if the dog tore into him like her growls warned. "I didn't lie to you about this. I was trying to save your life."

She didn't jerk free; she didn't even look at his hand. Her eyes held to his, trying to read the truth there, for she no longer trusted herself. If she was right, McCready was setting her up. If she was wrong, Maggie knew she was going to lose and lose big.

Trouble was, she wasn't sure she could continue trusting him. The long ride had made her yearn again for her freedom, but there was no way she could set aside the hours they had spent together. The hurt resurfaced over his refusal to tell her what had happened that brought Dutch to the cabin.

His eyes were intent on hers and very angry. Maggie reached up and uncurled his fingers from her shirt. "Do you trust me?"

"Trust you?"

"Yeah, McCready. You want mine, give over yours. Tell me why Dutch came."

McCready gazed at the still-rising sun. If he had been granted more time with Maggie, time to understand all that he was feeling for her, he would tell her what she wanted. But he hadn't been given time, and now everything was going to hell.

"You'll find out as soon as we get back. Trust me."

"That's your answer?"

"That's it, Maggie."

"This is mine. You asked me to trust you when you said that Dutch had Satin an' nothin' would happen to her. I did an' she's the one got hurt. You asked me to trust you an' said we'd share equal, like partners about me mines. I did. You asked an' I gave meself to you with nothin' held back. Now you're askin' for me trust again but refuse to tell me what's wrong." Maggie grabbed the reins from him. "Guess you'll wait to find out."

She put her foot into the stirrup and held the saddle horn, flowing smoothly up onto the saddle. She wavered when McCready put his hand on her leg.

"Maggie, for what it's worth, I *am* sorry that Satin was hurt."

"I wish I could believe you." She jerked her horse around and kept at a walk for Satin to follow alongside. But she wished McCready had told her that he was sorry he had hurt her.

When Cooney Camp came into sight, Maggie veered off to go to her cabin. McCready cut his horse in front of hers.

"Come down to the Rawhider. It's not safe for you to be alone."

"Get out of me way. I'm goin' home an' getting me gun. Then I'll come down to deal with Cora Ann."

"You go beyond mule, Maggie. You go all the way to hard rock."

"I've never denied it, McCready." Maggie deliberately began shortening the reins and making her horse rear.

McCready had no choice but to back his horse away and let her go. He turned to look at Dutch. "Your call—stay or go?"

"I'll stay."

"Take this," McCready said, tossing him the rifle. "And I'll hope you won't need to use it."

Dusk was fast closing by the time he got to the Rawhider, and he was in no mood to listen to Ira and Slick's questions when he had one of his own.

"Where is Cora Ann?"

"Upstairs," Ira answered. "Just like Dutch told us to keep her."

Slick came from behind the bar to follow McCready up the short flight of steps. But when McCready turned and he got a good look at his face, Slick backed down. "Was just coming to see if you needed help."

"The only help I need is to find the man responsible for shooting at Satin. You spread the word, Slick. You know I'll be generous in rewarding the man or men who find him."

"Ain't no call for you to be offering to pay. That's why no one's around. They're all out looking. Pete was damn good to a lot of men, McCready. Ain't one of us forget that. We'll do all we can to help Maggie without you asking."

"Yeah. Maggie's got herself an army of knights and doesn't even know it." McCready went up the stairs, but instead of going directly to Cora Ann's room, he headed for his own. Never had he craved a drink so badly as now.

He held the bottle and suddenly stopped himself from pouring the drink. He didn't need liquor; he needed Maggie. And once she met Larson Vladimir, she was going to kill him. Much as McCready wished it was the other way around that Larson would be the man killed, he wasn't going to waste time wishing for what couldn't be.

What he could do was to make sure that Maggie remained alive. Cora Ann held the key.

When he reached her room and saw that the key was missing from the lock, he cursed his own stupidity for not getting the key. It also hit him that it was too much trouble to bother.

"Stand back from the door, Cora Ann."

"McCready? Oh, thank goodness you're back. Dutch locked—"

The splintering door silenced and frightened her at the same time.

The second resounding kick that McCready gave the door sent it slamming open.

Cora Ann found herself in the corner of her room, with her hands spread on the walls as if to keep them from closing in on her. But when she read the fury in McCready's face, her heart beat, jumped, and pounded just like his boots pounded across the floor and brought him in front of her.

"I warned you when you came here looking for work that I didn't want any cheating at cards. And no damn trouble. I never took a cent that you made up here, did I? I told you to keep it all but don't bring me trouble, right? And I warned you what would happen if you brought me any, didn't I? I told you you'd answer to me."

Cora Ann squeezed her eyes closed, trying to brace herself for the blows she knew were coming.

"Stop cowering," he ordered, disgust filling him. He knew she expected him to beat her; most working girls were battered daily no matter where they plied their trade. He raked back his hair with both hands, wishing he had never given in to the miners' demands to hire any women. And it was too late now to worry about it. But he had never hit a woman, and he wasn't about to start now.

As the seconds passed by and she didn't feel his fists, Cora Ann let herself hope. She peeked up at McCready's face through her tangled length of hair but didn't find any softening of his features.

McCready's disgust deepened when she opened her eyes and gave him a terrified stare. "Stop it. We both know I won't hit you. But you're going to tell me all about Bill and what he wants with Maggie. You," he emphasized, "are going to tell me everything I want to know. And when you're finished, you're getting the hell out of here."

She believed him. But because he had showed himself to be soft, she dared make a demand of her own. "Swear to me that you'll get me away from here before he finds me."

"Who? I want his name."

"The man called Bill is William Berger. Now, will you swear to help me?"

For a moment McCready was tempted to tell her to go to hell. That he wouldn't lift a finger to help her after what she had done, not only to Satin but to him. But Cora Ann knew no other way than to bargain for every deal thrown her way.

"All right," he agreed. "I'll make sure you get out safely. Now talk."

"Yeah, you do that, Cora Ann," Maggie said. She stood in the open doorway, glancing from the rumpled bed to where McCready stood in front of Cora Ann.

"Maggie, you don't think—"

"Don't much matter what me thinks, McCready," she answered, cradling her rifle and coming into the room. Wrinkling her nose, she added, "Sure does stink up here. Don't you open a window?"

"Never mind the window," McCready admonished, pointing to the bed as the only place to sit. "Have a seat. Cora Ann was just going to begin."

Maggie chose to stand, but she listened quietly as the woman spoke.

"Berger threatened me into helping him. It doesn't matter over what, it's enough that I did."

"More," McCready stated very softly, retaining his stance in front of Cora Ann, not so much to protect her, but hoping Maggie would think twice about shooting her if he was in the way. A whimsical thought if he ever had one. Maggie's eyes were about as friendly as the bores of the rifle she carried.

"Berger is working with a man up in Santa Fe. He's the one that hired Quincy."

"Berger hired Quincy?" McCready asked.

"No. Thadius Cornwallis. William's partner. Quincy was supposed to marry Maggie and then kill her." Cora Ann peered around McCready to see how Maggie took that news, and shivered at Maggie's hostile look. "Quincy was supposed to have her make a will just like he would, so when she was dead, the mine would belong to him."

"You sing a pretty song, Cora Ann," Maggie said, coming closer. "But how do we know that you're tellin' the truth?"

"She wouldn't dare lie to me."

Maggie gave McCready a quick once-over look. "What's to stop her, McCready? You gonna stop playin' stud an' not service her?"

He rounded on Maggie. "That's enough. I said she wouldn't lie, and that's all there is to it. You're the one wasting my time and your own, Maggie. Keep quiet and let her finish."

Cora Ann's smirking smile confirmed Maggie's own fear. McCready was back to being McCready. His telling her off in front of Cora Ann stung her to the quick. Maggie had to drag out her defenses. She swore she'd never lower them again for him.

"Go on," McCready ordered.

"There's no more. Quincy was here looking for you with four men that he hired to help him. He left and a few days later Berger showed up."

"Where is he now?"

"I don't know, McCready." His slight move had her add, "I swear that. I haven't seen him since before I let the dog go."

Raking his hand through his hair, McCready turned to look at Maggie and found she was gone.

"Pack your bags. Slick and Ira can ride a ways with you." He ran after Maggie, calling her, but she had already walked out by the time he got downstairs.

"Where's Dutch?" he asked Ira.

"Left right after Maggie walked in. Said he had some business."

McCready started running for the door. "Not now, Dutch," he whispered to himself. "Not when Maggie's primed for firing."

But he was too late to stop Dutch.

CHAPTER
19

From his vantage point in the Rawhider's doorway, Mc-Cready saw Dutch leading the big blond lumberjack down the street while he yelled for Maggie to wait for him.

What McCready read in Larson Vladimir's face sent a cold fury through him. The man was shocked to see Maggie. He wasn't making any attempt to hide it. McCready wanted to rush out and tell him not to make the same mistake that he had. Maggie shouldn't be judged by her looks; she was all the woman a man could want and more.

But that was his Maggie. The one he alone knew. The Maggie who stood in the middle of the rutted street, her legs spread for balance, her rifle cradled in her arms. The wild, proud Maggie, who would take on both Dutch and the lumberjack without a thought for herself.

McCready longed to take this moment and plunge it into freezing water until he had figured out a way to keep the last shreds of trust that Maggie had for him from being ground into dust. But he had no freezing water and his sleight-of-hand was strictly confined to being able to deal what he wanted from a deck of cards.

He should be thinking about saving his own neck. But he couldn't tear his gaze away from Maggie. As if he were inside her mind, he knew she watched Dutch with all the wary instinct of a hunted animal. Her trust was shaken because of one C. V. McCready. He almost called out to her, almost turned his back to go inside, but he had never been a coward.

McCready walked out to stand beside Maggie.

Maggie didn't know where her strength came from to stand there, waiting for Dutch. She needed to be alone. Needed to sort out Quincy's betrayal and lies. But she needed to be held in McCready's arms while he held everyone at bay for a time.

"Maggie," Dutch said, "this is Larson Vladimir. He's come all the way from Washington Territory to meet you."

She kept her eyes on Dutch, having read the other man too well. He was looking at her like something that had crawled out from under a rock, and he didn't know what to do with it. She'd seen that look enough times so that it shouldn't have bothered her, but with McCready standing alongside, taking it all in, she felt unable to defend herself.

Dutch elbowed Lars's ribs. "Go on. Talk to her."

Lars felt he was choking, and it had nothing to do with the freshly starched linen collar he wore. This was Mary? She was no slender softwood sapling, easily bent to a man's way. She was hardwood locust, ready to dull the edge of a man's ax time and again from the look in her eyes.

"I ain't got all day, Dutch. Maybe he's swallowed his

tongue. Send him back where you got him. I'm goin' huntin'.''

Lars's gaze dropped to the rifle she held as if she knew how to use it. Bad business this letting a woman carry a gun.

Dutch slapped him on the back. "You've got something important to say to Maggie, so get on with it."

"*Ja.* I will do it." Taking courage in hand, Lars tried to smile. He couldn't manage one. He glanced around, looking for someone to offer them a place to talk in private. This matter was not . . . He lost his thought. Maggie turned heel and walked way. This was an insult not to be borne.

"You will wait until I say you go, Mary."

Maggie took a deep breath, then two more. She turned slowly to face Lars. "Mister, you got somethin' figured all wrong. No man tells Maggie O'Roarke what she does and when. An' if you don't want to find yourself eatin' the wrong end of this here rifle, you'll 'pologize right fast.''

"Right! I will give you what is right!" Lars tore papers from his inside jacket pocket, brandishing them as he advanced on Maggie. "You are a shameless woman. No more the wearing of men's pants. No more the carrying of a gun. No more the rough talk.''

Maggie stopped him by placing the barrel tip in his gut. "Take a deep breath and back off, or I'll use this. I don't know what you're in a lather about and don't care. Just back off.''

"Do it, Mr. Vladimir," McCready suggested. "Those of us who have come to know and love Maggie as she is, also know that she'll do what she says." He strolled to where they stood. "I would also suggest that you just tell Maggie what you're holding.''

Lars glanced at the forgotten papers in his hand. He tugged at his collar. "The paper, it tells that you are my wife."

"*Your* wife! I can't be your wife. I'm his," she hissed, jabbing the rifle at McCready.

McCready almost felt sorry for Lars when relief flooded his

eyes. His body lost some of its stiffness. But McCready knew it was time for the real fur to fly.

"You will not question my word," Lars demanded. "Dutch has read my papers. Your uncle lent me money to buy stands of timber and to build a sawmill. He asked no payment. But—"

"Seems it was a poor deal on Mohawk's part," Maggie cut in. But the words were spoken from a part of her that was still here. The rest of her was running. Running from the confusion that McCready's continued silence caused. Why wasn't he saying anything to stop this man?

McCready shoved his hands into his pants pockets to stop himself from grabbing hold of her and not letting go.

But Maggie was turning to him. "McCready?"

Her whisper cut through his turbulent emotions. He heard the silent questions she was asking him, begging for denial. And his silver tongue failed him.

"All Mohawk Pete asked in return from Mr. Vladimir was that he marry you by proxy, and if anything happened to Pete, the man was to come—"

"But you said—" Maggie stopped. Something was wrong.

"I had good reasons for what I said."

Her eyes glazed over. Maggie moved because they were all waiting for action. She gave them what little she could. Without sighting, she peppered the front of the Rawhider until her rifle came up empty. No one tried to stop her.

She saw Pamela run from the mercantile and stop when she saw them grouped in the street. But Maggie wasn't worried about Pamela. She was worried for herself. Somehow she had to walk back to her cabin. Somehow she would do it.

"Maggie, please, listen," McCready implored.

With a shake of her head she focused on him. "You know what you are, McCready?" she said very softly. "You're fool's gold. Glitterin' all fancy under dark waters, callin' out for a dreamer to come get you. But bring you up to the light, an' the shine's all gone. Ain't nothin' left to hold but worthless rock. Like you.''

He whitened with every brittle word she spoke, but anger for himself, for Pete not trusting him alone to take care of her, and anger for Maggie so easily forgetting what they shared held him silent. He was not going to defend himself.

Lars cleared his throat. ''I will call on you, Mary.''

''Don't bother,'' she snapped. ''I ain't for the likes of you. I don't care what paper you have. No man's telling me what for.''

Maggie closed her eyes, willing herself to move. She had a need so deep to crawl away and hide to lick her wounds in peace.

Pamela's scream cut through the air. ''Get down, Lars! All of you, get down!'' Wringing her hands, she backed up until the solid wall of the store stopped her. She should have warned them after she overheard her father with Quincy and Ryder. Lars could be killed! The fool dived after Maggie, but McCready was already covering her body with his as the three men rode them down. Dutch had rolled clear and was inside the Rawhider. She had never felt so helpless in her life.

''Pa, don't kill him!'' she yelled as he rode by. ''Please don't kill him.''

Maggie ate dust. From her shoulder to her hip, she had her empty rifle cutting into her. McCready's familiar weight pinned her down, and she knew that Lars had flung himself partly over them. It was too much to believe that McCready was shielding her with his body.

The ground beneath her cheek vibrated from horses at a full gallop. Maggie tried to make herself smaller, knowing what the trampling horses could do to a body. She couldn't think, couldn't move to do anything to stop them. Her belly heaved against the helplessness that gripped her.

Two warning shots kicked up dirt on either side of them. Maggie felt the tension in McCready. Questions and doubts were stripped in an instant. They were going to die. The terror of the storm came back to her. She had needed McCready that night, and he had come to her. She needed him now, needed to feel that he would care. Wiggling one hand out from under her body, Maggie managed to reach his arm. She gripped him tight, feeling the pounding of his heart against her, the slight move he made to gather more of her beneath him. His breathing was as labored as hers, but Maggie knew he had somehow understood, and she wasn't really alone.

From the doorway of the Rawhider, Dutch watched the three men pull up with their guns drawn. The horses danced in place, making it almost impossible for Dutch to get off a clean shot. He was no marksman and knew it, but he swore when Burton and Quincy dismounted, followed quickly by Ryder. With them holding their restive horses, Dutch had no chance to shoot them without risking the three on the ground. He clutched his rifle tight and eyed McCready's rifle by his side.

"Ira, you and Slick try getting around behind them. But don't open fire unless Maggie, McCready, and Lars are clear."

"We're gone," Slick answered, running for the back door with Ira.

"Get up, fancy man." Lars felt cold iron press against his neck. For his slowness to obey, the gun was jabbed in warning.

"Peeling them off each other is almost as much fun as watching that little fat man peel off his money."

"Shut up, Ryder," Quincy ordered.

Andrew Burton nervously watched as Lars came to his feet. The man was as big as Dutch, red-faced with fury, and Andrew caught himself backing away. "Don't take your eye off him," he told Ryder. Looking up and glancing around, he worried that their shots would bring the miners crawling all over them.

"Settle down, Burton," Quincy said. "This time I won't fail." But he, too, sent a quick searching glance around, dismissing Burton's daughter cowering near the store. "Hurry up, Ryder. Get Maggie so we can get out of here."

"Maggie," McCready breathed into her ear, "run when I get up."

"C'mon, McCready, you're next." Ryder hunkered down beside him to make sure that McCready felt the gun barrel he jammed against the back of his head. "Ain't the big man now, flashing your money an' giving orders."

McCready knew everything rode on Dutch, and he prayed that Dutch wouldn't fail him.

He rolled against Ryder, forcing him to lose his balance. Ryder's shot went wild. McCready's kick landed on his jaw and sent Ryder sprawling. Dutch called out and flung McCready his rifle. Andrew's shot spit dust up between McCready's feet, but McCready came up from his half-crouch, levering and firing in a blur of motion.

Maggie, ready to swing her empty rifle like a club, froze seeing McCready in action. Ryder's gun was shot out of his hand. Quincy tried to stem the flow of blood from a shoulder wound, and Andrew writhed on the ground, churning up more dust, holding his bleeding leg. Lars's solid punch flattened Quincy alongside Ryder.

The three of them—Maggie, Lars, and McCready—stood with chests heaving, ready to do battle. McCready was the first to recover and grabbed hold of Maggie, crushing her against him.

Time and place blurred for Maggie. McCready was holding her as if he would never let her go, and she was back at the cabin with him, safe and warm.

"Maggie, hold me," McCready whispered. "I need you to hold me."

She hugged him tight, but then pulled back to look at him. "You *can* shoot, McCready."

"On occasion, Maggie mine, on occasion." His blood still surged with the rush of fear he experienced for her.

"You could've been killed."

"Yes, and you, too. So stop sounding so accusing, Maggie.

What I want to know is how Andrew got involved with these two.''

"You go ask, McCready," she said, jerking herself free of his arms. "I don't want to know." Bewildered by the need to get away from everyone, Maggie looked at Lars and found herself meeting Pamela's tear-filled eyes while Lars cuddled her close.

Shouts and yells roared down the street from both ends, as miners, drawn from their search by the gunfire, ran to see what had happened. Maggie found herself pushed and shoved out of the way by the men crowding around McCready. Ira and Slick joined Dutch in slapping McCready's back, then, screaming McCready's name, the Rose came running, forcing everyone aside to get to McCready.

Maggie backed away from them, absently smiling and nodding to the miners.

"You see it? Mighty fancy shootin' for McCready! Didn't know he had it in him. Three they say—that true?''

Trying to clear her thoughts, Maggie shook her head. She felt as if she had to do something, but her blood was pumping at an alarming rate, and her heart felt as if it intended to pound its way free of her body. She stepped aside and looked down the street only to be jolted when she saw tiny Miss Mae standing on her porch with her dead husband's dueling pistols in hand. She waved one and Maggie waved her arm, signaling her it was over.

But the first voice that yelled, "String 'em up!" told her it was just beginning.

"That's Texas justice!" another man shouted.

"Hush yore fool mouth," someone else ordered. "This here's the territory of New Mexico."

"Justice is justice," came the rejoinder.

"Hold on, hold on," Slick said, shushing those closest to him. "We'll let McCready decide."

There were murmurs of agreement, but McCready ignored

them, trying to see over the heads of the men to where Maggie was.

"Can you see her?" McCready asked Dutch, then called her without waiting for an answer. The voices were louder now, demanding his decision of what to do with the three men, and McCready held up his rifle and fired the last shot in the air. He got the silence he wanted. "These three are guilty of trying to jump Maggie's claim. She'll decide what's to be done with them."

Maggie found herself facing a collective group of miners with blood on their minds. Jumping a claim rated a rope just like horse stealing. They expected her to order swift, harsh justice.

And too late, McCready realized he had made a mistake. She was ashen and he sensed that she was trembling but fighting to hide it. He shoved open a path for himself and reached her, only to have Maggie step away from him.

"Don't make me do this, McCready," she pleaded in a soft whisper that only he could hear.

Her voice was low and shaking, and he leaned close. "Maggie, stop being afraid to let these men know you're a woman with a woman's feelings. They won't respect you less." But he could see even when he finished that Maggie was afraid to reveal a softer side. He couldn't blame her. Taking her hand with his, he squeezed it gently. "Think a tar-and-feather party will satisfy everyone? I can't just let them go."

Relief flooded her, and she knew McCready felt her shiver before she pulled her hand free. She even managed a lopsided smile for a few seconds until she remembered Andrew Burton.

"Pamela's sure to be upset about her father."

"I think she's got other things on her mind right now," McCready said, turning, and knew that Maggie had to follow his gaze to where Pamela appeared to be arguing with Lars. "I think your husband has his women mixed up."

''He's not me husband. An' the next man that says so will find out I'm not a soft woman.''

McCready ignored the warning in her voice, glad to see color return to her face. Her eyes were losing that glazed look, and that was all he cared about. Well, it was for a moment. From the corner of his eye he saw a man step out from behind the miners clustered around the three wounded men. His russet hide vest, chaps, and bowed walk pointed to him being a cattleman, and when McCready heard the jingle of his spurs, he confirmed it to himself. He moved closer to Maggie just as she did to him. He didn't think either of them would forget how easily they dismissed Quincy as being harmless.

''Mighty nice shootin', fella,'' the man said, tilting his hat back and squinting at them. ''Name's Mike Grant and I call Montana home. Sorry I couldn't take a bit of the action.''

Reading no guile in the man's eyes or in his crooked smile, McCready took his offered hand. But he felt a ripple of jealousy at the way the man's eyes darted to Maggie.

Mike touched his hat brim. ''But you're the little gal I've come to find.''

Maggie bristled at the male gleam in his eye. She only had McCready to judge by, but the look was the same. ''Seems I'm gettin' to be a bigger draw than a newly staked claim.''

''An' any fool can see why, darlin'.''

''Maggie needs to go home,'' McCready cut in, every male instinct sending him an alarm about Mike Grant.

Maggie wanted the same, but she wasn't giving McCready the satisfaction of ordering her. She wasn't this Mike Grant's darlin', or his little gal, but there was an open honesty in the warmth of his dark eyes and the deeply tanned face that set off his ready smile.

''We've got business?'' she asked him.

''Sure do, honey. You see, Mohawk Pete, your uncle, is the one that staked me so's I could buy a ranch I had my eye on. I'd helped Pete out of a mite of trouble, an' he figured this was a way to repay me. Generous man, Pete was. Made sure there was enough money to stock the place. It's been five years, an' I'm doin' real well. Was right sorry to hear about his dying. Wish I could've been here to help you. But that's why I'm here now. Just learned of Pete's passing.''

"Whatever you owed Pete, forget it," Maggie said, liking the way his eyes crinkled up at the corners.

"Much as I'd like to, darlin', I can't be doing that." Mike smiled at her and winked. "The man made me an honorable proposition, and I accepted it."

"This is all very interesting, Grant, but Maggie can hear this later," McCready once again cut in. "She's had a rough time and—"

"Heard it all," Mike said, turning serious. "I'm obliged to you for taking care of her the way you did. Ain't many men that would put their life on the line for a woman."

"Maggie's not just any woman. She's damn special to me," McCready grated from between his clenched teeth, ignoring Maggie's stunned expression. This cowpoke was getting under his skin, and he no longer cared if the man knew it. McCready turned to Maggie, basking a moment in her smile, intending to take her arm and drag her away if necessary, but Mike's arm snaked between them and caught hold of Maggie's hand, pulling her to his side.

"You did real fine, mister. But I'll take over caring for her now. Maggie's got packing to do so we can get a fresh start in the morning."

"Packin'?" Maggie looked up at Mike in confusion. She peeled his hand from hers. She couldn't make sense of this. "You're mistaken. I'm not plannin' on goin' anywhere with you or anyone."

Mike's jaw angled out and he tugged his hat brim forward. "Right sorry to hear you feel that way. But, darlin', you ain't got a choice. This here paper I've got says we're married—"

"Married!" Maggie yelled.

". . . married, like I was saying, all nice and legal. My wife's gonna obey me."

"Wife!" Lars pushed his way to them. "No. You make a mistake. Mary is my wife."

"Who the hell are you?" Grant glared at the newcomer, taking his measure and figuring he wasn't all that big.

"Me," Lars announced, pointing to his chest, growing tired of having to explain. "Larson Vladimir from the territory of Washin—"

"Washington and he owns his own sawmill," Maggie finished for him. "Pete staked him to buy land and the mill. Right generous of old Pete, wasn't it?" she asked of no one but herself, not understanding her uncle's conniving. It was bad enough when McCready first had told her they were married— but two more? And she didn't even want a husband!

"*Ja.* Mary tells this true. So she is my wife."

"Can't be, fella. I got papers right here." Mike dug into his pants pocket and pulled out a crumpled piece of paper. He almost tore it in his hurry to get it open and wave it under Lars's nose. "Read that. Says here that Maggie O'Roarke was married by proxy on the seventeenth of June, eighteen-eighty."

"But that's almost four years ago," Maggie cut in, rubbing her hands over her arms. What had Pete done to her? She saw Lars frown at her and wondered what he expected her to do. Behind them, the miners were listening and buzzing with their own speculations. She looked to McCready for help, but he was staring at Mike.

"That's right, darlin'." Mike nodded. "Mohawk Pete married you to me, Michael Grant, just like what's written here, in Billings, Territory of Montana. And it's signed by Captain Earl Austin, justice of the peace."

"*Ja. Ja.* I see your paper. You look, too, at mine. My paper says that Mary O'Roarke is married to Larson Vladimir on the seventh of April in eighteen-eighty."

Voices rose and fell from the crowd, but Maggie didn't hear

them. Why wasn't McCready shutting them up? Why didn't he tell them that she couldn't be a wife to either of these men since she was already McCready's? She turned to him. "McCready, show them the date on your paper." Her demand was followed by a silent prayer that his date was older.

"His paper?" Lars and Mike chorused, facing Maggie.

She raked her hands through her short hair, trying to stop the growing feeling that something was horribly wrong. "Crazy. All of this. Crazy as Pete thinkin' he could marry me off to three men. I ain't married to you," she told Mike, grabbing his paper and tearing it in half. "An' I don't want to be married to you, any more than you want me," she informed a stunned Lars. But he wouldn't let her grab hold of his paper.

"McCready? Tell them, damn you!"

McCready was seething for what Pete had done. He could put a stop to this by telling them that Maggie was married to him, but she and they were demanding a paper he didn't have. Temper glared from Maggie's eyes, and he knew she had been pushed as far as she would allow. Another woman would be flattered to know that men wanted her without her gold mine. But not his Maggie. She wanted his proof of marriage. And he didn't have a shred of paper to show.

"Maggie, I can't. I lied to you."

"Just back off an' leave me be!" Maggie knew she was about to start screaming. A roaring filled her ears, and she saw that McCready was talking, but she couldn't hear him. Her insides felt as if they were crumpling and she helpless to stop it.

Then everyone was looking at her, making her feel caged. Shaking her head and whispering no, Maggie raised her fists.

Pamela provided unexpected rescue. She came to Maggie's side, sliding her arm around Maggie's waist, and confronting the men with tears glistening in her eyes.

"While the pack of you are tearing at Maggie, I tended three wounded men. No matter what he did, Andrew Burton is still my father. But how any of you could do this to Maggie after what she's been through shows what a bunch of stupid men you are. Shame on the lot of you. Women need comforting, not badgering by a passel of men. I'm taking Maggie home to her cabin, and if one of you dares come near us, *I'll* be the one doing the shooting!''

She caught their attention. Everyone knew that Pamela couldn't hit a bucket unless she stuck the gun inside, but no one wanted to find out. There wasn't one protest to be heard, least of all from Maggie.

''Belly up to the bar, boys,'' Dutch offered and waited until the men turned away. He touched McCready's shoulder. ''You, too. She's not going to want to see you at all.''

CHAPTER
20

McCready started to walk back with Dutch, trying to block from his mind seeing the same terror in Maggie's eyes that she had the night of the storm. His hands clenched with the need to hold her, but he knew Dutch was right. She wanted to be left alone. Maggie was back to not needing anyone. Certainly not him. He had lost the soft woman he had found in his isolated cabin. And the loss right now was more than he could stand.

The sight of the three wounded men lying inside the doorway stopped him. "Berger," McCready whispered, having forgotten about the other threat to Maggie. "Ira, get up to

Maggie's cabin and keep watch. There's still one more we
need to catch.''

Ira slugged down the drink he had just poured and, grum-
bling, left them.

Once Satin accepted her presence, Pamela bullied Maggie
into using the warm water she heated to wash, then ordered her
into a clean shirt and bed.

There was little in the way of food supplies, but she didn't
want to eat, and Maggie refused the moment she mentioned it.
Pamela brought Maggie a cup of whiskey-laced coffee and sat
on the edge of her bed to sip at her own cup.

Maggie thought Pamela looked as lost as she felt. No matter
how bad her own untenable situation was, Pamela had to face
the fact of what her father had done.

''You called out a warnin' to us, Pamela. When did you find
out about your father?''

''I thought you'd be snapping and snarling like a scalded
dog, Maggie.''

''Well, I've had the snap and snarl shook out of me.''

Pamela busied herself rimming the edge of the cup, unable
to look at Maggie. ''I'm so ashamed of my father. I never knew
he was involved with those men. The night before, Ryder came
looking for him, but Pa was still in Clairmont. And . . .
and . . . Oh, Maggie, I don't know how to tell you what I've
done.''

For once Maggie was not annoyed with Pamela's sniffling.
She wished she could do a little of it herself. But she had shut
down all thoughts about McCready and his betrayal. She
closed her eyes for a moment, fighting to regain the wall she
had painstakingly erected.

Pamela sipped the hot coffee, hoping she would have the
courage to tell Maggie the truth. But when she glanced up,
Maggie had her eyes closed and she looked away.

''Maggie,'' she began softly, ''have you ever in your life

done something that you knew was wrong, but you did it anyway?''

Wanting to be with McCready in spite of his lies was damn wrong to Maggie, but she couldn't deny that right now it was what she wanted. Pamela's expectant look forced her to answer.

"Yeah, I guess I have."

"Oh, Maggie, you don't know how much easier you've made this for me." Almost shyly, Pamela reached for Maggie's hand and held it. "I never really felt close to you, but I always liked you, Maggie. That's what makes telling you this so hard."

"Maybe if you just get on with it, it won't be so bad."

"It . . ." Pamela released Maggie's hand and wrapped both of hers around the cup. "It's Lars," she finally whispered.

Maggie recalled the instant when McCready's gaze had led her to see Pamela cradled against Lars. "You're not the kind of woman to carry on over a stranger, Pamela. Did you know him?"

"Know him?" She couldn't help her guilty start. Maggie couldn't know the truth. And a look confirmed that. "I . . . I met him right after Ryder came looking for my father. Poor Lars," she said, shaking her head. "I held a gun on him, but I was shaking so badly I think he knew it. But he didn't make a move; just reassured me that he meant no harm. I was so relieved that I invited him to stay for coffee."

Biting her lip, Pamela sought encouragement from Maggie for her to continue. She had to make do with Maggie's nod.

"Pa usually comes back the same night, but this time he didn't. Lars stayed to have supper with me."

Maggie read the growing shrillness of her voice as a sign that Pamela was upset and afraid to tell her the rest. "Havin' him to supper wasn't so bad."

"But there's more," she whispered, bending to set her cup on the floor. Clasping her hands together in her lap, Pamela stared at the wall. "I did more than have supper with him, Maggie. I seduced him into my bed."

Seeing her head bow, Maggie had the feeling Pamela was waiting for the kind of condemnation a preacher was best at giving. She had never shared talk with another woman, not like this, and didn't quite know what to say. She certainly couldn't blame Pamela for doing the same thing she herself had done. And Maggie knew she didn't want to open the door and think about what happened with McCready. It hurt too much.

She really felt uncomfortable saying anything, but when Pamela once more turned to her, her gaze pleading, she had to say something.

"My pa always told me that if doin' somethin' made you happy an' didn't hurt no one—"

"But it did hurt, Maggie." Pamela clasped her hand over her mouth.

"Then why did you do it?"

Slowly Pamela lowered her hand. "The kissing part's all right. And men seem to want to. It really wasn't so bad the second time."

Maggie's hand shook, and she handed Pamela the cup so as not to spill the coffee. Those few words triggered memories of McCready. The hungry kisses they had shared, the taking and the giving that went on and on, without pain, until Dutch had come and McCready had refused to talk to her.

"Maggie, have you ever wanted a baby? I mean, you do think about getting married someday and having children, don't you?"

"No, can't say as I have."

"Well, I did. And now with Lars married to you, and after what we did, I might be having a baby without being married."

"A baby?" Maggie couldn't look at Pamela's tear-filled eyes. She had never thought about babies. McCready didn't, either. And now . . . She couldn't help but look down at herself. She could be carrying McCready's child and not even know it.

"Now, you know why I had to talk to you, Maggie. You've got to give up Lars. He's got to marry me."

"Yeah, Pamela, he's got to marry you." But she wasn't prepared for Pamela flinging herself against her for a quick hard hug. "Oh, Maggie, I just knew once I explained that, you would understand. With goodness knows what's going to happen to my father, I'll be alone. I've never been so scared in my life."

Maggie untangled herself from Pamela and slipped off the bed. She had to think. With Lars and Mike both claiming her as a wife, she couldn't tell McCready he had to marry her. She wouldn't do it anyway. The man had lied to her. Her trust had been betrayed.

Pacing, ignoring the other woman, Maggie knew she should figure out a way for revenge, but she hurt so much.

Watching her wrap her arms around her waist, Pamela began to realize that Maggie had troubles of her own. "What's wrong, Maggie? Can't you share with me? I know I'm not as strong as you, but sometimes just talking will help."

There was warmth and sympathy in Pam's eyes, and it reached down into the raw place inside Maggie. And she found herself saying, "You're not the only one that got fooled by a man and needs to think about babies."

"You?"

"Yeah. Me."

"It was McCready, of course," Pamela stated, instantly setting aside her problem for Maggie. "What are you planning to do? I know you'd like to skin him alive, but Maggie, that wouldn't make sense now."

"Nothin' much makes any sense. Look at what Pete did to me. Marryin' me off to two men. An' you're welcome to Lars. The man doesn't want me. I saw that right off." Pamela's hurt expression had her adding, "Not that he isn't a fine-lookin' man, but I'm all wrong for the likes of him. He needs someone like you. Someone soft and pretty who'll know how to do for him.''

''Well, what about the rancher? He seemed mighty taken with you just as you are, Maggie.''

''What do I know about ranchin'? The only way I like beef is on me plate. An' I don't want to be married to a man who calls me darlin'.''

She turned her back toward Pamela, thinking of McCready's voice whispering *Maggie mine* just before they joined together. Or the teasing way he called her . . . No, she wasn't going to drag up any more. She was only hurting herself.

''And McCready? How do you feel about him?'' Pamela asked in a timid voice.

Maggie wished she knew. She wished she could summon up anger at him. She wished she could rid herself of the ache that was growing inside her. Why did he lie to her? Pressing her fingers against her forehead, she rubbed hard. Did he want the mines so badly that he would pretend to care for her? Did he have to trick her? *There was more than that, and you know it*, a voice whispered.

''Maggie, did you hear that?'' Pamela ran to douse the lantern. ''There's someone outside.''

Satin was whining at the door, scraping it with her paw.

''Stay, girl. I'll not have you outside to get shot at again.'' The darkness was no hindrance to Maggie. She found the shelf that held her cartridges, took her rifle, and went to the table to load it. *Just goes to show how much McCready hurt me*. She hadn't even loaded her rifle when she came home.

''You're not planning to go out there,'' Pamela whispered at her back, startling Maggie. ''For one thing, you're not dressed. For another, you don't know how many are out there. It's all my fault. I never should've told everyone to stay away.''

In a surprising gesture for Maggie, she reached out and

patted Pamela's hand. "That's who it might be. Someone comin' to see if we're all right."

"Maggie, please be careful. I heard my father talking with those men. They were set on making you tell where that claim is. And they talked about someone else . . . a . . ."

"Berger," Maggie supplied. "We got his name from Cora Ann. Don't worry. I'm always careful."

Not so. You didn't do so well protectin' yourself against McCready.

That was the past.

Maggie swore it would be when she lifted the bar to the door. She had to order Satin to stay again, for the dog was nosing her aside, trying to get out.

McCready left the tar and feathering to the miners. They were none too pleased not to be having a necktie party, but when he told them that was what Maggie wanted, no one argued. None of the three wounds were serious; still, Mc-Cready warned Slick to make sure the tar and feathers were kept away from the bandages. He had even supplied Cora Ann's feather tick and watched Burton, Quincy, and Ryder taken outside with a flood of relief. By the time the miners got done with them, those three men wouldn't be able to show themselves in the territory, for nothing spread faster than miners' gossip.

Dutch brought the last of the glasses he had washed back to the bar. McCready looked up but didn't say anything and went back to nursing his drink. He stood alone at the bar, but behind him, at the far table, Mike Grant sat with Lars Vladimir discussing their wife-in-common, Maggie. The Rose sat at the piano, picking out notes and softly humming.

Pouring the last of the liquor from the bottle into his glass, McCready motioned for Dutch to bring him another.

"Don't you think you've had enough?"

"Just bring me another bottle, and I'll let you know when that happens, Dutch."

The whoops and hollers coming from outside had Dutch shaking his head. "Sounds like they're having themselves a party out there."

"Slick'll make sure it doesn't get out of hand. You can't be feeling sorry for those three after what they tried to do."

"Not me, boss. But you, you're another matter."

"Nothing's the matter with me."

"Hey, McCready," Mike called out. "Come sit with us. We need you to settle something."

"Not now," McCready whispered.

But Dutch heard him. "What are you going to do about those two? Maggie don't want either of them. Can't figure Pete doing such a thing to her. When you told me that day that you lied and told Maggie she was married by proxy to you, I thought it sounded—"

"You landed a fist or two in lieu of voicing an opinion, Dutch." McCready rubbed his jaw. "My lie wasn't as far-fetched as you seemed to think at the time. I just never thought Pete would have done that to her. Neither marriage is legal. And I—"

"McCready," Mike called again. "You want we should join you?"

"No. I'm coming." McCready took his glass and the fresh bottle with him. If he drank enough, he would forget the look in Maggie's eyes. If the burning in his gut didn't force him to quit sloshing liquor down first.

"Boss?"

"Yeah."

"You come down with something? Long before now you should've been quoting from that fancy education of yours."

"Never fear. I've been repeating one to myself. 'Alas, poor woodcock, dost thou go a birding? Thou hast even set a spring to catch thy own neck.'" McCready offered Dutch a grin.

"That from the play you like so much?"

"Shakespeare's *Hamlet?*" McCready shook his head. "Not so. John Dryden's *Wild Gallant.*"

Shaking his head, Dutch muttered, "You sure do savor those fancy words. Figure you got caught in your own trap?"

"I've got another one for you," McCready said, waving the bottle. "When the Spartan commander, Lysander, was told that he could not wage war by deceit, he replied, 'Where the lion's skin will not reach, it must be patched with the fox's.' And that's what I need to do. Patch things up."

"You think you can do that with Maggie?"

"What I think is, if I don't go over and have a few drinks with her two husbands, I'm gonna have a fight on my hands." He glanced from the glass to the bottle he held. "Can't. Got my hands full."

"What you've got is a belly full and don't know it," Dutch muttered to himself. He left the bar and went to the back door, satisfied that the job was almost done. By the torchlight he saw the three men were covered with pitch, and the last of the feathers were being tossed on them. Someone had used the tick's covering and made cloth signs to hang around their necks, announcing these were "Cooney Camp Claim Jumpers." "Nice," he called out to Slick, who was already seated on the wagon that would haul the men out of there.

"Figure I'll take them up to Clairmont first. Boys up there ain't had a good laugh."

"Whose wagon, Slick?" Dutch asked.

"Burton's. Fitting, too."

Dutch shook his head over that. Andrew Burton was a man he liked. Just went to show how one man could fool another. He turned and went back to the bar.

"They almost finished, Dutch?" McCready called out from where he sat with Mike and Lars.

"Just about. Slick's going up to Clairmont first."

"One problem down and the biggest one to go," McCready muttered, solemnly contemplating his fresh drink.

"I've been trying to tell you, McCready," Mike said, hunching himself over his glass. "We figured out between us what to do with Maggie." He was a mite disappointed to see that McCready's eyes didn't hold a flicker of interest, but he told him what they decided anyway.

"See, Lars here admitted that she's too rough and independent for a woman. A mite too tall. Now, me," he said, "I don't mind in the least. I need a woman that can take care of herself. She's a mite feisty, that's true, but she'll come to learn who's boss in our outfit."

McCready lifted his glass to his lips and didn't stop until he set it down empty. He smiled at Mike and poured out another drink for himself. *The man thought Maggie was going to learn to call him boss? She'd hold an Irish wake like she did for Pete before she let that happen.* And he knew he would be lifting the first glass.

"I believe you have disabused me of the myth that men living in the territories cannot settle their differences without resorting to violence. No fists, knives, or guns. A toast, gentlemen, to the gentlemen's way of fighting over the same bone. Good liquor, clear terms, and proper payment."

McCready didn't wait to see if they would join him; he slugged his drink down. The liquor wasn't gently blurring the edges tonight. His mind was sharp and clear, so he poured another one.

"So tell me, Lars," he intoned softly, meeting the man's steady gaze, "how much did Grant pay you to back off?"

"Five hundred dollars he offered."

McCready slouched back against the chair. "Only five hundred? Bad deal. Maggie's worth more." And to Grant he said, "She's young, strong, and has all her teeth. She can hit anything she aims at, does her own hunting, and really, when you come down to it, doesn't need anyone." The bitterness of his own words forced the glass to his lips once more, and he drained the few drops.

"Didn't ask you to come over here to stir up trouble, McCready. We have this settled between us. The only thing Lars and me want from you, since you seem to know Maggie, is to go tell her what we decided. I want to get started for home in the morning."

Jealousy floated like a cork on the sloshing waves of liquor in McCready's stomach. He reached for the bottle, eyeing its half-full contents, promising himself that he would drown the cork before the night was over no matter how much whiskey it took. But as he poured slowly, he saw Maggie's hair lit by firelight in the amber depths. Maggie, dancing on the table, telling him of the wee ones. Maggie, answering his demand that she give him her mouth with a dare of her own to take it. Maggie, giving and giving, filling the empty places.

He set the bottle down with a controlled motion and very carefully raised his glass. "I've heard that messengers get shot."

"That little gal ain't gonna shoot you."

"You, my friend," McCready announced in a slow drawl, "do not know Maggie."

"Seems you've made it your business to tell me some bad and good points. The rest I'll be pleasuring myself to find out."

Pleasuring himself? With his Maggie? McCready came out of his slouch and set his glass on the table beside the bottle. He turned in his chair just far enough to reach out and grab hold of Grant's shirtfront, pulling the other man's face close.

"You, cowpoke, aren't talking about buying a cow. Maggie, *my Maggie,* hasn't any 'points.' She's a flesh-and-blood woman who you'll treat with respect or answer to me."

Mike Grant had faced his share of mean. But McCready's eyes promised more than a good fight. There was death in his look. Since he was the stranger here, not McCready, Grant jerked free and slowly nodded. "I hear you."

Lars had sat quietly and watched the two men, but he had his own worries that needed his attention, and he wanted this settled.

"Now, you will go to her and say this is the man she is married to, *ja?* You are to blame that she is so angry."

"Lars's right. Just stop this hemmy-hawing and give us your answer, McCready. You gonna go tell her?"

If Maggie hadn't been barefoot, she would've never known that it was a body she stumbled over on the second wider circle she made around her cabin. By touch she knew it was a small man, still breathing but out cold judging by the lump behind his head.

"Pamela, get the lantern. Someone's hurt." Maggie spared a quick look down below, where the bonfire raged high behind the Rawhider. She could hear shouts coming from the milling figures.

Satin nearly made her fall when the dog rushed to her, licking her face and whining. Maggie pushed her down and ordered her to stay, but Satin sniffed and whined her way around the body. Before Pamela came with the lantern, Maggie knew the body was someone that Satin knew and no threat to them.

Holding the lantern high, and lifting her skirt to pick her way over the rocks, Pamela finally reached Maggie. "Why, it's Ira. I fixed that shirt for him a few weeks ago."

"Wonder what he's doin' up here?" Maggie turned him over, trying to be careful. "Whatever brought him up here, someone hit him. That knot he's got ain't from no fall. Ira's got feet like a mountain goat."

Nervous, Pamela looked around, swinging the lantern to throw light on the night's blanket. "What if that someone is still here, Maggie?"

"No. Satin would be growlin'. You'll have to go down an' get Dutch."

"Don't ask me to do that, Maggie. Please, I'm afraid."

"You can't keep bein' scared of your own shadow, Pamela. I ain't dressed an' Ira needs tendin'. You figure you can stay with him while I go down?"

"I don't want to be left alone, Maggie."

With a new understanding Maggie didn't poke fun at her. She owed Pamela for helping her, and, having her own fear about storms a secret she shared with McCready, Maggie knew she would work out another way. Satin lay beside her with her head resting on her front paws, and Maggie absently patted her before coming to her feet.

"This is what we do. You stay right here while I get me boots and pants. I'll send Satin to get Dutch."

At the mention of her name, the dog came to stand beside Maggie.

"Good girl. Now, go fetch Dutch for me." But the dog whined, then barked. "Go on. You obey me." Maggie gave her a little push, but Satin came right back. "What's wrong, girl? I need you to get Dutch. We have to get help for Ira. You like Ira, don't you?" Maggie took her barks as a good sign. She was finally getting through, but when she ordered the dog off again, Satin refused to go.

"Maggie, maybe she doesn't want to leave you after being away from you."

"No. There's somethin' else. But I'll be hornswoggled if I can figure what."

Pamela suddenly grabbed hold of Maggie's arm. "Look over at the ridge. Someone's walking across, carrying a lantern." She swung her lantern back and forth, trying to attract attention. For a few moments it appeared that they had been seen, for the other lantern hung motionless, but soon it was moving away.

"Stop wastin' time," Maggie ordered. "Satin, go get Dutch. I need him, girl. Go now. Go on," she added when the dog trotted off and turned. "Do it." Maggie swore when Satin's eyes gleamed in the light before she finally turned and ran. The dog actually seemed to be pleading with her not to send her away. Maggie shrugged it off. She was, without a doubt, losing her mind.

"Hang on to this," she said to Pamela, handing over her rifle. "It's loaded, so be careful. I'll be right back."

Maggie left the cabin door open, knowing that it would make Pamela feel safer. She pulled on her old pants and stuffed her shirt inside. Just as she sat to pull on her boots, a bloodcurdling scream from Pamela had her running to the door.

"What's wrong, Pamela?"

"There's a fire!"

Maggie almost snorted and went back inside. "Yeah," she called out. "I saw the bonfire they built behind the Rawhider."

"No! It's on the ridge across from us. Where we saw the lantern. Maggie, the tents are burning!" It took a few minutes for Pamela to realize that Maggie didn't answer her. She turned and saw the cabin door closed. "Maggie! Maggie!" Pamela ran back and tried to open the door, then pounded on it when she found it barred. "Answer me!" All she got was silence. Pamela screamed for help.

CHAPTER
21

Satin burst through the open door of the Rawhider and barked to get Dutch's attention. He hushed her, engrossed with waiting to hear McCready's decision about going to tell Maggie, as Lars and Mike wanted him to.

When she snarled and grabbed hold of his pant leg, he had to give her what she wanted.

But McCready was already running across the room. "What's Satan doing here?"

"Don't know, boss. And her name's Satin. Can't you remember?"

"Never mind. Maggie wouldn't let that dog out of her sight

after what happened. Something's wrong.'' McCready acted without thought. He dropped to his knees and reached out to grab hold of the dog's neck. "Easy, girl, I won't hurt you. Maggie sent you, didn't she? Nothing else makes sense. But Ira's up there with them, isn't he?'' His look caught Dutch's curt nod. Satin issued a low, steady warning growl, and McCready let her go.

"I hear you say that dog belongs to Maggie?'' Mike asked from behind McCready.

"That's right. Maggie's best friend. Where Maggie goes, so does Satan. Just like Ruth in the Bible.''

"Satan! Ain't a fitting name to be mentioning in the same breath with the Bible, but she's a fierce-looking critter.''

"This, gentlemen, is one of the devil's own, just like me. Right, girl?'' he asked, leaning toward the dog and holding out his hand. "You're going to take us to Maggie.'' He rose and took the rifle from Dutch. "Care to come along?'' he asked the other two men.

The faraway shots and faint screams stopped their talk. McCready and Dutch shared a look and spoke at the same time. "Berger!''

"Who is this Berger?'' Lars asked but found himself running to keep up with the others.

"A dead man!'' McCready shouted back.

"Up there, on the ridge!'' Slick yelled.

For a moment the sight of fire arrested McCready and every man that turned to look. But McCready was already gazing up to where Maggie's cabin was, relief flooding him when he didn't see flames leaping high. On the other ridge fire was spreading to the tents and shacks that belonged to the miners.

The miners moved like an angry horde around to the street where McCready and the others stood.

"Slick, bring that wagon. Dutch, break open those new barrels of whiskey and pour it out. We'll fill them with water from the creek.''

''You're ordering me to spill out good whiskey, boss?''

''You heard me. Take whoever you need to help you. Maybe we can save something.''

No one was more surprised than McCready to find Satin trotting at his heels when he broke into a run. There were enough men to form a bucket brigade up the ridge before the fire spread to the street. But Maggie and Pamela were alone, and Berger was still out there somewhere.

McCready ran, cursing the liquor he drank that slowed him down. Ira could have fired a few warning shots when he saw the fire. But a woman had been screaming. Warning them of the fire or someone more dangerous? The question was one McCready asked himself as he reached the bridge. He couldn't see any light coming from Maggie's cabin.

Satin streaked by him, running flat out, and he had no choice but to follow her. Every breath he drew was filled with the smoke drifting across to him. The only thing he could be thankful for was that there was no wind tonight. He heard shouts and yells as orders went back and forth from the men below as they filled whatever they could find with water.

But all he could think about was Maggie. That was why Pamela's headlong flight down the rocky path caught him unawares and sent them both sprawling in a tangle of arms and legs.

It took McCready a few minutes to recover, and when he did, he had to shake Pamela to stop her crying and get her to make sense of her babbling.

''Where is Maggie?'' he demanded.

''Up t-there. Ira's hurt. We found him. Someone hit him and he has a lump and Maggie wasn't dressed and I didn't want to be alone.''

''Slow down, Pamela. I can't make heads or tails of what you're saying.'' He helped her to stand and had to peel her clawlike grip from his arm. ''Now, tell me where Maggie is?''

''The cabin. S-she was getting dressed. I didn't want to be

alone outside with Ira, but she gave me her rifle. I saw the fire and started screaming. Maggie heard me. She came to the door but went back inside by the time I told her where the fire was. When she didn't come out, I turned and the door was closed.''

"So, she wanted some privacy to get dressed. It's no reason to try breaking your neck by running—"

"You don't understand! McCready, the door is barred. I called her, and when she didn't answer me, I tried to open the door.''

"Listen to me.'' He gripped her arms, shaking her. "Did you hear Maggie inside?''

"N-no. That's why I'm running for help. Maggie didn't answer me when I screamed, not even when I fired off her rifle.''

Her panicked words tore through him just as Satin's barking reached a new pitch. McCready released her and raked his hand through his hair. "I want you to go down, but don't let anyone come up here, Pamela.''

"But if someone has Maggie—"

"That's just it. I think it's one man, but I'm not sure. And no one knows what would happen to Maggie if he's cornered. I'll figure out a way, but you go on.'' He gave her a light push, already turning to run.

"Be careful, McCready,'' she whispered after him.

Within minutes McCready was kneeling by Ira's side, as the man moaned himself awake. He helped the miner to sit up, firing questions in a whisper at him. "Did you see anyone? Hear anything before you were hit?''

"Not a blasted thing. Can't you hush up that dog? She's making enough noise to make my bones rattle.''

"Just be thankful that she's ignoring us. That is one devil I don't want to tangle with, Ira. Can you stand now?''

"I'll give it a try. Maggie and Pamela all right?''

McCready shook his head, then realized that Ira couldn't see him. Coming behind the old miner, McCready helped him to his feet, steadying him with his own body when the man rocked to and fro. "Sure you'll be all right?"

"McCready, I'm tougher than I look, and you didn't answer me. Them women all right?"

"Pamela's down below. I told her not to let anyone come up here."

"And Maggie? Where's she?"

"Inside, Ira."

"Gawd damn!" Talking and trying to turn around cost him his strength, and he had to grip McCready's arm not to fall. "Guess I ain't as tough as I figured, huh?"

Lifting Ira's arm around his shoulders, McCready moved him away from the cabin. Lowering him to rest against a small rock outcrop, he planted his hands on his hips and looked down at Ira.

"You stay put out of harm's way. Pamela didn't see anyone, but it could be more than one man."

"That fella Berger?"

"That's what I think. How desperate he is, I don't know. All I want to do is get Maggie out and safe."

"Helped Pete build that cabin. Solid. If the door's barred and the windows shuttered, ain't no way you're going inside lessen they let you in."

"Nothing like a few impossible odds to make a challenge worthwhile."

"That's the spirit, son. How'd that get started across the ridge?" Ira asked, pointing to the fire.

"I didn't stay to find out."

"Someone tried fooling us by yelling fire. It almost worked. Could be the same man trying to draw us all away."

McCready nodded, but he was studying the dark outline of Maggie's cabin. Ira claimed there was no way in unless somebody opened the door, and that wasn't likely to happen. He tried to coax the dog away, but she ignored every one of his whispered promises along with the commands he tried.

Smoke drifted toward them in thickening clouds, and tiny figures were visible moving about as the men fought the fire. McCready kept glancing from the fire to the cabin and suddenly had an idea.

"Wish me luck, old-timer."

"McCready, what're you gonna do?" But Ira saw that he had already gone around back of the cabin and couldn't hear him. He rubbed the lump on the back of his head, then tried to call the dog away. But he had as little success as McCready.

Inside the cabin William Berger was having very little success in forcing Maggie to draw him a map to her gold claim. He couldn't kill her, but he thought his threats sounded as if he were desperate enough to do it. The woman was proving to be extremely stubborn.

"Gold isn't worth losing your life over," Berger told her once more. "Draw the map and I'll leave."

Maggie eyed the gun he held. There wasn't a quiver to be seen in his hand. She knew he had to be the one that started the fire to draw everyone's attention. And he had managed to catch her unaware with one boot on. She had been too far to grab her handgun and had no idea where her knife was. She hadn't seen it since the morning McCready had come with his breakfast peace offering. The badgering continued for her to draw him a map to the claim, and she tried to close out his voice, not understanding why she didn't do what he wanted.

"Can't you shut that dog up?"

"She won't stop lessen I let her inside."

"No. You aren't going to try to get me to open that door. This is the last time I'm going to say this. You either draw me that map, or I'll start shooting. It won't be pretty. You can still use one hand after the other holds a bullet and you could still walk with one leg if you force me to keep on."

Maggie clutched her hands together. It wasn't the threat of what he would do, but the edge in his voice that told her she was pushing him. It had been a long while since she had heard

Pamela at the door and didn't know if she was still outside with Ira or had run down for help.

The man, Berger, had the same habit as McCready of raking his hand through his hair, but McCready's hair was thick and Berger's thin enough to reflect the light off his scalp every time he touched it. She kept hoping that he would get careless and turn his back toward her, for he was short and slightly built. She might be able to land a few solid punches and get the gun away from him. But never once in the minutes that seemed to stretch and stretch had he given her an opportunity.

"A pickle," she whispered to herself.

"What? What was that? Did I hear you say you'll do it?"

Maggie looked at his eyes and didn't like what she was seeing. They had a desperate look. Satin ceased her barking and began scratching and whining at the door, so it was real easy to hear Berger click the gun hammer back.

"No. Don't start shooting. I'll make you a map." Fear for her dog made Maggie agree. But it was hard for her to swallow his gloating smile. "Trouble is, I don't have what's needed. Ain't got a pen or paper."

Berger eyed her carefully to see if she was trying to trick him. But he saw for himself the meanness of the cabin, and pen and paper would not number among this woman's possessions.

Backing away from her, never once taking his eyes from her, he reached the back wall and snatched down a shirt. Throwing it to her, he ordered, "Tear off the back and use that."

Maggie caught her shirt, crushing the cloth in her hands. This was the shirt she had worn that morning McCready came. The shirt she had worn when he taught her to play. The same shirt that she had so willingly taken off wanting him so badly. And where was McCready when she needed him this time? Likely getting himself drunk with relief being rid of her.

The cloth tore before she realized she was doing it. Pushing aside the clutter on the table, Maggie smoothed out the material. "That gives me somethin' to draw on, but me finger ain't gonna do you no good."

"Don't sass me. There's got to be something here you can use."

Maggie eyed the stove. Berger had set the fire across the ridge, of that she was sure. The smoke was beginning to drift in through the cracks in the chinking between the logs. It wasn't enough for him to notice, but Maggie smelled the smoke. Fire was everyone's biggest fear.

She pushed back her chair.

"Where do you think you're going?"

"You said I had to find somethin' to use to draw you the map. I just figured I could take a stick from the fire if they ain't all burned. If not, I'll just stick a piece of the kindlin' in." His glare told of his mistrust, and Maggie took a little of Pamela's meek manner and lowered her head. "That all right with you?"

"Just get on with it and remember that I'm watching every move you make."

"I'll remember," she muttered, kneeling down in front of the small wood stove. With the poker in her hand, she opened the door and knew she would find some glowing coals. The poker was a weapon, but with him standing on the other side, she wouldn't have a chance of hitting him before he fired a shot. She set the poker down and took up a split piece of wood. Carefully she held it against the coals until it began smoking. Soot began to filter down, and Maggie fought the urge to look up.

She turned her head and began loudly hushing the dog, hoping to distract Berger from what she was noticing.

Another clump of soot fell, and she saw the stovepipe shake. The temptation to look up, even as she strained to hear if someone was up on the roof, grew to be almost impossible for her.

She wanted to believe that someone was up there. Pamela

would have gone for help. But she had to get away from the stove before Berger noticed what was happening. Time was all she could buy for herself and whoever had come to her rescue. Once again she didn't feel so strong or certain that she could take care of herself and whatever came her way. First, McCready had shown her and now Berger.

The intense heat of the stove forced her to move. She closed the door and rose, moving slowly to the table, all the while keeping up steady loud commands for Satin to stop her whining.

Seated again, Maggie started at the lower end of the cloth to draw the map. She had no intention of showing Berger where the gold claim was, but she didn't know how much he knew. Her map had to have real landmarks. What she hadn't counted on was Berger coming to stand behind her.

"No tricks." He placed the gun to the back of her head and finally had the satisfaction of rattling her. The line she was drawing revealed the tremble in her hand.

"There's no marking for north or south. I warned you not to try—"

"I can't be markin' what you want. I can't write."

His exasperated explosion of breath told Maggie how close he was to her. She thought about poking his face with the wood, but there again she could end up shot.

"I might of known that you would be ignorant."

Once more Maggie eyed the stovepipe. She could see the soot filtering down. And the smell of smoke was getting stronger. Pointing to the line she had just drawn, she said, "This is the road leadin' out of Cooney Camp. Sun's at me back in the mornin'."

Berger shifted to her side, moving the gun and taking the wood from her hand to mark an *S* at the bottom of the cloth.

Maggie leaned away to give him room, trying to squirm off the chair. The ripping sound of the stovepipe being wrenched free from its place in the stove made Berger spin around, firing a wild shot.

Up on the roof McCready felt as if his heart stopped when he heard the shot. The heat of the pipe had blistered his hands even with his shirt wrapped around it. He managed to pull it free and threw it over the side. Smoke billowed up in his face when he tried to peer down and see if Maggie was hurt.

He could hear them coughing and worked his way to the edge of the roof. He crouched there and waited for them to be forced outside. His ploy had to work.

But fear for Maggie's safety had wormed its way inside him, and he found that he was sweating and shaking while he offered prayers and promises once again to a deity he had to believe in.

Berger knew he was cornered. He dragged Maggie from her chair, knowing that the smoke overcoming her as well as himself was the only reason she moved at all. She didn't have enough hair for him to use for leverage, so he grabbed her shirt and twisted it in one hand, holding the gun against her neck with the other.

"Get that bar off the door," he ordered, rapidly blinking his eyes against the sting of the smoke.

Maggie did as he ordered, offering no resistance. She would have to wait until they were outside. He held her shirt so tight that the material was choking her, but she threw off the bar and opened the door.

Teeth bared, Satin checked her lunge. Maggie couldn't utter more than a weak order for the dog to stay. The air tantalized her to breathe deeply, but Berger's grip didn't slacken.

She could see the dark shadows of men working to douse the fire across the ridge. There was no sign of Ira's body or Pamela.

"Don't move yet," Berger ordered, making his own sweeping search of the immediate area in front of the cabin. He, too, noticed the absence of the miner he had struck from behind, as well as the other woman. He had to assume she went for help, but he had no idea of how many men might be waiting beyond the circle of light spreading out from the cabin behind him.

Maggie O'Roarke was his only way out. Since she didn't get to finish the map, he had to keep her alive. With a sudden move he let go of her shirt but grabbed her wrist and twisted her arm up behind her back.

"Now we walk out," he managed before a fit of coughing overtook him. "Carefully." Once more he had to stop. The smoke was so thick that he couldn't breathe and knew he had to make his move.

Pressing the gun against her neck, he urged her forward.

Maggie knew that Satin backed away because she sensed the danger to her mistress. But the growling didn't stop, and Maggie also knew that, given the chance, Satin would tear into Berger until there was nothing left of him. Without his grip on her shirt, she dragged lungfuls of the fresh night air and felt its ease. Her eyes darted from side to side, trying to discover where help would come from so that she would be ready to do whatever she could to get away. But Maggie saw no one, not even a shadow for reassurance.

From his vantage point on the roof, McCready saw that Maggie was in an untenable position. He couldn't jump down as the man holding a gun to her came into view. His rifle had been left behind the cabin on the ground, for he was afraid it would clatter when he climbed and give away his position.

McCready needed something to throw. Both his shirt and the stovepipe had gone over the side. He looked down at his boots, knowing how much time was wasting. Once Berger saw that no one was there to prevent him from leaving, he would be moving fast. Easing himself down to sit on the edge of the roof, grateful for once that Satin was barking again, he tugged off his boot. Setting it down beside him, he tugged off the other one. Grabbing hold of the heel, he saw Berger move and had no more time to make his move. Swinging the boot he threw it in an arc but didn't wait to see if it hit his target.

McCready launched himself off the roof.

Maggie's acute sense of hearing had told where help was coming from with a bare scrape against the roof. She was pulling away from Berger when the boot hit his back. The pain in her arm brought her to her knees as she tried to twist free. But the weight of a body falling on Berger had her flattened beneath him when he fell.

She kicked her free leg and used her fist on whatever part of him she could reach. But it was only moments before he was torn off her.

For the second time that day Maggie had her mouth open without a sound coming out. In the light spilling from the smoke-filled cabin, she saw McCready punch Berger's gut. The gun was fired again, but the shot went harmlessly into the ground. She drew herself up and away from them, worried that McCready might trip over her, while they grappled for possession of the gun.

McCready managed to tear Berger's grip from the gun, but before he could back away and use it, Berger kicked McCready's hand, and the gun went flying. There were no curses, just the sound of their ruthless fists landing where they could as each man sought an opening to take his opponent down.

Maggie was held by the sight of McCready's lithe moves, the flex and play of his muscles, and the light and shadows thrown on his bare chest and bare feet. She had the damnedest impulse to call out a warning about the rocks so he wouldn't cut himself. But she kept quiet and began searching for the gun. Satin circled the men, nipping at Berger's legs. Berger landed a solid blow to McCready's jaw and sent him sprawling, then spun to kick Satin's chest before she could lunge at him.

The dog's painful whelp sent Maggie running to her, but she kept her eyes on McCready, willing him to get up. Berger was searching for the gun, too. Maggie prayed that she would find it first.

She urged the dog to move away from them. McCready was moaning, but he wasn't getting up.

Berger kicked McCready's leg, and Maggie couldn't wait any longer. She tackled Berger around the legs, thankful for her strength, furious that he dared kicked McCready while he was down. Berger fell, but he managed to twist himself around, facing her before she could plant herself on top of him. Maggie's punch danced off his arm while his blow sent her head snapping back. Lights danced in front of her eyes, and she fell back, her arms sliding uselessly away from him.

But she had bought McCready time, and he came to his feet in an enraged rush just as Berger went to hit her again.

"You son of a bitch! Get the hell away from her!" McCready ordered, lunging for Berger.

Maggie had witnessed lethal fighting in her trips with her father through Indian territory and later with her uncle as they roamed the mountains prospecting. But she had never seen such a feral look on a man's face as McCready's when the light caught him.

Berger staggered to his feet, swinging wildly.

Maggie heard Satin's warning growls and spun around. The dog launched herself at Berger's back just as his blow knocked McCready backward.

"Satin, no!" Maggie screamed, seeing the dog's bared teeth before they closed over Berger's neck.

McCready stumbled toward her, and Maggie closed her eyes, then turned away, unable to watch. But nothing could prevent her from hearing the vicious sounds of her dog vanquishing her enemy.

CHAPTER
22

It was over. Maggie told herself this, but stood shaking in the aftermath of violence. Warmth suddenly came from the feel of McCready's body behind her, his hands cupping her shoulders, forcing her around to face him. The race of his lips over her face brought heat to chase the cold inside her, her whispered name the only sound he made.

She burrowed against him, betrayal and lies forgotten, in her need to be held, to feel safe again.

But other needs surfaced, bringing with them a trembling that rocked their bodies together. The need to taste sealed their lips, and a softer violence erupted. Maggie drank her own tears from his mouth, hungry to know again the mindless wanting that left no room for questions. No soft words. No gentleness. She understood the raw passion they brought to each other. She could feel McCready's heart race to match hers.

McCready dragged her head back. Snarling one minute, giving him everything the next, she made him ache until he couldn't think.

She made him forget words and remember only needs. His mouth savaged hers, and she took, and took, then demanded more.

"Figure my two cents ain't wanted, but you've got company coming."

McCready froze, his chest heaving, and tore his mouth from Maggie's. Still holding her, he made a half turn and saw Ira, leaning on his rifle, standing no more than a few feet from them.

"Lucky for you, McCready, I'm friendly and that one's down for the count." Ira glanced to where Berger lay. "Best call off the dog, or there'll be nothing left to bury."

"Call the bitch off, Maggie," McCready ordered.

Maggie wasn't as quick to recover, and she didn't react until anger rode McCready's voice with the second order. His hands on her arms became a punishing grip as he forced her away from him and once more repeated it.

"Do it now, before your *husbands* get here."

She then heard the sounds of men running up the rocky path and pushed McCready away. "Satin! Come, girl." Still holding McCready's gaze, she wiped at her mouth. "I forgot who you were."

"Damn you, Maggie!" McCready spun away from her.

"Damn yourself, McCready! You're a hell of a lot easier to take when you're not pretendin'." *Tell me you want me. Tell me no one else matters.* But when he faced her, those weren't the words he gave back to her.

"Don't you dare," he said, fury coiling around every word,

"tell me that what's between us is anything but as honest as it gets, Maggie."

She had hurt him. He had saved her life, and she gave him hurt in return. "Honest, McCready? You're wrong." She lifted her hand to him, but he had already turned away, and then Pamela came running to her.

"Are you all right?" she demanded, taking Maggie's limp hand into hers. "I heard the shots and was so afraid for you."

"No need. McCready was here. An' Satin," she added, holding the dog's neck to keep her by her side. She watched McCready as he walked around the side of the cabin to recover his shirt, but instead of putting it on, he draped it over Berger's face.

A chorus of men's voices warned Maggie she would have no time to talk to him alone. She closed her eyes briefly, knowing she had made a terrible mistake.

Pamela moved away to make room for Lee Warren.

"Maggie, I wish I had been here to help you."

"It's over, Lee, an' that's all that matters."

"Maggie!" Mike Grant shouted as he spotted her. He ran to her, gripping her arms and turning her so that her back was to everyone. "Darlin', I should've been with you. Sorry don't say the half of it."

"It wasn't your fight," Maggie answered, tightening her grip on Satin's neck so the dog wouldn't lunge for the men milling about the body. Satin issued one long low growl, and Maggie was thankful that Mike released her.

"You should've told me about that gold mine. Now I understand why you ain't anxious to leave. When McCready was reading me off your good points like a heifer going to auction, he didn't say a word about you being rich to boot."

Maggie found McCready watching her. *The gold again.* Was that all he wanted from her? Was that all any of them wanted from her?

McCready read her bleak, accusing stare and wished he

knew why. In the next moment she looked away, and Ira was asking him what to do with the body.

For Maggie, McCready's ignoring her was an answer. But when Mike asked about the mine, she barely managed to talk to him. "Me gold mine has nothin' to do with you."

"Darlin', a wife's property belongs to her husband."

Maggie retreated. "You see that body? Satin did that. Leave me alone. Don't call me darlin'. Don't call me anythin'. Pamela," she called out, "will you spend the night with me?"

"We can't stay here, Maggie." Pamela glanced around for support, but Maggie surprised her.

"You're right." Maggie looked into her smoke-filled cabin. "I'll come down an' stay with you." She swayed where she stood, fighting the hollow feeling in her belly and the pounding in her head. She shrugged off Mike's offer of his arm and went into the cabin to get her other boot.

McCready caught the bemused expression on Mike's face and walked over to him. "Don't waste your time trying to understand. Maggie doesn't need help from anyone. She'll get around to telling you that eventually."

Embarrassed that McCready had seen Maggie's rebuff, Mike couldn't help his anger. "Seems to me you're on more than friendly terms with my wife. Only a fool would miss the looks you're exchanging."

"If you're looking for a fight, you've found it."

Maggie came back outside in time to hear McCready. She knew he wasn't a man quick with his fists. Everyone knew that he'd rather talk you to death than fight. She quickly stepped between them, ignoring the glare in McCready's eyes for her interference.

"You can't fight. There's been enough here tonight to fill everyone's belly. An' for you," she said, rounding on Mike, "McCready's nothin' but a claim jumper tryin' to get me mines."

Dragging her pride up to rescue her, Maggie walked away

from them and, together with Pamela, headed down the rocky path.

"She's one hell of a lot of woman, that Maggie."

McCready clamped his mouth shut when he heard Mike's admiring tone. His hand clenched at his side in an effort to keep from hitting the other man. He was trying to figure out why it hurt to hear Maggie dismiss him as nothing more than a claim jumper after her mines. She had sounded calm, too calm. That wasn't his Maggie. She should have been sassing them both and wishing them to the devil. But she was right about the belly full. He had had enough for one night.

Pamela insisted that Maggie have the first bath to rid herself of the dust and smoke that still lingered in the air. They had seen for themselves that the fire on the ridge was out, but the miners were still up there, so neither one knew how much damage had been done.

As Pamela bathed, Maggie listened to her humming in the kitchen, and looked down at the pristine white, voluminous nightgown that Pamela had given her to wear. She had never had a nightgown but liked its softness as well as the freedom it gave her to move about. The cotton was trimmed with tiny flowers and lace around the cuffs and neckline. Maggie felt strange seeing herself in the mirror over Pamela's bureau.

Pamela said she looked pretty. Maggie wondered if Mc-Cready would think the same. A flush stole into her cheeks, and she lowered her gaze to the bottles neatly arranged on the tray. Why would a woman need all these scents and creams? Seemed like nonsense to her. Bathing was fine when she had the chance, but she'd be damned before she would gussie up and stink for some man.

But she found herself lifting the stopper to a bottle and raising it to her nose. The scent was so light that she had to hold it beneath her nose and repeatedly sniff to know she was smelling flowers. But she didn't know what they were.

"Help yourself, Maggie," Pamela offered, coming into her room.

Feeling the same way she did the first time she was caught with her pants down, Maggie set the bottle back on the tray.

"Well, if you don't like the scent of lily of the valley, try the violets that I lent you for your wedding day."

"Ain't a need to."

"Of course there's a need to, Maggie. Women don't use creams to make their skin soft or pretty perfumes just for men. They use them because it makes them feel good about themselves." Bustling over to the bureau, Pamela lifted a pink glass jar with a seated cupid on its lid. "Give me your hands. Come on, Maggie, this won't hurt you."

Reluctantly Maggie held out her work-rough hands, feeling out of place in this room of lace and fancy pillows. She was embarrassed, too, that Pamela, not much younger than she, knew all about women's things while she was ignorant.

The cream Pamela rubbed on the top of her hands was silky soft, like the first pussy willows. It was cool and soothing, too.

Finished with one hand, Pamela lifted it to Maggie's nose. "Go on, smell that. Isn't it pretty? This is Madam La Roche's hand cream." Pamela dabbed more on Maggie's palms. "Now, you work that in and tell me if it doesn't make your hands feel smooth and nice. While you do that," she said, replacing the jar and taking up another, "I'll start working some of Miss Philippa Gosling's face wash into your skin. This is guaranteed to make your face feel like silk."

"Pamela, you do this all the time?" Maggie couldn't believe she was standing still for this, but she was. Blame it on all that happened today, she told herself.

"Of course I do. Every morning and every night. A woman has to protect her skin and especially her hands. It's the first thing a man's allowed to touch."

Their gazes locked, and Maggie was the first to smile, then chuckle as Pamela started giggling. Laughter eased the tension of the last few hours, and for long minutes they couldn't stop.

"Did you hear me, Maggie? Me worrying about smooth hands when I seduced Lars right into that bed."

Maggie caught the ragged note in Pamela's voice and slipped her arm around Pamela's shoulders, giving her a quick hug. "You can't keep blamin' yourself. He wasn't dragged there, was he? 'Cause if you did that, tell me how you managed."

The laughter bubbled up again, and Pamela couldn't help hugging Maggie.

To keep her laughing, Maggie dabbed a bit of cream on her nose, turned to the mirror, and decided Pamela could use the same.

Pamela returned her effort with a smear across Maggie's cheek, and not to be outdone by the shorter woman, Maggie managed two streaks across Pamela's forehead.

She listened to Pamela's mutterings that they were being silly and childish, but Pamela didn't stop and neither could Maggie. She had never played like this. Playing had only happened with McCready. Her hand was arrested in midair. *McCready.* Maggie closed her eyes. *We'll play, Maggie. I'll chase you and you'll chase me until one of us is caught.* And they had. But it was only a game. A game like all the other things they had shared. And games were for children.

"What's wrong? Maggie? Maggie, answer me."

With a quick shake of her head Maggie looked at Pamela, then set the jar she held down on the tray.

"It's McCready, isn't it?" Pamela asked, setting her own jar down and replacing the lids on both. "You can't stop thinking about him any more than I can stop thinking about Lars." With her hands resting on the edge of the bureau, Pamela bowed her head. "Maggie, what are we going to do?"

"You're marryin' Lars."

"What if he doesn't want me?"

"Fool's talk. He wants you."

"I wish," Pamela said, turning, "that I could be as strong as you, Maggie. I wish I could believe that you're right. But what about you?"

"Me? Why, you just said me was—"

"No." Shaking her head, Pamela went to the bed and patted the place next to her. "Sit and talk to me. I meant what are you going to do about McCready? Do you love him?"

"Love him?" Maggie felt the flush heat up on her face. "Love a man with a silver tongue that could have the devil himself givin' up hell? No way. Were you hearin' what that Mike Grant said to me?"

"When?"

Maggie started pacing the small area in front of the bed. "When he come rushin' up after it was all over. Said McCready had been listin' off me good points like I was some heifer up for auction."

"Auction? Well, Maggie, at least you would have enough men bidding on you if that was really happening. Pity me. I'd be lucky if Lars threw a bid my way. But he couldn't do that while he's married to you."

"Can't be married to me. Can't have two husbands. Ain't one of them Mormons."

Frowning, Pamela looked up. "I think you have that wrong. They have lots of wives, but I don't think the women can have more than one husband."

"Just like men to be thinkin' of that!"

"Maggie, that calls for a drink." Pamela was off and running to the small parlor and back with a bottle of her father's whiskey, and a sober mood, in moments.

While Maggie watched, Pamela tipped the bottle back and took a healthy slug. Coughing and with eyes tearing, she handed Maggie the bottle. "That one was for my father."

"Pamela, someone'll come along an' buy the mercantile. Tell you what. Soon as I get me mines open, I'll buy it. You take the money to your father an' start over. Slick'll only go to a few camps with them tarred and feathered.''

"I never thanked you for stopping the miners from hanging them. I still can't believe he was involved with those men. Give me the bottle if you're not going to drink.''

Maggie handed it over, thinking it was best that Pamela had some sleep. Her mind was churning with too many problems. And Maggie knew she was no better.

"Pamela, talkin' about that auction gives me an idea. We could—''

"You're going to do it? Maggie! You're really going to auction yourself off?''

"Auction meself?'' Maggie repeated, staring at the other woman, then turning the thought over and over. "Well, I wasn't figurin' that. I was thinkin' of all the supplies in the store. You'd have them sold out in no time an' have all the money you'd need for a fresh start somewheres.''

Pamela climbed onto the middle of the bed and curled her legs under her. "Think about it, Maggie. We could hold a double auction. Me getting rid of the stock of the store, and you taking the highest bid for a husband.''

"Crazy talk.''

"Wouldn't you like to see McCready bidding for you? Why, I'll bet you he would top every single bid that was made. You can't be blind and not see how the man looks at you, Maggie.''

"Slaves got auctioned. We fought a war to stop that. An' here you sit, Missy Prim and Proper, an' tell me to put meself up on the block.''

Pamela did not take offense at Maggie's name-calling. She smiled and nodded. "That's it. You put yourself up on the block. Can you think of a better way to get rid of two husbands you don't want? Think about it, Maggie. Think hard. Do you really want to be Mike Grant's ranch wife? He's good-looking, I'll admit, but not nearly as handsome as Lars. He would likely pet you and keep you tied to a kitchen and babies.

"And that's another little thing we've forgotten about. You could be carrying McCready's baby right now. Wouldn't be fair to bring another man's leavings to a marriage."

"Still think you're crazy."

"Do you? You want McCready—"

"He's a liar!"

"Stand still and look at me." Pamela squinted to make sure that Maggie did stand still. Three drinks were one too many for her, she decided, swaying slightly. She inched her way back until the pillows cushioned her. "That's better. Now, where was I?"

"You were tellin' me that I was wantin' McCready, an' I'm sayin' you're wrong."

"Do you get butterflies in your stomach when you see him?"

"Butterflies? Oh, you mean the wee ones."

"Wee ones? Well, you have them, and I'll keep my butterflies. But that proves what I'm saying. You don't have them around with other men, do you?"

Maggie sat on the edge of the bed and looked up in dismay. "No," she whispered. "Not even a tiny flutter."

Pamela clapped her hands with glee, her gaze suddenly wise. "Do you think about kissing anyone the way you do McCready?"

"I ain't ever kissed another man."

"And I know you wouldn't want to. I feel the same way about Lars, and I've done my share of kissing. It's the only way, Maggie. McCready wants the mines, right?"

"Yeah," she answered absently, her mind racing with this crazy idea of Pamela's.

"He'll do anything to have them?"

"Bet on it."

"That's it, then. You'll put up yourself and the mines for auction. We'll need signs, but I'll take care of those."

"Slow down, girl, you're like a wild bunch of mustangs, tramplin' everythin'. I need to think about this."

"You do that, Maggie," Pamela said in a smug little voice. "We'll both sleep on it and see what the morning brings."

"In the last hour that's the best suggestion you've had." Maggie blew out the lamp and crawled into the other side of the bed. "It's mighty soft," she whispered, trying to hang on to the edge so as not to roll into the middle, where Pamela lay.

"Get used to it, Maggie. You'll have to stay with me. We have what's left of our reputations to protect." She found Maggie's hand and gently squeezed it. "I'm glad we're friends. I couldn't get through this without you."

And in the dark Maggie squeezed Pamela's hand back, unable to answer her for the tears burning in her eyes and throat.

Pamela would likely never know how much Maggie needed her as well. She wasn't open like Pamela with her hugs and touches and her words. But she was learning that she could be strong and still share with someone else without losing anything.

She had promised Pamela she would think about her crazy idea of an auction, and she tried, but eyes closed or open, all Maggie could see was McCready's face with those dark blue eyes and that cocky know-it-all grin. Her sleep was restless. Her dreams filled with his taunting and daring her to reach out and take what she wanted.

Pamela asked if she loved him. Maggie wasn't sure what love was. But she knew she would rather be fighting with McCready than accepting any other man's kindness.

Dawn stole into the room, just as the answers she needed stole into Maggie's heart and mind. She slept peacefully then. Able to wait to tell Pamela what she had decided.

CHAPTER 23

Pamela and Maggie worked frantically all morning and argued every step of the way. Having set out a Closed sign and locked the door of the mercantile, Pamela ignored the few men that stopped by, but Maggie had to restrain her when Lars called out to her.

"We agreed," she reminded Pamela. "No one sees us till we're finished."

"You're right, but I didn't think it would be this hard to do."

"Never mind. You finish makin' the list of stores, an' I'll keep countin'. You'll have enough money to give to your father an' plenty left for—what was it you called it?"

"A dowry, Maggie. A woman should have money and things of her own to bring to a marriage. It gives her worth in her husband's eyes. The more she brings, the more he values her."

"That so?"

"Would I lie to you? That is exactly the way it's done back East, and I would imagine here in the territory, too. There aren't many women who get to pick their own husbands. Why, it's just like what Pete did to you. He made arrangements with Lars and Mike to marry you instead of paying back what they owed him. So, you see, Maggie, he already paid them your dowry."

Maggie turned from the stack of shirts she was counting. "Pamela, you figure that me havin' a bigger dowry might get McCready to do some biddin'?"

"Well, it couldn't hurt," she answered with a shrug. "But you don't have anything but the cabin."

"You'll wait a few days till I get back to put up the signs?"

"Maggie! Maggie, where are you going?"

"Why, I'm off to get meself a dowry."

Pamela ran after her. "You can't leave. What'll I say if anyone comes looking for you? Maggie, please." But by the time she reached the back door, Maggie had called her dog to her side, for Pamela refused to allow Satin inside. "Maggie, don't go," she whispered, leaning against the edge of the door. But Maggie was already working her way up behind the mercantile and was soon lost to sight.

"Where is she going to get a dowry?" Pamela didn't know.

By nightfall Pamela had run out of excuses why Maggie couldn't come to the door. To Mike Grant's two visits, she explained first that Maggie was still sleeping, then taking a bath. They worked as well for the two times McCready came calling. When Lars arrived for his one try, she refused to open the door at all, ordering him to go away, that Maggie didn't want to see him and she didn't want to talk to him.

But McCready didn't give up. He came back a third and then a fourth time. He didn't believe that Maggie was too distressed to see him. He certainly didn't believe that she was taking another bath.

Pamela didn't know what to do when he said he'd wait. And then asked about Satin.

"Why isn't she here by the door, Pamela? That dog gets within ten feet of me and starts growling. She can't be taking a bath, too."

Twisting the curtain that covered the upper half of the door, although there was no window, Pamela turned to search the small kitchen behind her, hoping for new inspiration.

"Pamela?"

McCready made warning and impatience roll through her name. She turned to look at him through the few inches of the open door. The light barely revealed his features, but what she did see set her stomach to fluttering. His bruises only added to her sense of unease. There was no charming smile, just a thin, grim line shaping his mouth.

Pamela forced herself to smile at him. "Ah, the dog got into the pickled beef barrel and ate so much she made herself sick, and now she's sleeping."

McCready lifted his hand and, using one finger, tapped her nose. "You're lying. Now, let me in to see Maggie."

"She's not here."

"My patience is growing thin, Pamela. I need to talk to Maggie. I won't go away until I do."

She knew he meant it. "Fine. Threaten me, McCready. Do your worst." Pamela opened the door and stepped back. "Go on. Come on in and see for yourself that she's gone."

He wasn't wearing a gun, but Pamela felt a chill when she saw him dressed in black, filling up her kitchen with his male presence. Maggie, she thought, was welcome to him. She dogged his every step, standing quietly while he knelt beside her bed and peered beneath it, silently laughing to herself when he grew desperate enough to begin lifting the lids of the barrels in the store, hoping to find Maggie in one of them.

When they returned to the kitchen, her smile was smug, and McCready's mouth had grown stern. His eyes, Pamela didn't look at. ''Are you now satisfied that I was not lying?''

''I'm satisfied that Maggie isn't here. But you know where she is, don't you, Pamela?''

She thought for a few minutes about putting him off. But she was worried about Maggie. And she really didn't know where Maggie had gone, only what she had gone for. If McCready could make sense of it, he might find Maggie before more trouble found her.

''All I can tell you is that she went looking for a dowry.''

Her level gaze told him she was telling the truth, but it made no sense. ''What dowry? Maggie doesn't need one. She's already got two husbands that—''

''One, McCready. Lars made it clear for all to see that he didn't like Maggie.''

''Well, Lars didn't know about the gold mine. Funny the way gold can make a man like almost anything or anyone.''

Pamela hid her hurt. Men knew things about other men that women were never told, and sometimes never learned. But she could strike a blow for Maggie. ''Is that why you want to find her? Is that all you care about, McCready—the gold?''

''What's between Maggie and me is just that—private. And it'll stay that way till Maggie decides differently.''

''I don't think so, McCready. Along about nine or so months from now, everybody might know about you and Maggie.'' Pamela turned her back on him, biting her lip to keep from crying. *Lars couldn't want Maggie. He just couldn't. What did McCready know, anyway? He'd made a mess with Maggie. No, she wouldn't believe him until Lars told her so himself.*

But the mere thought that he might have told her the truth forced Pamela to sit down.

McCready hunkered at her side, raking his shoulder-length hair back before he lifted her chin with the tips of his fingers. "Let's forget about Maggie for now. Why don't you tell me what has you upset? You know no one blames you for what your father did. And we'll make sure that you can keep the mercantile going, if that's what you want, Pamela. Ira said he'd come help you as much as he can, and there are others, if you're interested in selling, who might be able to buy the place and stock from you."

"Maggie already offered."

"But Maggie won't be here."

"Don't be so sure, McCready. Maggie doesn't want to be married to Mike Grant. She said as much. She meant it, too. And she doesn't like Lars any more than he liked her. So Pete just wasted his money trying to marry her off. But you," she said, turning in the chair to face him, "didn't understand what I said before. I'll make it plainer. A man has his pleasuring and knows it, and a woman, McCready, a woman has to wait to find out if she's the one paying for it."

"Maggie's—no, she couldn't be."

Pamela wasn't sure who he was trying to convince, but it wasn't her, and he was unsteady as he stood up and towered over her. "Like all men, you never thought about that, did you? Well, Maggie and I don't need the likes—"

"You? I never touched you, Pamela."

"I didn't say you did. But as I was saying, Maggie and I will work out our problems in good time. You'll just have to learn some patience and wait. And now, McCready," she stated coolly, "it is late and you'd best leave."

McCready slipped the leash on his temper. He gently pushed her back into the chair. With one hand braced on the chair's back and the other flat out on the table imprisoning her, he angled his face close to hers. "I'm not going anywhere till you tell me where Maggie is."

For all that he looked dangerous, Pamela wasn't afraid of him. But she had to make him understand that she wasn't lying.

"Do you really care about Maggie?"

"Would I have come over here looking for her all day if I didn't?"

"That is not much of an answer, McCready."

"It's all the answer you're getting. Now, tell me—"

Clasping her hands together in her lap, Pamela met his penetrating gaze. "I don't know. She said she was going to find a dowry. Do you know where she could do that? Because, if you do, that's where Maggie is."

"The mine," he whispered, releasing Pamela and turning away. *Maggie missing. Maggie and baby. Maggie and gold. Maggie and her damn husbands.* With both of his hands he raked back his hair. He had forgotten about the possibility of Maggie being with child. His child. And now she had run off. He spun around.

"Supplies, Pamela? How many days' worth did she take with her?"

"None. Not from here. And there wasn't much up at her cabin."

"Christ! That damn woman!"

"Now, now, McCready, she'll be back. She has to come back and settle the problem of one too many husbands. And you don't really want someone marrying Maggie and taking her away, do you?"

He glared at her. Pamela was taunting him. "Feeling feisty?"

"Wouldn't you do just about anything to stop one of those men from having Maggie?"

"Anything?"

She jumped up and threw her arms around him. "Oh, I knew you'd agree to help us any way that you could, McCready. I told Maggie that you'd be on our side.'' She ignored his gentle push to set himself free and hugged him tighter. "I can't wait to tell Maggie.'' She leaned into him, forcing him to step back.

McCready was a little less than gentle but not rough enough to hurt her as he pulled her arms away and backed himself to the doorway. Pamela's smile and sparking eyes warned him that he had agreed to something that he was going to pay for and regret doing it. But he didn't have the heart to steal the first smile he had seen from her. She had been there for Maggie when he couldn't be, when Maggie wouldn't let him near her. After all, he told himself, what could she possibly want from him?

And with Maggie on his mind, he let it go, wondering why Maggie managed to slip away every time he thought he had her where he wanted her.

"McCready, you'll remember to tell Maggie when you find her that I'll have everything ready.''

"Sure. I'll tell her when I find her.''

If you find her. Pamela smiled, then closed the door, leaning against it with a satisfied smile. It had taken her most of the day to figure out what sort of dowry Maggie was after. She started to laugh, and soon couldn't stop.

McCready wouldn't have a chance to run when Maggie was finished with him. But best of all, McCready still didn't realize that he wanted to be caught.

It was late the next night when an exhausted and furious McCready returned to Cooney Camp without Maggie, without having seen a sign of Maggie.

Standing in front of the mercantile, Pamela heard him tell Dutch that he didn't know where Maggie had gone.

With a sigh of regret Pamela wished that Maggie had trusted her and told her where she was going. She couldn't really blame her. McCready's lies along with Quincy's and what her uncle had done to her had wounded Maggie mighty bad.

But when Pamela saw that Mike Grant and Lars had come out of the Rawhider to talk to McCready, she hurried back inside. She didn't want any more questions about Maggie.

Even with the shorter trails that Maggie knew, it still took her almost three days to reach Santa Fe. The city sprawled from Mannitan Avenue to past Capitol Avenue. The market-place off the plaza was empty of the farmers that sold their produce and others selling cloth, leather goods, and pottery.

Maggie didn't waste time once she found the Camino Del Rosario. She headed for San Francisco Street, looking for St. Francis's Cathedral. She knew it would be easier to get the information she wanted from the padre there, rather than make the rounds of the cantinas. Men of the cloth, her uncle always told her, knew more about the sins and doings of folks than they ever let on.

The stately-looking padre took her for a young man, since he called her ''my son'' when questioning why she wanted to find Thadius Cornwallis. Maggie pulled the brim of her floppy felt hat a little lower to hide her grimed face, then explained that she had to pay a debt of honor to him.

Finding out that Thadius had rooms in the Exchange Hotel right on San Francisco Street was a bit of luck. Maggie quickly thanked the padre and made her way around the back of the buildings until she found the hotel. She didn't want anyone to see her if she could help it.

But she had rushed headlong into coming here without finding out what Thadius looked like. She fingered the small poke of gold in her pants pocket, wondering how much it would buy her. Thadius's room, perhaps? But that meant letting someone know that she was looking for him.

Her shabby appearance would likely have her thrown out of the hotel if she attempted to go inside through the front. But she had to find a way.

The creak of a nearby door had her spinning around,

searching for a hiding place. The rattle of pots and pans and the stale aroma of fried foods had Maggie's mouth watering. But the sight of a young boy, no more than ten or so, made her reveal herself. Here was someone who might help her and for some gold dust forget that he ever saw her.

"You are hungry, *sí*?" the boy asked with a faint accent.

"A little," Maggie admitted, studying what she could see of the boy's thin body, dark hair, and even darker eyes. "What I'm really needin' is a bit of help."

"I am Antonio. You are looking for a cheap place to stay?"

"Not exactly. I'm lookin' for a man that lives in the hotel. Maybe you know him? Thadius Cornwallis."

"His is *mucho* bad."

"So I've heard. But I've got to find him, an' I'm willin' to pay for the information of where his rooms is an' what he looks like."

From beyond the open doorway someone called for the boy. He turned and yelled something back that Maggie didn't understand, then came to her.

"How much?"

Maggie didn't hesitate. She drew out the poke from her pocket and handed it over but kept the drawstring clenched tight in her hand. "Feel the weight. There's more than enough for what I'm lookin' to know."

Antonio grinned. "He is a little fat man. Room six."

Maggie released her grip, and the bag disappeared inside the boy's shirt. He was gone before she thought to thank him. She wiped her damp palms down the sides of her pants and opened the hotel's back door. Far down the hall a wall lamp flickered, but it provided enough light for her to see the stairway.

Before she climbed them, Maggie checked her gun and made sure that her knife was untied from its sheath. She hadn't lied to the padre. She had a debt to pay Thadius Cornwallis for causing her uncle's death and the attempts on her own life.

She hugged the wall as she tested each step before she put

her weight on it. And when she reached the upper hall, it was with a sigh of relief that no one was about to stop her. Here were several wall lamps, turned up high, so that the gleaming brass numbers were clearly revealed.

When she came to number six, Maggie pressed her ear against the door but didn't hear anything that offered a clue as to whether or not Thadius was there. She had figured that the door would be locked, but a man living in a hotel wouldn't want his key lost and would likely leave it in the lock. She counted on Thadius having done just that and used the tip of her knife in the keyhole. It wasn't thin enough to fit all the way in.

Swearing, Maggie stood back a moment. She wasn't going to be defeated by a locked door. She could knock but that would steal the advantage she wanted of surprising Thadius.

No, she had to get that key.

Staring at the door number, Maggie realized that it was held in place with nails. A nail would come in handy, she thought, just the right thickness and length. But not those holding the number to the door. She took a few steps over to the wall lamp and pried one nail free with her knife.

Minutes later she was rewarded by a soft thunk as the key fell out of the lock and hit the carpeted floor inside the room. Her knife, flat side down, barely made it under the door, but Maggie was standing and holding the key seconds later. Please let him be inside, she prayed, fitting the key to the lock and turning it to open the door.

The light from the hallway did not penetrate the dark room. Maggie stepped inside, her boots sinking into a thick carpet, then closed the door behind her. She stood still, giving herself a few minutes to let her eyes adjust.

After sheathing her knife, Maggie pulled her shirt free from her pants and unwound the rope she had wrapped around her waist. Coiling it into a loop that would easily slip over her head and one shoulder, she tied off the ends, then secured it in place until she would need it.

Bending slightly, with her hands extended in front of her, she turned to her left and began to work her way around the room. Having come this far, the last thing she wanted was to trip over a piece of furniture. She shaped each bulky piece with the same delicacy of hand that she had used to learn how to skin hides.

The thick carpet muffled any noise, and Maggie found velvet draperies pulled across two windows before she found the bedroom door. It wasn't fully closed, so she heard a man's snoring before she stood by the bed with her rope in hand. While she listened to make sure that no one else was in bed with him, her nimble fingers quickly made a noose from the rope. Giving it a few hard pulls, she was satisfied that the knot would hold. Now, she knew, came the hard part.

Maggie eased the covers back from his head and shoulders. She could make out the lumpy form of his body, and by carefully listening to the uninterrupted snores, she determined that he was facing away from where she stood.

Giving the noose slack, she draped it over the pillow above his head, then slowly lowered the other side so it could drape around his neck. Two wraps of the rope around one hand gave her leverage she would need to pull it tight. Drawing out her knife, knowing that she didn't want to slice his throat when he woke up startled, she placed the tip of it below his ear.

"Thadius Cornwallis?" she whispered, bending lower. "You bastard bottom of the dung heap, wake up," she said a little louder and was rewarded by the cut off snore. She sensed he was awake and tense. "Listen to me," she warned, gently adding a bit of pressure to the tip of the knife.

Thadius raised his head off the pillow. "Who—" His word was cut off by the noose around his neck. He tried to bring his hands up to free himself, but the knife bit his skin.

"Lie still." Maggie had to turn away from breathing his

fetid breath. "If you move again, you good for nothin' cow plop, I'll slice you open an' feed you to the hogs. There's a whole pen full of them out by Fort Marcy. Just raise your hand a bit to let me know you're hearin' me."

Maggie wanted to see him badly, but she knew she would have to wait for that. It was enough that he obeyed her and managed to lift the cover and bring up his hand.

"Now crawl backward till you're off the bed." She backed away and gave the rope just enough slack to allow him to move. "An' if you touch that noose, I'll send you to the devil right now."

Thadius felt his panic die hearing her last words. She wasn't going to kill him. At least not yet. He didn't know who she was, but the trickle of blood from the cut behind his ear warned him that she was serious. He inched his way to the edge of the bed, trying to pull down his nightshirt, but a light tug on the rope forced him to get off the bed quickly. First Ryder had broken into his rooms and now this wild woman. He would have to hire himself a bodyguard before this could happen again.

Maggie was in the awkward position of having almost two feet of rope taut between them. If Thadius took it in mind to grab hold of it, she didn't know if her strength to hold on would be enough to stop him. She had to keep him worried and too busy to think.

"Find the lamp an' light it. Then you an' me are doin' some business. An' just remember I'm real quick with usin' this knife. I'll have your liver cut out an' fed to you before you can call out." Maggie cursed herself for her choice of words. They were the same ones she used about McCready on her supposed-to-be wedding day. But when she heard the rattle Thadius's shaking hands made lifting the glass from the bedside lamp, she pushed McCready out of her thoughts.

It took three tries before Thadius managed to light a match and hold it steady enough to fire the wick. His damp hand almost lost its grip on the glass, but he replaced it and faced his attacker. The battered felt hat covered her hair and grime was smeared over her face, but her green eyes held him, for he had never seen hate that was so cold it was deadly. She topped him by nearly six inches and Thadius began to understand he might not get out of this situation easily. His gaze dropped to the wickedly gleaming blade she held in one hand and the rope loosely coiled in the other.

Desperate, he opened his mouth to speak only to find that his voice was dried up. Swallowing was hard with the rope around his neck, but he forced himself to do it until he felt some moisture in his mouth.

"I've got money," he croaked.

"That's good. Real good. 'Cause you're gonna give me all you've got."

Robbery. That's all she was after. He almost breathed a sigh of relief, but she yanked on the rope, then with a quick flip of her hand twisted it once around his arms and chest.

Maggie had to force herself to look at him. He was as pink as a porker with the eyes to match. "Pick up the lamp an' we'll go into the other room. You're gonna do some writin' for me." Maggie almost snatched the lamp from him; he was shaking so bad that she was afraid he would drop it and start a fire. She was taking a gamble that he would have all that she needed in the other room since the padre didn't tell her that he had an office anywhere.

"Move, Cornwallis," she ordered, following him. His nightshirt flapped against his hairy legs, and he waddled from side to side into the other room.

A quick look showed Maggie a large wood desk set before closed dark red velvet drapes. She gave him a shove toward it. "Go on an' set." Once he was in the chair, Maggie eased the rope looped around him. "Free your writin' hand." Once he did, she wrapped the rest of the rope around him and the chair's back and tied it off.

Taking a place on the corner of the desk facing him, Maggie lifted the knife to his throat and shoved his inkwell forward. "Get your papers."

Thadius had been waiting for this. He eased open the top right-hand drawer, keeping his eyes on her. Beneath the leather case of writing paper was his gun. His sweating fingers closed over the handle and slowly began to ease the weapon out.

Maggie watched his eyes. She knew he was up to something by the sudden gleam in them. Leaning forward, she raised the knife and nicked his chin. "Put it back, fat man. You'll do no more hurtin' to me an' mine."

Thadius released the gun, flinching under her murderous look. He raised the leather case and brought it out to put on the desk. He didn't even wait for her to tell him, but removed a sheet of paper.

"That ain't gonna be enough for what you've got to say."

He took out another. Maggie shook her head, and he added a third sheet in front of him.

She backed up but kept the knife slightly raised in case he needed a bit more convincing. "This is what you say. You tell how you killed me uncle—"

"No!" Thadius reared back with shock. Now he knew who she was: Quincy's backward bride. "You're—" He stopped himself from saying dead. He stopped himself from asking her what happened to Ryder, Quincy, and Andrew Burton. If she had found him, they had talked. But he wasn't going to take the fall by himself. "Listen to me. I didn't kill him. Berger, William Berger—"

"Berger's dead," Maggie announced calmly.

Sweat beads popped out all over Thadius's face, and he longed to wipe them away. He closed his eyes, his mind darting from this corner to the next, searching for a way out.

CHAPTER
24

Maggie smelled his fear like that of a cornered rat searching for a way out. She wouldn't give him the chance.

"Start writin'. I ain't got all night, Cornwallis."

"But why? What do you intend to do? Surely you know that forcing a confession from someone is against the law?"

"Law? You dare talk to me about law?"

"You can't expect me to condemn myself on your say-so and not ask why."

Much as she hated getting closer to him, Maggie brought her face up to his. "You'll do what I tell you or you die now."

"There's money. Lots of it. I'll give you—"

"Yeah. You will. But later," she said, satisfied by his babbling that she had instilled fear in him. "Start."

Maggie spoke slowly, wanting him to get all that she knew had happened right. She was gambling that Thadius would write exactly what she said. She had no way of knowing. If McCready had spent more time teaching her to read than learning about loving, she wouldn't be so worried. She lost track of the time, fighting her own tiredness as he labored over the pages and finally dropped the pen after he signed his name.

Maggie had to risk a bluff. She snatched up the first paper and held it to the light. "Where does it say that Quincy was to kill me?"

"Here, here." Thadius shoved the second sheet at her. "Right there in the middle of the page. Just as you said it."

Maggie pretended to read and let him sweat.

"I wrote all of it just as you said," he whispered in a hoarse voice, hoping it was over.

"Now, you'll get me your money." Maggie scooped up the papers, folded them in half, and tucked them safely in her shirt.

"What are you going to do with them?"

"You'll find out soon enough." She slid off the desk and stood behind him to untie the rope. Keeping a tight grip on the noose, she ordered him up.

Thadius decided as he wrote out his confession that if she took his money and let him live, he was going to come out all right. After all, what could a backward, filthy creature do with a forced confession? No one would believe it. He had friends. Powerful people whom he had helped place in office. All he had to do was hurry and get rid of her. He anxiously walked across the room to his safe concealed in a lacquered cabinet. But for all his own feeling of urgency, it took him two tries to open the safe. He stood back and let her see what there was inside.

Maggie was smarter. "No. You take it out." But when he

started to put the money bags on the floor, she stopped him. "Stand up an' turn around. I'll be needin' somethin' to carry them in." Without warning, Maggie sliced down the front of his nightshirt. "Take it off."

"You can't strip me naked!"

His outrage would have been funny, but she was in no mood to laugh. Her voice became as cold as the look in her eyes. "I can't?" she repeated very softly. "You stripped me of the only family I had by killin' off me uncle. You stripped me pride an' tried for me life. You tried to steal me mines. Take it off, Cornwallis, or I'll make you fodder for hogs. Just be thankin' the devil that it ain't your hide I'm strippin' in its place."

The indignity was unbearable. He couldn't look at her as he took off the nightshirt. "You'll pay for what you're stealing from me," he blustered.

"Ain't stealin' a damn thing." Maggie quickly secured her bundle. "I'm takin' the money what was promised to me by Quincy to open me mines. An' some for Pamela Burton to give her a new start. You stole from her, too."

She caught Thadius's slight move away and rose to her feet. "Drag that chair from the desk over to the middle of the room."

Thadius no longer thought about arguing. He was mortified into silence by his naked state and the knowledge that she might still kill him. He dragged the straight-back chair from the front of the desk to a place under the crystal chandelier.

Maggie threw the end of the rope over the fancy light fixture. She tugged gently, feeling that it wouldn't hold the porker's weight, but it was the best she had.

"Get up on the chair."

"Wait a minute. This is too much. I'll yell and have help—"

"You got a choice. I'll have that chair kicked out from under you or slit your throat before the first sound comes."

Thadius climbed up on the chair, but his legs were shaking

so badly that he had to hold the top edge of the chair to steady himself.

"Listen good. If you stay real still, you might make it till someone comes lookin' for you. Move around an' you'll hang yourself."

He clawed at the noose, but she had pulled it taut, and he couldn't even get one chubby finger between the rope and his neck. He saw her wrap the balance of the rope twice around his desk and tie it off. There was no way he could pull the rope free.

"Have some pity. I did everything you wanted me to. You have the money you need. It pays for whatever you feel has been taken from you."

"It'll never pay for Pete's death, you bastard," she hissed. "An' while you're waitin', I'll be takin' these papers to the *Santa Fe Gazette.* Hear Hezekiah Johnson ain't got any use for the likes of you."

Maggie looked around. She had done all she could. But as she went to blow out the lamp, knowing how being in the dark would add to his fear, she spotted the chunk of ore that her uncle had had with him when he was killed.

Thadius saw her pick it up and smooth one hand over and around it. "Listen. I've got friends. Powerful friends. They've got money, too. We could work out a deal. You'd have the lion's share of ownership in the mine, and we'd make sure you never had to work again. You could buy—"

"Shut the hell up," she ordered calmly. Killing him would end it all too fast. She wanted him to suffer and let the law take care of him. Pocketing the ore, she hoped that Pete could rest in peace now. She wanted to go home.

"All your fancy talk an' even fancier ways ain't gonna buy your way out. You're a dead man." Maggie gripped the palm-size piece of ore in one hand and walked out.

Cooney Camp was in an uproar. Every search party that McCready organized trying to find Maggie had come up empty. Slick had returned from making his rounds of the surrounding mining camps. He had left the three tarred men down in Albuquerque. His tale was worth the price of a drink to more than a few men, and he didn't refuse their offer to head over to the White Elephant Saloon and tell his tale.

When he mentioned Mohawk Pete, a man pushed his way to Slick's side and introduced himself. Once Slick heard his story, he offered to take him back to Cooney Camp with him.

And now he faced a McCready lit like a stick of dynamite ready to blow the Rawhider sky high.

"How do you know he is who he says he is, Slick?"

"Now, McCready, I ain't a fool. Made him take me over to the foundry and machine shop he claimed to own. Men all called him boss. His name was on the sign out front. I took him over to Miss Mae's for a room and said to come down here when he was ready. Figured you'd be wanting to question him yourself."

Dutch set an unasked for drink in front of McCready. He knew McCready was suffering the guilt of the damned since Maggie had been gone. McCready couldn't deal cards, he wasn't drinking, and when Dutch thought about it, McCready wasn't even talking much to anyone. The man brooded the days away. But he wasn't ready to hear Dutch tell him what he knew was wrong.

"How many others did you tell the story to?" McCready finally asked when he had leashed his temper.

"Nearly every man I met heard it. Kinda of hard to be riding around with three tarred and feathered men and not explain why."

Slick sipped his drink, exchanging a look with Dutch. He couldn't help noticing that McCready hadn't touched his drink. He wondered if the man was sick. A quick little shake of Dutch's head warned him to leave the matter be. He slugged down the liquor, wiped his mouth, and headed for the door.

"Where the hell are you going?" McCready demanded.

"Figure I'd go find Ira and catch up on what's been happening around here. You ain't the most pleasant piece of business today, McCready."

"He ain't been pleasant since he lost my wife," Mike said from the doorway.

"That's a matter up for debate, young fella," Slick said as Mike joined him at the bar. "You're about to meet another contender."

Mike looked to McCready for an explanation, and McCready answered, "He found another one on his travels, and Slick, here, is feeling real proud of himself."

"Another one? Another what? You ain't making sense, McCready."

The door to the Rawhider opened again. Slick stepped forward to welcome the newcomer. "C'mon in and join us, Samuel. This here young fella is Mike Grant. He ranches up Montana way. This here's McCready, owns the Rawhider, and the big fella behind the bar is Dutch, best friend a man could have. Makes the best damn whiskey ever to slide down a man's throat." Slick turned to Dutch. "Pour out a drink for Samuel Taylor and make him welcome. He's here—" Slick caught McCready's murderous gaze upon him and backed away from the bar. "I'll just mosey out and find Ira and leave you all to sorta get acquainted."

"Slick," McCready warned, watching the man back all the way to the door. "Come back here or I'll—"

"Later, McCready." Slick was out the door before anyone could stop him.

McCready saw Mike give the newcomer a quick once-over, then dismiss him. McCready made his own assessment, not as quick or dismissing. The man had hard years behind him, but his dark eyes retained a sparkle. The man would need to find humor to help him get through this, McCready thought, taking in his slight build and slightly shorter height than his own. Judging by the fine tailoring of his suit, McCready knew that

Slick had not lied about this Samuel's foundry making him wealthy. But he knew that he was meeting a gentleman, something that McCready forgot at times he once was.

He was so deep in his thoughts that it took him a few minutes to realize they were all waiting for him to speak.

"Have a drink on the house," he offered. "Slick told Dutch and me why you're here."

"Wish someone would tell me," Mike cut in.

"I'll leave the pleasure of that to Mr. Taylor here," McCready snapped.

"Well?" Mike prompted, turning to the stranger.

"I've come to see Mary Margaret O'Roarke." Samuel spoke softly, revealing his southern drawl. "I don't quite understand why you gentlemen will find this of any interest, but I'm her husband."

"You don't say?" Mike asked, carefully setting down his drink and hitching his gunbelt. "Stand in line, mister, there's two more in front of you."

"*Two* more? But that's impossible. She can't have *three* husbands. No woman can."

Dutch took pity on him. "You see, it's like this," he began and went on to explain how Mike and Lars were both married by proxy to Maggie. When he finished, he looked at McCready with sympathy. The man was hurting, and hurting bad. "None of us can figure why Mohawk Pete did this," he added.

"Gentlemen, you realize that this is a shock to me. I had assumed when I agreed to forgo paying Pete what I owed him for setting up the foundry and machine stop that I would be offering to share my home with a respectable woman. But I certainly do not want to be involved with a woman—"

"Shut the hell up," McCready ordered but very softly. "Maggie had nothing to do with any of this. Pete is the one at fault. And he's dead, so there won't be a reason given for what he did."

"And just what, may I ask, is your interest in this matter? Are you the other husband?"

"Don't he wish," Mike answered before McCready did.

"Seems to me," Dutch said in an effort to calm them down, "that it isn't hard to figure why Pete married her off. To more than one," he quickly amended for the glares that both Samuel and Mike gave him. "If any one of you died, Maggie would have one less husband looking to collect her."

"I'll drink to that," McCready stated, finally lifting his glass, but the sip of liquor had his stomach churning, and he set the glass down. Since Maggie had run off for a dowry, if Pamela told him the truth, he hadn't been able to sleep or drink in peace. And now there was another man vying for her. If he wasn't so worried about her, he would cheerfully wring her neck when she got back.

But one thing was certain. He and Maggie had to have a talk and clear things up between them.

No one was more startled than McCready a few minutes later when Slick stuck his head inside and yelled, "Maggie's back! She's over at the mercantile!"

Slick was gone before they could question him. McCready saw Mike gulp down his drink, wipe his mouth, and head for the door. Samuel was right behind him, and Dutch followed. Only McCready remained where he was.

What he had to say to Maggie was for her alone. He could wait. She couldn't be surrounded by husbands forever.

When Maggie had accomplished her goal and retrieved Satin from where she left the dog guarding her horse, she wanted the miles to fly so she could get back home. But arriving in the middle of the afternoon to a sun-baked day and having a crowd demanding to know where she had been before she had gotten off her horse wasn't the homecoming she had hoped for.

McCready was nowhere in sight. Maggie smiled and nodded but soon understood that he had not come to see her. Maybe he didn't care where she had been or that she was back. The exhaustion that had ridden with her the last miles swamped her as she stepped down from her saddle into Dutch's waiting arms.

"Maggie, you had us worried," he whispered, feeling the slight tremble of her body. The press of men behind him had Dutch ordering them back to give her room, and he was rewarded by Maggie's lopsided smile. But he read the question in her eyes before she could ask. "He's inside, and yes, he knows that you're back."

"I need to talk to him, Dutch. Alone."

"You don't ask for much, do you?"

"Please. Help me."

He couldn't ignore the plea in her voice and her eyes. Pamela wedged herself a place next to them, and Dutch gave Maggie a quick nod to show he would do what he could.

"Pamela," Maggie said, suffering through a quick hug, "I've a bundle in me saddle bag that you need to take inside. You'll have your dowry an' I'll be havin' mine."

"Then you found what you were looking for?"

"That I did." Maggie scanned the crowd, disappointed that McCready still hadn't shown up. She noticed that Pamela was doing the same and leaned down to whisper, "Where's Lars?"

"He went to Clairmont when he heard there was a lawyer mining there. I guess he hopes to find a legal way to settle the matter of your husbands."

"I'll be settlin' that meself." She squeezed Pamela's hand to silence her. "We'll talk later. There's somethin' I've got to do." Maggie looked up at Dutch. "Ready?"

"Don't fight me," he said, stepping behind her. "Quiet! I know you've all got something that begs saying to Maggie, but it'll have to wait." Without any warning, Dutch swung Maggie up into his arms, the move widening a small circle around them. "Be still," he warned Maggie in a whisper. "Maggie's exhausted and thirsty, and I'm taking her over to the Raw-hider.''

Maggie wrapped her arms around him since he gave her no choice. ''Haulin' me like a sack will have them thinkin' I'm one of them helpless females.''

''You *are* a helpless female, Maggie. You just don't know it yet.'' Dutch started walking across the street.

''Why's that?''

'''Cause I believe McCready might feel partial to a helpless female along about now. And then, you got more trouble waiting.'' Dutch saw that Mike was blocking the door and ordered him to open it.

''No way. That's my wife you're handling a mite too familiar like to please me.''

''Fella, you ain't got the good sense the Lord gave your cows. Open the door and stand aside before I tear you apart.''

''Excuse me, please,'' Samuel said, joining them at the door. ''Am I to understand that *this* is Mary Margaret O'Roarke?'' His gaze was judgmental. Dust-covered and dressed in the same rough mining clothes most of the men around here wore, Mary Margaret O'Roarke was less than tolerable. At least her face was clean, and dressed in the right clothes, she might not be too bad. He couldn't forget the worth of those mines Slick had told him about.

Maggie glared at the man. How dare he call her Mary Margaret? No one used that name but McCready. But there was something unsettling about the man's eyes. Maggie was tired, but she began to understand what his calling her Mary Margaret might mean. ''Dutch! Dutch, it can't be true. This ain't the trouble I've got waitin'?''

''Afraid so. Meet Samuel Taylor from Albuquerque. And yes, before you ask, he's another one of Pete's proxy marriage males.''

Maggie buried her head against Dutch's shoulder, glad that he was holding her. She couldn't take any more. ''Go away,'' she pleaded. "All of you. Can't you be seein' I'm a helpless female in need of a glass of good whiskey?"

"She drinks?" Samuel exploded.

"You don't know the half of it," Mike answered, then opened the door. "We could all use a drink."

The mutters behind him forced Dutch to realize he wasn't getting away with taking Maggie inside alone. "Where did you leave Satin? We could use her help now."

"Up at the cabin. I didn't want to bring her here with me. She might remember what she did to McCready the last time. I really need to talk to him, Dutch, not kill him."

"I'll hold you to that."

"Well, get goin'. You're already doin' enough holdin'."

Dutch walked inside just as McCready came down the stairs. The sight of Maggie held in Dutch's arms held him immobile. Fearing that she had been hurt forced him to move, but there was a churning that fired his gut when he saw Samuel and Mike following closely along with men who appeared anxious to see what more could happen. His gaze sharpened on Maggie, but she was hiding her face against Dutch's shoulder. He couldn't see blood, and Dutch didn't seem overly concerned, so he slowly started down the steps, but Dutch warned him back.

"Don't bother. We're coming up. Maggie needs quiet, and you're taking her up to your room."

"I am? Since when are you giving me orders, Dutch?"

There was both threat and warning that Dutch heeded when he looked at McCready. Uncaring of who heard him, he said, "You can't turn her over to them. She only needs you."

"The lost maid and her entourage of knights?"

"I wouldn't be knowing about that, McCready," Dutch answered, almost daring him. "About her being a maid, that is."

"What the hell are you saying?" Mike demanded, trying to push past Dutch so he could face him.

"He's telling you that Maggie and I were lovers."

Maggie wanted to crawl inside Dutch to hide. She flinched hearing McCready's biting voice, even if she didn't understand what he meant about knights. Was he blaming her for having too many husbands? Even he wasn't that much of a fool. After all, she didn't go out and marry the passel of them. She closed her mind off from hearing Mike's demand that McCready explain. She didn't care that he told them they were lovers, but she was hurt that he sounded more bitter than proud.

She clung tight to Dutch, wishing she had never asked for his help, and never wanted to see McCready alone. But Dutch had his own plan, and without a word he handed her over to McCready.

"She's all yours for now, boss."

Maggie was afraid for a minute that McCready was going to drop her. He staggered a bit under her weight, then quickly recovered his balance.

Dutch turned and faced the men. "You're all welcome to the bar and the tables. But no one goes up the stairs."

McCready's continued hesitation cost Maggie her courage. She couldn't look up at him. What if he didn't want to talk to her? What if he wouldn't agree to what she wanted to do? Heat stole into her face that he wasn't moving. And then she wondered why being held in his arms felt like coming home.

"Guess you've left me no choice, Dutch," McCready said, his hard look at Mike and the others an added warning to the way Dutch's body blocked the stairway. Angling his head down, he whispered to Maggie, "So you're all mine and you need only me. Well, Maggie mine, I've a few needs of my own." He turned and started up the steps.

"McCready?"

"Quiet, Mary Margaret. You've come willing into the devil's den, and it's too late to change your mind."

Maggie was quiet. The wee ones were awake.

CHAPTER
25

McCready was breathing hard by the time he reached the door to his room, but this time he knew it wasn't Maggie's weight that caused it, just Maggie herself being in his arms.

"Open the door," he ordered, waiting until she did before he stepped inside and set her down. He kicked the door closed behind him.

"McCready?" Maggie looked at him, and the hard cast of his features warned that he was furious. "Wait—"

"I've waited long enough." He grabbed her hat and threw it aside before she could think about backing away from him.

Raking both of his hands through her short, coppery curls, he tilted her head back and satisfied the first of his needs with her mouth.

Maggie pushed him, but he nipped her bottom lip in warning. "Dare me to take your mouth now, Maggie mine," he whispered.

She started to, but the tip of his tongue ran lazily around her parted lips, slipped inside, and teased her tongue to play. If he had demanded, she would have fought, but he took a kiss that gentled into heat and left her defenseless. An emptiness twisted her belly like a hunger too long denied, and spread until it was an ache to be loved. Her body yearned for it, yearned to know again the fire and flight that McCready brought to her.

Her heart told her he was the only one she could share herself with, not without risk, she knew, but without pain. Her mind began to cloud. The feel of his strong hand skimming her back, urging her closer to his body, the heated intensity that deepened his kiss, combined to make her forget what she wanted from McCready. If she gave in, gave herself to him again with nothing solved between them, Maggie would be the loser.

His hot, spicy kiss stole her breath, his mouth demanding her attention. His hands skimmed her hips, grinding her against his aroused flesh, and Maggie knew the safety seconds that would allow her to pull away were flying past. Need was ready to take over, and Maggie struggled until he let her go.

"Stop it, McCready! No more of your kisses and touches and fancy words that leave me steaming like a kettle set too long on the fire."

He caught hold of her arm and with a jerk brought her stumbling against him. "Why not, Maggie? That's all you want from me, isn't it? All you'll let me give you?" His eyes were nearly black with fury. "No more—"

"I came here to talk to you, damn you, McCready." She clawed at his grip. "An' what's wrong with me wantin' you?

Can you say different? What've you ever wanted from me but me mines and me body?''

The words stung. He didn't think. He acted. He had never felt the same toward another woman. It went beyond physical need and had nothing to do with her damn mines. Still holding her arm, his other hand slid around her neck, exerting enough pressure to still her.

He gazed into her defiant and fearless eyes and smiled. ''You've made me ache, Maggie mine. Nights when I've longed for sleep, I can't find any. There's no ease with whiskey for me, either. One minute you're soft and giving and the next you're snarling. You can't make up your mind what you want from me or yourself. So I'll do it for you.''

His lips claimed hers so that she tasted desire and fury. Maggie fought against it even as it found its answering chord in her.

McCready knew he had hurt her, knew that her trust wasn't his completely and might never be again. The frustration of it made his kiss ruthless, his hands urgent. This was the only way she was completely his. He backed her toward the bed and, with their mouths still fused, tumbled onto it, feeding the fire that would take them both. Her slender body molded to the fit of his. Maggie, his Maggie, had no wiles, and he had no tolerance for them. She consumed him with need and fury, and he fought the assault on his senses.

McCready pulled his head back and stared down at her. Her mouth was swollen from his kisses. Her eyes were almost closed, and he couldn't read them. She lay still so that he could feel every tremor of her body. He wanted her so badly that he almost begged. And in the end all he could tell her was of the want that tore inside him, a wanting that she shared, for she drew his lips to hers and drank his groan of pleasure.

Maggie understood the honesty of desperation. She couldn't doubt the urgent search of his mouth or frantic touch of his hands. Shadows disappeared with the blazing light of desire.

His swearing as he tugged at her clothes made her laugh, breathless with the same need to have his gone. McCready knew her better than anyone, and he wanted her. He pulled the buttons on her shirt, then cursed. Maggie heard the material rip and only waited to feel his flesh against hers. Her hands wouldn't be still, and she drove him as he had driven her. She pulled his shirt from him and felt the loss of her own, greedy to have his mouth on hers again.

He raised himself up and rolled to the side, tugging the pants down over her hips, cursing when they caught on her boots. He came to his feet and stood between Maggie's spread legs, pulling off her boots while he watched her. Her chin was up, her eyes glowing and silently hurrying him. There was no fear, no submission. Her breathing was as labored as his own, and her look became challenging even as her second boot hit the floor.

"Daring me, Maggie?" He kicked off his boots and stripped off his pants. He knew he could take her, take her any way he chose. But McCready didn't deny to himself that he would be taken as well.

He covered her with his body, a muffled oath dying with a kiss.

Every deep, greedy kiss took her away from the narrow world she made for herself. He was relentless from the moment he touched her flesh, bringing hunger to a fever pitch that brought the words he had longed to hear.

"I need you, McCready. Need you." She felt his hair brush over her bare shoulder and the burn of his mouth on her breast brought fire. He could cherish her and rake passion higher at the same time. Her moan came from knowing that as much as from desire to have him inside her making her whole again.

McCready never had a woman snap his control the way Maggie did. One kiss, one touch from her, and he lost himself. She arched beneath him, more in demand than an offer of herself. Her eyes were dark with need, and he had what he wanted from Maggie. She thought of no one and nothing else.

"Maggie, love," he whispered, "take me inside you." He saw the change in her face as he moved slowly, her soft drawn-out moan bringing forth his own pleasure sound. Need surged in his blood and he fought it with a control that he had thought lost.

Maggie couldn't stop him, couldn't hurry him, and didn't think she could stand a moment more. Tremors rode her body as he did, leaving her weak and crying out his name, then breathing it over and over as if she knew no other word, no other sound, forcing his control to snap until they plunged into a dark swirling void where thunder ruled the skies.

Reason returned long minutes later when McCready moved to her side and tried to take her into his arms. "What have I done?" she whispered.

"Made me a happy man," he answered, nuzzling her neck. His arm rested across her waist, and once again he tried to gather her close.

Maggie would have none of him. She pushed his hand away and came off the bed, grabbing up her clothes.

"What the hell is wrong with you?"

"I've come to me senses, McCready. We need to talk about me mines. I want to buy you out. I've got the money."

"Money?" McCready slowly sat up, watching her haste to dress. "Woman, we just made love, and you're talking about those damn mines and money?"

"What's wrong with that?" Maggie couldn't look at him, afraid she would be tempted to fling herself once more into his arms. He weakened her—that's what the devil did. He wiped out her thoughts faster than a jackrabbit ran from wolves. "Never thought we'd be . . . well, lovers like you said. Didn't ask for that to happen. That's all we got between us, McCready, right?"

He hung on to his temper because he knew what would happen if he unleashed it. He hadn't even known he could feel this kind of hurt. His hand swept the rumbled bedcovers. "This is all there is, Maggie.'' McCready picked up his shirt from the floor, watching her almost dispassionately as he buttoned it.

Maggie was running scared. There was a coldness in his eyes that she had never seen, and when she caught his gaze with hers, he looked away. This wasn't the way it was supposed to be. They were going to talk, she would make her offer, and he would accept it. Then, once she had the mines open, she would tell him that she loved him. McCready was the one she wanted to be married to, no one else.

But things hadn't gone the way she planned, and now she didn't know how to fix them.

''McCready?''

''What?''

His sharp voice made her flinch inwardly. ''Don't you want to know where I've been?''

''I did. I worried myself sick over where the hell you were. No one could find you. Want a good laugh, Maggie? I had goddamn search parties out looking for you. I was afraid for you. But no, to answer your question, I don't give a damn where you were.''

She stood and watched him yank on his pants, then sit to pull on his boots. Her heart was in her eyes, but he wasn't looking at her. ''McCready, I'm not laughin'.''

''Neither am I.''

''I've got the money to open the mines,'' she said, lifting her boots in one hand and glancing around his room. He had rushed her into bed so quickly she hadn't noticed how large it was. A massive writing desk slanted across one corner, a wing-back leather chair behind it. She could picture him sitting there, the light from the desk lamp playing shadows over his face. But Maggie wasn't about to sit in that chair. It reminded her too much of the one Thadius had. She shivered, thinking about what she had risked, and now McCready didn't want her to share it with him.

The sound of water splashing made her turn, and she found him at the washstand, wiping his face.

"Help yourself," he offered, refusing to look at her. McCready went to the sideboard on the wall opposite the bed where a tray of crystal decanters was displayed. He hesitated a moment, then pulled out the stopper and poured himself a drink. He hoped that she didn't see the betraying tremble in his hand. He hoped that Maggie had the sense to get the hell out of here quickly before he exploded.

"Aren't you offerin' me any?" she asked, coming to stand behind him. She reached out to touch him but withdrew her hand before she did. Fury was coming off him like the heat waves of the desert. "I went to see Thadius Cornwallis."

"You did what?" He set the glass down carefully, closed his eyes briefly, and when he was sure that he wouldn't grab hold of her and shake the daylights out of her, he turned. "Why, Maggie?"

"He owed me for Pete's death. For other things. I took what I needed. What I was promised by Quincy."

"And that's all that matters to you, right? Those mines?"

"They mattered a hell of a lot to you, too, McCready." Maggie had her hands on her hips, anger flushing her face, set for battle.

McCready pushed by her. "I'm not selling you my share of the mines. And if that's what you have come here to find out, you can now leave."

"Don't fight me, McCready. You'll lose this time."

"This time? No, Maggie, you're all wrong. I've already lost. But I won't lose the mine, too." His gaze snared hers and he grinned. "If you're not leaving, Maggie, I'll assume you weren't satisfied. If that's true, the bed's behind you, and being a gentleman, I'll do what I can to accommodate you."

"You bastard!"

"True. Quite true, Maggie. My mother was raped and bore me against her will. She never let me forget it."

"McCready, please, I didn't—"

"Your pity is worth about as much as the dust on your boots, Maggie. I made you an offer. If you're not taking it, I suggest you leave." He opened the door and stood there.

Maggie snatched up her hat and held it with her boots in one hand. "I came here in good faith to deal with you."

"Another offer?" he questioned, crossing his arms over his chest, then leaning against the door.

"The same one," she whispered, walking toward the door.

McCready put out one arm to stop her. "Maggie, if I told you that you and what we share meant something to me, more than I've had with any other woman, would you believe me?" He knew he could lower his mouth to hers and make her forget, make her believe him, but he didn't move.

"Before, maybe I would've. But now, I ain't so sure."

McCready dropped his arm. She stepped into the hall. "Maggie, make sure you take your husbands with you. I'm damn tired of shepherding your growing flock."

"Me husbands? McCready," she snapped, "by the time I'm through with you, boyo, you'll be knee-deep in *me husbands!*"

"A threat, Maggie?" he taunted, knowing she wouldn't let him have the last word. He almost grinned when she spun around and shoved one finger against his shoulder.

"Just bet on it."

He waited until she reached the stairs. "Maggie, just remember that I always win."

By the following afternoon, when McCready returned from a solitary ride to clear his head, he finally understood what Maggie had meant. Knee-deep in husbands, indeed! Ira was daring to nail a sign to the outside wall of the Rawhider.

"McCready," he said by way of greeting. "Just doing a few odd jobs for Miss Pamela and Miss Maggie."

"Miss Maggie?"

"Yep. That's what she said folks got to call her now." He scurried away with the other signs tucked under his arm.

McCready stepped up on the wooden sidewalk. He instantly recognized Pamela's neat printing, but that didn't make what he was reading easy.

AUCTION!   AUCTION!   AUCTION!

One week from Saturday at the Rawhider Saloon in Cooney Camp. Goods from Burton's Mercantile will be offered to the highest bidder in one lot.

Mary Margaret O'Roarke will take bids on herself and her ownership of three ore-producing silver mines and one gold mine. Object is matrimony with the highest bidder.

ALL MERCHANDISE WILL BE AVAILABLE FOR INSPECTION ONE HOUR PRIOR TO THE START OF THE AUCTION.

Pamela Burton, acting auctioneer

McCready felt he was being watched. He wasn't about to give anyone the satisfaction of seeing his reaction. He even thought to straighten the edge of the sign that he wanted to rip into shreds.

He settled his hat, turned, and walked across the street to the mercantile. Tied before the door was Maggie's damn dog.

But instead of the growled greeting and bared teeth she usually offered him, the dog whined and lifted one paw.

McCready trusted her about as much as he trusted her mistress. "Don't try that on me, you devil's spawn." The dog cocked her head to one side, still whining. "So, they locked you out just like me. Or are you out here guarding the little darling inside from getting her neck wrung?"

Christ! Now Maggie had him talking to her dog! McCready spun around and headed back to the Rawhider.

"Dutch!" McCready yelled as soon as he stepped inside.

"Right here, boss," he answered, coming out from the store room. "Something wrong?"

"Wrong? What could be wrong?" McCready asked in a soft, silken voice, moving behind the bar to take one of his special bottles of whiskey down from the shelf.

Dutch eyed him. McCready had been riding, judging by the dust on his black clothes. McCready had taken to wearing a lot of black lately, now that Dutch thought about it. He carefully stepped behind the bar.

"I just figured, boss, that something was wrong by the way you hollered."

McCready slugged down one drink and quickly poured out another.

"Guess your stomach ain't hurting like it was, boss."

"The state of my stomach is not your business, Dutch. But there is a little matter I want to discuss with you. A matter I believe I don't have to waste time bringing to your attention, but I will give you the benefit of the doubt and pretend that you don't know what the hell I'm talking about."

"Truth be, McCready, I don't."

"Do I own this establishment?"

"Far as I know. You ain't got yourself in another game and put up the Rawhider, have you?"

"No. The point that I am trying to make, Dutch, is that I do own this building and the property it stands upon. But there is a notice posted on the outside wall of this saloon. I do not recall giving my permission to anyone to place a nail in my wood, on my property. Nor do I recall giving any son of a bitch permission to use my saloon for a goddamn auction!"

Dutch thought it best to wait until the second drink was gone and replaced by a third before he answered. "But you did give permission, if that's what got you riled. Pamela Burton was here bright and early right after you rode out and said that you told her you'd do anything you could to help her."

McCready groaned. His head sank down into his waiting hands. He did recall the night he went over to Pamela's to see Maggie. The night she told him that Maggie was gone. The night she conned him into this agreement, and big-hearted fool that he was, he didn't want to see her smile disappear.

When he lifted his head and met Dutch's gaze, he knew he had been outsmarted by Maggie and Pamela.

"It's true, ain't it, boss?"

"It's sort of the truth. Pamela is welcome to use the Rawhider to get rid of the stores from the mercantile, but I'll be damned if Maggie is going to auction herself off." *Knee-deep in me husbands.* Maggie's words rang in his mind like a death knell. "Dutch, do you know where Ira is putting up those signs?"

"Ira's already been over to Clairmont. Slick volunteered to hit the other mining camps."

McCready's elbows hit the bar, hard, and once more he buried his head in his hands. It was already too late to put a stop to it.

Dutch echoed his thought. "You can't try to stop it now. You'll have every man jack of them down on you."

"I know. That's what the Irish thief was counting on."

"Irish thief? Maggie? Now, McCready, that ain't true. She hasn't stolen from you."

"Wanna bet?"

Dutch decided he needed a drink, and for a few minutes left McCready to brood. "A man has a right to claim what's his. You could, if you're of a mind to, bid on her. If you won, why, you could get back what you've lost."

"Bid on Maggie?" McCready slowly lifted his head. "The hell I will," he grated, grabbing the bottle and retreating to his room.

"Then you're a bigger fool than I figured, boss," Dutch whispered to himself.

"Thief, damn Irish thief," McCready muttered to himself three hours later when he realized that Maggie had stolen the blurred-edge peace his whiskey had once brought him. What

had possessed her to hold an auction for herself? It made no
sense. Her and her mines, a little voice reminded him. Mines?
That sign said *her ownership* in four mines. But she didn't own
the mines by herself. They were partners, due to his generosity.
And she called him a liar!

He closed his eyes, but she refused to leave his mind.
Maggie learning her letters, telling him about her dreams to be
a lady, to learn to read, and to open those damn mines. Maggie
didn't need to change. He liked her just the way she was—
honest, giving, prideful, mule-tempered Maggie. His Maggie.

And her offering to let the merchandise be inspected before
the auction! Did she believe he would stand by while some
man put his hands on her? Didn't the woman have an ounce of
common sense? Men who loved—loved?

McCready bolted up off his bed, turning the word over in his
mind. He loved Maggie? That scrappy, independent, fight-at-
the-wrong-word Maggie?

Raking his hands through his hair, McCready knew there
was no help to be had. He loved Maggie. Somehow, he had to
get her to agree to call off this auction before he committed
murder. And he had to do it quickly, or he would be calling in
the army to keep peace in Cooney Camp.

Across the street Pamela was repeating similar words to
Maggie.

"You can't get cold feet about this. The signs are already
out, and you'll need the army here to keep peace if you try to
call it off."

"But McCready had to see it. He should've been here by
now, ready to fight with me."

"Duck your head again so I can rinse off the soap, Maggie.
When we're finished cleaning up, we'll talk about McCready."

With a towel around her head Maggie rolled up the sleeves
of Pamela's borrowed nightgown and helped her fill and empty

buckets, until there were only a few inches of water left in the wooden tub.

"Hold open the door, Pamela. I can drag it now, and we'll tilt it outside."

Pamela stood behind the door watching Maggie wiggle backward, dragging the tub.

Maggie managed to get the tub halfway out of the door when her bottom hit something solid. She wiggled from side to side trying to understand what was blocking her way.

"Pamela?" But even as she called the other woman, she was reaching back with one hand to discover cloth covering solid muscle and lower, a boot. Caught between the tub and whoever stood there, Maggie couldn't move, and Pamela wasn't answering her.

"Let me help you, Maggie mine," McCready whispered, bending over her body and placing his hands on either side of hers. "I like the smell of violets on your skin, O'Roarke; it brings to mind a fond memory and the freckles I never did get around to counting."

"You said . . ." Maggie was surrounded by his scent, his body warmth, and his lips against the back of her neck. "Help. That's what you were doing."

"Was I?" he returned, rubbing his chin over her shoulder. "I wasn't sure what kind of a reception I would find when I came here, Mary Margaret, but never, even in my mind, did I dare think you'd be ready for bed."

"Pamela!"

She stepped out from behind the door and looked down at Maggie. "Well, you said you wanted him here to talk. So go to it."

"Like this?"

"I like this just fine, Maggie mine."

"You would!" Maggie returned, glaring up at Pamela. The towel was slipping down over one eye. Maggie made a grab for it just as McCready leaned forward to kiss her cheek. He got her thumb in his eye, and Maggie reared back, throwing her weight against him. McCready lost his balance, and Maggie went sprawling with him into the mud the emptied buckets had created.

Maggie was stunned for a moment, then twisted around as he sat up. "Damn you! Look what you've done, McCready."

"What I've done! I came here to talk to you about calling off that damn auction. You poked my eye and gave me a mud bath I didn't need."

"Ain't calling it off!" Maggie struggled against his arms wrapped around her waist, but he held her tight.

"Listen to me, mule-head. I came with the best intentions. You can't auction off mines I own half interest in."

Maggie froze. That was it? The mines? Not her? "Go to hell, McCready, the devil's waitin' on you."

"Be reasonable—"

"Reason? I'll give you reason!" Maggie threw her weight forward, clawing at his hands, caught him unaware, and broke free. She sprawled on all fours in the mud, but McCready was only able to grab her ankle. She kicked him and twisted onto her back, flinging handfuls of mud at him. "You want those damn mines so bad. Bid on them, McCready."

Satin bounded up, barking, and Maggie yelled, "Get him, girl!" at the same time McCready ordered, "Down, Satan!"

McCready came to his feet in a controlled rush, slipped, then grabbed Maggie and hauled her to her feet. "Call off the dog and the auction. I'm not asking you, I'm telling you. You think I'll stand by while you parade in front of every man in the territory who feels free to paw what they're bidding on? Think again, Maggie. I won't let it happen. We've done our share of fighting, and now it stops." He shook her and Maggie motioned Satin to stay away.

"I didn't forget that you could be carrying my child."

Maggie felt her belly bottom out. She glanced from his

punishing grip on her arms to the glare of his eyes. "You're talkin' marriage 'cause there might be a child?"

"I'm not talking about marriage at all, Maggie. But I won't have you leave me out of my child's life, and I swear I'll take care of you." His grip eased and became caressing. "Maggie, what we share is good, damn good." He read the doubt in her eyes and knew he had to say more. "I love you, Maggie."

She fought the tremble that started inside her. She couldn't believe him, no matter how much she had longed to hear him say those words. How could she trust him? "Why—" She had to swallow and, staring into his eyes, finished. "Why didn't you tell me when Lars showed up? Why didn't you say it when Mike came or the other one showed up? Why now, McCready?"

"I didn't know it then. Maggie," he whispered softly, lowering his mouth to hers, but she turned aside. "I've never said those words to another woman."

"An' now you can?" She didn't try to pull away. She knew he wouldn't let her go. "You're askin' for trust again. But I can't. It's just your way of gettin' me to stop the auction, but it ain't gonna work. You'll have to prove it to me. Prove you want me more than anyone or anything."

He released her. "I'll be damned if I'll do that."

Maggie couldn't watch him leave. Satin's whine told her he was gone. "McCready, you're wrong. It's me who's damned."

CHAPTER
26

The morning of the auction dawned bright and clear, but Maggie's cross mood was better suited to match a storm. She had not seen or heard from McCready again. When she thought about it, Maggie realized that neither of her three husbands had been around, either. She had done all that she could to make sure the auction was the success she wanted. Now it was only a matter of time until it began.

Satin tugged her hand to get her out of bed. Pamela had agreed that the dog could come inside with them as added protection after one overly excited bidder came too early for the auction and broke into the store.

When Maggie opened the back door to let Satin out, she found Lars coming around, hat in hand. Maggie scooted behind the door to hide the fact that she was only wearing a nightgown. Living with Pamela this past week had taught her so many things about being a lady.

"I have come to see Pamela," Lars said. "To say goodbye."

"You're leavin'?"

"*Ja.* I will not stay for the auction. The lawyer I have spoken to tells me that I cannot be married to you unless we agree and have the marriage again."

"The others, Lars, do they know about this?"

"*Ja.* I told them. But they are staying. Please, you will let me see her."

"C'mon in an' sit. I'll get her up." Maggie's mood lightened with his news. One less to worry about. And if Ira and Slick did what she asked, McCready wasn't going to have a chance.

When she walked into the bedroom she and Pamela were sharing, the other woman was already up and dressed. "Lars is here to see you. He's leaving, Pamela."

"Leaving?"

"That's what the man says. I'd hurry an' find out what he came here for, 'cause it ain't just to say goodbye."

"But my hair!" Pamela grabbed for the brush with one hand and hairpins with the other.

Maggie took them from her. "Leave it. Don't waste time."

"Come with me?" But even as she asked, Pamela saw Maggie shake her head. Taking a deep breath, Pamela marched out to the kitchen.

Maggie closed the bedroom door to give them as much privacy as she could. Curled up on the bed, she tried to forget what would be happening tonight. Cooney Camp didn't have a spare blanket left or the room to spread it down. From her frequent peeks out the mercantile's window, she saw the constant flow of men going into the Rawhider. At least McCready couldn't complain about all the business she had drawn in for him.

Not knowing what he was going to do gnawed at her. If he had told anyone, they would have passed it along to her. But not even Dutch knew what McCready would do.

Not that Dutch had time to find out. He was busy tending bar and selling whatever chairs he begged and borrowed to use for the front rows. Ira had told her that he was charging two hundred dollars a seat so the serious bidders were assured of a place. Maggie should have been feeling pleased with herself, for there wasn't an empty chair.

But all she felt was scared. What if McCready was right and men tried to paw her? She didn't think she could stand to have another man touch her. Much as Pamela argued against it, Maggie knew she would have to take Satin with her. She couldn't depend on McCready being there to protect her. The thought didn't even startle her anymore. She felt less than whole without McCready, and there was no fighting against it. And it was too late to tell him that she was wrong to put the mines first. Gold and silver couldn't wrap their arms around her and keep her safe and warm. They couldn't make her feel the same excitement as one of McCready's kisses, even if she once had thought so.

I'll chase you and you'll chase me, Maggie, until one of us is caught.

Maggie prayed that every word McCready said was true. If she didn't catch hold of him this time, she never would.

An excited cry from Pamela made her turn toward the door, but Maggie didn't hear her cry out again. She hoped that Lars was offering her marriage. Pamela deserved it, and she would make him a good wife. At least Pamela wouldn't have to worry that they'd be fighting and scrapping. Larson Vladimir was too much of a gentleman to do that to her.

It was nearly an hour later that a rosy-cheeked Pamela opened the bedroom door. "Maggie! He asked and I said yes and he's going to wait until after the auction." She flung herself on the bed, bouncing up and down, accepting Maggie's hug and crying.

"I'm really happy for you, Pamela. You've got what you wanted."

"Yes," she answered, sniffling. "We talked it all out. Lars agrees that I need to sell the supplies, but, Maggie, he doesn't want me to take the bids on you."

"But we agreed—"

"I know. I tried to tell him, but he has his own notions about how his wife should behave, and I couldn't fight with him. But I'll be there. He agreed to that. And he's going to ask Dutch to do it."

"Dutch? He'll never—"

"He will. Lars," she said through misty eyes and a smile, "can be very convincing when he sets his mind to it."

Maggie didn't want to spoil her happiness, and so let it be. But she was sure that McCready wouldn't allow Dutch to auction her off.

By midafternoon Lars returned and proved Maggie wrong.

"*Ja. Ja*, he said he would do this. To help Mary."

Seated at the kitchen table, Maggie looked across at him. "You're sure? McCready doesn't know, right?"

"He was there when I asked Dutch. He made a toast to me and my bride and one to you."

"He wasn't angry?" Maggie stared down at the cold cup of coffee that she couldn't force herself to finish. Her belly was knotted, and the wee ones were dancing to a different tune. One that made her swallow a lot.

"McCready?" Lars shook his head. "He has said that only two drinks be allowed for each man. They are running out of whiskey. But, Dutch, he tells me that McCready is worried how men behave when they are drunk."

"See, Maggie," Pamela said, holding Lars's hand. "I told

you there was nothing to worry about. And now you know that McCready will be there.''

''Yeah. But will he be biddin'?''

No one answered her.

Pamela tugged the bodice of Maggie's gown up, but the blue, flower-sprigged calico wouldn't cover the bared curves of Maggie's breasts. Frowning, Pamela stood back. ''We could tuck a bit of lace, but you'd have to be careful when you moved unless I stitch it in place.''

''There's no time, Pamela.'' Maggie glanced at herself in the mirror. Pamela had labored over brushing her hair and securing it with combs so that it looked longer than it was. Around her neck was a blue velvet ribbon and a great deal of skin until her gaze lowered to the edge of the gown that didn't cover what it should have.

''You put on weight. That's all it could be. I know I took the right measurements. Let them wait and I'll sew on lace.'' McCready would be furious, but her little lie was worth it.

Maggie shook her head. With hands that were softened by Pamela's creams, she fixed the edges of the gown on her shoulders. She was wearing a gown to please McCready, and she would use whatever she could to entice him into bidding for her. Pamela had explained how a lady made a man jealous, and while she had been uncomfortable about the gown at first, she wasn't now.

Lars called out from the kitchen that they were late.

Pamela thrust a shawl at Maggie. ''At least wear this until we get there.''

That Maggie agreed to.

But Pamela stopped her at the bedroom doorway. ''Maggie, the day you were going to marry Quincy, I told you how pretty you looked. But tonight, Maggie, well, you're beautiful enough to make that parish stallion rip and snort.''

''Be right, Pamela. Just please be right.''

* * *

Stallion aptly described what McCready felt like. His territory was being invaded by every single man sniffing after his filly. Ira left to escort another small group of married men and miners whose luck had panned out and were looking for a stable way to earn a living over to inspect the store.

The Rose, Lee Warren, and Dutch were serving behind the bar, keeping close watch to make sure that no man had more than two drinks. The last thing McCready wanted was some drunk pawing Maggie or forgetting that she wasn't being paid to keep him happy.

"Boss," Dutch warned, then nodded toward the door.

McCready saw that Mike and Samuel were finally here, but it was the sight of Miss Mae between them that sent him pushing through the crowd.

"Miss Mae? What are you doing here?"

"She asked us to escort—"

"Shut up, sonny," the frail-looking sixty-year-old woman said to Samuel with an added poke to his ribs. "I can speak for myself. McCready, this is the most excitement we've ever had. You didn't think I'd miss it? Now. You take my arm and get me a chair up close. I don't want to miss out hearing one word."

McCready's offered arm was readily accepted, and Miss Mae held her parasol like a cane as they made their way up front.

"Causing quite a stir what your little gal did."

"She's not my little gal, Miss Mae. But you're right about the stir she's created."

"Came to see me this week. Had plenty to say about you, too."

"I'm sure she did."

"Called you names I had to think twice about to remember. Getting on, you know."

McCready led her around to the center chair of the row that Dutch had set up.

"Not here. Give me that one on the end. If I feel faint, you can take me outside without disturbing anyone."

"I wasn't planning on staying, Miss Mae."

"Horse feathers! You'll stay, McCready. A lady is asking for your company. You gonna refuse me?"

"I'm sure that Samuel or Mike would be happy to act as your escort. Let me—"

"Don't want either one of them, McCready. I'm old and I'm stubborn, but I'm a lady that knows fine breeding when I see it. You've got the lines of good stock and the manner when you want. A woman needs to be proud of the man standing by her side. And you're the best man around here. Take my word for that."

She was old, and she was stubborn. But within her face edged by a lace-trimmed mob cap, McCready saw her bright eyes that held his as steady as any rock. She reminded him of a time when a gentleman never refused a lady's reasonable request. But he hadn't planned on staying, just as he told her, and for a moment felt she had neatly trapped him.

"I'm all the excuse you'll need, McCready."

"You, madam, are a fraud."

"Set me down easy like and get this auction going. It's long past my bedtime as it is."

"We're just waiting for the prize of the night to show up," he answered, helping Miss Mae to lower herself into the chair. "Is this comfortable for you? I'll get—"

He never finished and never heard what she answered. The murmurs that quickly grew louder and the crush at the doorway told him that Maggie was here.

McCready straightened to his full height very slowly. He believed he had been ready for this moment since he understood that Maggie was really going to go through with this. But somewhere between the crowd parting and his first sight of her, his heart forgot to beat. Gone were the muddy boots—her steps were taken in high-buttoned pointy-toed ladies' shoes. He had prayed she would want to be his Maggie and wear baggy pants, a too big shirt, and a jacket to hide the body only he knew intimately. But Maggie's body was graced by a full calico skirt that might conceal a petticoat, but his gaze gave way to the lush fullness of her breasts. Too much of her breasts, for his peace of mind. But the worst offense to his sight were the freckles that the too-low bodice revealed.

Miss Mae tapped his arm. "Can't see her. You're blocking my view."

He stepped aside, but fury grew that no one else's view was blocked. Why the hell was Maggie carrying the shawl? It should be draped, wrapped, and tied around her! And where did that practiced smile come from? She had never smiled at him like that. Where was his Maggie? She would never flutter her hand about, lightly touching one man's arm, another's shoulder. Softly laughing at something Mike whispered to her. Arching her brow with a pout on her lips when Samuel demanded her attention.

She was flirting! Drawing men around her like flies, and those damn mines had nothing to do with it. He started forward, but Miss Mae's clawlike hand grabbed his. "Leave her be. The gal's getting her courting, McCready. Unless you want to join them? Bet you'd give those bucks a run for their money. But you don't want her, right?"

The sparkle in her eyes should have warned him, but he wasn't thinking clearly. "You're quite right, Miss Mae. And I thank you for stopping me before I made a fool of myself. If you will excuse me, I'll get Dutch to begin."

But Dutch had already come out from behind the bar and was clearing space before it. Those that had bought seats took them, and the rest had to stand behind them. "Quite a turnout, boss."

"Yeah. Well, get it going. The sooner this is over with, the better I'll feel."

"I'm betting on it. Folks!" he yelled. "We're ready to start. Now, I'm taking bids on the supplies from the Burton store."

Maggie stood at the end of the bar nearest the door with Pamela on one side and Lars on the other. Pamela had been right about just smiling at this one and pouting at the other being the way to flirt with men. But the one man she wanted to try her new wiles on hadn't come anywhere near her. She knew he saw her. The moment she walked into the Rawhider, she searched out McCready. The wee ones were kicking up their heels at the sight of him. She knew McCready was as handsome as sin and twice as bad, and the unrelieved black he wore only added to her belief. She closed out the sound of Dutch's voice and calls as bids were raised for the mercantile's goods. In a few minutes she would be standing up on the bar, parading back and forth while men made offers. Mike had assured her that he would put up his ranch and take his "little gal" home where she belonged. As for Samuel, she didn't like the idea of how charming she would be gracing his arm as his wife.

"Two thousand!" Dutch called out. "That's the last bid. Going once, twice, and sold to Joseph Applebee." Dutch directed the storekeeper from Silver City to Pamela and he watched the man counting out the money to her. He listened to the restless mutterings and knew he couldn't wait any longer. "Maggie? You ready?"

Nervous, Maggie rubbed her palms down the side of her gown. Finally she nodded and let Dutch lift her up in his arms so she could stand up on the bar. The whistles and catcalls surprised her, and she was grateful for the squeeze Dutch gave her hand before he released her.

"I'm right down here, and they'll have to go through me to get to you. I won't let that happen, Maggie." He turned and held his hands high for quiet. "Now, settle down. It goes without my saying that Miss Mary Margaret O'Roarke is a fine-looking woman. She's . . ." Dutch's voice was drowned out by the rowdy shouts of agreement. He gave them a few minutes more, then roared an order for quiet. From the corner of his eye he watched McCready, but the man had eyes for no one but Maggie.

Dutch began again. "Most of you men know me or of me. I'm vouching for Maggie's claim to the worth of the mines. Now I'll take an opening bid."

"Five hundred!"

"Two thousand," Mike Grant offered, having decided that no one was outbidding him.

"Three," Samuel said, unwilling to be outdone.

"Smile at them, Maggie," Pamela whispered as Maggie came to her end of the bar.

But Maggie was finding that being the center of attention wasn't pleasant. There was heat in the stares as the bidding climbed quickly. Strangers forced Mike and Samuel into offering serious money. She tried to block out the voices and the crude suggestions that came with them but saw that Ira and Slick were working their way through the standing crowd of men doing a little hushing of their own.

"The last bid was Taylor's at thirty-thousand," Dutch announced. "Where's the men in this crowd? You gonna let a fine gal like Maggie—"

"Thirty-five!" Mike shouted.

"Thirty-eight," Samuel shot back.

"Forty," came another voice, and both men craned their necks to see a gray-haired man lowering his hand.

"Who is he?" Mike asked Samuel.

"Lawyer. From Silver City. Came up with Applebee."

"Forty-five," Mike bid.

"Fifty," Samuel said almost before he was finished.

Maggie smiled at them, but the one voice she longed to hear was not making a sound. She looked at McCready as she walked the length of the bar and found his dark blue eyes were filled with storm warnings. Maggie never knew what made her do it, but she gave him an airy wave and turned her back.

"Cheeky little gal, McCready," Miss Mae said, cackling at the murderous look he shot her.

McCready wasn't surprised that the bidding was climbing by ten-thousand-dollar increments. Maggie was sashaying over the top of the bar. If she wiggled her hips any more, she'd be a harem dancer for them. He wanted to haul her out of there. But he wouldn't give her the satisfaction. She asked for this and she was going to see it through to the bitter end.

He pinned his gaze on two men in the second row of chairs, who sat with their heads together. They were tinhorns. No question in his mind at all, and he didn't like the way they were looking at Maggie. He had seen tinhorns who used women as shills when they gambled for high stakes, sure that the right kind of woman would distract a man from serious play while they dealt off the bottom or palmed a new hand of cards from a sleeve. When they combined their bid to top the one hundred thousand that Mike had just offered, McCready knew they were trouble.

"I'll put up my ranch. It's worth twice as much."

"Says who?" one gambler yelled back.

"Says me." Mike was up and around his chair too fast for anyone to stop him. "You feel lucky enough to step outside and repeat that?"

Dutch had to go settle it. "Listen, Mike, it's a fair enough question."

"Maybe. I'll allow it. But they can't combine their bids."

"I've never said different. I've got to accept it. Now, sit down and we'll get on with this."

"Dutch, if you question the worth of his ranch, then I can't bid my foundry, right?" Samuel asked.

"Cash bids is all I'm taking. And from what I see these two waving around, it sure looks like a hundred thousand or more."

Maggie almost fell off the bar. Pamela's gasp made her want to cry. This wasn't supposed to happen.

Dutch bought McCready all the time he could. He drank a glass of water that Lee handed him. Went over the last few bids until mutters began, then grew louder, demanding that he get on with it.

"Now, we're all agreed that the last bid was one hundred and two thousand dollars? Right?"

"Hurry it up, Dutch. I'm so parched back here you got me thinkin' I've been eatin' cotton."

Dutch laughed with the rest of the miners, most of whom had dropped out of bidding on Maggie when they saw how high it was going. But Dutch had caught more than a few sneaking looks at McCready wondering, as they all likely were, why he wasn't bidding. Every man there saw the way Maggie watched him. But he couldn't wait any longer.

"The bid's going once, going twice—"

"I'll make it one hundred and five, but I want to see some proof of the mine claims," the lawyer said.

Maggie expected this and took the ore sample from Pamela. She held it high for all to see. "This is from the gold mine. Should assay out to five maybe six hundred dollars."

"But I know nothing about raw gold," the man returned.

Maggie tossed the sample toward him and waited until he caught it. "Ask any miner here if I ain't tellin' the truth."

It took a few minutes and only three men confirming what she said before the man nodded to Dutch to let his bid stand.

Mike turned to Samuel. "Look, I want Maggie for my wife. Drop out of the bidding, and I'll give you half of the mines after we're married again."

"I could ask you to do the same. But it doesn't matter. I can't come up with enough cash money to top his bid."

Miss Mae was disturbed to see the two of them whispering. "You gonna let her go to some stuffy lawyer that'll lock her away and change her into something dead, McCready?"

"This is of Maggie's making, not mine, Miss Mae."

"She needs a man that understands her. One who'll let her be Maggie. A man, McCready, who ain't afraid of a strong woman. One who won't be pettin' her like that rancher and think she's soft."

"I am not bidding on her."

"You're not?" The fury in his eyes was more than enough of an answer. "Hold my parasol," she demanded.

McCready, with an exasperated sigh, lifted his hand to take hold of it just as Dutch repeated the last bid. Miss Mae waited until McCready gripped the handle before she shoved his arm high.

"McCready bids one hundred and ten thousand!" Miss Mae yelled out, then waved to Maggie.

"I never—"

"One hundred and ten from McCready!" Dutch roared so that he drowned out McCready's protests.

Maggie climbed down from the bar, running to him. "Oh, McCready, you do love me!" she cried out, flinging her arms around his neck, stopping his denial with her lips for a few seconds, then pulled back. "There's no child."

He held her gaze steady with his. "Let the bid stand."

The parasol slipped from his fingers. His arms closed around her waist, and he took every bit of giving softness that her mouth offered to him.

Samuel glared at Dutch. "The bidding isn't over yet."

"Top his, then," Dutch returned, only to have Samuel do just that.

Miss Mae frantically tugged on McCready's sleeve, but he was lost in Maggie's kiss. "I'll be his agent," she announced and promptly entered the bidding. "One hundred and twenty-five thousand."

McCready half heard what Miss Mae was doing, but he didn't stop her. Maggie was whispering against his lips that she loved him, only him, and every word was balm to his wound.

He had never had a woman's love completely his. And he didn't care what anyone bid, he was offering Maggie his love and his heart in return with every deepening kiss they shared.

"Two hundred thousand!" Dutch shouted, grinning. "Going once, twice—and sold to McCready! That's it, boys. Drinks are on the house."

"Did you hear that, Maggie mine, you really are mine," he murmured against the corner of her smiling mouth. He swept her up into his arms to stop her from being crushed by the men that surrounded them, and found himself facing Maggie's two husbands. "She's been mine from the start no matter who Pete tried to marry her off to," McCready said, then smiled when Maggie rested her head on his shoulder.

"Could've fooled me," Mike said. "In fact, you did. You weren't even bidding on her."

"But I would have."

"You would've?" Maggie demanded to know, wrapping her arms around his shoulders.

"Bet on it, Maggie mine. I said I always win. Besides, we have a partnership, right? Share everything, equal and together."

"But you stated that you wouldn't be bidding," Samuel added.

McCready grinned, then looked at Maggie. "I lied."

"Ah, McCready, you're a silver-tongued devil an' no mistake about it. But you'll be marryin' me to make an honest lady of me?"

"I'll marry you. I'll even make a lady out of you, if that's what you want. But a Maggie mine kind of lady. One who is honest, and warm as sunshine filling all the empty places inside me. A golden lady, dripping diamonds and draped in silks, satins, or calico, even mud, but still my sassy-mouthed Maggie. I'll tell you why you need seven forks to eat your dinner and why it's impolite to fall asleep at the opera. I'll share all there is if you share the world with me."

"McCready." She blinked back tears. "I don't cry. But I've an Irish temper."

"I'm arrogant."

"I'm mule-headed."

"Me, too. But I love you, Maggie."

"An' I love you, C. V. McCready." She kissed him with all that love in her heart, knowing he wouldn't try to change her, just as she wanted him as he was.

Poking at the men's legs with her parasol, Miss Mae ordered, "Get back, the lot of you. Can't you see they want privacy?"

McCready turned his back, holding Maggie tight, and swept the sweet taste of her inside himself. The churning in his gut subsided with every moment that the kiss lasted, and when it ended, he had his Maggie's smile and glowing green eyes.

"I'll be sayin' it again. I love you, McCready. I love fightin' with you an' kissin' you. But if you're marryin' me," she asked, shyly lowering her lashes, "could you be thinkin' to tell me what C.V. is for?"

"Later, Maggie."

"We're sharin', remember?"

He angled his head down, giving her his trust, and pressed his lips against her ear. "My name, Mary Margaret, is Clarence Valentine."

Maggie jerked her head away. Wide-eyed, she stared at him. "Clarence?" she repeated very softly. "Clarence Valentine?" She tried to stop her smile, she tried to swallow the laughter, but the challenge in his eyes seemed to encourage it forth.

"Maggie!" he warned. "I'll take you over my knee—"

"Don't you wish, boyo."

"Stop giggling. I've had to—"

"Clarence?" she repeated once more, lifting her hand to her mouth to stifle the laughter.

McCready knew how to stop her. He nudged aside her hand and sealed her mouth with his. And when he finally felt the tremors that racked her body along with his own, he slowly lifted his head.

"Tell me, Maggie mine, are the wee ones awake?"

"Ah, McCready," she said in a dreamy voice, "they're set to dance at a grand Irish weddin'."

"And you'll promise to forget about my first name? No more teasing? No more laughing?"

"You're a silver-tongued devil, like I've said, but I love you." Maggie lowered her lashes once more and solemnly nodded. "I promise, McCready." *Until after the wedding,* she silently amended.

"That's good, real good, Maggie, 'cause I lied. It's Calvert Vance."

"McCready!"

"Claude Verne? How about Chandler Virgil?"

"Ah, 'tis a grand marriage we'll be havin', 'cause I lied, too," she whispered, drawing his mouth to hers. "You're not fool's gold, McCready. 'Tis the luck of the Irish I'll be havin' with you an' your love."

He let her have the last word this time. How could he argue with a woman who promised him everything that mattered with her kiss?

It *was* going to be a grand marriage. Maggie, Satan, and him. And when the little darlings came, the good Lord help them all.

FREE
Romance
(a $4.50 value)

Send in the Coupon Below

To get your FREE historical romance and start saving, fill out the coupon below and mail it today. As soon as we receive it we'll send you your FREE Book along with your first month's selections.

Mail To: **True Value Home Subscription Services, Inc. P.O. Box 5235**
120 Brighton Road, Clifton, New Jersey 07015-5235

YES! I want to start previewing the very best historical romances being published today. Send me my FREE book along with the first month's selections. I understand that I may look them over FREE for 10 days. If I'm not absolutely delighted I may return them and owe nothing. Otherwise I will pay the low price of just $4.00 each: a total $16.00 (at *least* an $18.00 value) and save at least $2.00. Then each month I will receive four brand new novels to preview as soon as they are published for the same low price. I can always return a shipment and I may cancel this subscription at any time with no obligation to buy even a single book. In any event the FREE book is mine to keep regardless.

Name _____

Street Address _____ Apt. No. _____

City _____ State _____ Zip Code _____

Telephone _____

Signature _____
(if under 18 parent or guardian must sign)

Terms and prices subject to change. Orders subject
to acceptance by True Value Home Subscription
Services. Inc.

913-7